WITH

THE

NEXT

MAN

EVERYTHING

WILL

BE

DIFFERENT

WITH THE NEXT MAN EVERYTHING WILL BE DIFFERENT

EVA HELLER

TRANSLATED FROM THE GERMAN
BY KRISHNA WINSTON

 Random House / New York

This work was originally published in German as *Beim nächsten
Mann wird alles anders* by Fischer Taschenbuch Verlag GmbH,
Frankfurt am Main, in 1987. Copyright © 1987 Fischer
Taschenbuch Verlag GmbH, Frankfurt am Main.

*Grateful acknowledgment is made to the following for permission to
reprint previously published material:*
ACUFF-ROSE MUSIC, INC.: Excerpts from "Only the Lonely" by Roy
Orbison and Joe Melson. Copyright © 1960 and copyright renewed
1988 by Acuff-Rose Music, Inc., 65 Music Square West, Nashville,
TN 37203. All rights reserved. International copyright secured.
Reprinted by permission.
WARNER/CHAPPELL MUSIC, INC.: Excerpts from "Always Something
There to Remind Me" by Burt Bacharach and Hal David.
Copyright © 1964 by Blue Seas Music, Inc., Jac Music Co., Inc.,
and Chappell & Co. All rights on behalf of Blue Seas Music, Inc.,
and Jac Music Co., Inc., administered by Chappell & Co. All rights
reserved. Reprinted by permission.

Library of Congress Cataloging-in-Publication Data

Heller, Eva.
    [Beim nächsten Mann wird alles anders. English]
    With the next man everything will be different/Eva Heller;
translated from the German by Krishna Winston.
    p. cm.
    Translation of: Beim nächsten Mann wird alles anders.
    ISBN 0-394-57834-1
    I. Title.
PT2668.E423B4513 1992
833'.914—dc20   89-43425

Manufactured in the United States of America
98765432
First U.S. Edition

This book was set in 10.5/14 Avanta.

Book design by Debbie Glasserman

WITH

THE

NEXT

MAN

EVERYTHING

WILL

BE

DIFFERENT

1

I wake up in the morning and I am Princess Diana. Lying next to me on the champagne silk sheets—is it Charles, my husband and heir to the British throne? Yes, it's Charles. He's already been to polo practice. He got up very quietly so as not to wake me, and now he is beside me again, freshly showered. I think he is probably just pretending to be asleep. I, Princess Diana, run my fingers through my blond locks, which are a little disheveled, and perhaps my nose is shiny, as it sometimes is in the morning. To spare Charles this sight, I coquettishly bury my nose in the ruffled collar of my Janet Reger nightie and ask, "Oh, Love, are you still asleep?"

No, he is just pretending, because he thought I was still asleep. I gaze at Charles, my husband and heir to the British throne, with my blue eyes and say, "Oh, Love, please help me: what should I have for breakfast—coffee or cocoa? And what should I wear today? I am supposed to open the insect exhibition at your great-grandparents' museum."

Charles looks at me and says, "Oh, Love, whatever you wear will be perfect, because you're perfect. May I suggest your new pink blouse? And please, Love, try this new blend of coffee; it comes from your favorite colony."

Yes, Charles solves all my problems! I press a button on the intercom by our bed.

"Yes, Your Royal Highness?" replies the chief royal chambermaid.

"I shall wear my new pink blouse today."

"Very good, Your Royal Highness," says the chief royal chambermaid. "You will look ravishing in it!"

I was still thinking what my life would be like if I were Princess Diana—not that she's my ideal woman; she's way too bourgeois for my taste, too establishment, too conservative, not nearly intellectual enough; but Charles, now, in looks he's not my type, but at least he's a man who knows what he wants, I was thinking—when suddenly this rather large object hit me on the head. Everything went dark. The door to my room slammed. It was my bathrobe.

Albert had hurled it onto my bed, or rather onto me. Apparently I'd committed the heinous crime again of hanging it on his hook in the bathroom. Dear God—how I despised his pedantry! I once read that schizophrenics have this kind of obsessive compulsion about order. Albert was probably suffering from advanced schizophrenia. Any day now he'd insist that I place my comb, nail file, and toothbrush exactly twelve millimeters apart in the medicine chest, or something neurotic like that. For a year now he'd been hoarding his toothpaste because I didn't roll tubes up in the prescribed fashion; he claimed it was a waste to squeeze them from the middle because bits of toothpaste got trapped in the creases. He slit open one of my used-up tubes with a scalpel, trying to prove to me that there was enough toothpaste trapped in there for at least five brushings. I let him have the leftover toothpaste as a gift. What he completely repressed was the fact that with his method, about five times more toothpaste spurts out of the tube every time because he rolls it up so tight. That's a total waste. But there was no point discussing it with him.

I threw the bathrobe off the bed. It hit a wineglass that I'd left standing on the floor. I couldn't get up and clear away the broken glass while Albert was home, because he would go on and on about how he didn't leave glasses on the floor, and I was such a slob—the old broken-record routine. The glass was one of the ones Albert's hysterical old mother gave him. Served him right for throwing the bathrobe at me. It was 7:17; he never left for the hospital before 7:33.

At 7:38 he finally slammed the apartment door behind him. Finally I could breathe freely. I was so wiped out I had to go back to sleep for a couple of hours.

When I got up, I found a note on the bathroom sink. "The sink needs cleaning!!!" it said. I went and got a Magic Marker from Albert's desk. "Keen observation!" I wrote on the slip of paper, and put it back in the sink after brushing my teeth. As I did this, I spotted two hairs in the sink. Albert and I have almost the same hair color, dark brown, but my hair is much longer. These two hairs were long. Mine. I took the nail scissors, clipped the hairs to Albert's length, and laid them on top of the note, as a sort of garnish. Haha.

In the refrigerator I found another note: "You owe me 10.85 marks!!!" What gall. I counted my yogurts—he'd taken one again. Aha! There was the empty container in the trash. I knew I hadn't eaten it. But I paid for the yogurts. I pulled the container out of the garbage pail and used it to pick up the shards of the wineglass. A wineglass for a yogurt: we're even.

I was so drained by all these irritations that I got my coffee and went back to bed. I couldn't take it anymore. Albert and I'd known each other for three years, had been living together for the last two. But why? I hadn't the faintest idea! I couldn't ever remember wanting to waste my life away at the side of a schizophrenic tightwad. He was getting cheaper by the minute. He'd been doing his residency for a year already, and I'd thought he'd be more generous now that he was earning money; haha—just the opposite! Now he was making four times as much as my parents were giving me, but since all his money supposedly got swallowed up by taxes, it was me, the poor little student, who was supposed to buy the rich doctor his yogurt.

Christmas was the last straw. I'd bought the food: altogether it came to 79.85, I'll never forget. But instead of 39.92, he gave me only 39.48 because I'd bought two little cans of peas, and we only needed one for Christmas dinner. The other one, Albert said, I would no doubt eventually consume by myself. So he refused to pay his share of the second 92-pfennig can of peas.

And I'd bought that stinking tightwad a fantastic watch! All black, even the dial, except for the hands, which were white. I'd scrimped and saved to come up with 109 marks, and here he was fussing over a can of peas. And when Albert trotted out his measly Christmas present—stupid demitasse cups from the secondhand shop and a decorative flowerpot in shit-brown—that did it. I threw the watch in the toilet and flushed it down right before his very eyes. Yessir, gone. It's important to give expression to your feelings, right?

Then Albert threw the demitasse cups in the bathtub. That was typical. Whatever I did, he had to imitate. He was totally reactive. It got on my nerves. But of course *I* was the one who had to fish the shards out of the bathtub.

It was a delightful Christmas. Honest. Albert spent the whole time yelling about my rotten disposition, how I was just like my father; how I should just look at myself in the mirror—see how my eyes had a hysterical glint, and so on. The whole building could hear him yelling.

People would think I was mentally defective if I put up with it any longer. I got up and decided to change my life. Without delay. It was the second Wednesday in January, and to be proper I should have made my resolution to leave Albert on New Year's, but better late than never.

As I hunted for my pink wool tights, I swore I'd make Albert move out. After all, I was here first. My parents would certainly understand; their only child couldn't possibly be expected to *live* under such circumstances, let alone study. They'd just have to come up with the few extra marks I'd need as a single student. Besides, if worse came to worst, I could always fall back on the bank account my dear departed Aunt Frida left me, the money she'd put aside for my dowry. She would definitely approve of her legacy's being used to make me independent of men! Absolutely. But my parents couldn't find out that I was withdrawing more than just the interest. My father would have a fit. He has this crazy notion that a girl's dowry is meant for buying her a husband. When she finds a promising candidate, she shows him her dowry passbook, and then the guy makes up his mind whether he wants to become the proud owner of the woman *and* her passbook—that's exactly how my father pictures it! I wonder how much my mother paid for him. I don't need to sell myself that way—I'm never going to get married!

The pink tights were nowhere to be found. I bet Albert had thrown them somewhere. Actually I wanted to wear my new pink blouse, because this afternoon was the first meeting of Gottfried Schachtschnabel's seminar since Christmas vacation. But without the pink tights the pink blouse wouldn't happen. Shit. I had to get Albert out of my life as soon as possible.

I made up my mind. I wrote Albert a note:

Albert:
Get out of my life
A.S.A.P.!!!
& the apartment!!!
Sincerely,
Your Constance Wechselburger

Then I crossed out "Sincerely" and wrote over it, "With all due respect." That would do it. I threw the note on his bed. Today was the first day of the rest of my new life.

The note was still there when I got back from class in the evening. I read it again, crossed out "Your," but in a way that he could still see it underneath. Then I decided to go to my favorite bar. It was really too early—there was never anything happening at the Café Kaput till after nine, but I didn't want to be home when Albert found my note.

I've fired him without notice, I thought on my way to the bar.
I felt fabulous.

2

The Kaput was pretty empty, surprise, surprise.
No one I knew was there. Another woman
came in soon after me—I'd never seen her
before. She looked around hesitantly. Three
guys were standing at the bar, the regular boozers; you couldn't just go over and join them,
especially not if you were a woman. There wasn't a soul at the
three big round tables up front, each of which could seat at least
a dozen people. But if you sat there by yourself, you felt like you
were on display, and the next person would make a point of
sitting down on the opposite side of the table, which would just
leave you even more isolated. There were four small tables in
back; couples sat at the two by the windows. One couple was
totally engrossed in each other, the other couple looked bored.
At the table next to me was a guy, about thirtyish, alone. He sat
with his knees far apart, but had a likable face. The woman took
a quick look at the number of glasses on my table—aha, only one.
That settled it: she would join me. Women who come in alone
always gravitate toward women sitting alone.

"May I join you?" she asked.

"Sure," I said.

"Do you know if you can get anything to eat here?"

With my chin I pointed at the board above the counter,
where the cook scribbled the menu for the day.

"Weird selection here," she remarked.

"The cook's from Upper Bavaria."

"Oh, that explains it."

After she'd picked at her Upper Bavarian bean soup till about half of it was gone, she felt sufficiently fortified to start up the conversation again. "Do you come here often?" she asked.

"Yes."

"It's nice here."

"Yes."

"Do you live by yourself?"

"No."

Typical female, I thought. If a woman goes to a café by herself and sees another woman there by herself, each assumes the other has a lonely, frustrated existence. Even men are more tolerant than that. At least they can imagine that a person might go to a bar just for the hell of it. I was still trying to come up with a snappy comeback when she said, "So you're married."

"No."

"Very good," she said approvingly.

I didn't say any more. This subject was getting on my nerves. Obviously this bar-tourist was fixated on relationships. When she'd asked whether I lived alone, I should have just said yes. But I didn't. So I changed the subject.

"Say," I said, "is it true you're supposed to let potatoes steam after boiling them?"

"Of course," she said, "what a stupid question. Haven't you ever boiled potatoes?"

"Oh, I've made potatoes, but I read recently that you're supposed to let them steam."

"How old are you?"

"Twenty-seven."

Was she wondering whether it was actually possible for a woman to get to be twenty-seven without knowing that you had to let potatoes steam after you boiled them? "You pour off the water and put the pot back on the stove for two or three minutes. You have to shake the pot a few times," she said, tipping her head to one side.

"Thanks for the tip. How old are *you?*"

"How old? Oh, I'm thirty-one."

I'd guessed thirty-three, thirty-four. She had your standard brown hair, grayish-brownish eyes, not bad-looking, but nothing special. Your average student type, but older. Objectively speaking, I thought she seemed a lot older than me. Listen, it's not that I'm terribly pretty—my eyes are too small, my pores are too big—but people say nice things about my legs and mouth, and Albert once described my eyes as almond-shaped.

She gazed at me expectantly again, and I still didn't say anything, so she said, "I've only been in this part of town since January first. By the way, I'm recently divorced."

Well, she certainly didn't waste any time—she laid her cards on the table. Again she gave me an encouraging smile. But how were you supposed to behave with a newly-ex'd; did you congratulate her like a newlywed, or give her your condolences? Finally, I said, "Newly divorced, and thirty-one!"

"Exactly," she said. "We were married exactly three years."

"Why did you get divorced?"

"Well, we realized we'd grown apart, so we sat down and discussed it all calmly and came to the conclusion that the best thing would be to get divorced—for both of us." She smiled cheerfully.

"Just like that?"

"Sure, we're both mature adults." Still that cheerful smile.

I hoped she didn't notice I was turning pale with envy. Why were other people always so mature? They separated after a calm discussion—no screaming, no slamming of doors, no beatings, no insults, not even a smashed coffee cup. Why could everyone else do it? Albert and I were the only ones who couldn't pull it off. I felt ashamed for him—he'd never grow up. If it were up to me, we could separate in perfect harmony.

"We separated in perfect harmony, we're still good friends," she said, as if she'd been reading my mind.

I had to change the subject, otherwise I'd get furious with

Albert. I looked around—none of my bar buddies were there yet, nothing was happening. "So what do you do when you're not busy getting divorced?"

"Well, right now I'm here having a glass of wine."

What a jerk. This newly-ex'd wanted to play twenty questions. "Maybe you're a famous Hollywood star, and this divorce was your fourth?"

She smiled, flattered; she actually thought I mistook her for a wild woman. "No," she said, "one marriage is enough for a lifetime."

"I've never been married," I said, and I was glad I could compensate for that childish breaking-up business with Albert by rational behavior in other areas.

"That's okay," she said. "What do you do instead?"

"I make films."

"Oh, you work in a film lab?"

"No, I make films."

"How?"

"I'm at the film academy. I'm working on a film for my senior project."

"You make films?"

"Right."

That really floored her. She thought I worked in a film-processing lab. Charming. That a woman might strive for something higher, something more intellectual—that she couldn't imagine. She was probably a newly-ex'd housewife. That was what she looked like, anyway.

She ordered another glass of wine and said, "I'm a psychologist."

"Oh." Now *that* threw me. Psychologists gave me the creeps. But on the other hand I was very interested in psychology. Also I read psychology articles pretty often. I ordered another glass of wine.

"I use a lot of psychology in my film," I said. "See, it's going to be a film about breaking up, and I have to really work out the psychological dimensions of the characters."

"So you're making a film about a divorce?"

"Not exactly a divorce. More like a separation. . . ."

"Autobiographical, right?"

"Not exactly—actually it's going to be a political film."

"How's that?"

"My main task is to unmask the prevailing societal structures in a critical light."

She was staring at me with such a confused expression that I had to tell her about Gottfried Schachtschnabel. See, he was the instructor I'd be doing my senior project with. No one, and I mean *no one*, would ever have thought he'd have a name like Gottfried Schachtschnabel. He had a beard like Lenin's, but he looked a lot younger than Lenin. And he was at least as revolutionary as Lenin—I had to explain this to my bar companion first, then I told her that in his seminar "The Relevance of Bourgeois Romanticism to the Hollywood Ideal," Gottfried Schachtschnabel demonstrated how the bourgeois institutions merely served to perpetuate the existing power structure. And we should think about the implications of that. He also said that the illusion of "infinite sensuality"—he thought up that incredibly great term himself—that Hollywood films conjured up was the biggest romantic hoax you could imagine, utilized to throw dust in the eyes of the people, all in the interest of the ruling class, because, of course, there was no such thing as infinite sensuality. And bourgeois opposition to pornography was nothing more than an expression of the repressed sexual morality of the bourgeoisie, which was maintained in the interest of the ruling class. Then I explained to her what Gottfried Schachtschnabel said about monopoly capitalism and the petty-bourgeois imagination, but I was beginning to get the sense that she wasn't so interested in his analyses.

Suddenly she yawned and asked, "Are you living with this Schachtschnabel?"

Apparently this woman hadn't heard a word I'd been saying. Or she hadn't grasped it. I ordered a third glass of wine so I could explain the business with Albert. She'd told me about her divorce, so I had to tell her about myself—if for no other reason than not to be a mysterymonger. And besides, psychologists are fascinated by other people's problems.

So I explained that I'd just broken up with Albert, and that he was a physician, a resident. When we met three years ago, he was still in medical school and I was working and had more money than he did, so we were equal partners, whereas now he was a *Herr Doktor.* Even though he hadn't even started his dissertation yet, all his patients called him *Herr Doktor.* Albert was well on his way to becoming the Lord God Almighty in White, and I was well on my way to becoming a mere appendage, a film student with lousy prospects for employment. Not that it made any difference to Albert; he just assumed I'd be able to pay my own way somehow—otherwise he wouldn't have been so obsessed with me, the cheapskate. He always said he appreciated my independence; by independence he meant separate checks. Of course, his parents were convinced I wasn't a suitable match for their boy, Superson.

But apparently the psychologist didn't find these explanations very interesting; she yawned again. At first I thought she must not be a very good psychologist, but then I thought her lack of interest might be my fault; I'd been describing only the externals of our relationship, without mentioning the underlying psychological causalities. So I provided an analysis of Albert's character.

I explained that Albert and I were totally different. That he was nowhere near as mature as Gottfried Schachtschnabel, for instance. "Albert is like a child, but without the child's capacity for joy," I said. I'd read that sentence somewhere, and it was very apropos. I also told her he was convinced he should get everything without ever giving anything in return, and that he was completely blocked emotionally. I expected the psychologist to praise me for this accurate character analysis.

But she didn't say anything, so I assumed I'd have to delve into Albert's early childhood development—after all, I did read a lot of psychology and knew the kinds of things psychologists consider important. "Albert was born by cesarean. It was a very difficult birth, his mother says." As I'd expected, that interested her.

"Don't you also want to tell me how much he weighed at birth?" she asked.

But I didn't know that.

Then she yawned again and said, "Don't think you're boring me. It's kind of late."

"I've been wanting to leave for a while," I said promptly. "So when will you be back here?"

"Dunno, we'll see what happens." She got up and paid at the bar.

I took a quick trip to the ladies' room, and when I got back, she was gone.

On the way home it occurred to me I'd forgotten to ask her name. But she hadn't asked me mine either. Too bad; she'd been quite entertaining.

When I got home, I made a lot of noise on purpose. I threw my shoes onto the rack and knocked over the umbrella stand to wake Albert. The door to his room was closed. I cautiously pressed the handle to see if he'd locked it again. No, the door was open. The note was gone. Albert was gone, too.

3

The next morning Albert still wasn't back. He must have had a night shift, I thought. Then I realized that he'd taken the note. When I left for the Kaput at eight, the note had still been there. . . . If he'd really been on at night, he wouldn't have come home after eight, because he'd have gone on at six. For a second I thought he'd already moved out. But all his stuff was still here. His savings passbook was in the secret compartment in the fridge. His electric shaver was still in the bathroom. But then again, he kept another shaver in the car.

I was positive he'd picked up another chick. Another of his dumb nurses, guaranteed. He wanted to get to me, that was obvious. But I couldn't care less. No way was I going to put up with that. I'd get even with him, just wait. There was only one problem: with whom? Spontaneously I thought of Gottfried Schachtschnabel. But he wasn't as easy to get as Albert. Unfortunately. Still, I didn't give a damn what Albert did. The main thing was, I wanted him out of here.

I decided to work on my screenplay day and night so I could discuss it with Gottfried Schachtschnabel next week. It had to be a fantastic screenplay so he would be impressed by the acuity of my analytical intelligence.

I sat down at my desk and made up my mind not to stop thinking till I had the whole concept for the film worked out, at least theoretically.

Of course I could have made a film with some of the other students. But in collaborations, people constantly fight over who has the best ideas, and it's the men who always win because they can keep on drinking longer; they just drag out the discussions till all the women go home. And when the women are out of the way, they decide what they're going to do. They let us do the cutting and the uncreative stuff, and I didn't feel like getting into that. But if you could come up with a fantastic screenplay, all worked out, you could get money to make a film by yourself. And of course I wanted to create a work of my very own.

I found a piece of paper and wrote at the top, "Theoretical Film Concept."

Then I began to think. Basically the concept was clear: I'd make a film about breaking up with Albert. An analysis totally free of emotion. Tough, objective. But a film with emotional impact. That was it!

I'd have to very subtly work in the psychological factors of our relationship. And the most important thing would be how I revealed my political agenda. And there had to be something about the environment in it. Gottfried Schachtschnabel had recently talked about another student's senior film, which had a huge impact on him. He said the film made it clear that the destruction of the environment, the dying of the forests, actually signaled the end of patriarchy. "The kind of analysis one would really have hoped to have come from a feminist," he said, and then he'd added in a sorrowful voice, "I don't know why it's only men who come up with such things."

The film really had been incredible. There was a recurring sequence with soldiers falling on the battlefield (they were soldiers of all nations), juxtaposed with cuts of trees being chopped down (the trees were all different, too). Get the symbolism?: falling soldiers, falling trees! Incredible!

Why didn't I ever think of things like that? But considering what my daily life with Albert was like, it was no wonder I wasn't capable of profound thought.

Aside from that, the film was a kind of love story—political, of course. The hero was an ex-urban guerrilla who moved out to the country to teach the farmers about the ecological-psychological cycle of nature. But the farmers didn't get the point, and didn't want to accept the ex-urban guerrilla as their leader in an agricultural revolution based on psychoanalytic principles. The film was set in the Black Forest, by the way, and was called *The Desert of My Imagination*—also deeply symbolic.

What was most incredible was how the film subtly revealed the farmers' sexual repression. Very symbolically, too. You saw a farmer trying to open the door to an old hut with various keys. "Ingenious, to visualize the key scene as a key scene," Gottfried Schachtschnabel had said. See, the farmer suspected that his wife was in the hut with the revolutionary. But the farmer couldn't get the door open because his wife's lover had barricaded the door from the inside. When the farmer finally got violent and tried to rip out the lock with his hand, his middle finger got stuck in the keyhole. Then the film cut to the inside of the hut, where the revolutionary and the woman were screwing, and juxtaposed with that was a shot of the farmer's finger jammed in the keyhole; the farmer kept wiggling his finger back and forth, and it swelled up. Gottfried Schachtschnabel roared with laughter at that, and of course all the rest of us did, too.

The film ended with the farmer's wife running away with the revolutionary. She sold her tractor, and the revolutionary bought himself a Jeep with the money, intending to go on a Third World agitation tour. Of course the film also made it clear that the revolutionary had correctly recognized that consumerism had completely fucked up the Black Forest farmers' revolutionary potential. At the end you saw all the trees in the Black Forest falling over.

It really was an incredible film. It was even shown at the Young Filmmakers' Festival in Passau and got very good reviews.

Gottfried Schachtschnabel passed the reviews around very proudly—after all, the film was made by one of his students. The review in the *Voice of the KounterKulture* said:

> That love relationships and capitalist-patriarchal structures reveal themselves from the vantage point of human needs as a substitution of willingness to oppose that striving for happiness that threatens the power structure for the guarantee of psychoanalytic stability, and that they differ from each other as much as they resemble each other in their formal multiplicity—all this, this film makes alarmingly clear.

I copied out this sentence and hung it above my desk, as inspiration. That was the kind of film I wanted to make!

The review in the *Frankfurter Allgemeine,* which Schachtschnabel also handed around, wasn't so good. But that was typical. The paper didn't even go into the film's political explosiveness . . . all it wrote was that the really shattering thing about the film was its intellectual level. And apart from that the paper just whined that, "in spite of compulsively graphic sex scenes," the film was rated PG6.

"We don't give a damn what the bourgeois lackeys at the *Frankfurter Allgemeine* write," Gottfried Schachtschnabel had said. "No member of the underclass can understand their power structure–perpetuating ranting in any case, and those are the people we want to reach with our films."

A woman student added that it was typical how this capitalist rag ignored the problems of the single mother: if the film *wasn't* rated for six-year-olds, the ones who would be hit hardest would be the single mothers again, because they wouldn't be able to take their kids with them to the movies.

"Exactly," Gottfried Schachtschnabel said.

Then we talked about the role of women in this film. Actually it had bothered me that the women never said anything in the film, except to admire the men. Also, I found the rape scene pretty brutal.

But then Schachtschnabel explained that this rape scene had to be interpreted abstractly, because it really meant the rape of the forest, and he thought this transposition was a brilliant stroke.

Then another woman, Beate, said she thought it was sexist when the farmer's wife told the revolutionary, "What I admire most about you is your power to impress. You sounded just like the federal chancellor." And the revolutionary replied, "Just wait till you've experienced my power to impregnate!" And then he said, "What I admire most about you are your tits. You have the same tits as Dolly Parton." So my fellow student said she thought that was "tendentiously" sexist.

Actually I'd had the same totally spontaneous reaction. Only I'd kept my mouth shut because I'd wondered if my spontaneity might show a lack of reflection. And sure enough, Gottfried Schachtschnabel explained it all to Beate; he pointed out that after this dialogue the man plus the woman laughed together, and that made it unmistakably clear that the film viewed man plus woman as naturally complementary. And besides, he explained, in the context of the emancipated sensuality advocated by this film, this exchange should be viewed as emotional honesty.

"You can't just switch the roles, like you picture it, Beate," Chlodwig Schnell chimed in. He was always showing off, as if he were Schachtschnabel's assistant or something. "A man happens to be built differently than a woman, as perhaps you've noticed!"

"You mean a man doesn't have tits!" said another woman, with an impossible hairdo.

"I refuse to let this discussion descend to the level of popular feminism!" Chlodwig Schnell bleated. We women just giggled because Schachtschnabel simply ignored Chlodwig and asked whether there were any more problems, but no one else had questions.

He then summed up by saying he found laughter per se terribly important, and anyone who tried to make a political film nowadays without humor could hardly hope for acceptance by the working masses. Well, I thought so, too. That was something I'd really have to keep in mind.

I looked down at my sheet of paper with "Theoretical Film Concept" written on it.

The most important part was the themes. If you had ambitious themes, you automatically came up with an ambitious film, so most of us wanted to work up several significant themes. I suddenly thought of Harold. Last year I'd talked with him several times in the cafeteria. He was then in his fourth year. Harold was a real intellectual, with long gray hair and half-glasses. He often sat alone in the cafeteria, and when I could sit down at his table as if by chance I was always happy. He never seemed to mind, he was always very friendly and told me a lot about the film he was making for his senior project. Also under Schachtschnabel. Last summer Harold had worked up a list of themes for his film, and after he showed me the list and mentioned casually that Schachtschnabel had been terribly impressed, all I could do was nod with admiration. Wow, Harold really had it together. I copied down the list, to help me with my own film when the time came. Harold was nice enough not to mind. "If you want to plagiarize, I'll include you in my list of imitators," he said. He was a true intellectual. Of course I didn't want to plagiarize him, but in October he left school—without making his film. It wasn't worth the trouble, he said, everything here was on too low a level for him; he was going to New York or L.A.— that's where he belonged, not here in the provinces. To accumu-

late the pocket change he'd need for his projects, he was going
to take over his father's wholesale delicatessen-supply business.
I was sorry Harold left school, but now I could use his list of
themes for my film. But where the hell had I put it? I hunted
around for at least three quarters of an hour.

Finally I found the piece of paper in the binder where I kept
all my important documents. It was filed under "P," after "Po-
lice Registration." At the top I'd written in big red letters,
"Practice-Related Themes"—that was why it was under "P."
How dumb I'd been in my second year, still considering praxis
more important than theory, in my petty-bourgeois naïveté!

I read the sheet of paper and was delighted. Ten points were
listed:

1. Capitalism/Monopoly Capitalism (critique)
2. Progressive Consciousness-Raising
3. Environmental Crisis and Destruction of the Animal World
4. Liberation Struggle from Habitual Prostitution
5. Analysis of Bourgeois Institutions
6. Arms Race (international)
7. Feminism (critical discussion!!!)
8. Chronic Consumerism
9. Psychoanalysis
10. Unmasking Prevailing Ideologies

Yes, those were the very themes I wanted to deal with in my
film. Because I was a woman, no one thought I was capable of
it, but even as a woman I certainly could make a politically
ambitious film. Yessir, I would make a film like a man!

I wondered briefly whether as a woman I should replace the
critical discussion of feminism with a critical discussion of sexism, but I decided I should first ask Gottfried Schachtschnabel
what he thought—of course, he was a man, too, but absolutely
objective, thanks to his nonbourgeois consciousness.

I copied the list just as it was onto my "Theoretical Film Concept" paper. Very good.

But I added one point: "11. Humor!" Now I had everything I needed. Excellent.

Next I had to come up with a title. The title of a film is of tremendous importance. Script-Hoffmann had dictated to us that the function of the title is to:

a) sound the main theme or themes
b) raise curiosity about the content of the film
c) suggest the style of the film

And as a creativity vehicle in finding a film title one should compile:

a) a list of the themes
b) a list of the main plot elements
c) a list of the key phrases in the dialogue

I debated whether I could spare myself all that work listing the main plot elements and the key phrases, because that wasn't clear to me yet, and besides, I didn't want to inhibit my own spontaneity. Chaplin never knew what would come next in a film he was making. And Chaplin was a genius.

Totally spontaneously, four titles occurred to me:

Political Diary of an ERA Woman
My Love for You Is Like the Dying Forest
The Woman with Cemented Pinions
The Revolutionary and Her Man

Very good. I wrote above them: "Suggested Titles."

It was always interesting, Script-Hoffmann said, when you had an allusion to a classical author in a title. Only you should really know your classical author, he said. I thought about it: instead of Schiller's *Cabal and Love,* how about *Class Struggle and Love?* That would be original. Except that I'd have to read the play first, and I didn't really have time. What other classics were there? *Minna von Barnhelm!* I'd read that, and it would be very appropriate—wasn't she also separated from her guy? *The Liberation of Minna von Barnhelm!* Wow, that would be a powerful title! It had everything. Positively Fassbinderesque. With a title like that I'd be guaranteed a review in *Der Spiegel.* All the films reviewed in *Der Spiegel* had titles like that. I could already see the review before me. . . .

> . . . *The Liberation of Minna von Barnhelm,* the first feature-length work by Constance Wechselburger (twenty-seven), is a film that has powerful emotional impact. The attractive filmmaker portrays a woman's attempt to free herself from an emotionally repressed and incredibly stingy physician. Although the film is based on the dark-haired filmmaker's personal experiences, it must not be misunderstood as an act of revenge: the film's strength is based on its unsentimental objectivity, further legitimized by psychoanalytic facts. *The Liberation of Minna von Barnhelm,* an oeuvre out of the Schachtschnabel school, provides a positively scathing analysis of the prevailing societal strictures, the likes of which have seldom been seen in this intensity, and it reveals an intuitive capacity to plumb the depths of the psyche of the emotionally repressed and incredibly stingy physician. . . .

Yes, my dear, won't you be amazed when you read that in *Der Spiegel.* I could already die laughing at Albert's face.

Suddenly I had a super idea for how to begin the film: Albert, in an American gas-guzzler, races through the Black Forest at 120 mph. We see the needles raining off the trees. Albert rolls down the window and, with an aggressive leer on his face, tosses a cigarette butt into the forest. . . .

That was exactly how I'd begin. That would make a lot of things clear right from the start.

 **4** On Thursday night Albert came back, right after work. As if nothing had happened.

"Where were you last night?"

That was none of my business, he said. Then he claimed he'd unexpectedly had to take night shift for a colleague.

I told him he could tell that to his grandmother, but not to me. "Where were you?" I asked again, acting real cool.

"I was looking for an apartment."

"At night!"

"At night you can tell better whether the location's quiet." He grinned shamelessly.

He'd cheated on me quite often, the rat. But I'd done the same to him. After all, I hadn't come into the relationship a virgin. And then you read everywhere that a little fling now and then lends excitement to any steady relationship. I didn't have anything to be ashamed of.

But when a man's unfaithful, that's something else again—I'd just read that in *The Ladies' Journal*, or was it *Greenbook*, or *Modern Woman*? Or *Cosmo* or *Boss*? Whatever, I'd read it in my gynecologist's waiting room. In any case, when men play around, that's something else again, all the psychologists agree. An affair often reveals deeper underlying psychological problems, and for that reason wives should first try to understand what's bothering their husbands. So the first thing I did was insist that Albert and I talk.

"I don't want to talk, I want to move out," he said.

I was speechless. Who did he think he was? This would not do. "But you always said I was the 'love of your life'," I screamed.

"Well, that was a mistake on my part. You said you never loved me, you didn't feel an emotional bond with me, apparently I was just a stopgap for you!" he screamed back.

"And you pulled my hair and left four bloody scratch marks on my face! You're too much of a coward to say what you really think—you agree with everybody, nice little conformist, except that when you're drunk you let all your pent-up hostility out, on me, of course, 'cause I can't hurt you professionally. You remember how you hit me in the face, you brute, and my nose was dripping blood, and you just got in the car and drove off?"

"What has that got to do with it?" Albert screamed. "You were prancing around with that total idiot! What was I supposed to do, escort the two of you to bed?"

"That would have been perfectly in character! You're such a little conformist!"

"You're not such a bad conformist yourself! Why do you spend all your time in bars? You always talk to other people, and me you just ignore, as if you didn't know me! Your big liberated-woman act only works because I play along with you!"

"Well, why should I talk to you? You never say anything anyway. You just sit there, never opening your mouth, to show me you find me boring. Have I neglected to mention that you bore me to tears?"

"All you care about is your leisure-time activities! Whenever I make an attempt to tell you about my professional problems, you yawn!"

"You and your endless problems! The only things you want to share with me are your problems. Those I can have for free. When it comes to anything else, it's strictly separate checks!"

"Get a grip on yourself!" Albert bawled. "I'm moving out!"

"What I'd like to know is when!"

"You'll find out! Soon enough!"

At that moment the phone rang. I answered it. "Ooo," said this dumb woman's voice, "did I dial the wrong number? I wanted to speak to the doctor. . . ." Without a word I slammed the receiver down on the table. "One of your superintelligent nurses, I presume," I said so loudly to Albert, that the hag on the phone had to hear it.

"Auerbach speaking," Albert said, every inch the doctor. "Oh, it's you," he said. I was heading for the kitchen to get myself something to drink when I heard Albert saying, "How did you get my number?"

That sounded fishy. I stayed in Albert's room.

"I don't have time now," he said to the hag. Then he said "Yes, yes, yes" a couple of times, then "How awful!" and "Unbelievable!" and then he said again, "I don't have time now," and then he said, "Don't be ridiculous," and then, "No, not every doctor makes house calls," and then, "Take an aspirin," and hung up without saying good-bye.

Interesting . . . Interesting. "Who was that?" I asked.

"You don't know her." Albert grinned shamelessly. "When are you going to learn to control your jealousy, sweetie pie?"

Ha. I wasn't jealous. Why should I be? I reached the generous conclusion that I didn't really need to cheat on him to get even. Not right away, at least.

5 Sieglinde Schadler and Wolf-Dietrich Lamar lived two streets away. I'd met the two of them last year at a party. When Sieglinde heard I was living with a doctor, she said, "Well, we should get together more often." She explained that she belonged to the same profession—she was a dental hygienist. A very fine profession, but it came with a lot of responsibility. Her boss only took private patients, but if I needed a couple of teeth capped, she could put in a good word for me, because that was something her boss was willing to do for health plan patients. "Well, of course he does that for health plan patients," Albert said when I told him about it. "Dentists make a killing on caps, even with health plan patients."

When Sieglinde introduced her Wolf-Dietrich to me at the party, she told me right away that he was tax consultant. I didn't realize what show-offs the two of them were until we'd seen each other several times.

Only the best was good enough for Sieglinde. She identified completely with her boss, the rich dentist. He was her second most important topic of conversation. "Guess what kind of car my boss just bought!" she'd say, or "Guess what my boss's new desk cost!" or "Guess where my boss is going on vacation!" Sieglinde's boss was married, and Madame Dentist wore haute couture exclusively, or at least that was what Sieglinde claimed. To her, every pot holder Madame Dentist bought was a status symbol. Some day I was determined to ask her, "Guess how much I care about your boss's financial assets?" Up to now I'd bitten my tongue.

When I called her at work to tell her about my upcoming separation, she said, "My boss just purchased a new apartment house, maybe he'd be willing to rent to Albert, if I put in a good word for him, Albert's a colleague, after all." That really irked me, and I told her in no uncertain terms that her idiotic boss shouldn't give a moment's thought to Albert's idiotic housing needs.

But Sieglinde's absolutely numero-uno topic was Wolf-Dietrich. She was only a year older than me, but Wolf-Dietrich was much older than Albert. Except for the fact that Wolf-Dietrich didn't earn as much as a dentist, he was the ultimate superman. Sieglinde thought Wolf-Dietrich looked fantastic. "Wolf-Dietrich looks fantastic," she would say whenever he happened to be out of sight. Recently she'd even told me I should try to imagine how fantastic he would look in a tux. See, her boss had just had a tux custom-tailored because of all his civic and cultural duties, she said. But I had no desire to try to imagine a dentist in a tux, or a tax consultant in a tux for that matter. Then Sieglinde said that actually Wolf-Dietrich needed a tux in the worst way.

But Wolf-Dietrich wasn't just fantastically good-looking; he was also an intellectual, Sieglinde said. Every Monday he read *Der Spiegel* from cover to cover, and he had a subscription to a highbrow intellectual magazine that cost eight marks per issue. It was worth the money if it was for Wolf-Dietrich, Sieglinde said. Of course it was over her head, and she even found the pictures in that magazine boring. But Wolf-Dietrich needed something like that. Albert once asked him if he actually read his intellectual magazine every day, because every time we went over there, the most recent issue was lying on the coffee table. Wolf-Dietrich explained to Albert that it was there because he never had time to read it. But next vacation he was going to take the last two years' worth of issues along and plow through them.

Albert asked me later if I thought Wolf-Dietrich really believed what he said. I didn't really think so, but I thought Sieglinde believed him.

I was just wondering again why a woman like Sieglinde would worship a man like Wolf-Dietrich, when the doorbell rang. It was Sieglinde.

"Think of the devil!" I said.

"Why, am I interrupting something?"

"I was working."

"You? Working? On what?"

"Oh, I'm writing my screenplay."

"Oh." She scooted past me into my room.

"What's wrong?" I asked, genuinely concerned. Of course Sieglinde lived only five minutes away, and it was Saturday afternoon, the best visiting hours, but she had never come by without announcing herself ahead of time. On the contrary: every time we all got together, we had to have at least three phone calls to set a time. She would have to cancel at least twice for every time we met because Wolf-Dietrich had some objection. And if you wanted to see her by herself, the only time you could do it was when he was otherwise engaged. Even though they weren't married, Sieglinde had already internalized the housewife's ironclad credo: a man may go out alone, but under no circumstances may he be left alone at home.

Sieglinde threw herself down on my bed. "I'm still shaking, I'm so angry," she said. "It's unbelievable!"

"Does Wolf-Dietrich have someone else? Or has he left you. . . ."

"I'm going to leave him!" she exclaimed, and smoothed her Burberry kilt. "If this keeps up!" But she didn't say what was supposed to keep up; she just ordered a schnapps. All I could offer her was tea, but tea was good enough to fortify Sieglinde for further revelations.

"Just imagine." Sieglinde opened her eyes wide. "Wolf-Dietrich wouldn't let me put his photos and my photos in the same album!"

I didn't see the point.

"He wants his photos kept separate from my photos," she moaned. "He claims his are composed according to aesthetic principles, whereas all the people in my photos look mildewed. As if that were a reason not to have them together in the same album. . . ." For a couple of seconds her voice gave out, and then she suddenly shouted at me as if I were Wolf-Dietrich: "I wanted to create a monument to our togetherness, and that tyrant just blithers on about aesthetics!"

Exhausted, she slammed my pretty art nouveau cup down on its saucer. I tried not to show my concern for my cup.

"I bought six albums! Why shouldn't I put our photos together? They're memories we have in common! It's a terrible waste of money to have two prints made of every photo, which is what he wants. We can't afford it! And I already bought the albums! And the photos he took for himself—of his stupid plants and his parents and stuff—I could arrange thematically, to complement our shared memories."

"What kind of albums did you buy?"

"Oh, regular albums."

"What do they look like?"

"They were offer-of-the-month at Tchibo's Coffee and Closeout Sale Shop. Only six ninety-five apiece. A good buy."

"What do they look like?"

"The way photo albums usually look. Brown, Naugahyde leather, I think, with a gold border or something."

"You bought *those?*" That's typical Sieglinde, I thought. She always acted so hoity-toity, constantly talking about designer this and designer that, but if she could lay her hands on cheap pleather with a gold border . . . "At least if they were covered in cloth . . ." I said.

"You can cover them with cloth later. Wolf-Dietrich couldn't complain about the price."

"How do you cover those plastic things with cloth?"

"Wolf-Dietrich's good at stuff like that." Sieglinde realized she wasn't going to get much sympathy from me. "You're just like him—you won't listen," she moaned.

That made me mad, so I said I wouldn't let brown plastic crap with a gold border into my house.

"When you really love each other, it doesn't matter what color album you put your shared memories in."

"I can do without memories in brown pleather," I said mercilessly.

Sieglinde wanted to go home—she had shirts to iron.

Luckily for her, at this very moment Albert came home from the Laundromat. Since our blowup yesterday he was being real low-key. He was scared of losing me for good. Sieglinde was delighted to see the doctor, and put off ironing the shirts. Albert was delighted to see a woman who ironed her lover's shirts, and put off hanging up his own.

"How's Wolf-Dietrich?" Albert asked.

"I have no idea," Sieglinde said.

"You've split up?"

"Well, we may split up in the near future," Sieglinde said grimly.

Albert frowned.

Sieglinde began to shake with anger again as she told the story to Albert, and she said that Wolf-Dietrich had prevented her from creating a monument to their togetherness. Albert, that old opportunist and tightwad, sided with Sieglinde, of course. He said he likewise found it very nice to have shared photo albums, and it was a waste of money to make two prints of common memories.

It got on my nerves to see them chatting in such perfect harmony, so I said I could understand Wolf-Dietrich completely and I wouldn't let that kind of brown plastic crap into my house. Only over my dead body.

"She's just like Wolf-Dietrich," Sieglinde said, and gave Albert a sympathetic look.

"But you could cover them in cloth," Albert said to me.

Albert's solidarity restored Sieglinde's faith in the male psyche, she said, and she cordially invited him to come to dinner soon. I was invited too, of course.

"When?" I asked.

"Next Friday I'm giving a dinner," Sieglinde said, "but I'm not sure whether I can invite you with this group of people, or whether it wouldn't be better for you to come the next time I give a dinner, and in any case I have to ask Wolf-Dietrich first, after all, it does make a difference for his career whether I invite the right people."

While Sieglinde explained at length that she simply loved to cook, I was feeling annoyed at length that in spite of all her gratitude to Albert she still had to ask Wolf-Dietrich first whether we were suitable guests for next Friday.

"But there's one thing I can tell you for sure," she said, when we were almost through saying good-bye. "Guess what I'm giving Wolf-Dietrich for his birthday?"

"Photo albums bound in white glazed paper," I said, "or in black patent leather, or in brown paper—that looks great, too. . . ." I had a few other ideas, but she wasn't even listening.

Instead, she smiled at Albert, who hadn't said a thing, and exclaimed, "A tandem bike! I'm going to buy Wolf-Dietrich a tandem bike!"

"Great!" Albert said, "Great; then the two of you can ride together."

"Right," Sieglinde said. "It's always bothered me that Wolf-Dietrich could zoom around on his stupid racing bike, but I'm too slow on my regular bike to keep up. With a tandem, we'll always go biking together."

"Great," Albert said again, just to agree with her.

She made us promise not to breathe a word about it to Wolf-Dietrich.

6 Because of all that aggravation with Albert, I didn't manage to get my screenplay written by Wednesday afternoon. And I'd been planning to discuss it with Gottfried Schachtschnabel.

Still, I waited at the door after our seminar, and after the others had gone. "Was there something you wanted of me?" Gottfried Schachtschnabel asked spontaneously when he saw me standing there. "Let's go back inside; it's so impersonal out here in the hall."

Back in the seminar room he actually perched next to me on the table. "Well, what is it?" he asked in an incredibly nice way. I told him that I was planning to unmask the bourgeois illusion of infinite sensuality in my senior film project by using concrete examples. "In line with your theory," I threw in. "I wanted to ask you how that sounds to you."

"Sounds good to me, Constance," he said.

Of course we called each other by our first names. Gottfried was the first instructor who let the students call him by his first name. Now there were quite a few who did, but we didn't do it with the older instructors and the real professors. Recently Gottfried had said that the other instructors were just copying him; he had been the first, and had wanted to break down the hierarchical structures between teachers and learners. I thought it was fantastic, except that when I talked to him privately like this it was a little embarrassing to call him by his first name. I tried to avoid calling him anything—it was probably my bourgeois upbringing blocking my spontaneity.

Since he liked my basic approach, I went ahead and showed him my list of themes, which I had typed up all nice and clean just before the seminar. Not only had I analytically thought out the order of the topics, I'd also made such obvious improvements in Harold's list that I could honestly describe it as my own work. For the first item I had "Illusion of Infinite Sensuality"—that hadn't even been on Harold's list. I kept point 2, "Progressive Consciousness-Raising." I'd cut out point 3, "The Environmental Crisis and the Destruction of the Animal World" because so many people were doing it, and besides, it was really complicated to film animals. So for 3 I had "The Liberation Struggle," and under 4 I'd combined Harold's first point, "Capitalism/Monopoly Capitalism (critique)," and the "Analysis of Bourgeois Institutions." I wanted to keep the critical discussion of feminism, now point 5, because as a woman I would of course be expected to take a position on that, but I'd also integrated sexism into my catalog of themes: "6. Chronic Consumerism and Sexism"—somehow those things went together. Probably Albert was so stingy because he was a sexist. When I got to "Unmasking the Prevailing Ideologies," which I'd originally had as point 10, it seemed to me that that was really covered in the other points. So I took that point off the list, and instead left a space and wrote: "Purpose of the film: unmasking the prevailing ideologies. Stylistic means to be used: humor."

So now I had three less topics, which left only seven, but it seemed to me that that should be plenty.

Gottfried Schachtschnabel thought so, too. "It's all in there," he said. "Quite an ambitious program."

I pointed out to him that the only problem was how to link the topics, and that I had in mind the concept of a separation story; did he think I could work this story into the themes? Yes, he said, in fact that was just what was needed.

Because he was being so incredibly nice, I got up my courage to say that even though I already had the concept in my head, I didn't know where to begin. "It's always best to begin at the beginning," he said. And then he added, incredibly nicely, "You'll manage to pull it together, I'm not worried about that." I was proud he had such a high opinion of me.

All evening I thought about whether I should begin the film with the rise of capitalism or with an analysis of the arms race, or with the origins of feminism. These points worked best when combined with the critique of prevailing societal conditions, that I knew, but unfortunately you'd need lots of extras to film these topics. For that reason it's better to visualize the problem cluster by symbolic means. The janitor of our academy was proud that he'd played Karl Marx in three senior film projects so far—even though he was a die-hard Christian Democrat—and he took special care of his beard for the next time he might be needed.

For the international arms race I'd have to manage with footage from documentaries anyway. But in order to get such footage you had to talk to that dumb Tetschner, who ran the archives, and you had to tell him exactly what you wanted, because otherwise he wouldn't dig out anything for you. So the international arms race was pretty much a bust.

Finally it occurred to me that maybe I could begin the way Albert and I had begun. That would be a beginning in the true sense and good to visualize, because the scene would have to take place in a bar.

I could begin with the beginning of the end.

Scene 1: We met in a bar. It was the Owl's Nest, on December 8, three years ago. I was standing at the counter with Jürgen, an old pal. Years ago we'd had a brief, painless relationship—we didn't talk about it when we saw each other—but in the film I could make something more of it. Jürgen was telling me how fat his ex-girlfriend Gisela had gotten, and how their daughter,

Yasmine, suffered from growing up without him, her real father, around, and now, because Gisela had a new boyfriend, Yasmine was having trouble in school. She was bad in math, of all things! But she'd inherited a gift for mathematics from Jürgen! Of course, if her mother chose to fool around with this new guy instead of nurturing her child's talent, what could you expect?

"Why don't you and Gisela get back together?" I asked him.

"What am I supposed to do?" he said. "Whenever I want to, Gisela doesn't, and whenever she does, I don't."

I knew the story, knew all the details of this back-and-forth that had been going on for years, so I nodded and concentrated on the conversations around me. It was pretty late. Pretty much only men were left in the bar, droning on about cars.

"Gisela's still mad at me because I didn't marry her when she got pregnant. Are you always supposed to get married right away?" Jürgen moaned.

"How long before your car has to go through inspection again?" I asked one of the car buffs who happened to be looking at me at that particular moment.

"Doesn't look promising," he said. "We're going to have to split up soon, my little car and me."

That was the first sentence Albert spoke to me. That's how we met. That car had been junked long ago, and now I hoped our relationship would be, soon.

The stars were favorable when we met. Both of us had a lover in reserve. I didn't need to go out looking for a man, and Albert didn't need to pick up a woman. He split up with his girlfriend, Dörte, right after he met me. I've forgotten the name of my then-occasional bed partner—nothing about him worth remembering.

That was how it was. As I thought about it some more, though, it seemed to me that this scene wasn't romantic enough. And the prevailing societal conditions wouldn't be unmasked enough. The meeting between Albert and me had to be different

in the film: him and me, two halves wandering through the world
and finally finding each other.

I would just have to show, somehow, that these two halves
weren't compatible.

1   Actually, I hadn't planned to clean the apartment till after Albert moved out. But that
might not be for a while. And the place was a
mess.

It was Thursday, and Thursday was my day
off. Otherwise, I was completely booked up:
Monday I had Film Law first thing in the morning, at ten. It
was a total bore, and no one would go if it weren't required; if
you had three unexcused absences, you didn't get credit. Law-
Müller scheduled the course early on purpose, to aggravate us.
Monday afternoons I usually went to the library and worked my
way through the new photo magazines, the psych journals, and
the international film publications. Tuesday was my worst day;
I was busy from morning till night with Editing 3, History of
Film 2, and Script and Dramaturgy Practicum. The only interesting one was History of Film, because we got to watch movies.
Then on Wednesday I had the theory seminar with Gottfried
Schachtschnabel. He scheduled his seminars at "student-
friendly times," which meant from five to seven. And on principle he didn't have any seminars on Mondays, for the sake of us
students. On Fridays he had another seminar, but that was for
fourth-year students, and I was only at the beginning of my third
year. But the next semester Gottfried would definitely let me
into his senior seminar. After all, I was already working on my
final film.

Up till now I'd worked in the women's film group on Fridays.

Our goal was to infuse life into the theoretical superstructure, so we were on the lookout for topics that reflected the actual practice of our lives, but we hadn't found a topic yet because we'd only met twice this semester. Because of the traditional double role of women we all had so much to do that it was hard to find a time when we could all make it. On Thursdays, for instance, I couldn't, because on principle I kept my Thursdays free. That was when I had to work at home. The atmosphere in my apartment stimulated my creative intuition. Except that now I had to clean up the place.

While vacuuming, I thought about what I'd do if Albert really moved out. The apartment was small—two rooms plus kitchen and bath in an old building—and not expensive. I'd lived there before with Christiane. Then two years ago she went to France with a French teacher who was with the army—we called him our occupation force—and was now teaching German there. Albert moved out of his commune and in with me. We'd known each other for thirteen months by then.

At first we discussed whether I should move into his commune. He lived with three women and a guy in a five-room apartment in an old building, and one of the women was just moving out. At the time I thought I really should get some commune experience—Christiane and I had been only two, and you couldn't really call that a commune—but Albert's commune got on my nerves, like, totally. All day long they had these discussions: What is dirt? Where does dirt come from? Where does dirt go? Who's responsible for it? They also squabbled a lot because Albert stayed out of the group activities on purpose. He didn't want to join in the communal bread baking, and he didn't have any interest in encounter group weekends. The third time I visited the commune, Dagmar put me on the list for cleaning—because I'd stood around on the kitchen floor—their common space! Most of the time Albert was at my place, so I spent considerably less time on their communal kitchen floor than the others. But that didn't count. Albert called the commune women a "terrorist cleaning ladies' gang." I got him out of there.

If Albert moved out now, I could catch up on my commune experience. In a commune you always had someone to talk to, and that would be better than what I had now. Albert left in the morning and came back in the evening, which meant zero conversation all day.

On the other hand, I could definitely handle living alone. And the women who lived in communes talked about nothing but cleaning all day. Maybe, even, Albert was the lesser evil.

I found my pink wool tights. Finally. After washing them, I wrapped them in a towel and stretched them lengthwise, because I'd bought them a size too small. Somehow the damp towel had slipped down between two sweaters. The one underneath was wrinkled and smelled mildewy. I had to wash it with Albert's shampoo, because the Woolite was all gone. While I was washing the sweater, the sink automatically got cleaned. Then I cleaned the bathtub and the kitchen window, put clean sheets on the beds, including Albert's, ran the dust cloth quickly over everything, even dusting all the photocopies for his dissertation that he had on his desk, then sharpened a bunch of pencils for both of us, put all the shoes on the shoe rack and the typewriter under the bed, polished the mirror in the hall, scoured two filthy frying pans, scrubbed the telephone, and finally called Albert at the hospital to tell him what I'd done. He was very pleased and invited me to have dinner with him at the Bistro. It turned out to be a nice evening.

On Friday Irmela from our women's seminar called up at the crack of dawn and told me that her Benjamin had been coughing all night, and the child's father didn't have time to watch him, so the seminar would have to meet at her house, and she'd already told the others. So she'd called me last! In Irmela's eyes you didn't count as a full human being unless you had a child. I didn't like the idea of going to her house. Gottfried Schachtschnabel's seminar and the women's seminar let out at the same time, and there was the chance I might meet Gottfried in the hall, and then I could ask him something about my film. But now that was out for today. I called up Albert and asked whether he wanted to meet somewhere after the women's seminar. He said he didn't feel like going out again this evening, and he'd be home at six.

The women's seminar was bedlam. There were only five of us—Beate, Gudrun, Regina, Irmela, and me—but Regina had brought along her Benjamin, too, because her boyfriend didn't have time to watch the child either. Regina's boyfriend never had time, but she seemed to find that okay. For twenty-five minutes Regina's Benjamin and Irmela's Benjamin ran around the table, and the whole time they were shouting "Mother-fucker" and "Shithead." The mothers were sorry they didn't have a video camera so they could capture the little ones' spontaneous play. Regina and Irmela decided to make a children's film, no matter what. I didn't say anything, because it bugged me that the kids yelled "Motherfucker" and "Shithead" every time one of us grown-ups said something. Gudrun never said anything anyway, and Beate just said, "Oh, aren't they cute!"

But then Irmela's Benjamin started to cough again, and Regina's Benjamin coughed right along with him, so we adjourned the seminar till the children were healthy again. I asked Gudrun and Beate whether they felt like going to a bar for a while and chatting about political films, but they wanted to go home and work.

So I went home, too. In the hall, on the floor, I found a note: "Had to go to a friend's farewell party. Greetings, Albert."

That was strange—wouldn't he have known about that when I called him earlier? I didn't feel like staying home alone waiting for that fine gentleman to get back, so I headed for the Kaput.

 The psychologist I had met last week was there, with a man in tow.

"Ah," she said when she saw me.

"Is this your ex?" I asked immediately, because the two of them had an air of partnerlike harmony about them.

The psychologist laughed, but he didn't. "Certainly not," she said, "this is an old, old friend. We've known each other since we were in the sandbox, so to speak. Karl-Heinz Müller is his name. A name to remember!"

"We're like brother and sister," Karl-Heinz said, and gave the psychologist's knee a brotherly pat.

"And what's your name?" I asked the psychologist. This time I wanted to get the question out right away, because later it would be embarrassing.

"Juliet's her name," Karl-Heinz said. "Juliet—she has the most beautiful name in the world. Juliet, so indescribably . . . *feminine!*"

"He knows perfectly well how I hate the name Juliet," she said.

"But Juliet's the symbol . . ."

" 'You won't believe this, but I heard once that Juliet's the symbol of romantic love. . . . Romeo and Juliet . . . olala . . . hahaha . . .' —that's what every man says when I tell him my name, every single one, from your old-school gentleman to the kid who's just gone through his confirmation. And each one thinks he's hit on something terribly original. And what disgusts me most of all is that each man immediately checks to see if I match his sexual associations with Juliet!"

"Well, soon you'll be past all that," Karl-Heinz said.

"What do you mean?" Juliet asked.

"You'll be over thirty soon, right?" he explained.

Juliet gave Karl-Heinz a hurt look and didn't respond.

"And what's your name?" Karl-Heinz asked me.

"Constance."

"Constance's a very beautiful name, too. Also very feminine," Karl-Heinz remarked with the air of a connoisseur.

"I've been told that," I said. This Karl-Heinz obviously had no idea how much I'd hated my name when I was younger. I'd always called myself Connie, because Constance was so old-fashioned and prim. It was my mother's fault I was called Constance. My father would have preferred something nice and ordinary like Gisela or Waltraud. But my mother wanted to impress her girlfriends with her chic child, so she named me after the most popular women's magazine of her day. She would have done better with a poodle—the name would have fit a poodle just fine—that's what I yelled at her one time. Oh, well, in the meantime the magazine had gone out of business, probably because it went out of style. And stopped minding having the name Constance. But when I thought about my name, I was glad I didn't have any brothers or sisters—just imagine them having children, and the children calling me Auntie Constance!

"I'd like to see some romantic parents call their son Romeo," Juliet said, "but of course no one would dream of inflicting a curse like that on a boy."

"My father almost called me Tarzan," Karl-Heinz said.

"Almost," Juliet said.

"So how are you otherwise?" I asked Juliet.

"Super, really super. Since I got divorced I've begun a new life. Honest! I've never felt this good. For the first time in my life I feel really free. I'm full of energy, believe me."

"I believe you," I said.

"But most women suffer from an inferiority complex after a divorce," Karl-Heinz said.

"Not me. I'm happy to be divorced," Juliet said. "I'm never going to marry again."

"I believe you," I said.

"Are you married?" Karl-Heinz asked.

"Hell, no."

"But she has a long-term relationship," Juliet said to him.

"And where's your friend?" he asked.

I told them Albert was at a party for someone from work, and I'd also been invited but hadn't felt like going, because I couldn't stand this particular colleague, blah blah blah. I lied because I felt I had to justify to this Karl-Heinz why I was here alone.

"And when your friend doesn't have the time, you come to the bar alone," Karl-Heinz said.

"Sure." I told the two of them that I'd even worked in a bar once, after I graduated from secondary school and was working odd jobs while I tried to make up my mind whether to become a set designer or a photographer or open a bar or study philosophy. Then I decided on film, because it combined all my interests. A really logical decision. But the three years of working odd jobs was really important for my development, I said.

"It's one thing if a woman works in a bar, another if she goes there alone," Karl-Heinz said.

"Basically I think it's great that you go out by yourself," Juliet said.

"I know lots of people here," I said, and waved to Dieter, who'd just come in with his girlfriend, Jutta.

"Does your friend come here, too?" Karl-Heinz asked.

"Sure."

"I meant, does he mind you coming here by yourself?"

I almost said I didn't have to get Albert's permission to go out and wondered whether I should ask this Karl-Heinz if he was allowed to go to bars by himself. But now the two of them were discussing mutual friends. Juliet asked Karl-Heinz whether he had any news about Ulrich recently. Ulrich was Juliet's ex. But Karl-Heinz had no news.

I couldn't concentrate on their conversation, because I kept wondering who Albert had taken to the party. Basically I didn't care where he went, and I certainly didn't care who with. After all, I wanted to put an end to this whole damned relationship. Juliet was lucky—she already had her divorce behind her, and she'd carried it off so perfectly. Well, she was a psychologist. When you know the depths of the human soul, it's no trick to have a harmonious separation, I thought.

"You're a psychologist. Can you give me a hint how to pull off a painless separation?" I asked Juliet when Karl-Heinz went to the men's room and to make a phone call. I didn't want to lay myself open to attack with him there.

"You have to learn to stop thinking in terms of possessiveness," she said. "You can't possess another human being. A relationship is mutual give-and-take, you know."

I already knew that. I told her again that the real problem was Albert's emotional block, and that he was always so indecisive.

"Maybe you're indecisive yourself. Maybe you don't know what you want. Or maybe you want something that doesn't exist."

No, all that was too superficial for me. But before I could really challenge her, Karl-Heinz came back.

"I've got to go now," he explained to Juliet. "You want to stay here alone?"

"Alone" to this Karl-Heinz meant the same thing as "without a man." Pretty insulting—after all, I was still there. But Juliet wanted to go home. We quickly exchanged names and addresses. Her last name was Lämmle—Juliet Lambie, how cute. Juliet paid for Karl-Heinz's drinks.

"I'll call you when I feel like going out alone," Juliet said to me. And as she was leaving, she said, "Good luck."

I went and joined Dieter, Jutta, and the others at the big table. When I got home at a quarter past one, Albert wasn't back yet. Well, he could just wait and see what was in store.

9 At four in the morning the umbrella stand fell over. Albert came into my room, took off his clothes, and crawled into bed with me. He was totally smashed. I pretended to be sound asleep.

When he began to snore, I yelled, "Get lost, you drunken pig!" right in his ear.

He almost jumped out of his skin. "Who is it?" he asked.

Unfortunately I burst out laughing.

"Oh, it's you, my giggling, howling monkey."

At one in the afternoon he was still snoring. I pulled the covers off him and told him the stores closed at two and it was his turn to go shopping.

"What am I supposed to get?" he groaned. "Oh, God, I feel awful!" I told him it served him right and we were all out of laundry detergent. Albert said he didn't need detergent, just peace and quiet. I asked him where he'd been yesterday. He said that without the blankets he couldn't remember a thing. I gave him the blankets, but I still had to repeat the question.

"Oh, yes, it was a party with my colleagues," he said, and added, "Is that right?"

"So why didn't you take me?"

"Why?" was all he said. Then he got up, went into his room, and locked himself in.

I knew it wouldn't make sense to continue the conversation from the hall. He kept a box of earplugs on his bedside table. All afternoon I fumed to myself.

At five he watched the sports roundup, as usual. The critics of television were right when it came to Albert: our culture is going down the drain. In the old days people would read a good book in the evening, Goethe's *Faust* or something of cultural value. But nowadays it's normal for a doctor to be obsessed with the sports roundup. If I watched TV, it was only socio-political commentary or films of artistic value. I was the one who bore the sole responsibility for culture in our relationship. In his entire life Albert hadn't read a single piece of cultural criticism. But he knew every Donald Duck story by heart! Chained to this philistine, all I could do was wait for better times.

That evening I really felt like going out to eat. Albert promptly sent up a howl. "You want to eat out every night," he whined. "You with your luxurious tastes. All because you're too lazy to learn how to cook! You just use me and I'm supposed to pick up the tab!"

Because I didn't want to get into a fight, I said perfectly objectively that he never paid because he always forgot to bring his wallet when we went out. Quite by accident, of course.

"When it's a question of money, madame doesn't say a word about equal rights!" he squawked.

I told him very objectively that it was cheaper for me to eat out because when I shopped for the two of us I only got back a fraction of what I'd laid out for him. "You remember when I bought the food for Christmas dinner?" I asked him.

"Because of those stupid peas, you threw my watch in the toilet. You're a mental case!" he screamed.

"Don't yell!" I warned him. But I was slowly losing my cool. "You know perfectly well that your stinginess makes me sick. It's you who made me understand why the Catholic church considers avarice a deadly sin! They're no dummies, those Catholics! When I think of your crummy Christmas demitasse cups, it makes me sick!"

"Nothing I give you is ever good enough! I've never managed to satisfy your sophisticated taste. All you really care about anyway is having something to bitch about!"

"You could at least try to come up with something I'm going to like! Those art nouveau cups I got from my parents for my birthday—*those* are great! But your demitasse cups—the most hideous demitasse cups ever! Just because they were cheap! You wouldn't want to strain yourself!"

"I have better things to do than grovel at your feet and guess your every wish. I have to do a little work now and then, in case you hadn't noticed!"

"The only thing I've noticed is that the way to your heart is through your wallet. You can go to hell with your crummy demitasse cups!" Then I slammed the door.

I had no choice but to open a can of ravioli for supper. The evening was a total loss.

On Sunday afternoon Albert went out. Without making any phone calls. So he must have had something prearranged. Probably with that cookie who'd called the other day. He hadn't even asked me where I'd been the night before last. I simply didn't matter to him.

Well he didn't matter to me either. My decision to get rid of this tyrant was irrevocable. One thing I didn't want: that he leave me before I had something better lined up. What would people think of me! Me, a jilted woman. . . . My enemies would rejoice!

Neverever would I let that happen.

10 The days were as shitty as those cups. But suddenly, just as the sun after long winter days breaks through the clouds and gives all life new meaning, my life changed the following Wednesday.

I'd asked Gottfried Schachtschnabel after his seminar whether he had a moment, because I wanted to ask him something about my film. But he said that unfortunately he had to leave right away; was my problem urgent? Well, not exactly. I'd meant to show him the list of possible titles and get his opinion on them. Because he said he was in such a hurry that he wasn't even going up to the faculty lounge on the fifth floor, I walked him to his car. Gottfried Schachtschnabel drove an old Mercedes! Painted denim blue, with denim seat covers! Fantastic seat covers. Handmade, by his mother, probably.

He said he had to go to Kreuzberg. What a coincidence— that's where I lived! Gottfried said he lived in Lichterfelde, but since he was driving to Kreuzberg he could take me part of the way. "Come on, hop into my capitalist coach!" he said, and laughed.

What a feeling: me, a student, next to my instructor in a blue-denim Mercedes. I looked around to see if anyone from the academy was watching. Great: Chlodwig Schnell, Gottfried Schachtschnabel's self-appointed assistant, was coming across the courtyard. Chlodwig was pretty amazed when I waved to him from Gottfried's Mercedes. Haha!

We got around to the problem I was having with the title of the film. He asked me to read him the titles out loud. When I got to "The Liberation of Minna von Barnhelm," he said we would have to see whether it fit the film contentwise. He was right, of course. "The Liberated Woman with Cemented Pinions" he liked immediately, and said the title was deeply symbolic. I didn't read him the second title—"My Love for You Is Like the Dying Forest." Somehow I was embarrassed to read that to him. Besides, it seemed to me that it sounded too commercial. I told him that the title I preferred was "The Revolutionary and Her Man." But of all things, he objected to it. He asked whether I intended to degrade the man to a sex object. And he personally viewed feminists who merely wanted to commit the same mistakes as men very, very skeptically. I had to admit he was right, because I was very skeptical, too. I promised to take another hard critical look at the title.

We were going right by the Kaput. I told him it was my regular hangout, because I lived nearby, and that I was planning to go there right now, and that it had a great atmosphere. "Excellent," he said. "There's an empty parking space right in front."

I was hoping he'd join me for a beer or something, but he said he was sorry, that today of all days he didn't have time; he had to work on a lecture. I asked him what the lecture was about.

"About the illusion of infinite sensuality, using the cliché of the typical married couple in Hollywood films as the basis for the analysis."

That was incredibly interesting. I told him I'd given a great deal of thought to that subject and asked if students could come to the lecture. "Everyone's more than welcome," he said, "and bring all your friends." He said that the talk would be Tuesday evening at eight, at the Center for Alternative Popular Education, and that he'd already mentioned it in our seminar, but I hadn't heard him because I'd gotten there a little late. I blushed, because I'd come late on purpose so everyone would see my new trench coat, which I'd luckily gotten on sale. The coat was white and an incredible bargain. Gottfried said he was going to post an anouncement for his lecture in the academy in any case. And he'd only found out this weekend that he was supposed to give this talk. Actually they'd had another speaker scheduled for that Tuesday night, on some nice domestic subject, he said, and laughed so hard that I had to laugh, too. But because the lady speaker had been taken ill, he'd been asked to fill in, though he was actually scheduled for March. And he had to work hard on it, because those APE Center audiences expected political theory to be presented in its praxis-relevant dimension, and that was the hardest thing to do.

"I know what you mean," I said, thinking of my film.

"I have to go now," Gottfried said. And then he said, "I'd love to see you there on Tuesday."

When I said good-bye, my voice was all high and scratchy with excitement, and then I realized I'd shut the car door on my new coat! Shit! Well, I could get my coat dry-cleaned by Tuesday. I was incredibly anxious to hear that talk.

I ran into some friends at the Kaput and asked them whether they felt like going to a practice-relevant political lecture. No one felt like it. A bunch of ignoramuses. I didn't want Albert to hear about the lecture—with his complete lack of interest in politics he'd just be an embarrassment.

 **11** On Sunday Juliet Lambie called. I was home alone; Albert was on call that weekend. Juliet said she wanted to stay in touch with her new neighborhood. I thought it was very nice that she called—most people you give your phone number to never do call. I'd really meant to call her, but I just hadn't had the time.

Juliet said she wasn't feeling so good, she was in some sort of depressive phase.

I told her Gottfried had driven me home.

"Well, well!" she said.

"Times change, and we change with them!" I said, but I didn't mention that was a quote, because I wasn't sure whether it was Camus or Catullus. I told Juliet that Gottfried was giving a lecture at the APE Center.

"Very interesting," Juliet said.

I told her she could come along, in fact anyone who was interested could come along. But she didn't want to. I told her she might be able to point out some psychological angles to Gottfried's analysis that I hadn't picked up on. Even so, she didn't want to come. Then I talked to her about the lack of prospects in my relationship with Albert. "Everything's bullshit anyway," Juliet kept saying. We talked for at least an hour and a half. Then I asked her again whether she wanted to go to the lecture. I also told her we could go to Cookies afterward, the best pickup joint in the whole city, right near the APE Center.

Juliet asked, "How long will the lecture be?" I didn't know. But then she said, "Okay, I'll go with you. It's all bullshit anyway," and, "I'm dying to have a look at this fabulous Gottfried Schachtschnabel."

On Tuesday Juliet got to the APE Center at 7:47. She was coming straight from work, and had on a weird pleated skirt. I'd decided to wear my neon-blue mohair sweater with my best faux pearls, and in honor of the occasion I'd washed my jeans. Unfortunately I hadn't had time to take the trench coat to the cleaners, but the stain gave the coat a real casual look.

Aside from Juliet and me, sixteen people turned up. Beate from my class was there. She was sitting in the last row, already knitting. There were some first-year students and two women from the graduating class, who also had their knitting with them.

Other than that, there were several fortyish women and an older man. The old folks all sat up front.

Gottfried got there at five past eight and was incredibly cool. First he tested the microphone. "Testing one, two, three, we're very pleased to have you here for our lecture, one, two, three," he said. "Can we do something about this hum?" Gottfried said to the janitor who'd hooked up the mike.

"No, we can't," said the janitor. One of the older women said we didn't really need the microphone. "The gentleman can make himself heard just fine, with this handful of people."

But the janitor said it was part of his job description to hook up the microphone and the amplifier.

"Well, we'll just have to talk over the hum," Gottfried said, and he began his lecture. The janitor controlled Gottfried's voice the whole time. I had the impression that every time Gottfried said "socio-political" or "socio-critical" or used any other expression containing "socio," the janitor would turn down the volume. But for any expression that began with "sexual," he'd turn it up.

Everybody clapped really hard when Gottfried finished. The knitters even put down their knitting. Juliet whispered to me that she needed a beer. The older ladies surrounded Gottfried, all agitated and talking at once. One of them said she didn't understand it, one of them said she suspected there'd been a change of program, and one was explaining something to Gottfried about the graceful art of flower arranging.

"Let's go," Juliet said. But I wanted to ask Gottfried a quick question first. "Tear yourself away," Juliet said, "the dream is over." So I followed Juliet to the exit.

"Hey, wait, ladies, Constance!" Gottfried called when he saw us leaving.

"Well, well, well!" Juliet said, and looked at me. "Should I go on home?"

Gottfried simply walked away from the ladies and came over to us. "Are you going somewhere after this?" he asked. "I'm really in the mood for a drink—my throat is parched."

I told him my friend Juliet and I had planned to go to Cookies. Gottfried asked if he could come along, or if he'd be in the way.

"No problem," Juliet said.

While Gottfried was getting his coat, Juliet asked me if she'd be in the way, and if she should call Gottfried Schachtschnabel by his first name. I whispered to Juliet that she should chill out, for God's sake. "What do you think he'd think of me if you called him Doktor?" I warned her.

"No problem," Juliet said.

Gottfried asked whether we'd gotten anything out of the lecture. Juliet admitted that she didn't know a thing about this field, but certainly he'd presented things in a very interesting way. I agreed. She said she'd never thought that the problem of bourgeois romanticism was so deeply rooted in the basic structures of capitalism. Take her grandmother, for instance; she'd been a real movie fan, Juliet said, and she'd gone to every sad love movie and had talked about them incessantly, but then on the other hand her grandmother had married a socialist.

"Back when your grandmother was going to the movies, it was still the early stages of the oligopolitical competition that originated in the twenties," Gottfried explained. Juliet said she didn't understand what that meant, but in any case the lecture had given her a lot of mental stimulation.

Gottfried ordered our first round of beers and said again that he was glad we'd come. There hadn't been that big an audience, but of course quality was more important than quantity. Then he asked Juliet what she did.

"Juliet's a psychologist," I said.

"I work for the public school psychological services," Juliet added.

I didn't know that. I almost felt guilty for not asking Juliet for more precise details, and was reminded of Albert's constant reproach that I didn't take enough interest in his work. I was just wondering how to phrase my question about the particular problematics of modern school psychology, because with Gottfried there I couldn't ask just any old question, when Juliet explained, "I test nervous kindergartners for their school-readiness." That was very interesting, Gottfried said. I thought so, too.

"When you spend your entire day talking with kindergartners, you sometimes get the feeling you are a kindergartner," Juliet said. Especially since her divorce she often felt the need for an intelligent conversational partner, she added.

"You're divorced?" Gottfried asked.

"Newly divorced," I said; that at least I was sure of.

"But I feel fantastic," Juliet said. "I've never felt so free in my entire life." She also explained to Gottfried that many divorced women suffer from low self-esteem, because without a husband they feel socially incomplete, but that with her God knows that was certainly not the case. Then she beamed at Gottfried and said, "You're not in favor of marriage either, as I gathered from your lecture."

"Good listener." Gottfried laughed. "It's a cruel illusion to believe that one can find happiness through the guarantee of legality as defined by the state, though that's what the capitalist romanticism industry, with its happy endings designed to perpetuate the existing power relationships, would have us believe," he said, repeating part of his lecture.

"I don't know of a single happy marriage," Juliet said.

"Nor do I," said Gottfried.

"I don't know of a single happy relationship," I added.

"So how's your Albert?" Juliet asked.

"Who? Oh, him," I said, totally cool. "Actually, Albert's already out of my life." Gottfried looked at me with great interest, and I blushed a little.

We had another beer and chatted about divorce. I advised Juliet to take back her maiden name. "No!" she exclaimed. "My name used to be Freudenreich—Juliet Joyrich! Never again!" We ordered another round to drink to that. Then another, in honor of James Dean.

The only thing I didn't like about this wonderful evening was that Juliet had taken her car and gave me a lift. Otherwise Gottfried would definitely have driven me home.

12 "That was a nice evening," Gottfried said to me the next day after our seminar, "and your friend Juliet's very nice." And then he said, "If it's okay with you, I have to go out to Kreuzberg again today, and I could give you a lift. Only I don't have time to go to your favorite bar this time either. But another time, definitely."

When we were sitting in his Mercedes, Gottfried asked how things were going with my film. Quite spontaneously I sighed. I explained to him that I hadn't had any inspiration all week to help me work out ideas for my film. I hinted that aggravation with my former companion was to blame. Gottfried was very understanding. "If you don't have any ideas, go read a good book," he said.

I asked him what he would recommend.

"Well," he said, "just read Kant or Hegel."

That was philosophy. I'd thought he would recommend something like *Gone With the Wind* or *The Neverending Story*, something film-related. But, of course, Gottfried was a real intellectual.

"What by Kant or Hegel?" I asked.

"Doesn't matter," Gottfried said. "Everything Immanuel and the other chap wrote is excellent."

Albert should try to be more like Gottfried Schachtschnabel, I thought. Gottfried really knew his way around with these great figures. "Immanuel" and "the other chap"—of course, that's how intellectuals talk among themselves.

"You have time during the semester break," Gottfried said, "or are you going somewhere?"

No, I said, I wasn't going anywhere. Then he asked whether I was going to the Kaput again and whether he should drop me there. But since he unfortunately didn't have time to come in with me, I said no, today I'd go straight home. I didn't want to give him the impression I went out every evening. So I said it was too much for me to go to a bar again today; I'd rather go home and do some work.

Gottfried drove me to my front door. I was in such a state I thanked him three times. "No problem," he said. "What one won't do for promising students." He laughed.

Just in case, I told him I'd probably be going to the Kaput tomorrow, and that Juliet sometimes went there, too, since she lived in the neighborhood.

I banged the car door hard because I saw there was a light on in our kitchen. Albert was home. Hopefully he'd seen me getting out of the blue-denim Mercedes.

And, in fact, he had. "Who was that?" he asked.

"You don't know him," I said.

The very next morning I went to the Clocktower Bookshop and asked the woman there what she had in the way of Kant or Hegel. She searched through the books-in-print listings and then went down to the basement. She was gone for ages. Meanwhile I flipped through the *Biographies of Great Women* and read that after her thirtieth birthday Madame Pompadour hadn't wanted to sleep with her Louis—she just didn't feel like it—but he still stuck by her. And Empress Eugénie, I read, had a ball-gown with 213 ruffles! Wow, what women! The clerk came back with a book by Hegel: *The Phenomenology of Mind.* Seven hundred pages, including the notes. I asked the clerk whether she recommended this one particularly. She said that was all the Kant or Hegel she had in stock, but she figured this must be worth recommending or she wouldn't have it. Made sense to me. Besides, the clerk said, it must be a classic, because this publishing house only put out classics in paperback, she was absolutely sure of that. "You can't go wrong with *The Phenomenology of Mind,*" she said. So I took it.

My Hegel didn't fit into my purse. I stuck it into my coat pocket, where it just barely fit. I passed a boutique and saw my reflection in the display window. The part with "G. W. F. Hegel" was sticking out. That looked impressive. In the other pocket I found a packet of tissues. I forced them deep into the pocket with the Hegel, so it would stick out even more.

Soon I'd be an intellectual, too. Georg Wilhelm Friedrich would show me the way.

13 "You know what today is?" Sieglinde Schadler asked me on the phone.

"February first. Why?"

"It's Wolf-Dietrich's birthday—he's turning thirty-eight. You wouldn't think so—he looks thirty-five at most! I've taken the day off, without telling him; I'm giving him a surprise birthday. Would you care to help me a little?"

"I could cut the cheese into cubes," I immediately offered; I was feeling pretty hungry.

"No, I need somebody to help me get the tandem out of the basement. Come over right now."

On the way I bought two Butterfingers at the newsstand. It was already two, and I should have been preparing for my women's seminar. Well, helping your neighbors is important, too. I decided to skip the women's seminar; after all, you have certain obligations even if you don't have children. But I made up my mind to get up early tomorrow and read Hegel all day. I hoped there'd be something decent to eat at Sieglinde's this evening, not just wine and cheese cubes.

The tandem was slime-green and unbelieveably heavy. When another tenant heard us banging it against the banister, he helped us haul it up to the fourth floor. Sieglinde was petrified she might get a scratch on it. Everything was fine, except that my sweatshirt and the man's light-blue jeans got grease on them from the chain. "Luckily you can wash it out," Sieglinde comforted us.

The tandem had to be hidden in Sieglinde's room until the gift-giving that evening. Sieglinde had the largest of the four rooms to herself, because she always hung the wash up to dry in there. Here, between Sieglinde's beige silk slips and bras and Wolf-Dietrich's beige underwear, the greenish-brownish tandem looked very attractive, I thought.

"How are you planning to wrap it?" I asked her.

She hadn't given it any thought.

"Maybe we can just put a few pink bows on it," I suggested. Sieglinde liked the idea. But she only had tons of purple ribbon in the house. She'd gotten it on sale at a fantastic price, she explained, and added, "not because I'm a feminist." Purple didn't go so well with the color of the tandem, I thought, but Sieglinde thought it didn't matter; the bike was expensive enough. She wouldn't reveal what it had cost until that evening, so I'd be surprised, too, and now she didn't need me anymore, she could handle the rest by herself. In any case I should come at seven on the dot, so I would be there before Wolf-Dietrich

got home; it *was* a surprise party. And if possible I should bring
Albert.

I called Albert at the hospital. He asked why Sieglinde hadn't
invited us earlier. She'd said the week before last that she wanted
to have him over. And now, all of a sudden she called. "I guess
this is her idea of a surprise party," he said, and then without
further ado he promised to be home at six and go with me.

"Do you have a present for Wolf-Dietrich?" he asked before
hanging up. I told him I'd been planning to give him the shit-
brown ceramic flowerpot Albert'd given me for Christmas. Albert grumbled that the flowerpot had been very expensive and
in general he thought it was inappropriate to give a man a
flowerpot. But I reminded him that Wolf-Dietrich loved house-
plants. Then Albert said it didn't make any difference to him.
He'd bring Wolf-Dietrich a bottle of wine.

We were the first ones there. But right after us Sieglinde's
brother, who I'd never met, and his girlfriend arrived, then
Sieglinde's friend Petra and her husband, then another man.
Sieglinde said these were all personal friends; Wolf-Dietrich
hadn't wanted anyone from his official circle, and she also
thought it was much nicer when people could really feel at ease
and everything just fell into place. Casually. Actually, I'd have
liked to know who the single man was, and was hoping there'd
be a chance to strike up a conversation with him, but Sieglinde
said we shouldn't stand around so stiffly, we should all sit down.
"Make yourselves comfortable," she said. Each couple sat down
in a different corner. I sat down right by the cheese cubes, so
at least Albert and I had something to keep us occupied. The
others were sitting too far away to get at them. Now we all
listened, feeling really at ease, to Sieglinde. "Wolf-Dietrich's
bound to be here any minute," she kept saying, and "I can't wait
to see what Wolf-Dietrich says."

It was as casual as a dentist's waiting room.

We were on the next-to-last cheese cube when Wolf-Dietrich appeared. He didn't seem especially surprised to find us in his living room. Except that he seemed really amazed to see Albert and me.

Then came the real surprise. We were all congratulating him, but Sieglinde just couldn't wait any longer. So Wolf-Dietrich left all our presents still wrapped on the windowsill. He had to sit on the couch with his eyes closed. Just to make sure, Petra put her hands over his eyes and ears. Sieglinde and her brother pushed the tandem into the living room. Everyone yelled "Ooo!" and "Wow!"

When Wolf-Dietrich opened his eyes, he was completely stunned. His jaw dropped. We all laughed.

"You're stunned, huh?" Sieglinde screeched. "What a surprise, huh?"

The bike looked really wild. It seemed enormous in that small living room. And it was totally covered with purple bows. Four purple bows on the luggage rack, four on the pedals, a bow on each handlebar, also on the hand brakes, four bows on the wheel spokes, a bow wound around the taillight, one around the headlight . . .

"Twenty-three bows altogether," Sieglinde screeched. "I worked like a fiend!"

"What is it?" Wolf-Dietrich asked, still sitting on the couch.

"A tandem bike," I said.

"Where did you ever get a tandem?" he asked. "Was it a special offer at the Tchibo Discount Coffee and Closeout Sale Shop?"

"It's not from Tchibo," Sieglinde said, "no matter what you think."

"Well, where is it from?" he asked softly.

"First you have to say you like it," said Sieglinde's brother's girlfriend.

"First I want to know where it comes from," Wolf-Dietrich said.

Sieglinde had gone a little pale, sort of slime-green around the gills, but maybe it was just a reflection off the tandem.

"It cost six hundred ninety-five marks," she said, "including delivery and three marks' tip. A good buy, huh? I got the last one they had. Everybody's going wild over tandems. It's an excellent make, and even though it is, it was so reasonable because I got it at Eduscho Discount Coffee and . . ."

"My God, Eduscho!" Wolf-Dietrich yelled. "So it can't be exchanged. I thought maybe I could exchange it for chrome rims for my racing bike! But you had to go and buy a bike from Eduscho!" Wolf-Dietrich closed his eyes.

"I'm sure you can exchange it for about seventy pounds of coffee," Albert said.

"My God!" Wolf-Dietrich yelled. "How I hate these cheesy coffee closeouts!"

We were all standing around the bike like a bunch of idiots. I tried the bell to see if it worked at least. It worked fine.

"Would any of those present like to purchase a tandem bicycle for a very reasonable price?" Wolf-Dietrich had opened his eyes again.

"But it's a great bike," Sieglinde's brother said. "The two of you can . . ."

"By Friday at the latest I want this thing out of here!" Wolf-Dietrich yelled. "It's either the tandem or me!"

"Well," Albert said, "under certain circumstances I wouldn't mind having a tandem. . . ."

"Excellent!" Wolf-Dietrich yelled. "You can take it with you right now!"

"No!" Sieglinde screamed.

"You just watch!" yelled Wolf-Dietrich, as he sprang to the window. "I'm going to throw it right out on the bicycle path!"

Sieglinde screamed, "No! No! No!" and we all hurled ourselves at Wolf-Dietrich because our presents were on the windowsill and he would have smashed the flowerpot.

"I just want to know one thing: what in the world was this old girl thinking?" Wolf-Dietrich sat down on the couch again and closed his eyes.

Sieglinde whispered to Albert that Wolf-Dietrich always found it difficult to express his feelings. Albert said loudly to Sieglinde that she could ride on the tandem with him some time—that would be fantastic. Sieglinde bawled at Wolf-Dietrich that all the other men rode tandems with their women; he was the only one who refused.

Wolf-Dietrich yelled that he wasn't going to make a fool of himself by riding around with his woman on his tail. Then he asked Sieglinde what she possibly could have been thinking. Hadn't she gotten it through her thick skull that he owned a racing bike for which he'd paid over three thousand marks? Was he supposed to throw that away and drag around with her on a coffee grinder?

Sieglinde's brother wheeled the tandem back into the laundry room. The single man, who Wolf-Dietrich had addressed as Georg, said the most sensible thing would be to just sell the bike at a loss. And the most sensible thing would be to put an ad in the *Crier,* where you didn't have to pay.

Wolf-Dietrich pulled himself together. Of all the presents, he liked the flowerpot best! Sieglinde brought out a reconciliation drink, as she called it: for each of us a plum and a cherry in liqueur. She'd dipped the rims of the glasses in crushed crystallized sugar—it looked great, but afterward my mouth was full of sugar. Then she brought out little rolls of ham filled with guacamole and avocado halves stuffed with meat salad and pasta salad with North Sea shrimp, which don't look as nice as deep-sea shrimp but cost more, Sieglinde assured us.

Shortly after this snack, Albert and I went home. That night we didn't fight. It's been my experience that when other people fight it has a very calming effect on your own relationship.

14 After Wolf-Dietrich's birthday I got sick. I even had to get a note from the doctor, because of Film Law-Müller. I lay in bed with a fever, coughed a lot, and was too weak even to read my Hegel. Albert kept me fairly well supplied with magazines and pizza.

By Monday I was better, but I still stayed home, because the nice woman doctor had written my slip out to cover the week up till Wednesday, especially for Law-Müller. So he'd still have to give me credit for the course. Besides, we were allowed three unexcused absences—so the way I figured it, I only had to go once more during the semester.

Albert was home, too. He'd been on call on Sunday, so they'd given him Monday off. He was sitting in the tub when the phone rang and a woman asked for him. "I can't reach the doctor at the hospital," the woman said. "Would you please give him the message that he should call back? We have a charming three-room apartment for him."

"Thank you, I'll give him the message," I said calmly.

Then she said the doctor should please ask for Frau Kunze.

Unfortunately the conversation about how Albert could have had the gall to look for a new apartment without telling me was anything but calm. Of course he hadn't thought for a moment about what would happen to me all alone in the apartment. He claimed I'd always said the apartment was too small for two people, and I'd always said I'd rather live alone, and in case I got too lonely, I could always set up one of my many male friends in his ex-room. Instead of discussing the problem calmly and objectively, he took the phone, went into his room, and called up this real estate woman.

When he came back, he said I should calm down—the place the lady had offered him was completely out of the question. He wanted an apartment, not a penthouse—this was much too expensive. Besides, he didn't like the location.

"So I can be your answering service till you've found something suitable," I said.

"It's primarily in your best interest," Albert said. Then he went into the bathroom and locked the door.

Actually I wanted to go shopping, but I absolutely had to have my Dior lipstick, which as luck would have it was in the bathroom. I had to rap on the door at least eighty times before Albert finally let me in. To pay him back, I threw his bathrobe in the tub, because it was hanging on my hook again—typical.

"I'm looking for a new apartment tonight," Albert yelled after me. "God forbid I should try your angelic patience any longer!"

Gottfried Schachtschnabel greeted me personally. "Glad you're feeling better, Constance," he said. Actually I'd only missed one of his classes. But of course he knew that nothing less than a serious illness could keep me away from his seminar.

Unfortunately right after class he was surrounded by three students from the senior seminar, who criticized his linking of the theory of psychoanalytic images with the theory of imperialist power structures as too theoretical. A pretty blond student in a totally skintight sweater made a really big deal of it. She

bitched loudly about the supposed missing link between Gottfried's theory and practice. She seemed determined to badger
Gottfried for hours with her practice. "Praxis" was the decisive
thing, she said, and patted her hair. I hated this competitive
behavior in women! There was no point in waiting for Gottfried.
But he said good-bye to me personally as I left.

Next week's seminar was supposed to be canceled because it
was Ash Wednesday. But Gottfried had pointed out that all the
Carnival hoopla was decadent and superfluous in light of the
world situation and especially the dying of the forests. Chlodwig
Schnell, that artful dodger, promptly added, "Carnival is capitalism in the Janus mask of the clown." But some woman immediately contradicted him and said that Carnival was the ancient
witches' festival and had absolutely nothing to do with the dying
of the forests and so on.

Of course Chlodwig immediately had to lecture her: "And
may I ask what you witches make your broomsticks out of? *Trees*,
right?"

But the woman didn't pay any attention to his whining. She
and her women's group were going to revive an ancient custom
by dressing up as witches on Carnival Monday and go through
the bars armed with scissors, and cut off men's ties. What a blast,
she said. Gottfried said that was a tremendously interesting
symbolic action, psychoanalytically, and he was glad to cancel
the seminar so the ladies could have Ash Wednesday to recover
from their delightful undertaking. But the ladies should please
take note of the fact that he personally didn't own a single tie.

I didn't go along for the tie cutting. I didn't know anyone in
that women's group. But Albert was invited to a costume party
at Barbara and Christian's secondhand shop and bar, and I
wanted to go along. Albert went as Donald Duck. And I went
as *The Communist Manifesto*. Typical: a *blind* person could see
we weren't compatible.

I'd taken a sheet and cut two eyeholes and one for my mouth.

On my stomach and back I'd fastened a map of Europe. Everyone asked me what I was supposed to be. It was really embarrassing that no one realized I was *The Communist Manifesto.*
Finally I quoted, "A specter is abroad in Europe . . . the specter
of Communism," and made a point of explaining that this was
the beginning of *The Communist Manifesto*—I was sure of that,
because Gottfried Schachtschnabel quoted it so often—only
then did everybody think it was incredibly funny. Then Christian asked everyone who came in what I, the ghost with the map
of Europe, represented. Later on, when Christian was three
sheets to the wind himself, he told the new arrivals that I was
Das Kapital by Karl Marx. He'd forgotten the quote, but people
still laughed like crazy, even though it didn't really make sense.

Albert distinguished himself as the authority on Donald Duck
stories. He was wearing a T-shirt with a sailor's bib and a little
red bow tie printed on it, and a sailor's cap from a novelty store,
where he'd also bought an itty-bitty duck's bill, which fit perfectly over his nose. He'd painted two white ovals around his
eyes, about the size of fried eggs—he really looked like Donald
Duck, totally ridiculous.

The whole evening he sat in a corner with a chemist, who
attacked Albert, shouting, "Donald, fancy meeting you at the
Duckwater Fair!" They told each other Donald Duck stories,
like they'd both grown up in Duckwater.

For a solid hour they discussed the question of how much a
Duckwater dollar was worth, judging by the price of a glass of
lemonade at the annual charity ball of the Duckwater Junior
Women's Club. The chemist claimed that earlier the lemonade
at the Duckwater Charity Ball had cost ten crowns; he was
absolutely sure of that, but now it cost twelve crowns. He was
sure of that, too. Albert suspected that the Daffy Duck Company had its webbed feet in the pie somewhere, but the chemist
thought the price increase had been long overdue; after all,

Huey, Dewey, and Louie had managed to get a 125 percent increase in their allowance. Then they made up a melody for the song for which Donald had won second place—after Gussy Goose—at the Duckwater popular music competition:

> *And when I cross the baaaar,*
> *please put my old guitaaaar*
> *with me into my graaaave.*

After that the two of them yelled for the rest of the evening, "If you don't have a soft gourd, buy hard apples from Appeldoorn." And "Hold me back—it's Gussy Goose!" I just wondered how the chemist could bear Albert's cultural niveau!

On Friday we had another fight because Albert wasn't prepared to have a harmonious separation. He wasn't prepared to promise that we could remain good friends after he moved out. I asked him how he visualized the situation. Reactive as usual, he asked how *I* visualized it. He said all my talk about harmony was empty chatter—I should go tell that to my kindergarten psychologist, he was fed up. I'd been fed up much longer than he had, guaranteed.

Albert said he wanted to end this discussion once and for all. He put on his coat. I asked him where he thought he was going.

He said, "I'm just going out for cigarettes."

I let him go without a word. The classic parting between two people who loved each other once but now just lived side by side in total alienation. I knew it, he knew it. He'd probably spend the night with that creepy broad who'd called up the week before and again while I was home sick. Recently he'd been out again without telling me where. Maybe the real estate lady had found an apartment for the Herr Doktor. Or was he moving in with another woman? Maybe he'd just send a moving company to come for his junk; that'd be just like him, to sneak off and never show his face again. The coward. Presumably he'd be avoiding me for the rest of his life. That was okay by me—better to end it with hate than to hate without end, even if it meant I might be alone for a long time. Maybe even forever. It still had to be better than putting up with this situation any longer.

Five minutes later Albert was back. He'd gotten some cigarettes. What had I expected?

16

In the last few weeks Juliet hadn't had time to go out in the evenings. She had to redo her new place, get stuff moved in and arranged. I'd called her several times, to bring her up to date on the latest developments. Since we absolutely had to see each other again, Juliet invited me over for coffee on Sunday afternoon. Birgit, a neighbor of hers would be there, too.

Birgit was lonely, Juliet had explained on the phone. She was twenty-five, but in some ways she seemed much younger because of her childish fantasies; in other ways she seemed much older, because the goal of these fantasies was nothing more or less than a perfectly sickening conventional marriage. Birgit worked at a branch of the municipal library. The rest of the time she just sat home waiting for the man of her dreams to tap on the window of her little fourth-floor apartment. But Birgit was very nice, and I simply had to meet her.

It was my first visit to Juliet's place, and I liked it. She had two big rooms all to herself, plus a kitchen and bath. It looked a lot like mine except that it was more colorful. Juliet had white textured paper on all the walls. And a potted palm, only bigger than mine. And an ornate desk from the secondhand shop. She had the same Conran's lamps, except that hers were orange, and mine were white. We had the same hardwood floors and in the hallway almost the same coco matting. And the same bedspread, except that Juliet's had brown-and-white stripes, while mine was black and white, because everything I had was either black or white. Juliet had painted her baseboards green, to match the potted palm, she explained. My baseboards were white. Juliet's kitchen was all in yellow.

In the other room she had a good-looking sofa from Conran's and a round table on which sat an egg-liqueur cake—Juliet had baked it herself. Birgit went back to her apartment to get a pint of whipping cream. "The more calories, the better it tastes," she said. She was absolutely right.

Birgit was a surprise. You would never have known by looking at her that she worked at the library. She was blond and wore her hair in a lion's mane, just the way I'd have liked to have mine, but that style never worked for me, no matter how closely I followed the instructions in the magazines. They always told you to just wash your hair, shake your head a couple of times, fluff your hair up with your hands, and then let it dry by itself. Even if I patted it for hours, my retarded hair would stick out in all the wrong directions. Besides, I could never get it shiny like Birgit's and the models' hair in the magazines. But I didn't have the courage to ask Birgit how she did it. I thought it seemed more appropriate for me to be interested in her job.

Birgit was responsible for checking the circulation records at the municipal library. She complained that she constantly had to work overtime because people borrowed too many books. Everyone seemed to take out ten books, but she could swear they didn't read more than one, even though they kept the books out three weeks past the due date. She thought there should be a system whereby a librarian could test these so-called readers to see whether they read the books and understood them. Only if he passed could the reader take out more books, and then only as many as he had actually read. "The way it's done now, all that unnecessary borrowing only results in overtime," Birgit complained. "And we don't even get paid for it!"

I told Birgit I was reading *The Phenomenology of Mind,* but that I'd bought my own copy.

"That's very good," Birgit said.

Then I asked her if she could recommend a good book for me to read during semester break. But she couldn't. She didn't read during her free time, because when you were surrounded by books all day long, you couldn't stand the thought of reading a book in the evening. That sounded logical to me.

Juliet's cake was fantastic. I took another small piece. She had gotten the recipe from her mother-in-law. "My ex really loved this cake," she said.

"Have you heard anything from him?" Birgit asked.

Juliet said yes, but left it at that.

"My sister has a very happy marriage," Birgit said. She told us her sister had a darling husband and a darling baby.

Juliet told me she'd seen the pictures of the baby's birth. Birgit wanted to run upstairs to get the pictures, so I could see them, but I said I'd rather have another piece of cake. So Birgit confined herself to an oral account of her sister's happiness. The darling baby was a darling little boy; even when he was born he'd had the most darling hair, and he had the most darling name: Benjamin. "Married only four months, and already my sister's so happy," Birgit enthused.

"I had to get married because of the apartment. We wanted a big place, and without being legally married you couldn't get anywhere with landlords in those days. Besides, my husband got a better position when he got married. He's a teacher, see," Juliet explained, and beamed. "Wow, am I ever happy to be divorced!"

"Everyone has to have their learning experiences," I said. "With some people it just takes a little longer. It's always been clear as day to me that I'll never get married."

"You can't overlook the fact that there are certain advantages to being married. As a married woman my net worth was greater. Now I have to pay more rent, and have less room. And I can't travel anymore—no one can afford to travel alone."

"But not being married doesn't mean you have to live alone and travel alone."

"Yes," Juliet said, "but unless you're married, your colleagues don't really take you seriously. Even the women. Especially the women."

Birgit nodded vigorously. "I always have a guilty conscience when someone calls me frau, when in reality I'm just a fräulein."

"Does that mean you only accept married women?" I asked Birgit somewhat spitefully.

"It's easy for you to talk—you have a long-term relationship." She sighed. Apparently she'd heard all about me from Juliet. "So why don't you marry him?" she asked.

I was speechless. What idiocy. But Juliet laughed and said she thought Birgit's idea wasn't all that bad. It'd be very advantageous for me to marry a doctor, considering how lousy my professional prospects were as a filmmaker. "And divorcing a doctor is worth his weight in gold," she said, laughing.

I explained again that I wasn't ever going to get married because I rejected the tyranny of the state and therefore didn't need any state legitimation for my private happiness.

Juliet said she needed something to drink, and went into the kitchen to get a bottle of wine. When she came back, she said, "So, you should marry your Albert."

"Never." I admitted that he and I might live together, though not under the present conditions, and that there were various things we had to talk out, but getting married was out of the question. I reminded Juliet that Gottfried Schachtschnabel had argued in his lecture that marriage was the death knell for romance and that she'd agreed with him.

"Your Gottfried Schachtschnabel talks a lot of garbage, honest. At least on this subject."

I was floored.

"Let me tell you, there are lots of other things that kill romance," Juliet said. "If you're living with someone and are unemployed, that doesn't do much for romance, believe you me."

I had to agree. "The problem in our case," I said, "is that Albert and I aren't compatible. What I'm looking for is an equal partner who shares all my interests."

"Common interests—don't make me laugh. If your goal is to do everything together, let me give you a tip as a psychologist: get married, have a kid, or three, build a house, go into debt— and automatically you'll have complete togetherness!"

"No!"

"Absolutely! When you have debts, or kids, or both, you can't spend the evening cultivating all your interesting interests! You sit there in grim togetherness in front of the TV and worry about the kids and the debts you have together."

"But that's so beautiful," Birgit said to Juliet. "See, my sister and her baby and husband also want to build their own nest together soon, and it's incredibly important for the baby to have a yard to play in and fresh air."

Juliet's idea of togetherness and Birgit's idea of happiness were getting on my nerves. I felt compelled to dissociate myself from them in no uncertain terms. "I'm looking for a relationship built on an intellectual basis, not a material one," I told them. "For me, a relationship has to be mutual give-and-take, not a capital investment. Besides, to me, free expression of your inner feelings is an indispensable component of any partnership."

"You can't even be unfaithful properly till you're married,

trust me," Juliet said. Then she drained her glass almost in one gulp and said grimly, "My ex talked about his innermost feelings all the time, too. Emotional blackmail." Then she went back to the kitchen to get more wine.

Was Juliet trying to convert me? Or had she had too much to drink? She came back and pointed the corkscrew at me. "You want a guarantee that romance will last a lifetime. You think if you don't get married that'll buy you pure, true love. You're making a big mistake, trust me. Your relationship with Albert is going down the tubes even though you're not married." She thought a moment. "Probably your relationship is going down the tubes *because* you're not married."

"Every marriage goes down the tubes anyway," I said.

"That's not true—take my sister and her husband, they're really happy. And, forget what you've read in the papers, I can guarantee you Prince Charles won't ever divorce Diana!"

I had to laugh. This Birgit was so corny!

"Right," Juliet said. "We have to find a Prince Charles for Birgit. What about putting an ad in the personals? For both of you?"

I thought that was a great idea, for Birgit. But not for me. I'd read somewhere that the people who answered the personals were all weirdos. And the people who put them in all had unrealistic expectations.

"You both have unrealistic expectations—you absolutely have to put in an ad together."

Birgit said she wasn't in any hurry. She'd almost been engaged once, and now she'd rather wait for the right man to come along instead of wasting her energy on casual affairs.

"How are you going to find out who's the right man and who's nonessential if you just sit home and mope?" Juliet asked.

Birgit said when she met Mr. Right, Mr. One-in-a-million, she'd know it.

Juliet claimed most people didn't marry Mr. One-in-a-million but someone they'd known from the sandbox. Which proved that most people hadn't gotten to know a million possible marriage partners, but five at most. "The eternal search for that one-and-only is the greatest illusion."

"I'm willing to sacrifice the certainty of here and now for the uncertain hope of something better," I told Juliet. I drank to her: "I can find something better than bourgeois marriage anywhere."

"Can I ask you a dumb question?" Juliet said. "Did you ever really love Albert?"

That made me angry, and I told Juliet she was right: it was a dumb question. And I didn't really see why she was against marriage. I was wondering what I should really believe.

"If my first marriage had been unhappy, I wouldn't want to get married again either," Birgit said.

Juliet said, "You two are full of illusions—"

"And in your extensive experience, what *is* the important thing?" I interrupted her.

Juliet hesitated. "Willingness to compromise."

"Yes," Birgit said, "of course you have to adjust in all sorts of ways."

"No," I said. "I'm not going to live with someone just to make compromises."

"This discussion is pointless," Juliet said. "I suggest we look at the personals in the paper. They're swarming with Prince Charmings."

We declined with thanks. That wasn't the right way to go about it, Birgit said.

"How did your sister meet her husband?" I asked her.

"It was an accident." Birgit laughed. "She rear-ended him after he cut in front of her when she had the right-of-way. And she had all kinds of problems with his insurance company, so they had to see each other quite often. He ended up taking care of the whole thing for her. After all, he was at fault." Birgit laughed again. "And then it turned out the two of them *really* hit it off." It was clear that Birgit had told this story often, with relish. "That's how I'd like it to be for me, too," she said.

On my way home I was wondering whether I shouldn't get another car. Another old tin-can Renault or a Beetle. If I had a car, I thought, I could rear-end Gottfried Schachtschnabel's denim Mercedes. Or ask Gottfried to jump-start me.

17 It was the end of February, and Gottfried Schachtschnabel's seminar was meeting for the last time that semester. Irmela gave me a stupid grin when I went up to the lectern to ask him something.

"Listen," he said, "I have to go to Kreuzberg again today. Okay?"

"Okay," I said.

When we were sitting in his Mercedes, he said, "Today I have some time. We could go to your bar and celebrate the end of the semester. Of course, only if you have time and are in the mood."

Again we found a parking place right in front of the Kaput. Niyazi, the proprietor, saw me getting out of the Mercedes and nodded. We sat in the back by the window, at the best table. "Are you hungry?" Gottfried asked. "My treat."

It was great. I ordered the Upper Bavarian lentil soup with sausage for 7.95 marks—that seemed about right—and Gottfried ordered the schnitzel with Upper Bavarian turnips for 12.80. I told him that Niyazi was a loyal Bavarian. His father came from Turkey, but Niyazi had Bavarian citizenship and was extremely proud of it. The regular customers said he wasn't an Upper Bavarian but a Super Bavarian. "And now he lives here because in Berlin he can be more Bavarian than in Bavaria," Gottfried said. Amazing how astutely he'd analyzed that right away.

After we finished eating I immediately showed him my *Phenomenology of Mind,* which I had in my pocket, because now I was reading it every free moment I had. By page 29 I'd already written "exactly!" several times in the margin, and at least a dozen times "wonderful!" I'd never have thought I'd get so much out of Hegel, I admitted to Gottfried. Hegel was full of relevant points that I could easily work into my film. Gottfried was deeply impressed. "I'm impressed!" he said.

As I was skimming the book, I'd found a major quote on page 208 that exactly characterized my separation from Albert. I asked Gottfried whether he didn't agree that it would make a good impression on the funding commission if I began my screenplay with a quote from Hegel. I'd already copied the quote on a slip of paper—in block letters, to see the kind of visual effect it made—and now showed it to Gottfried.

THIS SEPARATION
IS NOT IN ITSELF FOR THE CONSCIOUSNESS OF SELF;
WHICH, AS ITS OWN SELFNESS
KNOWS THE OTHER.
—GEORG WILHELM FRIEDRICH HEGEL,
The Phenomenology of Mind

Gottfried was deeply impressed. He said all I had to do was check whether the context in which Hegel spoke of this "separation" had anything to do with the separation I wanted to treat in my film. I asked how he'd interpreted Hegel in this case. Gottfried said he unfortunately didn't have the context of this passage in mind at the moment.

Then I asked him whether I could take his senior seminar next semester.

"Of course," he answered. "Why? What year are you?" He seemed absolutely amazed when I told him that after vacation I'd be starting the second semester of my third year. I was amazed at his amazement. True, there were a few ninnies in my class who were two or three years younger and had started right after secondary school, but they weren't any better-looking than me.

"Somehow you seem more mature," Gottfried said.

Aha, that was it. Of course: the others weren't reading Hegel.

"So why are you already working on your senior film project? If you're only in your third year, you still have another year, maybe more."

I told him I thought it was important to get started now because, as he'd said himself, I had a demanding topic, and I also had to work my way through Hegel.

"That should keep you busy during the vacation," Gottfried said. Was I going away? he asked.

I told him I probably wouldn't go away, or at least not for long, because I could do better theoretical work at home (and because Albert didn't get that much vacation, but of course I didn't say that).

"Yes, yes, without theory everything's dreary," he said. Then he told me he also had a lot of theoretical work to do during vacation. He had to finish his dissertation; it was pressing because he wanted to apply for a new position. Nowadays it was better to have a title. Nowadays everything was becoming hyperscholarly, even the training of creative artists, but it did have its advantages, of course.

"Of course," I said. I asked what his dissertation was on.

"The usual topic," he said, and laughed. True, it was a special subtopic, as was customary for doctoral dissertations. He wanted to trace the illusion of sensuality in Hollywood films, with special emphasis on the films of Rita Hayworth and Ava Gardner.

I thought that was fabulous. "Why did you pick those films?" I asked.

"Frankly, blondes don't do much for me," Gottfried said. "I just don't care for them." He laughed, and I laughed too. I had the same hair color as Ava Gardner.

At that very moment—Gottfried was laughing and I tossed back my Ava Gardner–colored hair with a laugh—Albert came in. "What are you doing here?" I asked him. "Isn't there anything on TV?"

Hunger had driven him out of the house, he said; I hadn't done any shopping. Without asking whether there was room, he sat down at our table.

"This is Albert," I told Gottfried, and to Albert, I said, "This is Gottfried Schachtschnabel, my instructor." I tried to think whether I'd introduced them to each other in the proper order.

"Ah, your instructor," Albert said.

Gottfried said we were there because we'd just had the last seminar of the semester and we'd decided to top it off with a glass of wine afterward. "Where are the other students?" Albert asked. Gottfried said he'd had to go to Kreuzberg anyway, and he'd taken the liberty of giving me a lift. But now he had to go; he had to be somewhere.

"Yeah, I bet you do," Albert said. I could have killed him.

But Gottfried didn't go immediately; he said he had time for one more glass of wine. When Albert told him he was a doctor, Gottfried said he'd had his appendix out when he was six, and since then he'd always been afraid of shots. I thought it was fantastic the way he could talk so openly about his fears.

Albert talked pure garbage and made a complete fool of me. He said he just watched movies to be entertained. To him political films were boring. When I kicked him in the shins under the table, he said loudly, "Ouch, what are you kicking me in the shins for?"

Then he felt the need to comment on my plans for the film. Since I apparently felt compelled to make an artistic contribution to saving endangered humanity and the poor animal kingdom, he had a good idea. He'd really like to see a film in which Jane Goodall or some other protector of animals put in a word for the poor bird spider, threatened with extinction. Not always the same old baby seals and kittens and so on. The existence of the bird spider was also severely threatened by civilization. And he could even imagine Brigitte Bardot looking beautiful with a few dark bird spiders in her blond hair. Gottfried laughed politely.

Then Gottfried came to my defense. He told Albert we still had to decide which subjects my film would treat. "We," he said! After that Albert spared us further comments.

Unfortunately Gottfried really had to go. If Albert hadn't come, I bet he would have stayed. He looked at Albert hesitantly and said, "Actually I wanted to pay for Constance, but only if you'll permit me."

"There's nothing I'd be happier to permit," said the cheapskate.

"Give yourself time," Gottfried said to me in parting. And, "It'll work out."

After he'd left, Albert remarked graciously that Gottfried Schachtschnabel wasn't as much of an idiot as he'd expected. But he looked like your typical revolutionary. Then he said, enviously, that when he was a student he'd never had an instructor drive him home. "The competition never sleeps," I said ambiguously.

It was very good that Albert got a glimpse of Gottfried Schachtschnabel. And in spite of Albert's embarrassing chatter it was probably also good that Gottfried had met him. "Nothing makes a woman more attractive than another man bidding for her favor," my mother always said. "Divide and conquer" was the principle of the successful woman, she said. I was in the best of all possible situations: a woman between two men.

And what had Gottfried said in parting? "It'll work out," he'd said. Got it.

18

"After March fifteenth there'll be two more one-person households in the Federal Republic of Germany including West Berlin," Albert said.

"Why?"

"Because Christian and Barbara are moving into a commune."

"Christian and Barbara of the secondhand store?"

"Right."

"But they're married! Or isn't she taking Christian? And what about her rabbit?"

"According to what I've heard, she's taking her husband and she's giving the rabbit up for adoption. Or was it the other way around?" Albert said, and lit a cigarette. "They want to move into a commune to get defixated from their fixation on an exclusive relationship, or rather their fixation on marriage."

"I can't picture that."

"I'm taking over their apartment."

"You're taking over their apartment?"

"Right."

"Why?"

"That's what you wanted. By the fifteenth I'll have the place fixed up. If you want, I can move in a few days before that."

"Oh, I see," I said, perfectly cool. "But you just don't move into a commune when you're married," I added, and then I felt sick to my stomach because I was so sorry for Barbara and Christian. When I thought of the poor rabbit, I started to cry.

19 I made Albert pay me the rent for April, too. I couldn't line up a subtenant that quickly, nor did I want to. Even though Albert bitched about the extra rent, he knew perfectly well that he was getting a good deal; usually you have to give notice much further in advance. By the beginning of March he was already in his new place. The day after he'd told me he was taking over the apartment, he began fixing it up. And he had the nerve to ask me whether I wanted to help. That was all I needed. How easy he made our separation on himself. He had all the feelings of a doorknob.

"I'd advise you," Juliet said, "to be somewhere else when Albert moves out. I went away, too, when my husband moved out; otherwise I'd have felt I was witnessing my own defeat. And we would have fought over every shitty little thing. Trust me." Out of the solidarity one abandoned woman feels with another she offered to let me stay with her during "that period," as she called it. But I didn't want that—it would've looked as though I were running away. I wanted to go somewhere, that would be better all around.

Besides, it was high time I went to see my parents. My father was sulking because I hadn't been yearning for his company since my birthday in November, when I came to pick up the delicate art nouveau teapot and cups. He was still bitching that I hadn't even celebrated Christmas with them. He was probably jealous of Albert—not only because no man was good enough for his daughter, but because his daughter actually preferred Albert to him, that he couldn't handle. I read somewhere about the Oedipus complex, that supposedly all sons want to sleep with their mothers. I also read that all daughters are fixated on their fathers, hence the Electra complex; but that all fathers think their daughters . . . they don't have a complex for that; apparently that's considered normal.

I told my mother, after she'd lowered my defenses by asking how Albert was doing, that I was living alone now; my father's first reaction to this was that he guessed I'd need more money. As though Albert, that tightwad, ever gave me a penny. My mother was real cool about it. She'd said that now that I was independent—independent, she said, as though I'd been dependent before—I'd be able to come and see them more often. Typical: all my mother cared about was her needs, and all my father cared about was what something was going to cost him.

But at least my mother told me that my father had hinted he'd give me a little extra for my living expenses, provided, of course, I came to see them. So no money worries at least. With the money I got from Albert for the rent and a loan from my aunt's dowry account, I bought a mini-Fiat from one of the mechanically inclined dudes at the Kaput. Unfortunately it was spinach-green, but it wouldn't need to be inspected for a year. I needed a car. First, I wanted to go away; second, I was on my own now; and third, Albert's new apartment was quite far, and I'd probably have to drive over there now and then to work through our past.

With all the excitement I didn't have a chance to really deal with my head. Before I left, I had to switch over the registration on the car. And I had to lock all my worldly goods in my room to make sure Albert didn't appropriate any of my property. Probably he'd come by with some tramp to ransack the apartment.

March 15 was a Friday, but for safety's sake I left on Monday. I packed my dirty laundry and the other stuff you usually take home into the car and drove to L——. I couldn't stand that stupid little town; my parents only moved there four years ago, because my father had gotten a better job through my uncle, who lived there; my father had gone from an ordinary engineer to a managing engineer. But the main thing was he could buy a few square feet of land in a revolting bourgeois allotment-garden colony that people usually waited years to get into. So my father was happy in L——, and so was my mother, because she could sit around all day and yak with Aunt Katharina, but I didn't know anyone there, so my parents shouldn't have been surprised that I never felt like coming to visit them.

Actually I'd have preferred to take the train, with a seat facing toward the back. I never did understand why the seat that faced front was always the first one taken. I preferred facing backward—that way everything that went by the window was already in the past. But I took my car because driving is a good distraction—I had to concentrate on the other cars and on the weird noises the car was making, rather than on Albert's moving out.

My father took one look at me and began to treat me like a small child. My car wasn't safe for long drives, my hair was too long—how could I even see? Weren't there any hairdressers in Berlin? On the other hand, he launched into his speech the very first evening: I was too old to just hang around, it was time for me to think about getting married, this couldn't go on forever. He talked about my separation from Albert like I'd just lost my job through my own fault and had to go look for another one. My father was prepared to auction me off to the next man who came along.

The next morning, after my father had finally left for work, my mother said that he just didn't understand, I didn't really have to be in a rush to get married—with my looks, there was no need for that yet. The ones who got married young often made terrible matches. Oh, charming: at least my mother was willing to wait for the highest bidder. Then she went on and on about Albert as though we were still together. Actually she'd only seen him once, one time when they came to visit me. The fact that Albert was a doctor hadn't impressed my mother much, but it worked wonders on my father. My mother had been overwhelmed by how good-looking Albert was: "What cute curls he has," she'd said, sighing like a teenager. "What a handsome man! Your father was never that good-looking." It occurred to me that Gottfried wasn't nearly as good-looking as Albert, and I wondered what I'd done to deserve such superficial parents.

Well, did I have someone else already? my mother asked, so diplomatically that I suspected my father had put her up to it.

I didn't feel like telling my mother about Gottfried. After all, he was my teacher, and my mother and father always got incredibly upset when one of the secretaries in my father's company had a relationship with one of the men from the company. My mother really got upset—she was probably worried about my father—but she would act real cool. Besides, things weren't to that point with Gottfried yet. So I said, "No!!"

Did Albert have another woman? "No!" I said sharply. Well, in that case why had I left him? It was hopeless trying to discuss it with her.

Of course she told my father. That evening he asked me straight out why I'd left Albert if I didn't have someone else. I was ready to explode. I asked whether they thought I should keep using the old guy till I got a replacement. "Don't you ever think of anything but saving money and eating leftovers?" I yelled, and slammed the door.

I heard my mother yelling at my father—why in the world did he have to go and ask me that? "The child's going through a difficult phase!" My father muttered something.

It was my parents who were going through a difficult phase.

I couldn't take it anymore. I suddenly thought of Ilona Reuter, who'd gone to school with me. She lived only about an hour away. I called her and we talked for a long time; I told her my problem and she said I should come and stay with her, that she'd love to see me. Great. I had to get away from my parents.

My mother didn't mind me going to Ilona's, nor did my father. As a single woman I seemed to embody a failed upbringing to them. My father gave me some extra money for my "vacation at Ilona's." He had a guilty conscience. My mother, who hadn't gotten around to ironing my clothes yet, said she'd send them to me. They were glad to get rid of me.

Yes, the days of my carefree childhood were past. Now I was supposed to become the way my parents were. I decided it was time to cut the umbilical cord.

Being with Ilona was worth the trip. She'd separated from her husband six months ago, after six years of marriage, and without having another man in the wings! Since then she'd lived alone. She kept up with other women from our class, who, in the meantime, were all married and total morons. Not a single good marriage in the lot, Ilona assured me. And the worst part of marriage was the boredom.

"You can't imagine how bored I was."

"You bored? But you're always involved in so many things."

"I am now. But those evenings with Max were deadly. At night he'd go through his files, but otherwise he wanted peace and quiet. I have my work at the lab—I can't bring it home, and I wouldn't want to. But during the day I work pretty much in isolation, and in the evening I want some entertainment."

"Yes," I said.

"No," Ilona said, "my story won't be any help to you. Do you know how Tolstoy's *Anna Karenina* begins?"

I didn't.

" 'Happy families are all alike; every unhappy family is unhappy in its own way.' "

"Right," I said, and promised to read *Anna Karenina*.

"No, don't do that," Ilona said. "It has such a terrible ending. And besides, I don't think you'd like it."

I stayed with her for a week. While she was at the lab during the day, I just drifted around. The moment she got home the phone would begin to ring. We did things with her friends, on the weekend we cooked together, otherwise we'd go to the only student hangout in town, where everybody knew everybody else. "Since I've been alone I meet someone new every day," Ilona said.

I was finally able to stop thinking about Albert's not being there when I got back. I felt euphoric because the hoped-for change of circumstances had occurred. Finally.

"Every situation is better than the previous one," I had told Ilona.

Then I got depressed again, because I couldn't direct the course of change.

"Well, he hasn't left the country," Ilona had said.

"Now I intend to find myself," I had answered.

"Soon you'll find a new guy." Those were the words Ilona sent me home with.

I drove to Berlin feeling calmer. I was glad I'd driven; the train is only nice when someone's going to be picking you up.

Albert's room was empty and clean. He'd gotten someone to help him carry the old black table up from the basement, where we'd stored it for lack of space; it was in his room, where I'd asked him to put it. I looked for a note, a message. I couldn't find a thing. I called him up at his new place because I wanted to ask what that was supposed to mean. He wasn't home.

I checked the closet: nothing of Albert's in there. Two dark hairs in the sink. An old ski cap of his on the shoe rack in the hallway. We'd used it as a shoe rag. Otherwise no relics. Also no mail for him. His forwarding instructions were working flawlessly. The palm, which I hadn't locked in my room but had put in the kitchen so he'd water it, hadn't been watered in at least a week. So he'd moved out as soon as I left.

What had I expected? A bouquet of red roses, slightly wilted, and a note, somewhat yellowed, with words of farewell in a trembling hand: "I shall think of you always, forgive me. . . ."—some of the words smudged by tears. That would have been appropriate, the very least one could expect. That was how I'd do it in my film, I decided. My film would show Albert how a proper separation was done.

I looked around Albert's empty room. Nothing left. Just the facts. It was no longer our apartment, but now my apartment. Finally I had breathing room.

20 I had to begin the process of working through our separation alone; Albert wasn't home. Or at least he didn't answer the phone. I didn't want to go out, in case he called. I wanted to give him another chance.

Why had we separated? Because we weren't compatible—that sounded too general. Not analytical enough. I made a list of why other people I knew had split up.

1. Elke and Heinz got divorced because Heinz was always drunk and ran up debts. He only wanted to sleep with Elke on Christmas Eve and her birthday. She told me that herself. Heinz said it was just no good with Elke. He remarried soon afterward. It took her years before she'd found a new boyfriend.
2. Ilona and Max got divorced because Ilona got bored with Max. And, as she admitted to me when she was quite drunk, Max physically disgusted her. After she'd slept with other

men a couple of times, the disgust became overwhelming. Ilona said Max was going around telling other people she expected more of him than he could deliver.

3. Martin doesn't know to this day why Regina left him. Regina doesn't want to talk about it.

4. Friedrich and Monika got divorced when Monika found out that Friedrich had an affair going in another city. He even went on vacation with this woman—he told Monika he was taking continuing-education seminars. Friedrich remarried, but not to the mistress. Monika is still mourning Friedrich and blackmails him with their child.

5. Winfried and Sybille broke up because Sybille married Winfried just for his money and his status as a physician, Winfried says. They never paid any attention to their two children, and his stinginess was getting more and more intolerable.

6. Kurt and Irmtraud split up because Irmtraud wanted to grow intellectually, and besides she wanted children. But Kurt was stagnating mentally, and years ago a doctor had determined that he was sterile. Kurt says there was nothing he could do about it.

7. Juliane and Michael split up because Juliane had always worshiped Michael, who was much older, as supercompetent. When Michael lost his job, Juliane's teenybopper illusions collapsed, Michael says. Juliane says that in the last few years Michael went through a total personality change; he became more and more hostile. This wasn't the man she once loved.

8. Achim and Tina got divorced because Achim met the love of his life. He met her right after his wife had just had their fifth child. Achim moans and groans about being separated from the five kids, who of course stayed with their mother. He can't see the kids very often because he moved far away with the love of his life. Tina says Achim was afraid of getting old; he saw himself as a happening young guy, and the kids made him realize how old he really was. With his new wife, who is much younger, Achim can imagine that he is still happening. No children yet.

9. Bernd says Carola saw him as the Great Protector. Carola says she couldn't stand the way Bernd acted like her Svengali. Bernd's new girlfriend is eighteen; he's over forty.

10. Sonja and Andreas split up because Sonja was frigid, as Andreas tells everybody. In spite of his efforts, she didn't succeed in overcoming her parents' inhibited sexual morality. Sonja says Andreas thought he was the great sex explorer, but in fact he was just a little wiener incapable of love. Sonja ended the relationship.

I was just wondering how Sieglinde and Wolf-Dietrich would eventually break up when the phone rang. It was Albert.

His parents sent their best. How were things? Did I have a nice time at my parents'? How was Ilona doing? He'd been thinking of me. Especially when he was laying down the carpets—that was something I was much better at than he was. The whole apartment smelled of paint. Should he bother spending money on curtains? Was my car still working? We chatted for an hour and made a date for the next evening.

I read over my list again. Why do people split up? There are as many reasons as there are for people loving each other.

21

We met at the Kaput as if nothing had happened. Albert spent the night at my place because it was closer and because his apartment reeked of paint.

Three days later I visited him in his new apartment for the first time. Everything was neat and tidy, as always. Now he had a TV room and a bedroom. Because his old bed looked so small in the new room, he'd bought a wider one from Barbara at the secondhand shop, with a chrome art deco frame. He also bought a marble-topped table for the kitchen. He had a new lamp in the TV room, also deco. And light gray wall-to-wall carpeting. Very elegant.

Albert had laid the carpeting all by himself, he told me proudly. And painted the baseboards gray all by himself, too.

Albert made spaghetti. The sauce was lumpy. Even though he'd put in cheese, cream, ham, olives, butter, and vodka, it tasted like Italian dressing. Nevertheless, he was deeply impressed by his own domestic skills. And I praised the lumpy sauce. It was a very harmonious evening, until I suggested that we go to the movies on Saturday. Albert said he didn't have any time. He didn't say what he had planned. Probably trying to make me jealous.

Even though it was late, I decided not to spend the night there. What did I have the car for? If he had no time for me on Saturday, well, I wouldn't always be available either. Two could play at that game.

The next evening I spontaneously decided to go over to Juliet's for a chat. She was happy to have me drop in. Her new bed had been delivered that afternoon, a double bed like Albert's. We bounced around a bit on the new mattress. Juliet said, "I'm so glad to be rid of that old twin bed from my marriage."

"Albert has a new bed, too."

"He's doing the right thing."

"Why?"

"Why? Why?" Juliet said and bounced on the mattress. Then she asked how far I'd gotten with rearranging my ex's ex-room, and whether she should come over some time and help me rearrange things.

I told her it was incredibly nice of her to offer and she absolutely must come over, but I wanted to leave Albert's room empty. Juliet said psychologically it wasn't a good idea. I told her I wanted to leave it empty not for psychological reasons but for aesthetic reasons; I'd always wanted to have an empty room, and that had absolutely nothing to do with Albert. Besides, it had the table in it, and when I got back to my screenplay, that would be ideal—a room with just a table and chair in it, a very work-intensive atmosphere. "Well, if it helps you find yourself," Juliet said.

Suddenly she asked if I had a picture of Albert on me. I happened to have one in my wallet. I forgot to take it out. Rather embarrassing, because when you split up you're not supposed to carry a picture of your ex around with you.

"Not bad-looking, your Albert."

"Not mine anymore."

"Still, not bad-looking."

"Yes, he's not bad-looking. And he's a doctor, which is bad for a person's character," I said, making a point of sounding bitter, to hide my pride that I'd hooked such a handsome man and a doctor. Or had hooked him once upon a time.

"I thought that was him," Juliet said. "I saw him in the Kaput. Week before last, while you were away, I went there fairly late with a colleague, and when we got there he was just leaving."

"But how did you know it was him?"

"Someone said 'Bye, Albert,' and I thought, That's Albert!"

"When was that exactly?"

"If you really want to know *exactly*, he was with a blonde."

I didn't ask any more questions. I'd known for ages that he was cheating on me. With nurses. I feared neither death nor the devil, only nurses. But others mustn't talk about it. I don't want anyone to tell me I'm the loser, I thought to myself.

Still, Juliet noticed that I was pissed. "She looked like a bad version of you, at best. And she was all dolled up," she insisted. "She wouldn't stand a chance against you."

"Don't worry," I said, "she's only one of many." I placated Juliet, who was reproaching herself for telling me about another woman Albert was running around with. And I placated myself.

22

I ran into Sieglinde in the supermarket. I was in a hurry; it was Saturday, half an hour before the stores closed, and I wanted to buy a new two-colored ribbon for my typewriter so I could type my screenplay over the weekend.

We hadn't seen each other in almost two months, only talked on the phone once or twice. She greeted me silently, but with a warm embrace. Still holding on to me, she said, "Be glad you're rid of him—he was cheating on you anyway."

"I cheated on him, too."

"I don't want to remind you of the time he beat you up," Sieglinde said loudly. We were standing at the sausage counter with at least two dozen people around us.

"Sometimes physical aggression isn't as bad as verbal violence," I said softly.

"Hey, listen!" Sieglinde exclaimed. "He hit you!" I told Sieglinde I didn't really need any sausage. She followed me to the prepared foods aisle—no one was there. She clutched my arm, so I had to get the can of ravioli off the shelf with my left hand.

"I hit him back, you know," I said, "and once I whacked him first."

"But you're much weaker," she said.

"But I hurt him. Verbally I was much stronger."

"But he has someone else now," Sieglinde said.

"How do you know?" I told her in no uncertain terms that I hadn't heard anything about that.

Sieglinde admitted she hadn't heard anything either, but why else would Albert have moved out?

"Because I wanted him to," I said. "And Albert already had lots of others. Me too."

"I feel so sorry for you," she said.

"Albert's not doing so well himself."

"Say, why do you defend him all the time? I thought you split up with him. If I were you . . ." Sieglinde interrupted herself and finally released my arm.

"Theory and praxis are two different things," I said finally. Let her think what she wanted. She would anyway. In any case, I couldn't stand Sieglinde giving me advice. Wolf-Dietrich cheated on her, too. He also beat her up. And he didn't even sleep with her anymore—I knew that for a fact almost. She watched over him so jealously, and whenever he looked at another woman for even a fraction of a second, she immediately wondered if he was having an affair with her, so it was obvious he didn't have much to do with her, his ironclad girlfriend. Besides, he called her "my old lady"! And here she was giving advice! As if she were better off, as if Wolf-Dietrich were better than Albert. I had every reason to be offended. I told Sieglinde I had to go because I had some other errands to do. "I have to have you over again soon," she called after me.

When I got to the stationery store, they were just letting down the blinds. So I wouldn't make any progress on my screenplay, again. Exhausted and disappointed, I dragged myself home and lay down. I was pissed at Sieglinde.

23

Oh, how can I forget you,
when there is always something there to remind
me;
always something there to remind me. . . .

I used to think that was a love song.

Albert had taken everything that belonged to him, and everything I'd given him. But there were still memories everywhere, objects that became relics. My apartment had become an Albert Auerbach museum.

I LOVE YOU it said on the gingerbread heart, the first thing I threw in the garbage. Then came a portrait I'd sketched of Albert. If he didn't want to keep it, I didn't either. Then a wall hanging, no bigger than a doormat, a gift from his mother, who'd knotted this atrocity herself, with goofy fringes. It was lying in the back of the clothes closet and now I could finally throw it away. That was worth the pain of splitting up right there. I dumped the remains of my lunch onto the wall hanging/ doormat; the ravioli matched the pattern perfectly. And then the perfume from Albert, which always gave me a headache. I wondered what memories he had thrown in the garbage. When I was at his place, not one of my gifts had been missing. He was living in a Constance Wechselburger museum.

I took the antique silver bangle he'd bought me the year before last as a birthday and Christmas present, wrapped it in foil, and put it in the freezer. That was a good hiding place. I might wear it again in five years. The huge blue teddy bear that sat next to my bed was also from Albert. We'd won it at a fair.

"Which one would you choose if you could have any of these?" he'd asked me.

"No question; the blue teddy bear," I'd answered spontaneously.

Albert had snapped his fingers like a big shot. "Staff! Let's have one pale-blue teddy bear for the lady!"

So now I took it and carried it to the playground across the street. "Who wants a bear?" I asked.

Only three children were there. They didn't say anything; they seemed amazed at this unexpected gift. So I put the teddy bear on the bench next to the sandbox, thinking one of them would want it, and left. I watched them from my kitchen window. Half an hour later they buried the bear in the sandbox. What happened to it after that, I don't know.

I fetched a box from the cellar, and then shoeboxes from the closet. Then I started on the knickknacks from the shelf—all reminders of Albert. I took the large rhinestone brooch he bought me at the flea market and put it in the mother-of-pearl box, an Easter present. I also put in the little plastic pig with the little plastic piglets—the very first present he gave me; he gave it to me right in the middle of the department store. "Look what I pinched for you in the toy department," he'd said. I put the mother-of-pearl box in a shoebox, along with the art deco vase that I had wrapped in tissue paper. And on top, two windup tin butterflies. Once he gave me an ostrich egg. Wrapped in a lot of tissue paper, it would only fit in my biggest shoebox, but the ostrich-feather fan fit in the same box. An ostrich egg and a fan made of ostrich feathers: my memories were properly sorted.

A shoebox filled with pictures of Albert. And his letters. No temptation to reread them, but I wanted to save them. Later, when I retire, I'll want to reread all my friends' letters. But not till later. I still had more to my life than just memories.

I took the photo of us out of the black art nouveau frame over the toilet. I hung the empty frame back on the wall. Without our picture, it was free of the blot of memory.

The little bronze owl, the box with the painted-on butterflies, the opalescent glass ashtray, the monocle, the baroque hand mirror, the Plexiglas egg with the rose inside, the tray with the Elvis picture, the tumbling clown, the two tiny ceramic frogs, the little checked box from England, the abalone shell, the pink heart-shaped notepads—I needed another box. I wanted to keep everything—they were beautiful objects—but I didn't want to have to look at them.

I wrote "Devotional Objects" on the large box containing the shoeboxes of memories. Very tasteful. Then I carried the box down to the cellar.

There was still so much left. The sugar bowl with the blue roses was also from him. The iron—we'd bought it together. The soup bowls with the narrow gold rim; the scissors shaped like a stork; the hot-pink hand towels. Things live through memory. Or they live through their function—then they acquire a history of their own; everyday life is more powerful than memory. "Let the towels die a natural death," I told myself.

Till then, there is always something there to remind me. . . .

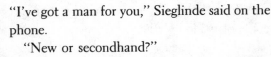

24 "I've got a man for you," Sieglinde said on the phone.

"New or secondhand?"

"He's a friend of my former acquaintance, the gastronomer, the guy I was once engaged to. He just moved here and doesn't know a soul. Incredibly nice. I've invited him to come over for fondue on Easter Sunday so you can meet him. Meat fondue—I have a new chafing dish. Come at eight, but don't be late, because of the fondue. The Sennebergs will be here, too."

So it had come to this: Albert's corpse wasn't even cold yet, and already I was considered fodder to be served up to tourists passing through. Obviously Sieglinde thought I'd be all alone for Easter and Albert would be with his imaginary lover. And again she invited me at the last minute. Probably one of her more elegant acquaintances had canceled.

I really wanted to tell her I couldn't make it. But then, I thought, how nice if I could tell Albert I had something better on tap for Sunday. And besides, I was looking forward to seeing the Sennebergs again. Gabi and Uwe, nice people. I'd met them twice before at Sieglinde's. Uwe was a lawyer and administered something or other. Gabi taught art and English at a prep school. When she talked about school, describing how nervous the faculty was, I could almost laugh myself sick. I could still see myself as a schoolgirl in her stories, and enjoyed the status of talking with a teacher on an equal footing. "What's this guy's name?" I asked Sieglinde.

"Bernhard."

Actually I wanted to ask why she thought I might like this man, but I didn't because I knew exactly what she would say: he's alone, you're alone, that's more than enough to have in common. What else do you want? But I did say, "I already know a Bernhard and he's a computer freak—what does your Bernhard do?"

"My Bernhard's very nice," Sieglinde repeated stubbornly. She was so status-conscious that she would only discuss someone's profession if she was sure it would impress someone. With her less prepossessing acquaintances she confined herself to emphasizing their outstanding personality traits. So all I could do was hope.

Besides, it was better not to ask. After all, I had to take my frustration in small doses. In any case it was a clever tactic to act disinterested. Not only toward Sieglinde—I had to assume she'd offered me to this Bernhard the same way she'd offered him to me. And if he got wind of the fact that I'd made inquiries about him before meeting him, he'd automatically take me for a desperate old maid on the prowl. I knew men. As a single woman invited to a party I had to be careful.

The minute Sieglinde hung up, I called Albert to tell him that I didn't have time to see him the day after tomorrow. "Oh," he said, then quickly said, "Never mind." When would I have time? I told him I couldn't really say at the moment, and I'd call him when I had my schedule worked out. Haha.

Sieglinde's Bernhard turned out to be a total sexist pig. He looked like a complete nerd, but that didn't stop him from talking the whole time. Since my appearance met his lofty standards, he made an effort to impress me. Every time I started a sentence, he would finish it for me. He didn't smoke, but snatched my lighter out of my hand, flicked it right in front of my eyelashes, lowered his arm, and then held the lighter directly over his crotch. He turned the lighting of my cigarette into a compulsory genuflection to his fly. I decided not to call him by his first name, to punish him.

"Please don't bother; I can light my own cigarettes," I said, when he tried to force me into symbolic fellatio for the third time. When he still refused to give back my lighter, I said, "Then please give me a light like a man."

He stared at me dumbfounded. "Wow, are you ever liberated! I guess you don't need a man for anything, do you!" He gave a bleating laugh and winked frantically at the two attached women.

"She didn't mean it that way," Sieglinde said.

Gabi Senneberg came to my aid. She said she also thought this chivalrous ritual of giving a woman a light was ridiculous; real courtesy would be men letting women get ahead in the professional world, but such a thing didn't exist, and she could also do without that stupid business of holding the door for a woman.

"Well, I don't smoke," Sieglinde said.

That topic was dropped.

He was employed at a bank, this Bernhard, and he boasted about his bank's assets. Whenever one of the women asked him a question, he would direct his answer to the woman's keeper. When I had the audacity to say something, he not only interrupted me but legitimized his interruptions with didactic comments about me, acting as though the others were his allies: "There she goes again with her typical female thinking, haha haha." Or: "No, you can't pigeonhole us guys that way!" Or: "Yes, I could have guessed that you'd see men that way, haha!"

Finally he announced, "Well, we don't want to bore the ladies anymore with this business talk," and asked the hostess to reveal the composition of the gray-green fondue sauce.

"They're all store-bought sauces," Wolf-Dietrich said.

"They are not!" Sieglinde said.

"Still very tasty," Bernhard said, and then, turning to me, "By the way, I need to find a cleaning woman, but a student would do fine, providing she's clean."

"Do you always have to be so hostile?" Sieglinde said the next day. "You act so progressive, yet you're so touchy."

"His kindhearted offer of employment as a cleaning woman was totally outrageous!"

"You misunderstood him completely. He'd never hire a woman like you as a cleaning woman."

I was speechless. I stuck my tongue out at Bernhard over the phone.

"You mustn't project your personal frustrations onto others." And in a particularly gentle voice she added, "Of course I understand your psychological situation perfectly."

I stuck out my tongue at Sieglinde.

"You know, if you can't make it with men, you'll just have to learn to live alone."

I told Sieglinde I was late to meet someone and had to run, and forced myself not to slam down the receiver.

25 On Easter Monday, in the afternoon, who should drop in but Albert. He wanted the iron. I explained that it was mine—yes, we'd both paid for it, but before we got it Albert had shared the iron my mother gave me till it died.

In exchange for the iron he wanted to leave me his old coffee maker, but I didn't want it. He urgently needed an iron right away, so he signed a note confirming that he was borrowing my iron and promised to return it. He could take the coffee maker in any case.

I gave him a tiny little chocolate egg. I'd bought it especially for him. It had cost five pfennigs. He asked me what I was up to these days. I told him he was wasting my valuable time and I had to work on my screenplay. He said he didn't have time, either, he had to get his dissertation written.

Right after he'd gone, I called Juliet. She didn't have time, either. But she said I should call Birgit, her neighbor, and gave me her number. For weeks Juliet had been urging me to go somewhere with Birgit. Otherwise she'd never see people. "Birgit sits glued to the TV every night, and after the last show she does crossword puzzles." I should drag Birgit to a bar or somewhere and make sure she met some men. Even one man would be plenty. Maybe I'd find one, too, in the process.

So I called Birgit and asked whether she felt like doing something that evening. No, she didn't have time today. Tomorrow? No, that wouldn't work—she had to wash her hair. Day after tomorrow? No, there was a talk show on that she had been looking forward to for weeks. On Thursday evening she was expecting an important phone call. Friday? Saturday? Sunday? No, no, no.

I heard pages rustling over the phone—apparently she was consulting her datebook. I was surprised at how hard it was for her to find an evening when she was free. Was Juliet's information current? But I didn't give up. "Well, you tell me when you're free."

"I'm sorry," Birgit said finally. "Up to and including Friday after next I have absolutely no time."

"I see, and how about the Saturday after that?"

"That Saturday," she said, "I'm not sure yet."

"All right, then let's plan for that Saturday. Saturday's the ideal day for going out anyway."

"You were thinking of going out?"

"Yes, of course, what did you expect?"

"I thought I was supposed to come over. But if you want to come over here, that'd be even better." Again I heard pages rustling. "All right, come over this Saturday at eight. We can watch the *Rudi Carrell Show* together and play cards. Julio Iglesias is going to be the guest star. And then on Channel 2 they have the *Great Gala of the Stars,* also with Julio Iglesias, till twelve twenty-five A.M."

I didn't say anything because I was speechless. She said, "I'll make us a little something to eat at nine forty-five."

"Hey, listen, I wanted to go to a bar."

Birgit said she didn't go to bars anymore. She'd been in a bar once, and all the people there were creeps.

Nothing I could say did any good. I'd have to talk to Juliet again about this hopeless undertaking.

"Don't you want to come over and watch TV with me?" Birgit asked.

"No, I want to go out."

"I guess we could go to the movies," she said hesitantly.

"Good!" If I could get her to the movies, she'd certainly go to a bar afterward, I thought, and besides, I absolutely had to see the film version of Kate Millett's *Sexual Politics*. Birgit liked the suggestion. Two of the girls she worked with had already seen the movie.

I explained to her that the film probably wouldn't be playing much longer, so she agreed to go this Saturday. She couldn't absolutely promise, but she'd try to arrange it, and if I didn't hear anything from her by Saturday, she'd meet me at eight in front of the Capitol.

All week long I didn't hear from her, or from Albert either, and she actually showed up Saturday night at ten past eight.

I thought the movie was boring. Too much sex, too little politics. But Birgit was happy to have seen it. She adored books made into movies. And she was so thrilled by Robert Redford in the role of a despotic husband that she put up no resistance to going to a nice little place I picked out. The Nuns Cellar. There were twenty-eight men standing at the bar, and Birgit was horrified when she saw them:

"This looks like a real pickup joint!" she said.

"Right-o," I said. "I love standing at a bar, picking up men."

Birgit looked at me as though I'd made a bad joke. We stood at the bar for a while. She stood about eight inches away from me, even though the place wasn't very crowded. I gave her the freedom to choose—after all, we were looking for someone for her, so I put my own interests second. I let her decide which guy we would target. Then I'd casually strike up a conversation. That's my specialty: I'd just go and stand next to the guys who interested me, listen in on their conversation a while, then ask a relevant question . . . and in no time, I was right in the thick of it. And when you go somewhere with other people, it's even easier, because then you can position yourself next to men who are there alone, not talking, and they make for really rewarding objects of attention. You chat a bit with the people you came with, and then ask the guy, "How about you? What do you think?" Every man likes to have a woman ask his opinion. So it's not hard at all to start up a conversation. But now I was still waiting for Birgit to pick one of the men at our disposal. She was standing six inches from me and saying nary a word.

"Where do you want to stand?" I asked.

"I don't know." Birgit stared down at the beer-soaked, sticky floor. If we stood in this spot any longer, we'd be stuck.

"I'm just going to the bathroom for a minute. In the meantime, you make up your mind."

"I'll go with you."

In the bathroom she suddenly became talkative. Why did I have to put on mascara now? What mascara did I use? Had I ever tried her brand? She and the other girls at work were very pleased with it. How many times a day did I apply mascara? I told Birgit all her questions made me get mascara in my eye, and would she please wait for me at the bar. Finally she left. I purposely took my time. Besides, I had my own interests to look out for. I combed my hair, and put on blush—highly recommended in dark bars like this. Unfortunately my fingernails were grubby, but I hoped no one would notice. When I got back to the bar, Birgit was nowhere to be seen. For a moment I wondered if she'd already split with the man of her dreams.

"Looking for someone?" a punk type on a bar stool asked me.

"Yes, my girlfriend, pale-blue-and-pink-striped sweater, she was here a minute ago."

"Pretty?" asked a counterculture type sitting next to him.

"Bring her over when you've found her," said the punk, sizing up my unimpressive upper-body circumference.

I looked around the bar thinking Birgit was probably chatting with one of the big guys blocking my view. But Birgit wasn't there.

What I saw then was so gruesome that I still shudder to think of it. Birgit was sitting all alone in the back room—at a table for two, with a view of the door to the men's room!

It couldn't have been worse.

Except for the children's table—how in the world can you sit down at the table right by the men's room? Catherine Deneuve could be sitting there and not a single man would look at her. The area in a radius of eight yards around their bathroom is terra incognita for men. They're all still too preoccupied with their pants to see anything else.

"What are you doing here?" I asked Birgit, without sitting down.

"It's very cozy here."

I had no choice—I had to sit down. "Did you see that cute guy at the bar?"

"No, which one?" There was still hope. "Hey, there's no service back here. You have to go up and get your own beer."

"Really." Just as I was about to head for the bar, the waiter came over.

"What can I get you ladies?"

During the next half hour Birgit stared with interest at the men coming out of the men's room. Then she said, "Hey, do they have any peanuts or potato chips here?" I just shook my head. Was it possible that Birgit related to the men's room door as a giant TV screen?

Then I got a headache and had to go home to bed. Birgit wasn't sorry. An old thriller was on TV that Birgit had always wanted to see again.

26 Because I'd gotten home so early, I was pretty much awake the next morning at ten when Jürgen, my old pal and lover, called to ask if I was interested in a job, since I was on semester break.

The ad agency where he was some sort of director desperately needed someone for competition surveillance, and he'd thought of me because he'd been on the phone with his ex-girlfriend Gisela, and she'd heard that Albert had moved out.

"What's competition surveillance?" I asked.

"It has to do with pesticides."

While Jürgen talked about Gisela and I explained to him that Albert had left the house at my request, and how happy I was, I thought it over; I was bored anyhow. Maybe while I was doing this competition surveillance I'd meet the love of my life. Maybe a topflight ad photographer. Actually I'd wanted to go somewhere during the break, but I didn't feel like going by myself. My mother was already nagging me to come and see them again, but that was boredom that knew no bounds. Besides, I didn't have a thing to wear. And I also needed some more money for rent and utilities. It wouldn't be so bad to spend the rest of my vacation working. I asked Jürgen what I'd be earning.

"We always pay well," he said.

I was supposed to present myself to the personnel director the next morning, but not before ten. No one was in the office before ten on Mondays—they were pretty laid-back. If I'd promise that I'd really come, he'd call the personnel director right now. I promised.

On the stroke of ten I was there. The personnel director got in at a quarter to eleven. He was pleased to find me waiting for him.

He explained that my job was to keep the competition under surveillance. That sounded exciting. He took me through a back door up to a large room two floors above the other offices: "This is our library," he said.

The room was filled with newspapers and magazines. The personnel director said these were all publications of the pharmaceuticals industry and advertising vehicles for agricultural consumers. He explained that the agency had an important account with an important pharmaceutical company, and for that reason the competition had to be kept under surveillance. My job was to look through all these magazines and newspapers, cut out all the pesticide ads, then paste each onto a sheet of paper and write on it the advertising vehicle and the edition.

I asked what an advertising vehicle was.

The personnel director explained that the advertising vehicles were the newspapers and magazines. "We in the ad business call them advertising vehicles because they carry advertising, and whatever they publish besides advertising we call the ambient field." To compensate for my ignorance I told him I'd already worked at an ad agency.

"Aha," he said, very pleased.

Okay, so I didn't tell him that I'd only filed photos and framed slides.

I was supposed to make three photocopies of every sheet of paper with an ad pasted on it. Then something very important occurred to him: I shouldn't cut any ad out of an advertising vehicle until I'd checked to make sure there wasn't an ad on the back. In such a case I had to photocopy it first, and then proceed in the aforementioned way.

I asked whether I should throw away the magazines after I'd

looked through them. Certainly not; the advertising vehicles didn't only carry ads for pesticides; the other ads might be needed at some later point. So I should put the advertising vehicles back where I found them. Only if a page had no advertising—just ambient field—then I could throw it away. But that certainly wouldn't occur very often.

Then he showed me where the coffee and copying machines were downstairs, and I asked him where the ladies' room was and how much I'd be earning. Two marks more per hour than I thought!

Quitting time was six o'clock. By twenty to six I'd cut out and pasted 145 ads, gotten myself six cups of coffee, and not spoken with a living soul. The only person I ran into was the secretary whose desk was near the copier. Three times I'd come down with a heap of advertising vehicles to copy, and each time she was on the phone and just said to me, bruskly, "I'm totally stressed out."

At ten to six the personnel director came upstairs. I heard him approach from a distance as I was cutting out an ad like an old pro for a pesticide for bean spider mites. I showed him what I'd done, and he was delighted. "Excellent job," he said. "Keep up the good work." He said I was much more efficient than the theology student they'd hired last vacation. I was feeling very proud of myself. The personnel director said he'd always thought that competition surveillance was a woman's job. I asked whether I should organize the ads according to insects. No, that made no sense at all, he said; they had to be organized according to advertising vehicle. It was crucial to know how many ads the competition had placed in the various highly specialized advertising vehicles. I should organize them according to the issues of the vehicles.

How long was my vacation, he asked. I could continue to keep the competition under surveillance for at least four more weeks—there was a lot of material to work on. Every morning and evening I should report to the secretary by the copier, who would keep track of my hours. I was entitled to a forty-five-minute break, and I could have my coffee as I worked.

It was an easy job. The only thing was, on Tuesday I began to itch all over. I was afraid I'd been infested with lice, or those extremely dangerous spider mites, which apparently showed up everywhere. That night at the Kaput I saw an aphid-eating Proctotrupidae on the wall. And in the corner a bark beetle.

But it was also a very lonely job. Jürgen stopped by only once for a minute, said I had a cushy setup. He was under terrible stress, and he'd love to change places with me. After that I didn't see him anymore.

During the first few days I was amazed at the number of extremely dangerous insects threatening our agriculture. After I got to know all the pests, including the parasitic bacteria, I realized that there were significantly more pesticides than there were pests. About a dozen products per pest, dedicated to its extermination.

I also gave thought to whether I should buy the hot-pink satin skirt in the boutique across the street from the agency. It wasn't that expensive. On the other hand I had to consider whether the skirt might not be too elegant. Whether Gottfried Schacht-schnabel would like it, for instance. Albert would like the skirt, I was sure of that. But what he would think meant as little to me as a hops spider mite. Since Easter Monday, which meant ten days ago, I hadn't heard a thing from him, and he hadn't shown up at the Kaput, either. He didn't even know I was learning all about pesticides, even though twice this week I'd stayed home all evening to see if he would call. He still had my iron. Maybe he did have a new woman after all. Basically I should be glad of that; in three weeks Gottfried Schachtschna-bel's seminar would be starting up again, and then presumably I wouldn't have time for Albert anyway. LIFE MAKES NO SENSE WITHOUT PROPER DEFENSE! was the motto of an ad against the perfidious floury cabbage leaf caterpiller. Exactly. That was my motto, too.

On Friday morning I asked the secretary between two of her phone calls whether I could be paid on a weekly basis. I should ask the personnel director myself, she said, she was totally stessed out. "Oh, still here?" the personnel director said. Then he accompanied me to my library, and I showed him that I'd gone through almost a third of the advertising vehicles. He praised his good nose as a personnel director for hiring such an "efficient young lady." I got an advance; it would all be worked out when I left, which was fine with me. It was Friday, so I checked out at five and went across the street to buy that pink skirt.

27

I didn't call Albert till Saturday night. When he picked up the receiver, I kept spinning the dial. That makes it sound like a bad connection.

"Auerbach speaking, hello, hello," Albert said. I fiddled with the dial a bit more. "Hello, hello, hello," Albert said. Then I waited till he hung up. He fell for it. A good thing I'd never taught him how to make a bad connection. "A woman must not only have her secrets, but keep them to herself," my mother says. Now I knew: Albert was also sitting home alone on a Saturday evening. If he had a new woman, he'd be out somewhere. I was sure of that.

Sunday afternoon at five Albert called.

"Oh, it's you," I said.

"What are you doing tonight?" he asked.

"I'm not sure yet."

"What would you think of spending a few hours talking with an old pal? No obligation on your part, of course."

"And how about on yours? Also no obligation?"

"Of course. Where shall we go?"

I wore my hot-pink skirt and looked ravishing. We went to one of the better restaurants. Because now it meant something when we went out together. Besides, there's less risk of fighting in a refined atmosphere—you don't dare throw plates or knock over the table, and in any case the subdued tones in the better places automatically subdue your own tones.

The longer you go without seeing each other, the more you have to tell each other. Albert didn't know the first thing about insects. I informed him about the San José louse and the asparagus beetle, an insect specializing in asparagus tips. He told me about a film he'd seen that he was sure I'd like, too. He also told me his old coffee maker had finally given out. And he'd bought himself a leather jacket, medium blue; he'd called me to consult about the bold color, but I hadn't been home. His marble tabletop had red-wine stains on it; I advised him to try a paste of vinegar and salt. His supervisor had finally said something appreciative about his abilities, and in the presence of the senior physician he hated, which made it that much better.

How witty he is when he's telling a story, I thought, as he cursed the senior physician.

"Well?" he asked after we'd had our absolutely last glass of wine.

"Well?" I repeated.

"You can come to my place," he said. "Then we can see right away whether vinegar and salt will get out those wine stains."

"All right."

Albert paid for me.

The stains didn't come out, but it turned out to be a euphoric night. A night of miracles. I had nothing to lose. Could demand whatever I wanted, no inhibitions. The ultimate orgasm. I forgot the notion that maybe he wanted to show me what he'd learned in the meantime. We loved each other no holds barred. I knew him better than any other woman. He knew me better than any other man. We knew each other better than anyone else.

"Well, my old sweetie pie," he said.

"Well, my old honey," I said.

We knew each other's erogenous zones from way back, but we also knew each other's taboos. Now that we had split up, the battle over those taboos was over. The fact that he didn't like this and I didn't like that was no longer a sign of withholding; our dislikes became personal characteristics again. In the attempt to respect each other's wishes, we could now make each other the gift of overcoming our own taboos. We'd reached the goal: total surrender, without hurting ourselves. We'd paid the price.

"You don't need to get up right away," Albert said the next morning. "Here's a key. Bye." A farewell kiss: "Take care." At the door he looked back again: "Please turn the key twice. And throw it in the mailbox downstairs."

I acted like I'd already dozed off again. When I left, I threw the key in the mailbox.

28 I didn't have my makeup with me so I had to go home after I left Albert's, and didn't get to the agency till almost noon. The secretary said into the phone, "I'm totally stressed out."

On this particular day I learned what a menace the bark beetle was. I worked through two years' worth of an advertising vehicle specializing in forest pests. Toward evening I began to wonder why this publication only carried the ads of one pharmaceutical company, and then I realized that I'd written *Bavarian Forest Courier* ninety-seven times on my sheets of paper, instead of *Bayer-ian Forest Courier.* I hid those pages before I went home. That night I reproached myself for not picking up on this clever advertising ploy, even though I'd been staring at the title for hours. My subconscious, which, as every kindergartner knows, is responsible for our receptivity to advertising, had been sound asleep. On Tuesday I carefully peeled the ads off the sheets on which I'd written *Bavarian Forest Courier* and I took ninety-seven new pieces of paper and labeled them *Bayer-ian Forest Courier* so no one at the agency would notice I was as resistant to advertising as the bark beetle was to last year's pesticide.

Repasting the ads and rewriting the sheets was easy. I could concentrate all my thoughts on Albert. The night before had been a decisive step on the road to a harmonious separation. My problem was this: I wasn't really a forsaken woman, I just didn't have a new man yet. Albert wouldn't get over me that quickly. Actually we could continue our relationship on this new level of understanding. . . . Albert couldn't claim ownership anymore; he'd have to make more of an effort to please me, so as not to lose me completely. It had to become clear to him that he wouldn't find anything better than me. "The brand that guarantees quality"—that was me. "Experience shows: quite simply the best"—that was me. That evening I called up Sieglinde and mentioned in passing that I'd gone out with Albert last weekend. She picked up on it immediately and asked where we went. "Oh, his place," I said, and laughed.

On Saturday I called Juliet. She said she finally felt in the mood to go to the Kaput. Actually I had a date with Albert, but I seized the opportunity to cancel it. I told him I'd thought it over and decided it was better if we didn't see each other again so soon. It's well known that nothing promotes harmony more than absence. That suited him fine, he said.

Juliet looked different: she'd tinted her mouse-brown hair kind of mahogany. And she wasn't wearing her usual earth tones, but an unmistakably lemon-yellow pullover. And fancy jeans. Altogether overhauled, mousy no more. Since I'd called her three times in the last two weeks, she already knew all about vine fretters, woolly scale, and apple blight. So we got to talking about Albert right away.

Juliet was very glad to hear about this movement in the direction of a harmonious separation. "I guess that closes the Gottfried chapter," she said, and laughed.

I laughed too. "While there's life, there's hope. The semester starts up again in a week and a half. Who knows what'll happen."

"You're persistent."

" 'If at first you don't succeed, try, try again'—that's what my mother always said."

" 'Hoping and praying can lead you to braying,' mine always said."

" 'Time will tell,' " I said.

"Time will tell," Juliet said.

We toasted my immediate future with a glass of wine. Then we had another to toast Juliet's immediate future. She told me her birthday was on May 10, and on May 11, Saturday, she wanted to throw a party. Thirty-two already! But she already had her first marriage behind her. I should be sure to bring Albert, she said. I liked the idea of showing Albert to Juliet, but there also might be an interesting psychologist at the party for me to meet. I didn't share any of these thoughts with Juliet, I just said I didn't know if Albert had the time.

"I might have a surprise for you at my party," Juliet said.

"Are you making that delicious egg-liqueur cake?"

"I'm going to leave you in suspense."

The next week I got a call from Dörte, Albert's former girlfriend. She still didn't know that I'd made Albert move out. Then she asked what I was up to these days.

When she asked what I was up to, that was Dörte-code for did I have a new guy yet. Dörte's your typical nurse: right after Albert dumped her (for me!), she went and married another doctor. A senior physician, yet. Because of that she'd forgiven Albert. Since then, she'd call him up from time to time to report on the new investments her marital partnership had made.

I told Dörte that I was also setting my sights higher.

"A head physician?" she asked enviously.

"I can't name any names, but it's someone in the public nonprofit sector." I'd heard someone say that once and it had made a deep impression on me. It made a deep impression on Dörte, too. I gave her Albert's new phone number. First, I had no need to be jealous, and second, Dörte was married, and third, presumably she would pass on to Albert what I'd just told her. I stayed home the rest of the evening, thinking Albert might call. But he didn't. Well, I had time.

During the third week of my competition surveillance I took Hegel to work with me. I still hadn't gotten around to working through the theoretical aspects of my film. It was high time; I had to get ready for seeing Gottfried again. Anyway, my job provided the ideal conditions for an intensive study of Hegel. I sat there by myself all day, and if anyone was coming, I could hear them a mile off—plenty of time to put my book away. But no one came. I mechanically cut out ads while turning the pages of *The Phenomenology of Mind.* On page 202 I found an incredible quote:

That profundity which the spirit gives forth from within, but only propels into its conceptualizing consciousness and leaves there, and the unknowingness of that consciousness as to what it is and what it means, is the same linking of the sublime and the humble that nature expresses naively in the linking within the living being of the organ of its highest realization, the organ of procreation, with the organ of pissing.

Who would have believed this was Hegel! Hegel actually said "pissing"! I looked further, but didn't find any other passages like it. But this was more than enough. I absolutely had to show the passage to Gottfried and ask him what it meant.

29 The hours crept by like cabbage worms. Finally it was Friday. I showed the personnel director that I'd cut up almost all the magazines. Wringing his hands, he asked me if I could please work through all the rest. The new semester was to begin on Monday, but everybody knows nothing ever happens the first week. The only thing was Gottfried's seminar on Wednesday. So I said I'd come back on Monday and work through the last pest. The personnel director was very grateful.

Sunday morning Albert brought back my iron. I needed it desperately because I had to iron my hot-pink skirt for Wednesday. Then we went for a walk together because the weather was nice. Albert bought himself an ice-cream cone at a stand and didn't get me one. He was stingier than ever.

"Get your own ice-cream cone if you want one so much."

I told him that even if he had a hundred thousand marks in the bank he wouldn't be satisfied. At the words *hundred thousand marks* Albert swallowed hard. I could see the greed glittering in his eyes. It was a gleam that would never be extinguished.

Our parting wasn't harmonious. I continued the walk by myself. What Hegel said about unhappy consciousness fit Albert exactly. I absolutely had to read that chapter next.

"Destroy the enemy before it destroys you!" was the slogan for a product guaranteed to kill red mildew dead. That was the last ad I pasted on; it was Wednesday, exactly 1:47. My pay came to more than I'd expected. The secretary hadn't subtracted the hours I'd missed on Monday two weeks ago, or rather, she hadn't recorded any hours, because she was so stressed out, she told the personnel director, and I'd always gotten there at ten and left at six. I didn't contradict her. The personnel director said I had a natural talent for competition surveillance, gave me a farewell pat on the behind, and said he'd like to call me back again sometime.

I tore out of there and bought the gold stilettos with the four-and-a-half-inch heels at Heel of Fortune for 159 marks. I raced home; Gottfried's seminar began in two hours.

30

I entered the seminar room as though I'd been born on four-and-a-half-inch stilettos for 159 marks. I lowered my lashes with their seven applications of mascara and said to Gottfried, who was gazing at me with pleasure, "Oh, hi."

Then I let my denim jacket slip from my shoulders, exposing my black top, and sat down in my satin skirt in the last row. I placed my Hegel on the desk and smiled seductively. I wondered whether I should have said, "Oh, hi, *Gottfried*"—that would definitely have given my greeting a more personal touch, but perhaps it would've been a bit too obvious. Better to preserve some distance, I decided, and stopped smiling seductively.

As expected, nothing happened the first week of the semester.

After half an hour only three male students and two other women in hand-knitted cotton sweaters had shown up. I knew just one of the guys, and only by sight. Gottfried asked who wanted to sign up for a presentation on a chapter from Godard's *Introduction à une véritable histoire du cinéma*. There were twenty-two pages to read. One of the guys agreed to do it, if Gottfried would photocopy the pages for him. After that was taken care of, Gottfried said it was better to postpone further structuring of the seminar till next week. And he would postpone his Friday seminar, too, since the students doubtless wouldn't come drifting in till next week. "The average students, at any rate," he said, and looked at me. I smiled modestly.

"Okay, till next week, then," Gottfried said. I got up slowly. I stuffed my Hegel into the breast pocket of my denim jacket. The other students were already gone. Gottfried and I were the only ones left in the seminar room. He switched off the light. It was May, and still fairly light. He waited for me at the door, and I could see his eyes.

"Hey, Constance," he said. "Constance, how about a ride home?"

I smoothed my hot-pink satin skirt, ran my pink nails first over my neck and then through my Ava Gardner–colored hair, and said, "Well, Gottfried," and paused a moment. "Actually I came in my own car."

"Oh," he said.

"See you later," I said, and went to my mini-Fiat without keeling over. My golden stilettos glittered in the evening sun.

Afterward I was sorry—it had been a fantastic scene, but Gottfried was so sensitive. On the other hand, I could afford to let him wait. First, I still had Albert. But second, my mother had always said that nothing stimulated desire more than making a man wait: "He who won't wait anymore isn't in love anymore." Gottfried was still waiting. He had stared after me like a doomed San José scale bug.

31

I bought Juliet a golden-oldie record—appropriate for a thirty-second birthday, I thought. Come around eight, she had said. My offer to help her with the potato salad, pasta salad, or herring salad had been politely turned down.

Only eight or ten people were coming, and there wouldn't be much work. Albert didn't want to come; he simply refused. Juliet's neighbor Birgit also couldn't make it; she had to baby-sit her sister's child.

I got there around nine. "Guess who's here!" Juliet greeted me.

"Karl-Heinz?"

"Well, him of course."

"Christian? Gerd? Ingo? Werner? Alfred? Anyone else from the Kaput?"

Juliet shook her head.

"Did Albert come after all?"

"No." Juliet grinned. "Gottfried."

"Gottfried? Which Gottfried?"

"Gottfried Schachtschnabel."

"Gottfried Schachtschnabel? Gottfried Schachtschnabel! How did he get here? Did you invite him? God, I'd never have expected that. How awfully nice of you." In a spontaneous burst of warmth I threw my arms around Juliet.

"Oh, I'm so terribly fond of you," I said—just like those women who've learned to give full expression to the emotional side of their being, except that my voice was a little scratchy, not clear as a bell like the voices of those women. But I knew Juliet would believe me anyway.

"Nothing to thank me for," Juliet said modestly.

"Why didn't you tell me beforehand? I would have worn something else if I'd known he was coming. How did you invite him, anyway? Did you bump into him somewhere?"

"I'll give you the details later."

I was really incredibly happy that we women had such solidarity, and when it occurred to me that I'd already worn my hot-pink satin skirt on Wednesday, I was incredibly glad that Juliet had kept Gottfried Schachtschnabel a surprise.

No one was in Juliet's living room because the stereo was on. Gottfried was sitting with Karl-Heinz, Juliet's sandbox buddy, on the bed. I was fairly embarrassed when I saw him, and he was too.

"Long time no see," Gottfried said. How witty he was! We'd spoken with each other just yesterday! Even though his seminar had been canceled, I'd gone to the department, hoping he'd be there anyway. I'd waited by the door to the faculty lounge for about ten minutes, reading the announcements and displays on the bulletin board, when he came down the hall. I'd asked him whether the Broadway musical could aspire to be considered a tour-de-force, a masterpiece, a *Gesamtkunstwerk*—provided, of course, it was conceived in such a way that it could adequately reflect the prevailing societal conditions. Gottfried said that was a very good question, but he didn't want to give a globalizing answer, and we absolutely had to discuss it at the next seminar meeting.

"What do you want to drink, Constance?" he asked me now. Sweet how he was playing the role of host for me. I beamed at Juliet. "How did you get here?" I asked him.

"Oh, I was lucky enough to be invited." He winked at Juliet. It was so great that he'd come.

"Isn't he sweet?" I whispered in Juliet's ear, not realizing that Gottfried was standing right next to her. I turned bright red; hopefully he hadn't heard me—that would've been bad, for strategic reasons. It was also better, for strategic reasons, to let him stand around by himself for a while. So I went into the kitchen.

All the rest of the guests were sitting around the kitchen table. Three male colleagues of Juliet's were playing cards amid the various salads, and four women colleagues were knitting and smoking. "Incredibly cozy," one of the women was saying as I came in. I said I found the party fantastic, too, but no one spoke to me, or at least not directly. "Close the door!" one of the men said. "How can we concentrate on the game with that music blaring?" So I closed the door, ate some potato salad and two meatballs, and smoked two cigarettes before I went back into Juliet's bedroom.

Karl-Heinz was sitting cross-legged on the floor in front of the bed, monopolizing Gottfried, who was lying on the bed, perfectly relaxed. My knees were almost shaking. I sat down cross-legged next to Karl-Heinz.

"You have it real good," Karl-Heinz said to Gottfried. "As a professor, you have the girls lying at your feet."

I was totally furious at this crude allusion.

"What good are those dumb clucks to me?" Gottfried said, grimaced at me, and added, "Present company excepted, of course."

So witty. I giggled.

"And besides," he said to Karl-Heinz, "I'm not that much of a fool that I'd get involved with a student. Man, if that got out, they'd crucify me. I'm on a short-term contract, you know. Till I get tenure, I gotta conform." Gottfried looked at me and grinned again. "Of course you didn't hear any of this, right, Constance? I can't afford any gossip."

"Right," I said, and tried to stay serious.

"Shove over, old man," Juliet said to Gottfried, and sat down right next to him on the bed. It was too comical.

"You called Gottfried old man," I whispered to Juliet.

"Whoops, old man," Juliet said. "Did I call you Gottfried by mistake?"

Juliet must have been pretty drunk. I laughed so hard I almost burst.

At that moment a bloodcurdling yell came from the kitchen, and then one of the knitting smokers came in and shrieked, "Help! My husband threw my wool in the herring salad!"

Juliet and I laughed ourselves limp.

I went back into the kitchen. My mascara was already smudged. Karl-Heinz trotted along behind me. "So you're definitely single now?" he asked. "Juliet told me your friend is out of the picture."

Now this dude was actually starting in on Albert. Albert, who I'd put out of my mind long ago. I told Karl-Heinz so. Then I said, "Other fathers have handsome sons, too." I burst out laughing again. Karl-Heinz didn't get it. He stared at me so idiotically that I almost felt sorry for him.

"How old are you anyway?" I asked him, to maintain the appearance of a conversation.

"Guess," he said.

"Twenty-seven," I said promptly.

He looked flattered. Did he seriously believe a sighted person could take him for twenty-seven, this old fart with his triple chin, sagging cheeks, and potbelly? Karl-Heinz smiled. "Well, actually I'm a bit older than that."

"When a man tells me to guess how old he is, I always say twenty-seven, on principle." Did he get it? No, he didn't.

"Come on, guess again," he said.

"Forty-eight," I said—that's what I always say when I'm forced to guess again.

He looked miffed. Then he said, "You look frustrated, already got some pretty deep lines around your mouth."

Aha, now he'd realized what I was up to, and dudes like that always react the same way.

"So how old are you really?" I asked placatingly.

"I'm a so-called double twen," he said.

"Why don't you just say a teenybopper cubed?" I said, and laughed.

Karl-Heinz didn't laugh; he just walked away. Haha, I'd really let him have it.

I went to the bathroom and tried some of Juliet's perfume, because I'd forgotten my own—I hadn't known who would be here. I turned up the stereo a bit in the living room, so they could hear it better in the next room, and put on the golden oldie I'd brought Juliet. It had one of my favorite cuts on it: "Cupid," by Sam Cooke.

> *Cupid, draw back your bow,*
> *and let your arrow go*
> *straight to my lover's heart for me. . . .*

Very suitable. Gottfried was still lying on the bed and Juliet was now perched on the edge of it. "You smell nice," Gottfried said as soon as I came in. "Delicious."

I had to giggle again. Then I asked him, "Say, did you bring your car?"

"Yes, of course," he said.

The time had come.

"You're going past my place anyway," I said. Of course I knew that was pure fabrication, but what the hell. Everyone knows that men don't like it when women are too direct. Tomorrow I could always claim I'd only been so bold because I was drunk. To support my alibi I took another big swallow and looked at Gottfried expectantly—but in a way so that the others wouldn't notice.

"I think I'm going to sleep here," Gottfried said.

God, so witty! He kept making me laugh. I giggled at Juliet, and even though it was really dark, I noticed that Juliet had turned beet-red.

Now Gottfried laughed too. "Come on, Julietta," he said to her, "why are you so embarrassed?" Then he kissed her smack on the mouth.

I don't understand, I thought, or rather, I still hope I just thought it and didn't say it out loud, but got out of there without saying a word.

Juliet wanted Karl-Heinz to take me home; she said I seemed kind of out of it. Basically she wanted to shoo all of us out of the house, so she and Gottfried could . . .

Juliet and Gottfried Schachtschnabel!

Unbelievable!

Whatever happened to sisterhood?

32 Juliet and Gottfried Schachtschnabel. I can't explain, I can only express it in the most banal terms: I was, like, paralyzed. Juliet and *Gottfried Schachtschnabel. Juliet* and Gottfried Schachtschnabel. *Juliet and Gottfried Schachtschnabel.* It was all I could think of.

I waited for Juliet to come after me and apologize for two whole days. I wavered between the idea of refusing to let her in when she came crawling and the possibility of forgiving her. Or should I just act as though nothing had happened? That was a possibility, because her affair with Gottfried Schachtschnabel—if in fact there was anything to it—couldn't go on for long, as far as was humanly possible to judge.

She must have gone all out. How dumb of me to introduce her to him; I should have known she'd fall for him—it wasn't often she met a fantastic man like that. Certainly not in the school system. But what did he see in her?

She probably had him in sexual bondage. I'd read about such cases. Revolting. I felt sorry for poor Gottfried, really sorry. In spite of what he'd done to me.

I thought about the whole thing: Juliet didn't know the first thing about the romantic clichés of the Broadway musical. She had no idea what a visual super-sign was. Or what a water glass means in a Fellini film. True, Gottfried could teach her that a water glass in a Fellini film doesn't have any symbolic meaning per se, but represents a water glass as such—but presumably it would be years before she got it. She didn't even know the difference between a soft fade-in and a hard cut. What did she think she'd talk about with Gottfried, the intellectual? Had Juliet ever read Hegel? It was just a mystery to me. Besides, I was better-looking, objectively speaking.

After two days of waiting I called her. She was probably so ashamed she hadn't dared to call me.

At first she acted as though nothing had happened. I did the same. But then I said, "So how's your Gottfried?"

"Our Gottfried's fine," she said with an idiotic laugh.

I wondered how he could stand that laugh of hers. "You could at least explain how you happened to invite him. You really could have said something!"

"Oh," she said, "it just happened."

"You're lying."

"You're right." She laughed idiotically again, and I thought to myself that people who laugh at their own jokes are neurotic.

"Did you snag him right after that lecture?"

"Oh, nonsense!" she said, and now she made an effort to speak seriously, like a trustworthy person. "I wanted to tell you for a while, but somehow the right moment never came. . . ."

"How long have you two been together?" I'd almost asked, "How long have you two been cheating on me?"

"Just since Easter."

"Just since Easter? Where did you run into him?"

"In the café on the corner."

"But Gottfried lives in Lichterfelde."

"Yes, but he's in this neighborhood sometimes. You know that. His ex-wife lives here, on Sonnenallee somewhere."

"Pardon me?"

"I'd gone to the café with Karl-Heinz for a bite to eat, and he came in with a woman. Then he had fight with her and she stomped out."

"What were they fighting about? Who recognized who first, you or him? What do you mean, ex-wife? Are you trying to make a total fool of me?"

Juliet said that if I'd hang on while she got something to drink, she'd make an honest attempt to remember every "ah" and "hm" that was spoken that evening.

What she told me next was absolutely amazing: after this woman had stomped off in a rage, Gottfried came over and joined Juliet and Karl-Heinz. Allegedly he had remembered her. And the woman he'd come in with was his ex-wife.

I really couldn't believe it. "Ex-wife or ex-girlfriend?" I asked. "Gottfried Schachtschnabel was never married, was he?"

"Of course he was married. The man is thirty-six. What do you expect?"

"But hasn't he always had a very critical attitude toward bourgeois institutions?"

"He told me he got married because of his mother-in-law, otherwise she would have written his wife and him out of her will."

"Have they been divorced long?"

"They haven't lived together in four years."

"I didn't know Gottfried Schachtschnabel had marriage experience."

"But they don't have any children."

"Well, I think it's fantastic that he still cares about his ex-wife and would even go out with her after the divorce," I said. "I'm sure they must have had a very harmonious separation."

"She left him for a lover from the city Building Department."

"I wish Albert had that much character," I said out loud to myself. "He didn't even give me a farewell bouquet of roses." I was still irked by his lack of style.

But Juliet didn't engage me on this point. "The problem is that the guy from the Building Department is still married and doesn't want a divorce, because he and his wife built a house together. And apparently, Inge, that's Gottfried's ex-wife, has frequent attacks of depression because she can't live with her lover as long as he's still married."

"I don't get it," I said. "Why shouldn't she live with the guy from the Building Department? Love doesn't require a marriage certificate. On the contrary, it's well known that bourgeois institutions are the antipodes of romance. Hasn't Gottfried explained that to her and the guy from the Building Department?"

Juliet interrupted me. "Gottfried's ex-wife's lover is a total moron. Gottfried says so, too. It's really awful for poor Gottfried."

Then Juliet told me that she and Gottfried talked a lot about both of their messed-up and unnecessary marriages and that it really gave them something in common to be divorced. She laughed again, and I had the feeling she was kind of showing off.

"So, are you going to marry him?" I asked, quite sore.

"Who knows?" she said. "I'd have to ask him first." Then she laughed idiotically again and asked, "Say, are you sore?"

I told her I wasn't sore at all, just incredibly sad because she'd lied to me.

"You know perfectly well how happy I am that I'm divorced, and I don't have to tell you that Gottfried doesn't give a damn about all that bourgeois marriage crap. We have a simple, spontaneous, open relationship without possessiveness. So don't take it so hard." Then she added, "Gottfried likes you a lot, too. Really."

My mood softened a little. "You know, I think we can still be friends, in spite of everything," I said. I'd often read that it was not only noble to renounce stuff, but that renunciation was the source of true happiness. I examined my feelings after I'd said that sentence. I felt total hatred for Juliet. Somehow she seemed to sense it.

"I'm so sorry about all of this," she said. "I hope you can forgive me. I didn't mean to hurt you."

"That's all right."

"You know, Gottfried and I—it has nothing to do with you that . . ."

"Well, with who then?"

"You're still emotionally fixated on Albert anyway. And for that reason incapable of forming new relationships."

That almost took my breath away.

"To you Gottfried Schachtschnabel was only the abstract idea of a Band-Aid solution," Juliet continued. "So don't let your wounded vanity blow a casual affair up into the romantic love of your life."

"Wounded vanity"—what gall.

"Just my advice as a psychologist," Juliet said arrogantly.

"So when are you getting married?" I asked when I got my breath back.

Juliet laughed her idiotic laugh again. "We'll tell you next week. We're all going to get together and you're going to bring your Albert finally. Gottfried's already met him, I'm the only one who hasn't. So, see you then, take care."

What should I do now?

So it was that easy for her. She nabbed Gottfried for herself and me she just sent back to Albert. It didn't matter a bit to her how I would look to the others. And that she ignored my intellectual bonds with Gottfried and just jabbered about wounded vanity—superficial observations that really didn't show her psychological abilities in a very good light. But then again, she only worked with schoolchildren.

It was still a complete mystery to me what there could be between Gottfried and Juliet. I had the feeling that she must have thrown herself at him shamelessly. True, both of them had marriage experience, but what did that add up to? So what if Gottfried in his youth had once been driven into a disastrous situation by his mother-in-law? I'd made mistakes in my youth, too. But Gottfried learned from the experience, which I could hardly believe of Juliet. After all, she was constantly preaching to me that I should marry Albert. With her passive acceptance of the bourgeois institutions she certainly wasn't a suitable partner for Gottfried.

And what made her think she could send me back to Albert? I wanted something better than that, I deserved something better. Albert just couldn't keep up with me, with my keen, critical awareness of political issues.

True, Albert could be quite witty sometimes, and he also didn't have that domineering manner that most men exhibit toward women, but that was about it. We had no interests in common. The intellectual bond between us was as fragile as a spiderweb. Albert wasn't the intellectual partner I sought. He wasn't the man to help me work through the damage that a bourgeois upbringing had wreaked on my psychological development. Life with him was just a constant hassle over his stinginess, his passivity, and whose turn it was to clean the toilet. He was driven by the petty concerns of everyday life. Gottfried and me—we had more of a bond. We had a common basis: the unity of our interests.

Gottfried—the broad vista of the great theories; Albert—the broom closet of petty deeds. My mind would never be able to liberate itself if I stayed with him.

But now Gottfried belonged to Juliet. If I hadn't taken her along to his lecture, none of this would have happened. She'd exploited my spontaneity. She'd been my best friend. She'd sacrificed our friendship to her sexual cravings. Didn't she know sex was out? I was sure of one thing: if Gottfried could stand that laugh of hers, she had him in sexual bondage. That kind of relationship never lasted—with the exception of perverse fixations, but Gottfried didn't have any of those, of course. This mismatch couldn't last more than a month. Three months tops. Or could it?

What should I do now?

Give up on Gottfried?

Go back to Albert?

Wait for Gottfried?

I decided to go back to Albert—until Gottfried had had enough of Juliet and was free again. Maybe that wasn't entirely fair to Albert, but he was totally insensitive anyway. In the meantime I could try to open his eyes to broad vistas. So this interval would be a decisive contribution to his intellectual redemption. And then Gottfried would find his way back to me, to experience the joy of shared intellectual interests in my arms.

33 I didn't feel like reading Hegel anymore. Instead, and to prepare myself for dealing with Albert, I went to the Clocktower Bookshop and bought myself an almost scholarly how-to book on constructive quarreling and sat down to read it right away.

But Albert didn't call. On Wednesday I didn't go to Gott-fried's seminar; I wanted him to feel my absence painfully. Thursday was a holiday. At two I called Albert, but when he picked up the phone, I hung up. At three I was at his door. "What a surprise!" I said.

"That's my line," Albert said. "What a surprise."

It was such nice weather we went for a walk. We chatted about this and that.

Suddenly he asked, "How do you picture your future?"

"How do you picture yours?" I parried, because I'd read that a question was often not a question but an expression of one's own problems.

"Somehow I can't get a sense of what you really want," Albert said.

That wasn't an answer to my question, so I asked him to formulate his statement with greater precision, to avoid misun-derstanding as to what was at issue here.

"What do you really want?"

I told Albert about the revolutionary necessity of unmasking superficial commonality of interest and liberating oneself from phoney bourgeois forms of institutionalized emotionality. I told him I was looking for a partner on equal footing, who could offer me communicative structures focused on the essential. I said that, for instance, Gottfried Schachtschnabel gave my thinking a deeper meaning by ascribing to the structures of my everyday life a very specific, conscious, concrete political significance.

"Oh, Gottfried Schachtschnabel," Albert said. "How is he?"

"The same," I said casually. I had no desire to tell Albert what had happened at Juliet's party. To steer away from this topic, I said Albert had lost all connection with the working class, and how it affected me deeply that he was trapped in the conventions of the ruling class and wasn't prepared to question traditions, let alone analyze them critically.

After I'd spent at least another half hour precisely laying out for him the possibilities and opportunities for a nonbourgeois relationship based on political intellectuality, he asked, "And what do you really want, in concrete terms?"

I suspected he hadn't even been listening. But since you're not supposed to verbalize that kind of thing, I asked, per instructions, "Let me ask you whether I've succeeded in making myself understood. Please give me some feedback."

"So far as I can tell, you're looking for a guru who'll do the thinking for you."

I'd read that it was wrong to respond to hostility with hostility, so I didn't say anything.

"Are you looking for some authoritarian bastard who shits authoritarian pronouncements and doesn't let anyone contradict him? Is that what you're looking for, sugar?"

Now he was trying to be sarcastic. It was obvious to me, but I still didn't say anything, because sarcasm is usually a hidden form of hostility.

"Well, don't strain your pretty little head," Albert quacked on. "Would-be gurus and would-be revolutionaries can be found in every corner bar." I still didn't say anything, for carefully considered reasons, so he asked again, "Okay, what do you really want? Come on, tell me; we can discuss it."

So he still hadn't grasped what was important to me. I wasn't sufficiently trained in constructive quarreling, and I was ready to explode: "Discuss it! I'm sick of always having to spoon-feed you! I'm always supposed to say which movie we're going to, where we should go on vacation, who we should have over, when we should screw each other. Maybe you could take the initiative once in a while. But basically it doesn't make any difference to you. You're indecisive up and down the line."

"In concrete terms, now, where am I supposed to take the initiative?" That had to be the joke of the day! He was asking me where he was supposed to take the initiative! I wondered whether I'd spent the last three years with a robot.

Another nonharmonious parting. I just walked out on Albert and took the bus home. It was hopeless. He would never change. He was incorrigible.

When I got home, I threw the book on constructive quarrels in the corner. It was worthless, too. But at least one thing was certain: I wouldn't have to look far to find something better than Albert.

34 On Wednesday I came to my seminar dressed in black. To better underscore my intellectuality. Appropriate, I felt, to finally dramatize visually the difference between Juliet and myself.

I was wearing tennis shoes and slouch socks and had given myself a real natural look with skin-toned lipstick. I'd even wondered whether I should bring some knitting to the seminar, to emphasize my critical attitude toward the consumer society more forcefully. In the past I hadn't placed enough stress on this essential aspect of my political profile in Gottfried's presence. But in the end I didn't take any knitting with me because I was afraid he might notice that all the other women in the seminar were faster knitters than I was. I chose not to expose myself to this competitive situation.

Gottfried talked about an interesting aspect of our fantasy lives: he said when we really desired something we could imagine it very concretely, as visual scenes. The more you wanted something, the more detailed you pictured the fulfillment of your wish. Yet conventional moral precepts and norms that you just obediently repeated but didn't support wholeheartedly—these kinds of tacked-on ideals weren't visually realizable; in contrast to those emotional wish/fantasy images, they existed only as words.

When we conceived scenes for films, Gottfried said, we should be alert to the degree of concreteness our thinking acquired for specific scenes, and in that way we could gain insight into the realm of our secret fantasies.

He also said that many students had trouble translating their political convictions into convincing images. "What do you think of, for instance, when you hear the phrase 'bourgeois institutions'?" he asked, and looked at me encouragingly.

"Justice of the peace," I said promptly.

"Very good," Gottfried said. "It's obvious you've given thought to this."

"The Taxman," said a male student in the first row.

"Hmm," was all Gottfried said.

"Church-run nursery schools," said a woman who wasn't knitting.

"Federal railways," said another, and then Beate said, after lengthy consideration, "Registrar of voters."

But Gottfried had only praised me, which everyone must have noticed.

Chlodwig asked where you could read up on this visualization theory. Gottfried said he couldn't say off the top of his head—it was something psychologists had documented. But he'd have the reference for us next time. "Aha," I said so loudly that Gottfried couldn't help but hear. I only nodded briefly to him as I left the seminar room.

On my way home I thought about what Gottfried had said. I tried to imagine how it would be if he and I lived together. But no images came to me. At least nothing that would have been any different from living with Albert. But I knew it had to be

different with Gottfried. Still, I wondered why no images came
to me. I'd heard somewhere that some theories had limited
applicability. Juliet's theory was very limited, for sure.

When I got home I called her immediately. "So now you're
Gottfried's consultant?" She laughed and acted like she didn't
know what I was talking about. I told her frankly that that theory
of hers—that you could visualize things you really desired, but
abstract norms remained nothing but words—didn't apply
to me.

"That's not possible," Juliet asserted.

"Yes, it is." I said that concrete images of bourgeois institutions occurred to me spontaneously, but I couldn't picture a
nonbourgeois relationship between two politically and emotionally liberated partners based on intellectual commonality.

"Then maybe that's not what you really, truly want," Juliet
said.

"Of course that's what I want, you know that perfectly well."

"So why can't you picture it? Long discussions in the evening?
On the Common Market's pricing policy? Or on the influence
of the Protestant ethic on the investment inclinations of capitalist entrepreneurs? While washing dishes you chat about the
latest government to be overthrown. . . . You only vacation in
countries that are politically pure—even if their beaches are
totally polluted. . . . You only drink coffee from Nicaragua and
tea from the People's Republic of China—even though the
coffee from Nicaragua is much more expensive, and the tea, too.
. . . But the main thing is that you go to some political discussion
group every night—the wife rushes off to her women's workshop
and solves the problems of the German working woman, and the
husband goes to his men's workshop and solves the problems of
the world in general. If you happen to meet back home in bed,
you compare your assessments of the latest factional struggles in
Albania or in the Social Democratic Party, or deal with the

problems of retirement benefits in the industrialized countries.
. . . And on the weekend you go to a demonstration together,
or a party meeting, and in the evening, for relaxation, you watch
one of those superboring political films with subtitles—never
dubbed. . . . Need some more ideas?"

I was crushed. How come she could picture it all so concretely,
and I couldn't? Oh, of course—she had Gottfried. Jealousy
clouded my brain. Extinguished my fantasy life. I heard Juliet's
idiotic laugh as if from a great distance. "Why do you laugh so
idiotically?" My voice was hoarse. Was it possible that Juliet was
an intellectual, too?

"Because it's all so idiotic."

"Why can you picture it so well?"

"Picture it! Don't make me laugh! I experienced it! My husband was a teacher. One little political project after another. He
was forever busy solving the world's problems, just so he
wouldn't have to confront our problems. God, that got on my
nerves."

I was still crushed. I wouldn't have thought that Juliet had
experienced that kind of political socialization—yet she spoke
about it so negatively! That only proved that basically she wasn't
an intellectual, but had just latched onto her husband. And now
she was trying to put one over on Gottfried. The jealousy in my
brain mingled with the sorrow in my heart. I could have seized
the opportunity for my political self-discovery with Gottfried.
Juliet had the experience already. She didn't deserve it again.

Juliet said she didn't have any time now, she had something
to take care of, but we could meet Friday night, at the Kaput,
she hadn't been there for ages.

"Will Gottfried be there?"

"I don't think so."

"What do you two do together?"

"We don't see each other all that often."

She was lying again. Yeah, right. What I *could* imagine was what—rather *who*—she had to take care of now! That viper! I took a deep breath to keep from verbalizing my hostility. Juliet really wasn't the right companion for me: when she wasn't lying, she was making fun of my goals in life. Anyway, I arranged to meet her. My head was spinning all night. Somehow, the whole time I kept seeing this picture of Gottfried stretched out on Juliet's bed.

35

It doesn't bother me a bit to go to a bar alone, not a bit, but it drives me crazy when I have to wait for someone. We were supposed to meet at eight, and Juliet didn't get there till shortly after nine.

She'd barely sat down when she pulled out her pocket mirror and smoothed her eyebrows—obviously she'd just been plucking them because the skin was a little puffy, and she'd heavily concealed a pimple on her chin. Then she pressed on the pimple with her thumb, which smeared away the thick layer of beige, leaving the pimple red and shiny. She grubbed around in her bag for her comb, threw it back in the bag, and went to the ladies' room. When she got back, the pimple was disguised again and her hair was fluffed up.

"Something wrong?" I asked. Juliet still hadn't given any explanation for being late.

"No, what would be wrong?" she asked, ordered a cup of coffee, checked her nails, and glanced at her watch.

"Is Gottfried coming after all? Or do you have a date with someone else?" I was waiting for an explanation.

"Actually he said he . . ." Juliet said, then smiled. Gottfried had just come in, looked around searchingly, then caught sight of us.

"Hi," he said to me first, and I said real casual, "Hi," as though we still had our old, cordial relationship.

"How are you tonight?" he said to Juliet, putting his hand on her shoulder.

When he sat down, he still had his hand on Juliet's shoulder. I had a feeling I'd soon be superfluous. Did she tell him to come so I could admire the spectacle of their rotten happiness? I decided to leave right away.

"I'm awfully sorry," Gottfried said to Juliet, "I have to leave right away."

Juliet stared at him.

"Inge called," he continued. "She's sick, she can't walk, she hasn't eaten all day. I've got to go and cook something for her, maybe take her to the hospital. The pain is getting worse, she says, she can't even move her left leg. I may have to call the ambulance when I get there."

"An accident?" Juliet asked.

"What happened?" I asked.

"Yes, well, not directly. She had her first riding lesson the day before yesterday, and got incredibly charleyhorsed, and because of that she tripped on the stairs this morning and scraped her shin. I've got to go see her right away—please don't be mad, maybe I'll be back later if I can. How long are you two going to be here?"

"Don't know," Juliet said. I felt the question wasn't directed at me. I ordered another glass of wine from Niyazi. I could stay as long as I liked; I hadn't been stood up.

Not till after Gottfried had left did I ask Juliet, "Are you going to have a glass now?"

She poked at a cigarette hole in the tablecloth and ordered, without answering me.

After about half an hour, she said, "That's really too much."
"What is?"

"He calls up, just before eight, asks what I'm doing, I tell him I'm supposed to meet you here, and he says, 'How nice, I'll come, too.' "

"Did he really say that?"

"Those very words: 'How nice, I'll come, too.' "

Aha. So he'd come partly to see me.

"I thought you'd be happy to see him privately again, away from the academy. But now—now he just comes by to announce that he has to report to his ex-wife."

I could understand him. If he stood Juliet up, there had to be a good reason for it. I was sure of that. "Hey, listen," I said "the woman can hardly walk! I had a terrible charleyhorse one time . . ."

"This isn't the first time he's suddenly had no time," Juliet said. "We've only known each other four weeks—intimately, I mean," Juliet said, without blushing, "and in that time we've only seen each other eight times. And he's seen that ex-wife of his four times, at the very least. Even though they've been divorced for ages!"

I didn't say anything; I was amazed at Juliet's pedantry! As though you could add up the give-and-take in a relationship by the frequency of being together. She was so old-fashioned. She was a philistine.

Juliet was getting more worked up. "Gottfried's convinced he can't skip out on his ex-wife. When her lover doesn't have time, he has to go over there and service the lady. Not that she wants to sleep with him; no, that's her lover's department. But she likes to call on her old husband for all sorts of other services. Like now, for instance!"

"But I find it fantastic—"

"Oh, please! What's fantastic about it?"

"But you're such good friends with your ex-husband, too," I reminded her. "You had such a harmonious separation."

"Oh, please," Juliet said again.

Neither of us said a word for a while.

Then she said, "I don't want to talk about it anymore."

So again neither of us said a word for a while.

Then Juliet finally said, "This can't go on much longer."

Apparently she had a mistaken image of a relationship with Gottfried. I secretly raised my eyebrows. I'd known that she wasn't an appropriate partner for him. Even though she didn't want to talk about it, I asked, "What do you really want from Gottfried? You said the two of you had an open, spontaneous, nonpossessive relationship. . . ."

"A man who doesn't have time for me—that's what I had before," Juliet said, and sank into silence again.

"What should we do now?" I asked finally. Actually, though we'd arranged to meet here, I hadn't pictured spending the evening with a jilted divorced woman staring gloomily into space. I'd rather have gone to a different bar to check out the scene. It was the weekend of Pentecost, and any number of Pentecostally decked-out studs could be milling around.

"I could call Karl-Heinz," Juliet said.

"If you feel like it," I said, though I had no desire for the company of Juliet's bosom buddy. Juliet wasn't the sort of woman to go barhopping with another woman—this I was beginning to suspect. She had to have a man along as an alibi.

She went to the bar, asked to be handed the phone, dialed, and let it ring endlessly. She came back in an even worse mood than before.

"Not home, or at least he's not picking up. Maybe he's in bed with some bimbo."

"Karl-Heinz? You think so?" I wondered what Albert was doing this weekend. He was probably sprawled in front of the TV.

"All men are fools."

"I think so, too, in principle," I said, "but first you should try to empathize with the situation of those with differing opinions." I'd read that in the book on constructive quarreling.

"Thank you very much," Juliet said. "I think I'll go home. Maybe Gottfried will call later, when he's taken care of his ex-wife."

"Maybe."

"But I won't pick up the phone, I'm telling you right now. I'm not sitting there at his beck and call."

What a pill Juliet is, I thought. She, my model for the ideal harmonious separation, was making all this fuss. Couldn't she grasp that Gottfried had also had a harmonious separation?

"This can't go on much longer," Juliet said grimly, as we parted at the corner.

"You don't mean that!" I said vehemently. Actually, I was thinking the exact same thing.

36

Power belongs not to those who exercise it but to those who can afford to renounce it. I'd read that somewhere, and it made me think. I, too, could afford to renounce exercising my power, so I called Albert.

But he wasn't home. Or just not answering the phone. Or had he gone away for Pentecost? Maybe to see his parents? He would have told me. Did he forget that every year on the Saturday of Pentecost we go to our street festival at the little park down the street? True, Albert didn't live here anymore, but that didn't have to be taken so literally; a lot of people who didn't live in Kreuzberg came to our festival.

I waited till three for him to call. Then I went to the festival alone. He was probably there already. He couldn't have forgotten.

At least two hundred people were there. A neighborhood action group was selling bratwurst as a benefit for world hunger; another was selling beer, wine, and hot dogs for a save-the-forests campaign; a suburban commune was there with progressive T-shirts they'd silk-screened themselves; Planned Parenthood had an information booth, as did a citizens' movement to stop real estate speculation. Almost everything good and leftist was there. The atmosphere was fantastic. Now and then a sound would cut through the languid May air. The sound came from the rock group Peace to the People, which was trying to repair its amplifier. The group's equipment was set up in a small truck. Various freaks were sitting around the truck, guzzling beer and giving the four guys in the band pointers on where to find the problem. I didn't know the group but had seen their posters everywhere in the neighborhood for days. The posters showed the members of the band, and said they had a lot of street festival experience and had kindly agreed to appear for free—in spite of their many commitments—to make their contribution to fostering neighborly relations between Turkish immigrant workers and longtime residents. In the photo you could tell that the guys in Peace to the People were genuine counterculture types: they all had hair down to their asses, or at least down to their elbows.

Albert was nowhere to be seen. I should have expected that: without me he was incapable of doing anything. So what, I could have a good time by myself, too. I bought a T-shirt from the suburban commune for fifteen marks: it showed two women silkscreened in dots à la Roy Lichtenstein; above the first woman was a bubble saying MEN ARE ALL EGOTISTS, and in the bubble above the other, OH, SISTER, THEY'LL NEVER LEARN FROM US WOMEN. Very witty and very true. I would've liked to put it on right then and there.

I spotted a guy from the academy. He looked nice, but I'd

never exchanged one word with him. There'd never been an opportunity, but here, at the street festival, everything was very laid-back. So I spoke to him, like very laid-back, and asked if he lived in the area, too.

"Not really," he said.

I asked if he'd been at the festival long.

"Not really," he said.

I asked which instructor he thought was the best.

"Why do you ask?" he said.

Then I asked what his name was and told him mine.

"What do I care what your name is?" he said.

So I didn't say any more.

"Why do you ask?" he said again.

I said I was going to get myself a spritzer.

"Right," he said.

"Bye," I said, and thought this guy wasn't too communicative.

"Hey, you, Constance," he yelled after me. I turned around.

"Hey, you, let me have a cigarette!" he said.

He seemed to be the sort of guy who wouldn't do anything for free, not even talk. I can do without those guys. But now I had to give him a cigarette because people had heard him loudly bum one. It was dumb of me to tell him my name—it would cost me a lot of cigarettes at school. When one of these freeloaders knows your name, it's over.

But I didn't let it spoil my good mood. I bought myself a spritzer and went over to the truck where the four guys from Peace to the People were still trying to repair their amplifier. Their advisers had come to the conclusion that the problem had to be a loose wire in one of the countless plugs and cables.

"Man, dudes," said one of the freaks sprawled around the truck, "the cable's the source of all evil, you dig?"

"Shut yer fuckin' trap," said one of the Peace to the People guys. I went over to the Planned Parenthood booth to check out the latest styles in cervical caps. The atmosphere was getting better and better, and a bunch of old people from the apartment buildings around the park had come. The old folks mixed in perfectly naturally with the freaks and counterculture types, the old-style and new-style revolutionaries, and the professional mothers.

There was lots of entertainment for the kiddies, of course. The biggest crowd was around the Quiz Booth, a stand put up by the PR department of a baby food manufacturer. The stand was manned by an M.S.W. who specialized in street festivals, as the sign above the booth informed us. There were also pictures of the company's products. The social worker was showing slides on a large screen, slides of a car or a soccer player or an animal or a film star, a TV star, or a rock star. The children had to come up with the names of the stars, cars, animals, soccer players, or famous people. The one who yelled out the right answer first was given a little green card with the name of the company on it. Five little cards got you a plastic Smurf. The social worker was sweating like a pig, but he had a good hold on the crowd. If none of the kids knew the right answer, he would give a little speech about the unidentified car or rock star; the kids listened to him breathlessly every time. Some of the children were real experts; one of them had bagged about twenty Smurfs. He'd known not only Mick from the prehistoric rock group Dave, Dee, Dozy, Beaky, Mick and Tich, but even the last name of Udo Jürgens's former longtime girlfriend, Corinna!

"Incredible how much kids know nowadays," one mother said to another.

"Phenomenal," the other one said. "I wonder where they pick it up." A boy of about ten had just won another Smurf. This kid was an absolute whiz on soccer players. He knew all of them, and had already amassed twenty-three Smurfs. "Stupid Smurfs," he said every time he won another one. The other children gazed at him admiringly and stared enviously at the Smurfs, which he'd lined up in groups of ten in front of him.

The social worker acted as though he suddenly had an idea. He said that anyone who'd won more than twenty-two Smurfs had to drop out to let the others have a chance.

"I've got twenty-three Smurfs," yelled the soccer whiz. But then he said that on the real TV quiz shows you didn't have to drop out, so he didn't want to. But the social worker was smarter than that. He said everyone who had over twenty-two Smurfs was a champion, and he'd make the champion his assistant, and the assistant got to press the button on the slide projector. Everyone knows, the social worker said, that the game-show assistants on TV were former champions. That made sense. Except that a girl raised her hand and said that on TV only women could be assistants.

"We believe in equal rights here," the social worker said. "In our show boys can be assistants, too. So," he said to the champion, "what's your name? Please introduce yourself to our viewers."

"Benjamin Harzer," he said, and bowed like a real TV assistant.

The next slide showed a bird. No one knew what it was. On the eighth try a girl got the right answer: it was a chickadee, not a vulture, as two other children had guessed. Then Benjamin Harzer was allowed to press the button again. The social worker praised him. Suddenly a little boy next to me began to bawl. He was too young to play the game, but he'd been listening closely for many rounds. The kid threw himself on the ground and pounded it with his fists.

"What's wrong, Hubby baby?" his mother screeched. She threw herself down on the ground, too. The kid was gushing like a fountain.

"I'm always left out!" the child screamed.

"But Hubby baby, that's not true!" The mother was almost crying herself. The other kids stared.

"All the other kids are called Benjamin except me!" blubbered Hubby baby.

"But that's not true," his mother said again.

Now a little girl of about four joined Hubby and his mother on the ground. "Hey, you, why are you so hostile?" she asked Hubby baby. Hubby baby kept on crying.

"Look, Hubby," the mother said, "I'm sure this little girl's not called Benjamin, and she's not crying."

Hubby's sobs became a little quieter.

"Right?" Hubby's mother said conspiratorially to the little girl.

"Every baby knows only the boys are called Benjamin, not the girls," the little girl said scornfully to the mother. The mother blushed. "My name's Juliet," said the little girl proudly, "and all the other girls in my play group are called Juliet, too."

"I want to be called Juliet!" screamed Hubby.

"It's vagina-envy," another woman told Hubby's mother. Now Hubby wanted ice cream to comfort him for his sad fate. I turned a bit to let Hubby and his mother get to the ice-cream stand, and way in back, by the hot dog stand, I saw Albert.

He'd come after all. He looked in my direction. I wanted to call to him, and had just opened my mouth, when a noise crashed over me. It sounded like a ballistic missile had exploded three feet overhead. I almost dropped dead. It was the loudest noise I'd ever heard. All life ground to a halt. I thought the whole city would sink in rubble and ashes. I stood there with my mouth open so my eardrums wouldn't burst.

Cheers, clapping, stamping, whistles, roars, hurrahs filled the neighborhood—though no one standing around was clapping or even saying a word. Peace to the People was playing an applause track on their sound system to warm up the audience. The noise bounced back off the facades, was magnified in the rear court-yards, and echoed back.

Like most rock groups with a political agenda, the instruments were much louder than the vocalists, so you could only make out the lyrics now and then, and only in snatches. Still, by the third song my ear had adjusted enough so I could catch some scraps of words: ". . . violence-free . . . liberate your souls . . . war on all who oppress us . . . we bring you tenderness . . ."

They were singing in German. I found it really great that Peace to the People used German lyrics, because that way they could really communicate with their audience much better. As one of the guys in the band announced, the next song had been composed especially for street festivals. It was called "Speak to Each Other, Turks and Old Geezers." But I couldn't follow the words because of the electric guitars.

The old folks hobbled back into their houses. The ones who'd been hanging out the windows closed them and pulled down the shades. The Planned Parenthood women packed up their stand. The social worker in the quiz booth handed out the rest of the Smurfs to the kids who hadn't won any yet. The rest of the crowd moved away from the immediate vicinity of the speakers. Me, too. Two followers of the Bhagwan danced with their little children right in front of the speakers. A couple of freaks with a lot of beer bottles were still sprawled on the benches in front of the truck, drinking to the band, totally laid-back in the here and now. Apparently they were the Peace to the People groupies.

Next to me a child was screaming; I only saw it, couldn't hear it, because the music drowned him out. "Okay, folks," the lead singer screeched through the microphone, "let's really heat it up now!" He turned up the sound. The applause tape came on again. Even more deafening roars, stamping, screaming, whistles.

One of the Planned Parenthood women went up to the group and took up a position on the platform. The woman was shaking, probably because she was standing near one of the amps and was rocked by the sound waves. I moved a little closer because I thought she was going to do a solo piece. Between songs she said something to the lead singer, which was inaudible because even when the group wasn't playing, the sound system produced buzz saw sounds. The lead singer, the one with the longest hair, gesticulated at the woman.

"Comrades and ladies," he suddenly screamed into the mike, "here's a broad who wants to muzzle us!"

The woman said something again. The lead singer roared at her through the microphone. "We're performing for free here! And you come along and claim we're anti-communication! Do you have any idea what this sound system cost?

"We're fighting for integration! Of old geezers! And Turks!" screamed the lead singer. "And all you can do is bitch!"

Now the percussionist of Peace to the People bawled into his mike. "Comrades and ladies!" blared through the neighborhood. "Our sound system cost over thirty thousand marks! We! are performing free here! We! won't let any representative of the establishment dictate to us how loud we! can play! Especially not this bitch!"

The woman opened and closed her mouth again, tried to get to a mike, but the guys shoved her away. One of the Peace to the People groupies threw an empty beer bottle at the woman. I really didn't like that.

"Let's ask someone from the audience how he likes us," the percussionist bawled, and held out the mike to the guy who'd thrown the beer bottle. "Ya stupid bitch!" the guy screamed, and shook his fist at the woman. "You need to get laid!" The Peace to the People group laughed, and the woman disappeared.

Actually I felt sorry for her. And I really thought they could have turned down the sound a wee bit. For the old folks' sake. But none of them had complained. It wouldn't have done any good if I'd shown solidarity with the woman—I didn't have a mike either. Besides, everyone else thought it was great. Otherwise they'd have spoken up. These were all antiauthoritarian types. So it went on like before. The group played their applause tape again. "The struggle continues!" the guitarist screamed. "We! won't let ourselves be oppressed!"

The brides of the Bhagwan and their two children continued to demonstrate how laid-back they were in the here and now.

The festive group scattered, most went home. There were still about fifty people back by the hot dog and wine stands. I looked everywhere for Albert but couldn't find him. The group was too loud for him, no doubt. He must've taken off as soon as they began to play. That would be just like him! He would never make any sacrifices for the integration of old people and Turks. But he couldn't expect a street festival to be like a funeral.

I was getting hungry. I wanted a bratwurst; the man working the grill looked at me uncomprehendingly, even though I was shouting as loud as I could. He pointed to the beef hot dogs, then the brats, then he looked at me with raised eyebrows, then held up his hand, first stretching his thumb in the air, then the index finger, then the ring finger, and then the little finger. He looked at me impatiently. So did the others standing around. Ah, I got it. He wanted to know which kind and how many. I pointed to the brats and signaled with my thumb that I only wanted one. I was a little ashamed that I'd tried to communicate verbally. All the people standing around must have realized I had limited street festival experience. Of course. Nonverbal communication: most old people were hard of hearing, and Turks don't understand anything. It was only logical that Peace to the People played so loud. Language has always been one of the ruling class's most subtle instruments of control.

I took my bratwurst and stood in a doorway, a little shelter from the music. A young man was helping an old woman down the stairs. Another old woman came out of the first-floor apartment: "Could you take me along, please, Frau Schmidt?" she said. "It's louder in my apartment than on the street!" Then she said to the young man, "I don't have anyone to come and get me." From the rear building an older woman came leading a very old man. "Come with us," said the man to the woman from the first floor, "we're taking the bus, wherever it goes."

Peace to the People was playing the applause track again. I saw that old people from the surrounding houses were being picked up by their relatives. Apparently every one who was ambulatory was being evacuated. Involuntarily I had to sigh. My goodness, I thought, how much has to happen before people are ready to support grass-roots political action?

The Peace to the People groupies were still sprawled on the benches in front of the truck. By now they were totally soused, and a similarly soused derelict was drinking with them; four women with their babies in Snuglís had joined them, too. One after the other, the women pulled their breasts out of their T-shirts and nursed the babies. The boozers drank to the babes. The two brides of the Bhagwan were still spinning their little children around in circles. Right smack in front of the speakers.

I didn't know what to do now. Most of the people had already left. Behind the stands were mostly single mothers with their kids. I didn't want to go home, but nothing was happening here. Nothing left to do but go home.

I lived only four streets away from the park, so Peace to the People was only slightly quieter in my flat. When I walked into the apartment, they were just singing a song that protested running a highway through a residential neighborhood.

The windows were rattling.

I tried to call Albert. If he'd gone straight home from the park, he'd have been there long ago. But he wasn't. It was almost seven. Why didn't he call? I went to bed early. At ten o'clock

Peace to the People fell silent. I opened the window and fell asleep at once.

But at four in the morning I woke up and couldn't get back to sleep. I was furious that Albert hadn't called. Maybe he was on night call. I phoned the hospital, direct-dialing the doctors' lounge. After it rang for an eternity someone picked up, a colleague of Albert's. The colleague didn't seem particularly wide awake. Only one doctor was on call at a time so Albert wasn't at the hospital. I hung up without saying a word. I wanted to call Albert and hang up on him, but he would have suspected it was me.

On Pentecost Sunday it rained buckets. Albert called in the afternoon. He claimed that hadn't been him yesterday at the street festival. I must have been seeing things. But today I could see him. What did I have planned? I was still bitter that he hadn't called yesterday. I said the festival had been really fantastic. What had he been doing, if he wasn't at the festival? He said he'd had something better to do.

"Well, what?"

"None of your business," he said.

It was impossible to go for a walk with all the rain. It was too early to go to the movies. Besides, I wasn't at his beck and call, waiting till the gentleman graciously condescended to phone. "I don't feel like going out with you," I said.

"So what are you going to do?"

"I have to think."

"About what?"

"None of your business."

"So you don't want to go out with me?"

"No."

"Well, okay then!" He slammed down the receiver.

Two hours later I was very bored. I didn't have anything in the refrigerator. The canned food was all gone, too. And it was still pouring. I resolved once more not to exercise my power and

called Albert. The line was busy. He was on the phone for an
hour and a half. Then he didn't answer the phone. Or had he
left the house as soon as he hung up? Where had he gone? And
with whom? Or was he just trying to get to me?

True, we were separated, but still; I was trying to achieve a
harmonious separation. Albert could use Gottfried Schachtschnabel as a model, the way he looked out for his ex-wife. But
Albert wasn't in the same league. For a moment I wished we
were married. Then we'd really be getting divorced. And he'd
have to do everything I wanted, otherwise I'd take him to the
cleaners.

37 It rained all week, and nothing else was happening. Then, on Thursday, summer broke
out. In a matter of hours all the muck dried up
and it was much too beautiful to stay inside.
The few bars in Kreuzberg that had a so-called
garden turned into sidewalk cafés where everybody who was anybody gathered. I went to the Collection Box,
looking for familiar faces.

She was sitting next to Albert. They'd turned their chairs
toward each other; she had one foot on the rung of his chair, her
other leg between his legs, and it was clear they had something
going. She was smiling happily.

She also nodded happily when I asked her whether there was
room at the table. Albert sighed, lit a cigarette, and said, "This
is my old friend, Constance Wechselburger." He sighed again
and tossed the pack of cigarettes on the table. She was very taken
aback. With her mouth open, and without saying a word, she
edged her chair away from him and stared at the tabletop.

"This is my dear colleague, Anna Mannersfeld," Albert told

me, more resigned than annoyed. He should have known I might come by here. I hadn't been spying on him—this was my territory, he was the one who'd moved away; if anyone was out of place, she was.

This Anna was small, thin, with blond hair and round gold-rimmed glasses. She was wearing jeans, a T-shirt, and one of those ethnic sweaters draped over her shoulders, one of those brown-beige rags with hoofed animals embroidered all around. I wondered if I'd seen her before; she was like her sweater: you see it a dozen times without remembering it. Was it camels or llamas or cows on those sweaters? Was she the type who tans easily in the summer? So average you didn't even take a moment to wonder whether she colored her hair.

Only on second glance did I notice irritating features. She was wearing wooden shoes with a natural-colored leather strap, but with high gold heels. Silvery particles glittered on her face, from her eyelids to her throat; she had sprinkled Carnival glitter over her face—at the end of May! Didn't go with the sweater, with her glasses, with her. I didn't want to honor her with so much as a glance, but I stared at her. She noticed.

"A little while ago a man at the next table said I looked like a Christmas tree," she said. She smiled uncertainly at Albert. "I usually don't wear makeup," she said, more to me than him.

"It shows," I said.

Albert said, "I think it's sweet," and wiped the silver glitter off her nose, where it had stuck to the blackheads. Anna began chattering in a shrill voice about hospital goings-on. Insider talk. She was some kind of dietitian's aide and was filling in on Albert's ward. Just as bad as a nurse.

She was laughable, and yet I was scared of her. I'd been jealous of her predecessors, Albert's other women, but I hadn't felt threatened. Threatened in my role as the only woman who was really compatible with Albert. But this Anna made me afraid, because she seemed prepared to risk everything for him. It wasn't enough for her to please him as she was; she wanted to conform to his wishes.

The fear that Albert could have found something better before I'd lined up something better for myself made my throat tighten. I don't know how long I sat there with them, not saying a word. "Take me home, please," I heard myself begging at some point.

"Okay," Albert said. He wanted to avoid a power struggle. Anna had tears in her eyes when Albert and I left the place. But he hadn't paid. What did that mean? Did he assume she would pay for him? Or was he planning to come back? Whose feelings was he trying to spare—Anna's or mine?

Albert refused to come upstairs with me. But we sat and fought in his car so long that I was sure Anna would definitely have left if he did go back to the Collection Box. I bawled all night long, because now I felt so . . . single.

 "He's dealing with the consequences," Juliet said. "You split up with him. Did you think he'd go into a monastery and mourn you forever?"

Well, actually I would have hoped . . . what else?

"Don't sniffle into the phone," Juliet said.

She was heartless. I shouldn't have called her, shouldn't have told her I'd seen Albert with that other woman. It was too late now. "And now? What do I do now?" I asked her.

"Even a harmonious separation is a separation," Juliet said. "Sometimes theory and practice are one and the same." She laughed that idiotic laugh.

I didn't understand what she meant. I wondered whether I'd

wanted to separate from Albert more in theory or more in practice. But no answer immediately came to me. And anyway, Juliet was a fine one to talk. She'd gotten her claws into Gottfried Schachtschnabel.

"By the way," Juliet interrupted my silence, "I've persuaded Birgit to try the personals."

"Really?"

"Yes. Tomorrow we're going to buy all the papers that carry them and see if there's something there for her. By the way, you could try one, too." Juliet sounded as enthusiastic as if the idea had just occurred to her. "Why don't you come over tomorrow afternoon?"

"Me—reply to an object—matrimony ad? But I'm not getting married, ever!"

"Oh, come on! If you answer an object—matrimony ad, do you think that means you have to get married? Most of the personals aren't for marriage anyway, just acquaintance."

I relented.

Juliet and Birgit were in a splendid mood when I got there on Saturday afternoon. They were drinking coffee and egg liqueur, and the rug was strewn with newspapers.

Birgit, who had so strenuously resisted this approach before, was now enthusiastically searching for Mr. One-in-a-million. Unselfishly, she'd even thought of me. "Listen," she said, "here's one for you, listen: 'Don't claim you're sincere—just be it. . . .' "

"Let me read it myself," I said. I read:

Don't claim you're sincere—just be it. I would like to live as a twosome with a woman who feels as I do. I have consciously avoided the usu. advt. lang., for, as we know, paper lies. I am no beauty, but certainly presentable. Early thirties, 5'10", 180 well-exercised lbs. (golf). I have a creative profession, which supports me handsomely, & would like to enjoy all the beautiful things in life, from art to the erotic, with a pretty blond partner (ca. 25). I know precisely what I want: a woman for whom togetherness is as important as it is for me. I'm not available for an isolated adventure, but if you've waited for a man like me and want to help luck along, I look forward to hearing from you with a photo, Box . . .

"He sounds really sincere," Birgit said.

I thought this man sounded too talkative and too fat. "Besides, I'm not a blonde and I'm over twenty-five."

"Oh," Birgit said, "that's true."

"*You* should respond to this ad," I said to her.

"Me? Are you crazy? You really think so?" she said.

I grabbed a page with the heading ACQUAINTANCESHIPS, MALE. I read:

55 years young, I love life and would like to share this love with a partner. I am financially independent and for reasons of equity want my partner to be the same. I have no complexes, am good-looking and very athletic: tennis, cross-country skiing, hiking, sailing. If you are between 18 and 25 and love life like I do, I look forward to a loving encounter. Box . . .

What very young kitten, yearning for tenderness, would let herself be stroked by a lonely tomcat and accompany him for part of his life's journey? The only thing you should have is tolerance and a womanly figure. Details in a nice little bistro (Dutch treat). Box . . .

Above-average, attract. male Pisces with above-av. emot. devel. and ythfl. aura, tolerant, hi intell. & artist. inclinations; 38, 5'9", dark, non-smok., Prot., civ. eng., hard working, very nat'l., loves childr. & anml., multi-faceted ind., seeks "Her": a stunning, attr., very ythfl. lady. You should be as much at ease in hi soc. circles as in a concert hall or the woods. Femin. allure and nat'l. appeal expected. Send rep. with tel. no. and recent photo to Box . . .

I (42, youthful entrepreneur, 6'2", 196 lbs.) recognize that my life and love are shaped by aesthetic considerations and therefore seek a partner who is: sensitive and cuddly, elegant in jeans or evening gown, max. 25, preferably with boyish figure (redheads also welcome). Feminists and girls who've missed the boat need not reply. . . .

I was overcome with rage, and not only because I didn't own an evening dress. Maximum twenty-five—that was the oldest these gentlemen were willing to tolerate at their sides in higher social circles or in the woods. And I was already twenty-seven and a half. Didn't anyone want me anymore?

I scoured the ads for the age limits. I discovered, with relief, that some men, who described themselves as "looking considerably younger" or called themselves "a man in his prime" (without mentioning their age), were willing to consider a woman up to thirty, provided, of course, she was stunningly attractive, had a flawless figure and character, was tender, chic, sensuous, athletic, loved animals, etc. I could meet those requirements—well, I wasn't athletic, and I didn't love animals, but you'd never know that by looking at me. But most important, I could offer qualities the men themselves boasted of: I was very interested in politics and culture, I was open to anything new, honest, nondogmatic, thoughtful, intellectual, with a good sense of humor . . . it should certainly be possible to find something in common with one of these men in their prime.

"What's a man in his prime?" I asked Juliet and Birgit.

"An older man, fifty at least," Juliet said.

"That old!" I thought for a minute. There were no couples

with that big an age difference that I knew. Albert was two years older than me. Sure, he was pretty immature. But a man twenty or thirty years older? The men I knew of that age were fathers with families who spent their evenings in front of the TV. The men in the ads seemed to spend the whole day involved in various athletic pursuits. I tried to picture these men playing sports: in my mind's eye I saw two soccer teams in their prime— old men with beer bellies and bald spots. Ridiculous. So I thought again and tried to picture the men in their prime as "looking considerably younger": holding in their tummies and with a few strands of hair combed over their bald spots—still ridiculous. What was wrong with these pictures?

Once more I checked the athletic types' self-descriptions, and I realized that none of these sports fans played soccer. That surprised me, since most men are soccer fans—but the ones who put ads in the paper played tennis, skied cross-country, sailed, mountain-climbed, and hiked.

I could more easily picture the older gentlemen cross-country skiing. But I didn't feel like spending the rest of my life panting along a cross-country trail. I wanted to discuss political problems with my partner, exchange views. But none of the men in the ads seemed interested in that.

I didn't get it. "Why do all men dream of a woman who could be their daughter? Do they have incestuous tendencies?"

"A mature man has a lot more to offer," Birgit said.

"How am I supposed to build a lively partnership with a man who has one foot in the grave?" I said to her.

"This is the male version of finding yourself," Juliet said. "They think if only they had a young woman they could finally live life to the fullest. Yet they don't want to change the way they live—on the contrary, there's nothing they're more afraid of! Because then they'd have to change themselves. So they're desperately looking for a young girl who'll let herself be dominated, who's inexperienced enough not to know that what these gentlemen dish out as the wisdom of age is really the obstinacy of old age."

"What do you mean?" Birgit exclaimed quite indignantly.

"How do you imagine an old man like that treats a young woman? My mother died very young, you know, and five years ago my father remarried. The old man's sixty-seven now, and his wife is forty-two—not a baby, but that's how he treats her! His wife isn't allowed to have any opinions of her own—allegedly she lacks experience. But aside from that he's incredibly worried that she's going to cheat on him with a younger man."

"So—you're saying go to bed with a grandpa," I said. "Do you think they can still get it up?"

"Well, they think if they can't get it up, it's only because the woman isn't attractive enough. And I think all my father needs is to know that other men envy him . . . he's happy if the other guys think that if he has such a young wife he must still be in the running. . . ."

"Even so, an older man is in a much better position to provide a cozy nest for his wife," Birgit said.

"I want a man to have sex with, not to inherit from," I said to needle her.

She stared at me in horror. Then she asked Juliet, "And why did your stepmother marry your father?"

"I'll give you one guess," Juliet said.

"Are they happy together?" Birgit asked.

"She's waiting for him to die, and he's hoping he has another twenty years to dominate her. Jolly prospects."

Birgit stared at Juliet in horror.

Juliet laughed. "I read a psychological study where they asked men what motives they would attribute to a pretty young woman who married a considerably older man. Well, the younger men usually assumed they did it for the money, hoping to inherit as soon as possible. But the older men, those over sixty, said that a pretty young women would marry an old man for love—because she appreciated his experience! Wild, isn't it?"

We drank a glass of egg liqueur to men and read on. I found an ad with the heading TOTALLY CRAZY INDIVIDUALIST. He was thirty-five and longed for a "girl-woman, age 26 ± 8 years." I subtracted: $26 - 8 = 18$. Of course. Even for a totally crazy individualist an eighteen-year-old was ideal. I added: $26 + 8 = 34$. "How does he happen to pick thirty-four as the upper limit?"

"It's obvious you don't read the personals regularly," Juliet said. "Very simple: if a man's looking for a woman of 'about twenty-five,' he's between forty and near-death. But if the ad says 'up to twenty-seven' or 'up to thirty-four,' in other words, if an exact number is given as the upper limit, you can bet the man's exactly one year older. He has to be at least a year older, because otherwise his masculine superiority would collapse. The men who put in ads that follow the second principle are usually younger. The younger the man is, the older the woman can be. The search for lost youth doesn't begin till forty."

"Here!" Birgit exclaimed. "Here someone writes 'age and appearance unimportant.' "

"Read it to us!"

"Best-selling author of the future seeks: solvent publisher for book, friendship; possible later marriage. World-traveler, athletic, stunningly handsome, and independent academic, fifty-five, five-nine, wishes to establish contact with woman of same métier. Age and appearance unimportant. Serious replies only to Box . . ."

"He doesn't want a photo, just your bank records as a reference," I said.

"Hm," said Birgit.

"An exception—worse than the rule," Juliet said. Then she read an ad from a nonconformist teacher who was looking for a nonconformist, sensuous woman who rejected city life and bras. And he wanted a full-torso photo.

Why does a woman have to be beautiful rather than intelligent? Because men can see better than they can think. I was reminded of bathroom-wall graffiti.

Nobility of heart was another quality much in demand in the personals. I wondered whether Juliet had more nobility of heart than me and if that was why she'd been able to snare Gottfried Schachtschnabel. I asked the personals expert, "What's nobility of heart?"

"You don't have it!" she replied.

"You don't even know me that well. . . ."

"Women who've graduated from prep school don't have nobility of heart."

"I graduated, too," Birgit said.

"For men, nobility of heart is the opposite of nobility of mind. So only stupid women have a good heart. I thought everybody knew that!" said Juliet, and laughed.

I read the next ad: "I like idealistic, creative people, children's laughter, children's sorrows, family joys. . . ." I stopped reading—the ad reminded me of Juliet's visions of total togetherness: children, debts, evenings in front of the TV.

Farther down I at least found an ad for Birgit, who wasn't averse to older men. I read it to her: "It's all right for you to set high standards; I do so myself. I am a young-looking man in the mid-forties; life and marriage experience have made me attentive and tender, and you are invited to lean on my youthful and athletic five feet eleven . . ."

"Lean on," Birgit said. She sighed.

". . . provided you are a many-faceted, romantic, tender young lady with a good heart and breeding. For reasons of equity I want a partner of substantial means. . . ."

"Too bad," Birgit said, "that these rich men only want to marry rich women."

In the next ad, too, some man was looking for a well-heeled woman, for reasons of equity. In addition to all the other positive attributes, of course. "Why doesn't anyone want an intelligent woman for reasons of equity?" I said.

"Luckily there are still some generous gentlemen out there," Juliet said: "Here, take a look at this one."

> Millionaire (50), gnrs., seeks attr. you. lad. for all love/ life sit. Reply w. pict., Box . . .

"You can tell by the abbreviations what a generous guy he is," I said. "A cheap, dirty old man is what he is!"

Now I was sure; it was idiotic to place any hopes in these morons' ads. Suddenly I noticed another ad, much bigger than all the others, but in a lower corner, so that I'd overlooked it till now.

> Your fine qualities cannot be formulated in the language of advertising. . . . You have found your own path, beyond the tranquillity of stasis. . . . You feel much that others repress. . . . You seek to take up arms against philistinism per se. . . . For you, being is more important than having. Your free spirit despises norms and is open to the deeper meaning of existence. You like politics. . . . Tolerance and aesthetics are as vitally important to you as to me: you are intellectual to the depths of your soul. The laws of eroticism are terra cognita. . . .

Shivers ran down my spine. I read on:

> . . . I, 32/5'6"/143 lbs., capable of enthusiasm and self-motivation, flexible and disciplined, but completely undogmatic and nevertheless reliable, have learned to orient myself in absolutely unstructured space, to discern organizing principles. I like clear language and clear people; unorthodox as I am, I prefer to view things other than

stereotypes. We are seeking each other, so that all this may be self-evident. Box 48763 UZ.

Here was what I'd been looking for: a kindred spirit! Finally an ad from an intellectual. And such a large, generous ad! And the ad was in a local paper, so the man must live nearby.

Really, a sign from fate. He was a little short, only four inches taller than me, but we intellectuals don't care about externals. I wondered whether I shouldn't respond to an ad after all. To this ad. Birgit disrupted my thoughts.

"A photo, I need a photo," Birgit exclaimed, "a full-length photo, otherwise I can't answer a single ad."

"Yes," I said absentmindedly.

"I don't have a picture of myself," Birgit said.

"You must have one lying around somewhere," Juliet said.

"No, I don't. At least none that would be suitable for something like this."

"Any old picture will do," Juliet said.

"I can't send a man I don't even know just any old picture! That'll be the first impression he gets of me, and you know how important that is. . . ."

"Should I take a picture of you?" I said. "I'm pretty good. I worked in an ad agency for a while after I graduated, and I learned how to use a camera. I have a fantastic camera, I'll be glad to shoot you."

"Honest?" said Birgit.

"Honest," I said.

"Well, I don't know . . ." she said.

I reminded her that I was at the film academy, and photography was my profession and my passion. I promised her the most beautiful pictures, in color. She'd look absolutely natural.

"Absolutely natural," Birgit said, and looked at us distrustfully. "Who knows what I'll look like?"

"We'll take the pictures tomorrow," I said, "at Holy Cross Cemetery."

"You're crazy," Birgit said.

"Because of the trees," I said. "There are such beautiful trees there; no trees like 'em anywhere else in Berlin." I swore to her that no one would be able to tell from the pictures that I'd photographed her at the cemetery; I promised her that if she didn't like the pictures, I'd pay for everything myself, and that she would only pay for the prints and the film if she really liked them.

"That's an offer you can't refuse," Juliet told her.

Because we didn't seem to be getting anywhere, I finally said that the most fantastic pictures of Catherine Deneuve had also been made in a cemetery, because of the soft light that you only find in cemeteries. Not true, but finally Birgit came around.

But tomorrow, she said, wouldn't work. She had a pimple on her chin, and of course she had to go to the hairdresser's before having her picture taken.

After a lot of back and forth we made a date for Thursday. That was Birgit's floating holiday, which worked out well because that was my free day. We agreed to meet at two, at the ice-cream stand across from the main gate of the cemetery. I told her that if she didn't like the cemetery pictures, I could always photograph her at the National Garden Show.

On the way home I bought the paper which carried that ad that had caught my attention. I didn't feel like admitting that I was toying with the idea of responding to it in front of Birgit— and especially Juliet. Besides, I wasn't totally sure. But now that Albert had someone else, I had to act. On the other hand, maybe he'd already left that standard-issue dietetic sour pickle. I knew Albert better than she did. She didn't really stand a chance with him. I decided that I wouldn't call Albert—I had no need to. But if he didn't call me soon, well . . .

39 I could kill him, I thought.

Not that I still wanted him. But no one else should have him either. Not without a fight. It would serve Albert right if I killed him.

How? I could tell him to visit me, one last time, and then I'd hide behind the door with an ax—thwack, thwack, quick and painless. Of course then I'd be a suspect. But I don't want to end up in jail; I only wanted to enjoy my revenge to the fullest.

Pills? I could see Albert writhing with stomach pain. It made me sick just to think about it. The best thing would be to run him over with the car. Spontaneously, in the grip of emotion—I could plead extenuating circumstances. But the blood would be everywhere. And maybe he wouldn't die right away. And if he realized I'd run him over, he probably wouldn't say these dying words: "Constance! I've always loved you! Only you!"

Maybe I'd put poison in a pudding. But if I went to his place with a bowl of pudding under my arm, he'd think something was fishy. I could throw a radio in the bathtub. Or a blow-dryer. But then maybe the whole place would burn down and I'd perish in the blaze, too. And I'm too weak to throw him out of a boat— he'd take me down with him. Or I'd drown and he'd be saved.

If he died in another woman's arms, I wouldn't have to deal with the corpse. In court I could come to the aid of the other woman, who'd naturally be suspected of the murder.

"No, Your Honor," I'd say, "I don't think the defendant killed him. He was so depressed after I left him. In those last weeks he often spoke of suicide." And in a voice blinded with tears, I could add, "I think he died of a broken heart." No one would dream of suspecting me.

Dressed completely in black, with a black veil, and leaning on two handsome men, I'd lay five hundred red roses on his grave. Poor Albert, he wouldn't survive the separation from me. It brought tears to my eyes to think of his self-inflicted fate.

Albert's funeral would make a great scene for a film.

40 Birgit showed up right on time—perfectly made up, her hair freshly curled—and full of distrust. She said she'd never been to the cemetery and thought the whole thing was weird. I didn't say anything, just lugged my camera bag and tripod to the headstone with the beautiful weeping willow next to it. Birgit trotted along behind me. You could smell her perfume miles away, though you wouldn't see it in the pictures. She was wearing Opium, the most penetrating scent since mothballs. That stuff had a strange effect on me. The sun was shining through the branches.

"Here!" I said.

"Here?" Birgit said, horrified.

I set up the tripod, screwed on my lens, and told her to lay her right arm over the gravestone—it was just the right height so she could lean against it in a relaxed pose. I told her to pull a branch of the weeping willow toward her face with her left hand. To appear professional, I spoke in an authoritative voice.

"Why?" Birgit said.

"Because it'll look fantastic."

Birgit examined the black polished marble for anything that would leave spots. She reluctantly reached for a branch of the weeping willow and examined the leaves for thrips. "What now?" she asked.

"Now smile."

Birgit smiled like a shark.

The most important thing in photography is that the model look perfectly natural. When I was working at the ad agency, I noted how one star photographer relaxed his subjects: "You're a total goofball, Desirée!" or, "You're a total goofball, Jennifer!" Such compliments always totally relaxed the models.

"You're a total goofball, Birgit!"

She stared gloomily. "I know, I look terrible. I should've combed my hair over my ears. But then you can't see my earrings!"

I told her I'd only said that to relax her, that I knew for a fact that all models relax when you tell them they're goofballs.

"All right, let's try it again," I said. "On your mark—you're a goofball, Birgit!"

She let go of the branch and frantically rubbed her left ear. She looked totally uptight. This wasn't going to work. She tugged at her gold neck chain as if she wanted to strangle herself with it. But that gave me an idea. "What was it your sister got as a present from her fantastic husband when her fantastic baby was born?"

"A really fantastic heart locket," she said, relaxing already.

"What kind of locket?" I asked, watching Birgit through the viewfinder.

"A gold heart," she said, and suddenly her eyes glowed from within.

"Nice," I said, and snapped the shutter. "Where'd he get it?" I asked. "At Tchibo?"

"No, at a little second-floor jewelry store in the center of town. The heart is really fantastic. And at Christmas he's getting her a chain to match."

"Say 'jewelry store' again."

"Why?"

"Because your mouth looks so sweet when you say 'jewelry.' "

I shouldn't have said that. Now she said it without moving her lips. That gave her mouth a sort of calculating look. But I wanted her mouth round and a bit pointed, and a yearning expression in her eyes. The sexiness of Marilyn Monroe and the elegance of Catherine Deneuve—that was what I was after. But Birgit was behaving like Margaret Thatcher.

"What kind of gold heart?" I asked. "Is it hollow? For 49.95?"

"No, solid gold. Real gold! Eighteen-karat!"

When Birgit said "gold," I got what I wanted. Those lips, half opened, the engaging smile that suggested faithfulness, the gleam in the eyes that promised lust, but not so strongly as to suggest that the average man couldn't satisfy her. "Say that again: 'Eighteen-karat gold'!"

"When I send in a photo in reply to a personal, I can't use one where I'm leaning on a gravestone," Birgit whined. I said at the very most a corner of the stone would be visible in the picture, and it would look like a black chest of drawers.

"Why would a chest of drawers be standing under a weeping willow?"

Both of us thought about that silently. Then we put Birgit's raspberry-colored jacket over the gravestone and she put her arm on the jacket. I assured her that none of the gravestone showed in the picture. Through the viewfinder I saw the leaves of the willow above Birgit's head. To her right was more of the willow. It all looked very pretty. Birgit's golden hair against the green of the willow, the structure of the leaves offsetting the pattern of her white lace blouse, with gold threads woven through the collar and cuffs, and the raspberry jacket picking up the color of her lipstick.

"Okay, now say 'Fourteen-karat gold.' "

"Why am I supposed to say that instead of 'eighteen-karat'?" Birgit said in alarm. "My sister's gold heart—"

"Okay, okay," I said. All I cared about was her saying "gold," at which time I would press the shutter.

"All right, eighteen-karat gold," Birgit said.

The gleam in her eyes had grown harder. I changed the f-stop from 3.6 to 2.8. At that setting, in spite of the sun, Birgit's face would look like a painting.

She was now all loose and natural. She turned her head to the left and tossed her hair back; once she supported her chin on the thumb of her right hand, then she looked dreamily at her jacket on the gravestone. Each time she said "Eighteen-karat gold," I pressed the shutter. And it looked fantastic every time.

"You're real eighteen-karat gold," I said.

Then I noticed a new grave with heaps of flowers back in the corner of the cemetery. I went to check it out, looked around cautiously—the old man who'd gone past us earlier was nowhere to be seen. I pulled a short-stemmed, dark red rose out of one of the arrangements. It was fading fast. The arrangement had a black bow, on which was written in gold letters, IN ETERNAL LOVE.

I gave Birgit the rose. She crossed herself.

"We'll put it back later," I said.

"What should I do with it?" she asked.

"Look at the rose and say 'Eighteen-karat gold.' "

It was almost four o'clock now. The sun broke through the branches of the weeping willow, no longer with the white brightness of the afternoon; now the light was warmer, more golden. I went back to a 3.6 setting. The shadows of the leaves played over Birgit's face, and she looked like a madonna by Riemenschneider or a whore out of a Fassbinder movie. Outside, a passing car had its stereo turned up loud: Udo, Heino, or one of those crooners blared out of it. The music drifted into the branches of the weeping willow, became soft again. . . .

Little Annabelle, you must forgive this man
who'll never forget you, however long he lives!
Somewhere he'll always be thinking of you,
and of the mouth that no one else has kissed!
Little Annabelle, oh, don't be lonely,
with your dream of long-lost happiness!

Then the car was out of earshot. Tears were glittering in Birgit's eyes. I stared at her through the viewfinder: f-stop 3.6, distance one and a half yards. Birgit moved her arm, wiped her eyes, and her jacket slipped down from the gravestone and fell onto the hardy grave plantings. The sun was now reflected in the black marble, a gold-black glow fell on the right half of Birgit's face, while on the left the shadows of the weeping willow leaves played. The gold threads in Birgit's collar gleamed with an other-worldly intensity. Suddenly, in the sunlight, the rose opened. It mustered its last strength to achieve its ultimate perfection; the delicate little hairs on the petals cast velvety shadows.

"Say it," I whispered. "Please say it for me."

"Eighteen-karat gold," Birgit whispered.

The wind drove a cloud of Opium into my face, I pressed the shutter and crossed myself. Dear God: I pray the shutter speed was right, I thought.

"I'm so excited!" Birgit said when we said good-bye, after getting a sundae to celebrate. I asked whether she knew which ad she'd answer, and she said she'd wait till the photos were ready. She said that in any case it had been fun to have her picture taken, and I'd done it like a real pro.

I didn't tell her that I'd decided to reply to an ad. I'd decided to because Albert hadn't called since we'd seen each other last week. I felt shaky knowing the time had come to take action. I also asked Birgit whether she felt it was time to make some life changes. But she didn't understand my question. Instead, she asked me how long it would take before the photos were ready.

41 What none of us would have thought possible had happened: the women's seminar was actually scheduled to meet. After much phoning back and forth, we figured out that five of the women had time on Friday—though we had to arrange to meet at three rather than five because Irmela wanted to go to a party with her Benjamin that evening, and he was supposed to take his nap beforehand so he'd be wide awake for the party. The earlier meeting time was fine with me; now that Gottfried was with Juliet, I didn't care to go to the senior seminar anyway—I couldn't have stood seeing him twice in one week. If the women's seminar met two hours earlier, I might at most bump into Gottfried in the hall. I'd just nod to him and leave him to ponder whether he'd made the right decision.

Because it had been too late on Thursday to drop off the film, I went by the camera store on the way to the film academy. I ordered high-gloss prints. They'd be ready on Monday. As I drove on—I was on the Alleenring, just before the traffic light at the crossing for the subway entrance—a blue-denim Mercedes drove toward me. Even though I could have easily made the light, I put on the brakes. I recognized his car by the license plate: GS1. I was on the other side of the pedestrian crossing, diagonally across from Gottfried, but he didn't see me. I cranked open my window, wanted to honk and wave, but at that moment I realized where he was headed. He was going to Kreuzberg—at 2:36 in the afternoon. What would he be doing there at this time of day? Love in the afternoon with Juliet!

As the light changed to green, I saw red.

Love in the afternoon with Juliet. And after that he'd teach his seminar. Disgusting. I was ready to burst apart with rage when I got to the academy. There was a note stuck to the door of the seminar room: "Seminar canceled today. Gottfried Schachtschnabel." So, he'd even canceled his senior seminar. . . . Wasn't she ashamed to use her psychological tricks this way?

During the women's seminar I couldn't concentrate at all, even though there was a lively discussion about how to convey the everyday life of a housewife in a film. The click of the knitting needles was getting on my nerves. Rosi said Hitchcock or someone like that had said you should picture the following scene: a woman ironing, cleaning, washing dishes. Then she takes off her apron, fixes her hair, goes to the movies, and sees a film in which a woman is ironing, cleaning, washing dishes . . . that would get to people, right? Rosi said. It annoyed me the way she tacked "right?" onto every sentence. I hated women, each and every one of them.

By four-thirty I couldn't take it anymore. I mumbled that I had an important appointment, and left. Beate left at the same time. She had an important appointment, too.

Shortly after five I was home. I immediately called Juliet to confirm my suspicions. She answered the phone on the first ring.

"Lämmle speaking," she said cheerfully.

Actually I'd meant to hang up if she answered, but I was taken by surprise when she picked up so quickly, so I said hello.

"Hi, Constance," she said, totally cheerful.

"How are you?" I said, totally grim.

"Fine, and how about you?"

"Is Gottfried there?"

"No, he just left. Why do you ask?"

"He canceled his seminar, and I happened to see him driving to Kreuzberg."

"Yes, he stopped by here before setting out."

"For where?"

He had gone to Hannover, for his father's birthday—the old man was going to be sixty-five tomorrow. Gottfried had to cancel the seminar because otherwise he wouldn't have made it to Hannover today. "But on Wednesday he'll be back. Your seminar won't be canceled," Juliet said, as if she were Gottfried's personal spokesperson. Of course she said nothing about spending the past two hours in bed with him, the snake.

"And what are you up to otherwise?" she asked, sweet as honey.

"I dunno, nothing special."

"We should get together. It would be nice," she said.

We arranged to meet at seven at the Mykonos, around the corner from Juliet's, where you could sit outside. I'd feel Juliet out, I decided, ask her about her sexual practices.

I'd just hung up when the phone rang.

"What is it?" I asked, because I assumed it was Juliet again.

"Is that you, Constance?" It was Sieglinde Schadler.

She was irritated, and asked what I was doing this evening. I said I'd just made plans.

"Oh," Sieglinde said.

"Why?"

"I was hoping I could invite you over this evening."

"Why?"

"Well, I don't want you to think I'm just calling because someone else canceled. . . ."

"Why ever would I think that?" I said.

"Well," she said, with a heavy sigh, "I invited a married couple, he's a colleague of Wolf-Dietrich's, and a former co-worker of mine who married a dentist and has a really sweet child. And now the wife of Wolfi's colleague just called and said her Tamara-Juliet's baby-sitter is sick! And my former colleague, the wife of Dr. Ziegler, can't make it either—her Benjamin got the hiccups earlier, so of course she can't leave him alone with his daddy for the evening, so here I am with my dinner. . . ."

"What are you having?" She wouldn't get me there if all they were having was a few miserable cheese cubes.

"I've discovered this great cheese soufflé recipe," Sieglinde said.

"Hm."

"And you can't freeze it, so . . ."

"I see." Again I had to admire Sieglinde's knack for being insulting without seeming hostile, even camouflaging insults as emotional openness. In her eyes I was just a poor student, without a life companion, no longer suitable company, but, rather, the recipient of a charitable deed.

"Before I throw out the soufflé—" Sieglinde said.

"But I'd have to bring someone," I interrupted her.

"Oh," Sieglinde said, "fine, if you have someone. Bring him along. Please be here promptly at seven-thirty. We're both looking forward to seeing you," she said, sweet as honey.

I immediately called Juliet and told her we could get a free meal tonight, prepared by someone who loved to cook. At first Juliet was reluctant, since she didn't even know Sieglinde and this Wolf-Dietrich Lamar.

"You're not usually that shy."

"Oh, all right."

Juliet got to my place at a quarter past seven. She'd never been there before and looked around while I quickly put on nail polish.

"Nice place," she said. "It's almost nicer than mine. You have a more consistent style."

"What do you mean?"

"With you everything's either black or white. It looks nice."

We were standing in Albert's former room, which was painted all white. Only the door and the window casings were black. The only furniture was the black table and chair, but I'd also put all my books in the room, piling them along the long wall like cigarettes in a cigarette machine. Over the books I'd hung a large poster of Dürer's *Melencolia*: this grumpy angel slouching around, totally bored. I told Juliet I'd once read that the picture was a symbol for the phase of calm before the creative storm, and that it was my favorite picture.

"It also matches the decor perfectly," Juliet said. "It's black and white, too."

We had to get going. At twenty to eight we walked into Sieglinde's.

"Oh! It's a woman!" She exclaimed when she saw us. "But you should have told me that—I thought . . ." Sieglinde didn't have to finish the sentence; it was clear what she thought.

"This is my *girlfriend* Juliet Lämmle," I said.

"Don't take me for a lesbian, Frau Schadler," Juliet said to Sieglinde.

"Why would you think such a thing, Frau Lämmle!" Sieglinde said.

"Why are you two being so formal?" I said.

"Oh, yes, how silly!" they both said, laughing.

"She talked me into coming," Juliet told Sieglinde, pointing at me and laughing.

"I know her little tricks," Sieglinde said, also pointing at me and laughing.

"My boyfriend is out of town," Juliet explained.

She immediately gave the same explanation to Wolf-Dietrich, who was on the sofa and straightened his intellectual magazines on the coffee table. The table was already set, and the soufflé had cooled enough so that it was ready to eat.

"Whatever happened to your tandem?" I asked, after I'd finished my first helping of soufflé.

"Would you like some more?" Sieglinde asked.

"Yes."

Sieglinde told me to help myself.

"What about the tandem?" I asked again.

"Which tandem?" Sieglinde asked.

"Which one? The one you gave Wolf-Dietrich for his birthday."

"Oh, that." Then she asked Juliet, "Would you like more soufflé, too?"

"So where is it?" I asked again.

Wolf-Dietrich had sold it, Sieglinde said.

He smiled. "I even got twenty marks more for it than it cost," he said. "That special price at Eduscho turned out to be a real bargain. When I went there to ask if they might be willing to take it back, the saleswoman said the tandems had already sold out, and they'd had so many people asking for them—"

"Everybody else wants a tandem," Sieglinde said, and poked around in her soufflé.

Wolf-Dietrich continued, "So I left my phone number—"

"And that same day four people called and all of them wanted a tandem," Sieglinde interrupted again, and stabbed at her soufflé.

"And one guy, who was just crazy to have a tandem, actually offered twenty marks more—so we made a tidy profit on the thing," Wolf-Dietrich said, and laughed.

"I think a tandem's very nice to have," Juliet said. Sieglinde looked gratefully at her. "My boyfriend used to have one," Juliet said.

"What?" I said.

"You didn't know that?" Juliet said to me.

No, I hadn't known that. I explained to Sieglinde and Wolf-Dietrich that Juliet's boyfriend was the instructor I was going to make my film with. But I didn't say that Juliet had met Gottfried through me—I didn't remember whether I'd told Sieglinde about Gottfried by mistake.

But then Juliet said, "So I met Gottfried Schachtschnabel through Constance."

"Do you ride tandem with Gottfried?" I said matter-of-factly.

"No, he owned it with his ex-wife. I assume she sold it."

"Schachtschnabel," Wolf-Dietrich said, and acted like he was trying to think of something. "Schachtschnabel—the name sounds familiar."

"Of course," I said. I didn't want to give him a chance to boast about all the people he knew.

"Is his wife named Inge?" Wolf-Dietrich asked.

"Yes," Juliet said.

"I know her," Wolf-Dietrich said.

"How?" Sieglinde asked.

"Him I hardly know," said Wolf-Dietrich. Sieglinde immediately looked suspicious.

"She's a certified feminist," Wolf-Dietrich said. Sieglinde smiled. "Works at the Women's Center."

"I see," Sieglinde said.

"Yes," Juliet said.

"How long have they been divorced?" Wolf-Dietrich asked.

"I don't know exactly," Juliet said. "At least four years, I think."

"No, I don't think so," Wolf-Dietrich said.

"Why not?" I asked.

"Because I know Inge," Wolf-Dietrich said.

"I'm divorced, too," Juliet said.

"Oh, you've been married already," Sieglinde said.

"I'd be the first to know if they were divorced." Wolf-Dietrich said. "Inge would have called me. I know dozens of lawyers. We've talked a million times about how much better off she'd be financially if she got a divorce."

"I didn't know you took care of feminists," Sieglinde said.

"But because she's involved with a married man who doesn't

want to get a divorce, she doesn't want to get one either. She doesn't want to be left in the position of a single woman vis-à-vis her lover."

"But I thought she was a feminist," I said.

Wolf-Dietrich made a sign that meant "cuckoo." "Inge also thinks it's to her advantage to wait till her husband gets a better job—on the other hand, there's always the danger that when his contract runs out he'll be out on the street, and then she'll get less out of him. I've explained it to her a million times."

"And Gottfried can't do anything about it?" I said.

Even though Gottfried was going with Juliet now, I felt sorry for him. How rotten of his wife!

"No, he doesn't even want a divorce," Wolf-Dietrich said. "Otherwise he'd have been divorced a long time ago." Wolf-Dietrich looked at Juliet. "The two of them still see each other fairly often, don't they?"

"That I wouldn't know," Juliet said stiffly.

"Oh, so you're going with a married man, Frau Lämmle?" Sieglinde said.

"You can still call her Juliet," I said.

"You're right," Sieglinde said, "that really isn't a good reason to be formal."

"Well, say hello to your boyfriend," Wolf-Dietrich said. "Tell him if he really wants a divorce, Lamar can recommend an excellent attorney."

"I thought you could recommend an excellent attorney for this Inge," Sieglinde said.

"What's the difference?" Wolf-Dietrich said.

"Thank you, I don't think that'll be necessary," Juliet said.

"It really makes no difference whether he's married or not," I said, because in spite of everything I wanted to declare my solidarity with Juliet (at least against Sieglinde).

"So, that's what you think, is it?" Juliet said, and looked at me as though I was the one who'd turned out to be married. I decided it would be better not to say any more. I was secretly wondering how we could get out of there as quickly as possible, but nothing occurred to me. Sieglinde suggested that we come into the kitchen to see her new microwave.

We finally managed to make our escape and said good-night.

"Should we go somewhere else now?" I asked, once we were on the street.

"I want to go home," Juliet said. So we headed for her car, which was parked in front of my building.

"Do you really believe Gottfried is still married?" I asked after a while.

"Yes."

Then we didn't say anything for a while. "He never really said he was divorced. He just acted like he was, and I projected it onto him. So, he's still married, and that's why he's always seeing his wife."

"A harmonious sep—" I said, but Juliet wouldn't let me finish.

"It's true he doesn't live with his wife anymore, but he's not divorced. Now it's all clear." She paused, "So that was it."

"What?"

Juliet was groping around in her pocketbook and found a paper handkerchief. She looked at it, crumpled it up, and threw it back in. Then she said, "It's over."

"Between you and Gottfried?" I asked cautiously.

"Yes."

"I don't understand why you didn't notice that Gottfried's married. I mean, you're a psychologist, after all."

"What was there to notice?"

"Everything."

Juliet acted as though she didn't know what I was talking about. "You have strange ideas about marriage!" She shrugged.

"Of course I'd have noticed if he'd been living with a woman—
that kind of thing you notice right away. One look in the medicine cabinet is enough. But he doesn't live with his wife. And
since she doesn't want to have sex with him and doesn't sew his
buttons on for him—what would give me the idea he was still
married?"

"But you did know he goes to see her often, and you even said
that couldn't go on much longer."

"Ever since I told him in no uncertain terms that I didn't like
it, he's stopped going. Or maybe he just doesn't tell me anymore."

"But you should have noticed he wasn't divorced," I said. I
hadn't known either, but then I hadn't had a physical relationship with him.

"I should have made him show me his tax return," Juliet said.
"That would have been the only way to know for sure." She
sighed. "When a man shows you his tax return, it's a sign of true
intimacy nowadays."

My heart was beating so loudly I was afraid she could hear it.
"Don't you at least want to talk to him about it?" I said, and
noticed how hoarse my voice sounded.

"If he's not divorced after everything his wife's done to him,
he'll never get divorced," Juliet said grimly. "There's no point
in clinging to illusions." For a while we walked in silence.

"When's he getting back?"

"Tuesday night. He wanted to come right over to see me."

"What are you going to tell him?"

"I'm going to throw him out. He can go right back to his dear
spouse. He made a point of going to say good-bye to her today."

"But it certainly didn't take him two hours," I said, without
looking at Juliet.

"What's that supposed to mean?"

"Come on, don't act so innocent."

"He only spent a few minutes with me, and he was in an awful rush, because he still had to go by to see his wife; he said he had to get an old picture frame from her that he wanted to bring to his father. He only spent five minutes with me, just before you called."

"Come on," I said. "I saw him driving out to see you at two-thirty."

"He didn't get to my place till shortly before five."

"And where was he in the meantime?" I asked.

"You can bet he was with his wife. And then he went back to her." Juliet stood still. "And then he took his wife along to his parents'. All nice and proper, I guarantee you."

"You think so?"

Juliet didn't say any more. Now we were standing by her car.

"You can think it over some more."

Juliet said, "No."

"Take care," I said.

A strange feeling came over me. If Juliet actually broke up with Gottfried now, he'd be free again. Even before I fell asleep, I was dreaming that he would get a divorce, because of me.

42 I lay in bed all weekend, thinking. Would Juliet really break up with Gottfried? First thing on Tuesday, when he got back? Or was she just making empty pronouncements again? I had to be careful, couldn't believe everything she said. On the one hand she kept telling everyone how happy she was to be divorced, and on the other hand she wasn't at all as radically opposed to marriage as she said. In fact, maybe she really wanted to get married again. In that case it would certainly be like her to break up with Gottfried just because he was married.

I thought about Gottfried: there must be theoretical reasons for him to still be married. I was sure of that.

I thought about Albert: my pain over him subsided in proportion to the new hope that filled my heart. Let Albert do as he pleased.

I thought maybe I shouldn't reply to that personal, given the circumstances. But then, it wasn't a sure thing Juliet would really break up with Gottfried. Maybe she would continue to try to mask the fundamental differences between them. Besides, there was the old wives' wisdom: Two men are better than none.

But what should I say in my reply? I didn't have any experience in this. Juliet had answered an ad once, I was pretty sure of that. I considered whether I should present my worldview, my concept of a free, partnerlike relationship, in the letter—or was it better to wait for a personal conversation to talk through our existing commonalities and in that way slowly but surely reach an understanding? Finally I decided in favor of the personal conversation, because I only had two pieces of my nice pale gray stationery left, and that wouldn't have given me enough space for a really thorough account of my position. I spent an eternity looking for a suitable photo, then chose one that Albert had taken one time when I was mad at him. I looked beautiful in it, but very critical toward society. Then I decided to write just a short note; after all, the main thing was that the man should get my address and phone number. I wrote them nice and clear at the top of the page, then the date, and then the problem was how to address him. I didn't have his name, after all, just the box number.

"Dear 48763 UZ"? *Please.* Finally I wrote:

Dear Intellectual,
I think your personal is fantastic, because it reached out

and touched me directly. Yours was entirely different from what all the other men wrote!

I would be very pleased if you called me. Please keep trying, since I'm often out.

Sincerely yours,
Constance Wechselburger

Short but friendly. I figured it would make him anxious to meet me. Especially the picture: I really looked good in it. I mailed the letter right away, to get that over with. As I threw it in the box, I felt a little shaky.

Then I went back to bed and thought about Simone de Beauvoir, who, as everybody knows, was involved not only with Sartre but often with various other intellectuals on the side.

On Monday afternoon I didn't go to the library. After class with Law-Müller, with whom I had to suffer through Film Law II this semester, I drove straight to the camera shop. The prints were ready. They exceeded all my expectations. Details I'd hardly been able to see through the viewfinder, or maybe I'd just intuited, had come into their own in the picture. The rose petals' color was reflected on Birgit's lips, the tears glittered in Birgit's eyelashes, and the sun was mirrored in the tears. When I spread out the photos on the counter in the camera shop, I had the feeling that there was a microprocessor in the photographic paper, and every time you looked at a picture it gave off an electrical impulse and made music play: "Little Annabelle, oh, don't be lonely, with your dream of long-lost happiness . . ." the microprocessor played in my head. There was a fragrance of Opium in the air.

The camera shop man, who'd discreetly gone away after giving me the envelope with the photos, came back to ask whether the pictures had come out all right. Did I want to return any of them? No, I had no complaints.

He glanced at the photos, then he said, "Did you take those?"
"Yes."

"You do nice work for a woman."

I'd just walked in the door at home when Birgit called to ask whether I had the photos. "You're going to drop dead," I said.

She wanted to come by right after the library closed. But I didn't want her to come to my place; I preferred to go to her place, so Juliet could see the photos, too—besides, I absolutely had to know whether Juliet was definitely breaking up with Gottfried tomorrow.

I got to Birgit's just before eight. Her apartment was just like her, spick-and-span. Everything in the kitchen was washable and looked as if it had just been hosed down. You could have eaten out of the garbage can. Even the dishrags were spotless.

"Where are the photos?" Birgit asked at least three times in the two minutes I took to look around her apartment. Her bedroom was like a young girl's room: the wallpaper was colorful, white-and-yellow daisies on a pink background; the bed linens were colorful, brown-and-yellow sunflowers on a white background; and on the pillow lay a big pink stuffed mouse. One side of the bedroom was taken up by a huge wardrobe with mirrored doors, and everything was immaculate—no fingerprints, no traces of squeezed blackheads on the mirrors. Birgit wasn't one to squeeze out blackheads. Perfect Birgit of course had a perfect complexion.

Birgit phoned down to Juliet on the third floor. She came up right away.

We sat around the Formica-topped scrubbable coffee table. Birgit brought out a bottle of wine and some glasses, and placed a coaster under the bottle and each of the glasses. To increase the suspense, I ordered Birgit to turn off the TV. I didn't want any evening-news catastrophes undercutting my photos' sensational effect.

"Why should I turn off the TV?" Birgit said, but at least she turned off the sound.

"Okay, let's see what we've got!" Juliet said.

Birgit almost fell over when she saw the photos. "Incredible!" she said. "Incredible!"

"Who's this?" Juliet asked.

"Me, me!" Birgit shrieked. "That's me!"

I, the photographer, smiled modestly.

Birgit threw her arms around me and kissed me out of sheer enthusiasm.

"Incredible," Juliet said.

"That's me!" Birgit kept saying; she was totally beside herself. "I look like Catherine Deneuve in these pictures, but younger."

"You're right," Juliet said. "Why didn't you just cut out a picture of Catherine Deneuve? You want to send this in a reply to a personal. . . ."

"Well, like it or not," Birgit said, "that's me."

I gave Birgit the bill for the film and the developing. She insisted on giving me an even hundred—forty marks more than it had cost!

Juliet said, "The two of you are totally nuts. Two romantic narcissists at once, that's too much."

"I don't know what's wrong with you," Birgit said. "The photos bring out my character to a T."

"Now which personal are you going to answer?" I asked Birgit. Her mind seemed to have gone blank.

"But that's what you had the photos done for, wasn't it?" Juliet said, and looked at her disapprovingly. Juliet really seemed to be in a bad mood today, I noticed.

Birgit said firmly, "I'm not giving up a single one of my beautiful photos."

I looked at her in amazement. She really meant it. But then it occurred to me that you could have copies made, and it would only take two days.

"Yes," Juliet said.

Birgit certainly did want copies. Three of each picture, and of the last photo, the one with the rose, she wanted ten: for her mother, her father, her sister, her pretty cousin, who would really be amazed—everyone was to get one. And if one picture was left over, she could use that for the personal. Maybe.

Birgit said I should order the copies and tell the people at the camera shop how the copies were supposed to look. I was a real pro. But because Birgit wasn't willing to give me even one print as a sample for the color, I told her to go herself, take a photo along, show it to the people in the shop, and tell them the coloration should be on the pinkish side; they'd know what to do. All right, Birgit said.

Juliet didn't say a word the whole time. I was secretly watching her. She didn't look good.

"Have you spoken with Gottfried already?" I asked finally, because she wasn't telling us anything.

"But he's away."

"Didn't he call you?"

"Just briefly. From a phone booth. Fifty pfennigs' worth." Juliet wrinkled her nose. "At any rate, he was cut off right away, and he didn't call back."

"And?"

"I'll bet you anything he has his wife along."

"What are you going to say to him tomorrow?"

"Tomorrow I'm throwing Gottfried out." And then she said, "Maybe I'll answer a personal."

"You want me to photograph you?" I asked promptly.

Juliet said she wasn't in that much of a hurry, and besides, she had some relatively new pictures. And then she said again that it was all over with Gottfried, no matter what. Over. Finished.

That was all I needed to know. I went home, relatively satisfied.

43

"Can I ask you something after class?" Gottfried said softly, and held the door to the seminar room open for me. I hesitated as I went in, and looked at him. "Wait for me by the car," he said even more softly.

Chlodwig Schnell was sitting in the front row with his scripts already spread out. He stared inquisitively at Gottfried and me.

What did Gottfried want to ask me? Had Juliet thrown him out last night?

A woman who was new in Gottfried's theory seminar this semester was giving an oral presentation on the difference between qualitative and quantitative portrayal of emotional content. The question was whether the moviegoer would be more moved by the spectacle of thousands suffering or whether people had a psychological need to identify with one person. Also, the question was whether it was politically responsible to individualize social suffering. Also, she analyzed the problematics of whether the subject's suffering was standardizable and whether there existed an ahistorical imagery of mourning that reflected the prevailing societal conditions. I had trouble following; I had personal problematics.

We finished a little earlier than usual because no one had any questions on the presentation.

I didn't know whether Gottfried had meant I should wait by my mini-Fiat or by his Mercedes. His car was on the left to the rear, in the area reserved for faculty. My car was on the other side of the lot. I decided on a spot under the plane tree halfway between the two—that was less conspicuous. I only had to wait ten minutes.

Gottfried looked troubled. He had dark circles under his eyes, and with his Lenin beard he looked like an endangered baby seal. I didn't say anything, because my heart was in my throat.

"Your friend Juliet doesn't want to have anything more to do with me," he said.

I plucked a hair off my sweater so as not to have to look at him, and acted as though I knew nothing about it.

"It's true," he said, and cleared his throat. "You know there was a certain connection there." He cleared his throat again. "I don't know what's going through her mind."

"Did she break up with you?"

He shrugged. "It was a misunderstanding, I can't explain it any other way. I don't know what she's got against me." He looked at me with a puzzled expression.

"Is it true you're still married?"

"I forgot to tell her. Honest." He looked at me despairingly. My heart melted.

"To get so upset just because I forgot to tell her I'm married! Sometimes I just don't understand you women," he said. "And the fact that my wife went along on this trip—that was just for the sake of my elderly parents! Why can't Juliet understand that?"

"I guess Juliet has very traditional values," I said softly.

"I'd be sorry if she really meant it," he said very softly. "She doesn't see that I simply can't afford a divorce." Gottfried cleared his throat, then he spoke louder again: "I don't even know what a divorce would cost—I'm just a member of the working class, and so long as I have a short-term contract here— just think of what people would say! Some discretion is called for—Juliet just doesn't understand that. Or doesn't want to understand."

"*I* understand," I said, and nodded several times.

"I just forgot to tell her." He looked at me despairingly again. "After all, it doesn't make any difference to our relationship."

"And what did she say?" I asked.

"Who? My wife?" Gottfried said.

"No, Juliet."

"Oh." He thought for a moment. "She said I was emotionally incapable of making a commitment so long as I was still married."

"I don't think your problematics can be characterized that simply," I said.

"Yes," Gottfried said, and plucked a hair from the sleeve of my sweater that I would never have seen myself. "You . . . you understand that."

"What difference does it make that you're still married?" I said. "It really doesn't matter."

Gottfried put his hand on my arm. Well, not really—it looked as though he had his hand on my arm, but I couldn't feel it. "Do you think there's any point to talking with her again?"

"With whom?" I asked. I was looking at my sweater—100 percent lambswool, and not a fiber had been bent by Gottfried's touch, but the little hairs on my arm were standing on end. Fortunately he couldn't see that. I wondered why I couldn't feel his touch.

"With Juliet," Gottfried said.

That touched me to the quick. Was I supposed to go to Juliet and beg her to take him back? Why me, of all people? I said I was afraid it was hopeless.

"Has she met someone else?" Gottfried looked at me sharply.

"No," I said spontaneously. Then I thought a bit and added, "I mean, I don't know." I really didn't know, so it wasn't a lie.

"Can't you ask her? Go ahead and ask her, then call me. Please."

"Me?" I said.

"Why not?" he said. "I'll give you my phone number, so you can call me at home. I don't mind if you call late. Just keep trying."

His hands were steady as he wrote his number on the first page of my ring binder. Of course I'd looked up his number long ago—I'd copied it out of the phone book after the party at Juliet's, because I actually meant to call him and ask him what was going on. Now, I was glad I'd restrained myself. Now, after he'd given me his number personally, I could call him without seeming pushy.

"You can call me anytime," he said again, "but I have to go now."

"Are you going to your wife's?" Now that he'd acquainted me with his problematics, it seemed appropriate to ask.

He looked at me, grateful for my understanding.

"Yes," he said, "I have to help her. She bought herself an herb rack at Conran's that requires some assembly, and she can't manage it herself. I have to help her. I can't leave her alone in a situation like this!"

I just nodded. He knew I could also express my understanding nonverbally. He looked at me gratefully again, then saw me to my car. When I was about to drive away, he knocked on the window. I cranked it down.

He bent over and said softly, "After all, Marx was married, too."

"Yes," I said.

"And in spite of that he was involved with his housekeeper."

"Yes," I said.

"There's something we can learn from that."

He waved to me briefly as I drove out of the lot.

44 I was sure Gottfried must have theoretical reasons for wanting me to talk to Juliet. Gottfried knew that he could trust my critical perspective on society and its conventions. Whereas Juliet might have picked up a certain political education through her ex-husband, but she didn't have a progressive consciousness.

I thought for a long time about what I'd say to her. After all, I had interests of my own to protect. Morality won out: I'd promised Gottfried. So I called Juliet and said I had to have a woman-to-woman talk with her about Gottfried. Juliet said she had no time for such crap and she changed the subject. She was going to a continuing-education seminar on the weekend: "New Testing Methods for School Beginners." The testing methods didn't interest her in the slightest, but under the circumstances it was better if she simply went out of town. And besides, you could meet good people at seminars—not such a bad idea. She wouldn't be back till Tuesday, and when she had time she'd call me.

There was nothing I could do.

Then I called up Albert. He was in a splendid mood.

"Oh, hi," he said, "don't we know each other from somewhere?" He seemed to have completely repressed that day I'd seen him with Anna. "So how's it going?" he asked.

I told him various things. Then I asked him what he would think if a person was married.

"Do you want to get married?"

"Nonsense!" I said, and then explained that my question was

purely theoretical and concerned strictly with the principle of the thing.

Albert said it so happened that many people got married. Most people, even. And it also had financial advantages, because marriage was rewarded by the state. If I had any other questions, I should feel free to ask. As usual, he wasn't willing to engage in any sort of serious discussion. His references to the empirical facts of bourgeois society weren't exactly enlightening.

"And how's your dear colleague?" I asked him casually.

"Fine."

I waited but he said nothing else about her. Then he asked whether we shouldn't get together one of these days.

"When?"

He wanted to see me right away. He could come right over. If he was in such a hurry, fine.

He came to my place—formerly our place. We sat in the kitchen just like before. He immediately claimed the porcelain coffee filter was his. That wasn't true, and besides, he'd bought a new coffee maker, so why did he need the old porcelain filter? He said it didn't matter to him, he just wanted to establish that the old porcelain coffee filter belonged to him, as a matter of principle. I changed the subject.

"How's your dear colleague?"

"You already asked that."

"Are you still seeing each other?"

"Of course."

"Often?"

"Every day."

"Every day!"

"We're working on the same ward."

"And otherwise? Do you see each other otherwise?"

"Otherwise we see each other, too. Any further questions?"

"So what's she doing tonight, your Beatrice?"

"Anna's seeing an old girlfriend; she's had it planned for quite a while. So it was very convenient that you called."

"It was *convenient?*"

"Yes, very." He laughed.

"She gave you a day off!" Rage was building in me. Was I at the mercy of this natural woman? But I didn't let it show. "And you're all right otherwise?"

"Oh," he said, "she's very different from you. More the gentle type. But very nice." He laughed again.

I looked him over. He looked exhausted. Didn't seem to be getting much sleep these days.

He looked me over. "Say, Anna, do you still have my egg timer? The little hourglass?"

Anna!

"I'm not your Anna!" I yelled.

"What's wrong with you? Not in my wildest dreams would I think of comparing Anna with you," he said.

"So why are you calling me Anna?"

"Did I? Sorry."

I found the stupid egg timer and threw it at his feet. "There's your stupid egg timer. Take it to your stupid Anna."

The sand dribbled onto the kitchen floor.

"Well, I guess that's it again," Albert said, and walked out.

I tore open the kitchen window and threw out the porcelain coffee filter. By the time Albert came out of the building, the filter had already detonated. I yelled that he should take his stupid shards with him. But he didn't turn around.

Every human being has weaknesses. Jealousy was not one of mine. Okay, sometimes I flew off the handle. But rage was only an expression of honesty. I was always honest: with others and especially with myself. No one could reproach me on that score. Because I wasn't envious normally, my self-critical honesty enabled me to reflect that I'd been overcome with envy. Albert had achieved a seamless transition. Why wasn't I allowed to find happiness without pain?

Nothing was working out. When I went to the academy on Friday for the women's seminar, there was a note taped on the door: "Seminar canceled today because of menstrual cramps. Irmela."

Why hadn't one of the women called me? I wasn't feeling so great myself.

I went up to the fifth floor to the faculty lounge and knocked. Hesitantly I went in. Gottfried was there with someone I didn't know. I said I had a message for him.

"Yes?" Gottfried said. He looked at me as unemotionally as if I had come to read the meter. Probably because the other guy was in the room and was obviously listening.

"Well, what I wanted to say was, Frau Lämmle is out of town till Tuesday, and for that reason I can't submit my report any sooner." I winked at Gottfried. Clever, the way I'd formulated that, eh?

"Ah, yes, Frau Lämmle," Gottfried said. "Thank you very much for letting me know."

I thought he might see me out so as to continue the conversation in the hall.

"All right, see you on Wednesday," Gottfried said.

With my characteristic honesty toward myself, I acknowledged that Gottfried was more interested in news of Juliet than in me. I became painfully aware that I had a long and rocky road ahead of me. Did he view me as merely the agent for the gratification of his extramarital needs?

On Saturday afternoon Birgit called up. She'd picked up the copies of the photos. They'd turned out just as fantastic as the originals. I asked whether she'd made up her mind about a personal.

"I don't know," Birgit said. "But I took a look at the ads in today's paper, and there was one that was darling." Birgit rustled a newspaper.

"Read it to me," I said.

"Should I?"

"Go ahead."

" 'Knight of the Blue Blossom of Romanticism . . . thirty-three, five foot seven, a hundred forty-seven pounds, seeks sweet princess. Who wants to come to my castle with me? Motorized steed available. Replies with likeness please,' " she read. "Darling, isn't it?" she said.

What a romantic! "Darling. Go ahead and write, so at least something happens around here."

"You think I should?" Birgit said. "I don't know, really. I think I'd better wait till Juliet gets back. I want to ask her what she thinks."

"Why do you have to ask Juliet?" I said. "You're old enough to make up your own mind. Go ahead, write *now*."

I wanted something romantic to happen. Nothing else was happening.

Nothing rescued me from my depression. Every morning I went to my mailbox with a pounding heart. Every time the phone rang I jumped, but nothing—no reply to my letter.

On Tuesday night I called Juliet.

"I just got back ten minutes ago," she said.

"How was it?"

"All married men. I could have had the same thing without leaving home."

"And contentwise?"

"Nothing new there either. I did hear that most of the girls entering school this year are called Juliet. They say there's no end in sight. Romanticism is in."

"And what does that mean for you?"

"For me? In the future, if someone calls 'Juliet,' I'm not going to react. I'm one among millions." Juliet laughed, almost hysterically. "And how did things go with you?" she asked, when she'd calmed down again.

"Contentwise nothing new either," I said truthfully. Then I asked, "Aren't you in the mood to go to Café Kaput?"

"Tomorrow."

"When tomorrow?"

"I'd rather go fairly early, right after work. See, I absolutely have to get together with Karl-Heinz, and he could come along, if you don't mind."

I said I wouldn't mind having Karl-Heinz there, even though I did. But on the other hand, if Karl-Heinz was there, Juliet would certainly stick to her decision not to have anything more to do with Gottfried. Karl-Heinz, that old philistine, would advise against continuing such an unbourgeois relationship.

"I could be there at five-thirty," Juliet said.

It occurred to me that the Kaput didn't open till seven, so we decided to make it the Collection Box, which was nicer in good weather anyway. I wasn't worried that Albert would be there—he wouldn't dare show up there with his Beatrice again.

Not till I'd hung up did I realize that if we were meeting at five-thirty I'd have to skip Gottfried's seminar. Or had Juliet arranged for us to meet that early just so I wouldn't have a chance to see Gottfried? No, I didn't think she'd be that calculating. With a heavy heart I accepted the idea of skipping the seminar. Maybe it was better that way: I wouldn't appear in Gottfried's presence till I'd accomplished my mission and overcome the last uncertainty.

45 Juliet and Karl-Heinz were already at the Collection Box when I got there. Although I'd made Karl-Heinz mad at Juliet's party, he greeted me with two little pecks on each cheek. Actually I didn't think much of his little pecks, and even less of the possibility that people sitting nearby might think I was as close to him as all that.

"Nice to see you," Karl-Heinz said. He put his hands on my shoulders and held me at arm's length to gaze deep into my eyes.

"Hello," I said. Juliet greeted me with a wave from the other side of the table. "Hi, hi," she said.

"Hi, hi," I said, and waved back.

"Can I order something for you?" Karl-Heinz asked, and placed his hand over my hand. He ordered wine for me.

"I had to skip Schachtschnabel's seminar to be here on time," I said.

Juliet grinned at me. "And how is your revered instructor, Herr Gottfried?"

Her grin made me suspicious. "You probably know better than I do."

"No, I swear. I haven't heard a thing from him since I broke up with him. And I don't want to hear anything from him. I've returned him to his spouse—for reuse, as she sees fit. I swear!" She raised her left hand and made the "Scout's Honor" sign. She actually swore.

"Gottfried told me he had no idea why . . ." I hesitated, because I realized I'd given away the fact that I'd talked with Gottfried about his relationship with Juliet, and I wasn't sure it was good tactics to let Juliet know that.

"He told you that! That can't be true!" Juliet laughed, and Karl-Heinz shook his head meaningfully. "If he doesn't have any idea, let me explain. I have no interest in a married man whose wife lends him out from time to time, when she has something better going. And especially when she reserves the right to call in the loan whenever she pleases."

I didn't like the way she was talking about Gottfried. After all, he was my instructor in nonbourgeois film theory. "Gottfried rejects marriage as an institution, if I may remind you."

"And he's married," Juliet said.

"But his marriage has no theoretical significance," I said, and was proud of this explanation. Secretly I felt like a true Schacht-schnabelian.

"Constance," Juliet said, "don't believe everything people tell you. Just try to think why Gottfried doesn't want to get divorced, even though he rejects marriage." She looked at me as though I were a learning-disabled schoolchild.

"Because it would mean financial ruin for him."

"Would it really be that expensive?" Karl-Heinz butted in.

"Don't believe it," Juliet said. "It wouldn't cost him any more than it cost me; his wife works, and they don't have any kids. And no savings. You know what he told me?" Juliet struck the table with her palm. "He said he'd rather spend the money on a large-screen color TV!" Juliet scrabbled around on the table, almost knocking over my glass. "A large-screen color TV! When he told me that, my last doubts evaporated."

"How come?"

"Because when a person admits he'd stay married for life to a woman he wants nothing to do with, for the sake of a color television, something's wrong!"

"But what difference does it make? Whether he's married or divorced? If they aren't living together anyway?"

"It does make a difference," Juliet said firmly. "I got divorced, after all."

I was annoyed. Juliet was acting as though Gottfried had to get a divorce just because she'd gotten one.

"Ah, yes," Karl-Heinz said, and now he laid his hand on Juliet's arm, "our poor Juliet had no other choice."

"Listen," Juliet said, and pulled her arm away from Karl-Heinz's hand, "I could have played tug-of-war with Ulrich for years."

"No, Ulrich's not the type," Karl-Heinz said.

"I'm not the type, either," Juliet said. Then she said, "This business with Gottfried really isn't a problem. The shorter the time you've known each other, the easier it is to break up."

Juliet was an expert in painless separations.

"I can learn a lot from you," I said. "It's amazing how you always pull it off! You also separated so harmoniously from your husband!"

"Well, that's one way of putting it," Juliet said.

"Well, that's one way of putting it," Karl-Heinz said.

"Would you still have gotten divorced if you'd known you'd meet Gottfried after the divorce and if you'd known Gottfried was married?" I asked, in order to find out what Juliet really thought.

"Of course I'd have gotten divorced," Juliet answered. "Stupid question—that had nothing to do with Gottfried."

"Our poor Juliet was abandoned by her husband, you see," Karl-Heinz said.

"That has nothing to do with it," Juliet said, and gave Karl-Heinz a warning look.

"What do you mean, abandoned?"

"Well, Ulrich has someone else now," Juliet said.

"Someone else? What type is she?" I wanted to know about the woman who could make a man abandon a clever psychologist like Juliet.

"She's a year older than Ulrich. Otherwise Ulrich hasn't told me anything about her, except that she's a secretary. She's the 'love-of-my-life' type; oh *no,* the fact that beauty fades will never pose any threat to *this* relationship."

She laughed, but I didn't laugh with her. I didn't like her sarcasm. I couldn't help thinking of that Anna Mannersfeld.

"I don't understand what Ulrich sees in that woman either!" Karl-Heinz said. "She doesn't have a shred of sex appeal! You remember you came across that photo of her? I could see at a glance that the woman's frigid." Karl-Heinz shook his sparse head in horror.

"By chance I came across a photo of her in his wallet," Juliet explained, and added quickly, "I was looking for a dry-cleaning receipt."

Karl-Heinz laughed.

"I'd have combed through everything till I'd found some evidence," I said generously, because the story pierced me to the quick, and Karl-Heinz's snotty laugh was getting on my nerves. "And where's your husband now?" I wanted to get the conversation away from past sufferings.

"He's living in a village now, right near the town where he grew up. He applied for a job there and got it right away, because nobody moves there of his own free will. But he moved because of her—she's also from there. Ulrich found true happiness in the home of his youth."

"Your husband's lucky," I said thoughtfully. "He really had a painless separation. He achieved a seamless transition. He traded up." As soon as I'd spoken the words, I was sorry. Juliet looked as if she hated herself. I tried to backtrack. "I think it's fantastic that you separated from him so harmoniously in spite of that."

Karl-Heinz asked, "Say, did he take the silver candelabras?"

"No, he didn't want them—they're only plate. But he did take the silver flatware. Half the set was mine, even though the

name on the sales slip was his." She shrugged. "But his grandmother's gold chain that he gave me for the wedding, that I
kept. Legally he didn't have a leg to stand on. The return of
wedding presents on that order of magnitude can't be demanded, so long as the marriage was legal. I was able to prove
to him beyond any doubt that he wouldn't get the chain back.
Of course he wouldn't have dreamt of returning the stereo I gave
him for the wedding, and that was somewhat more expensive."

"Fantastic, how you stuck to your guns," Karl-Heinz said.

"Well, but he got the car, too; it was registered in his name,
so I had to give in. But to get back at him, shortly before the
divorce I overdrew our joint account by three thousand marks—
the debts were divided up fifty-fifty, so at least I ended up a little
better off."

"Not bad," Karl-Heinz said.

"How clever you are," I said, just to have something to say.
Actually I was speechless. What Juliet was describing sounded
like a knock-down-drag-out divorce, not a harmonious separation.

"Besides," Juliet said, "he grabbed all the books we'd bought
together."

"Still, you got the furniture," Karl-Heinz said.

"The old living-room set, which wasn't worth anything anyway! The old kitchen hutch! He didn't want the old stuff, because it would have cost him too much to move it. So he
generously left me that garbage, and I had to figure out how to
get rid of it."

I was shocked. Gottfried wouldn't believe his ears if I told him!

"Fortunately I've almost repressed it already," Juliet said. "I
made up my mind not to think about it anymore."

And this Juliet had advised me to marry Albert! After a divorce like that! I didn't understand her at all.

"How can you advise me to marry Albert, and on the other
hand condemn certain other people just because they're married! You don't realize how you're contradicting yourself!"

"Gottfried is emotionally incapable of commitment, in case you still haven't figured that out," she said.

"No, I *haven't* figured it out," I said honestly and icily.

"Why not? Marriage creates more togetherness than any romantic infatuation. And if the only thing that binds two people together is a momentary explosion of feeling, it's much too stressful in the long run. But I told you that already, really." Juliet sighed. "Of course a marriage can go sour, but if you're afraid from the beginning to really throw yourself into a relationship, it won't work out anyway."

"And what's the deal with Gottfried?"

"That's precisely the deal with Gottfried! As long as he's married, he won't love anyone but his wife." Juliet looked thoughtful, then said, "But he loves himself more than his wife. If he weren't so vain, he might actually notice how she humiliates him."

Karl-Heinz put in his two cents again: "You're taking too narrow a view. If I were married and I met a pretty girl, I could certainly love her, even though I was married. Hey, no problem." He smiled smugly, placed his hand on Juliet's arm again, and then he whispered into Juliet's ear, "But you, you're already over thirty, and you won't find a partner that easily. If I were you, I'd think this through carefully."

"If I'm not worth a divorce, I'm also not prepared to emotionally finance his extramarital flings."

On the one hand I wasn't sorry to hear Juliet's assurances that it was all over with Gottfried. On the other hand I could hardly believe how calculating she was. Even though it was so warm out, I was feeling shivery.

"What time is it?" Karl-Heinz suddenly wanted to know. It was seven-thirty. He had to leave in a hurry.

"Where are you going now?" Juliet asked.

He had a date.

"With whom, if I may ask?"

He just smiled mysteriously.

In parting he kissed Juliet on the cheeks and me almost on the mouth. But I managed to turn my face away, so he only got my ear. After he'd left, Juliet and I sat there in silence—the other people in the place must have thought our mutual lover had just left us. Of course he hadn't paid for the wine he'd ordered for me. I was disliking Mr. Karl-Heinz Müller more and more. What an asshole. "Why does he slobber over me?" I asked Juliet. "I hardly know him!"

"He's trying to be a womanizer."

"Do you know any woman who really goes for that sort of thing?"

"Yes, women who consider themselves worthless. Who need a man in order to have a reason for existing."

"But he's a misogynist! Even if he does act so lovey-dovey!"

"You're just not frustrated enough. You haven't turned your hostilities against yourself. Otherwise you'd be happy to have someone slobber over you that way, never mind whether he's a misogynist or not. So long as he's a man."

I was afraid Juliet would proceed to give me some school-shrink explanation—sexual frustration is the essential prerequisite for happy togetherness, or true love, or something of the sort—so I said I had to get home because I had an important phone call to make. It was all right with Juliet, so we said good-bye and went our separate ways.

Actually I wanted to call Gottfried right away. But it was exactly eight, and the evening news was on. People like Gottfried Schachtschnabel, who have to keep up with politics, don't like to get phone calls during the news. So I waited till eight-thirty. Then it occurred to me that eight-thirty wasn't an unconventional time at all. I thought: if I call Gottfried Schachtschabel now, he'll think I go to bed with the chickens. I didn't want him to think that, of course. I thought some more. Finally I set the alarm for three in the morning. Now, that was an unconventional time. I'd sleep a little, so as to be in good shape. Then I thought three might be a little too late. I set the alarm back to two-thirty.

46 When the alarm went off at two-thirty, I was wide awake immediately. Even so, I didn't call Gottfried right away. If you call someone in the middle of the night, it's pretty much essential to have loud music playing in the background. That's the usual thing: whenever someone calls me very late, there's always loud music in the background. I looked through my albums. For an eternity I wavered back and forth between "Don't Cry for Me, Argentina"—I adored it because it was so old, but it wasn't quite suitable—and Elvis singing "Are You Lonesome Tonight." That would have been fantastically suitable, but I decided against it because it seemed kind of suggestive. Then I had an idea: "The Internationale." I had that on tape, and it was the ideal background music: "Peoples, hear the signals, rise up for the last struggle"—that was political, also very original for two-thirty in the morning. I turned up my cassette player to top volume; the retiree next door was practically deaf anyway. Now I was ready.

It took forever, though, for Gottfried to pick up the receiver.

"Whoisit?" he whispered.

"Gottfried!" I shouted, because "The Internationale" was so loud. "It's me, Constance! I saw Juliet, and she doesn't want anything more to do with you, and you know what I found out? She didn't separate harmoniously from her husband at all! Did you know that?"

"Whoisit?" Gottfried whispered again.

"Were you asleep already?" I asked cautiously, because he didn't recognize my voice. He didn't answer, I just heard him yawn.

"It's me, Constance! She doesn't want to have anything more to do with you, I'm supposed to tell you."

"Who are you talking about?" he asked, and sighed. I turned down the cassette player a little so I could hear him better. "About Juliet! She says hello, and she doesn't want to have anything more to do with you." I heard him yawn again.

"Who's speaking, please?" he asked again.

"It's me, Constance," I shouted again. "Juliet doesn't want to have anything more to do with you. She doesn't want to see you ever again, I'm supposed to tell you."

"Oh, I see. Yes, yes. Okay," was all he said.

"What do you say to that?"

"Nothing to be done." He yawned again.

"So?" I said, and waited for him to say something. But he didn't.

"Are you asleep?" I asked.

"Not exactly," he replied.

I was relatively disappointed that he didn't say anything else. Probably shock at Juliet's coldheartedness had left him speechless. "Okay, till next Wednesday," I said.

"Wait, I have to tell you something," he said softly, but sounding more lively than before.

I was on tenterhooks. "Yes?"

"You weren't there today. So you don't know that we're not meeting week after next. I told the others today. I have to go away, my elderly parents are celebrating their golden wedding anniversary."

"When?"

"Wednesday after next, July third, we're not meeting. Just so you can plan ahead."

I was totally confused. How was I supposed to plan ahead? I even forgot to ask whether his wife was going along.

"Well, good night," he said.

"Well, good night," I said.

Finally an answer arrived. The letter even came in an envelope with the newspaper's address on it—I was surprised, but pleasantly so: since I didn't have any personals experience, I didn't know that the response would be mailed to me so discreetly that my woman mail carrier would think one of the editors of the paper was writing to me. Very clever.

The envelope was fat—that was promising; it had even cost extra postage! I hurried with the letter to my desk, quickly got myself a cup of coffee from the kitchen, lit a cigarette, and then decided it would be better to read the letter in bed. As I ripped open the envelope, my hands were shaking so much that I almost shredded the envelope.

Inside the envelope was the envelope I'd sent my letter in—ripped open! My letter and my photo were in it, and also a message with the newspaper's letterhead and a sheet of paper with numbers on it. The page with the letterhead said:

Re: Box 48763 UZ, 6/1/pres. yr.

Dear Frl. Wechselburger:

As you certainly are aware, our newspaper has long served as an effective intermediary for persons seeking partners. Given the large number of advertisements that we process each week, occasional errors cannot be avoided.

In the case of the above-referenced box number, the advertisement, which was intended to be listed under females seeking partners, was mistakenly misplaced during typesetting and consequently appeared in the male column. Please excuse any inconvenience this may have caused. In order to spare our advertiser the awkwardness of replying, we have asked her to return to us the replies she received; you may, of course, count on our complete discretion.

In case you wish to join the many successful advertisers in our newspaper, we enclose our advertisement price list for your attention.

Enclosures: 1 advertisement price list
1 handwritten letter
1 photograph
3 advertisement forms

I don't know how often I read that letter—I held it up to the light; it sounded computerized, but it wasn't—before it became clear to me I'd replied to a woman's ad. So that was how my kindred soul looked! Was I a lesbian? No. It had all been a mistake.

Eighty pfennigs down the drain. Not to mention my hopes.

As always when my life had reached a new low, Sieglinde called. Or was it the other way around: was every call from Sieglinde a low point in my life?

"How are you doing?" she asked. "I'm doing terribly."

"Me too."

"Guess what Wolf-Dietrich has come up with to hassle me! He won't let me use his toothbrush, can you imagine? I made a point of asking my boss, and my boss said that when two people are intimate it's perfectly acceptable from a hygienic standpoint for them to share a toothbrush. But not for Wolf-Dietrich, oh no, he insists on drawing lines! The main thing, my boss says, is that you switch fairly frequently."

"Switch who?" I played dumb on purpose to annoy Sieglinde. "Does Wolf-Dietrich want to come over here and brush his teeth now and then?"

"Wolfi would never brush his teeth at your place," Sieglinde said sternly. To her this was no laughing matter. Not that anything else was, either; at least this time she admitted it. Nevertheless she had a lot of nerve to be so sure Wolf-Dietrich would never want to use my toothbrush. "Tell him not to get his hopes up, and say hello to him for me," I said equally sternly.

"I asked Albert, too, and he also said it really wasn't necessary to always buy two toothbrushes."

"When did you see Albert?"

"Oh, last week. He called and gave me his new phone number. I hear he has a very, very nice apartment now." Sieglinde fell meaningfully silent.

"Any other problems?" I asked.

Yes, she had other problems. She'd discovered these Laura Ashley sheets, satin, mocha brown, and her boss's wife had bought the same ones, of course, and did I know what temperature setting she should use to wash them and what iron setting she should use? The material was so delicate! And she'd already spoken with her boss's wife about it, and she wasn't sure, either. The problem was, they might shrink or run. Sieglinde sighed.

"Why would you buy sheets in mocha brown? Everything shows," I said during Sieglinde's sigh.

"What's going to show?" Sieglinde said, and then she said quickly, "I see you're no help." And then she had to get off the phone because she had to go shopping, and she only added the information that she'd discovered a fantastic cologne—not for herself, but for Wolf-Dietrich, her Adonis. . . .

So Wolf-Dietrich wouldn't let Sieglinde use his toothbrush. I should have such problems! Sieglinde hadn't asked, of course, why things were going terribly for me—and of course I hadn't told her. All my remaining hopes for happiness in the immediate future now rested on tomorrow.

To give Gottfried a chance to drive me home, I took the subway to the academy. All through the seminar I was thinking:

should I tell him afterwards that I wanted to get home right away? And then, if we parked in front of my building, invite him in for coffee? Completely spontaneously? I'd bought two bottles of wine and tidied the place up, just in case. Or should we go to a bar first, settle the topic of Juliet once and for all, and then go to my place? Or to his? Although I finally concluded that it didn't make sense to preprogram spontaneous developments, I still couldn't concentrate on the report some guy called Jürgen was reading. Anyway, he mumbled so much you couldn't understand him. I pretended to take notes, but in actuality I was just writing "Juliet," "Juliet," "Juliet" mindlessly in my ring binder, and then I slowly crossed out the name—so slowly and carefully that Gottfried, if he was watching me, had to think I was underlining crucial passages. Finally it was 6:45. By 6:47 all the other students were gone.

When we were alone at last, Gottfried said he didn't have any time. And today of all days he wasn't going to Kreuzberg, but straight to Lichterfelde. Someone was coming to his place to go over his tax return. He must have noticed how disappointed I looked, because he said again how sorry he was, but since he had to go to his parents' on the weekend, he couldn't postpone the appointment. But the week after next, when he was back, for sure; he'd make a note of it, we'd have to get together after the seminar for a good chat.

Even though Gottfried had been so nice and of course couldn't help it that he didn't have any time, I was totally frustrated. Was my life going to go on like this forever, totally uneventful? Alternating between unfulfilled expectations and expected disappointments?

So I wouldn't starve to death at least, I went to the Italian place on the corner and had a tuna fish pizza and two glasses of Frascati. After that I felt better. It was still much too early to go home. I went to Cookies.

48 I left at three in the morning with a guy named Martin. Or something like that. We went to his place, because he lived nearby and the subway wasn't running.

I already knew it would be embarrassing to wake up next to him, and a real strain on the social skills to stay and have breakfast. He was the type who puts new sheets on the bed after every one-night stand.

And what if I ran into him again? I'd just say, "Nasty weather for this time of year." In case I happened to remember him.

That's all there is to say about that particular night.

49 I can still feel his chest hair on my back. "Sexual frustration"—it always sounds like the only frustrated ones are the ones who don't do it. What a laugh. The frustrated ones are the ones who do do it! The ones who don't can at least preserve some illusions. He had these weird pimples on his back; I'd much rather have squeezed them than fucked. But such intimacies aren't allowed when you don't know each other.

What would it have been like with Gottfried? I was so frustrated that all day long I couldn't really do anything.

In the afternoon I dragged myself and my dirty clothes to the Laundromat. The whole time, I sat and stared at the wash tumbling in the machine. This eternal cycle made me think. I decided that every time the drum changed direction and something blue showed in the window, it meant that soon something would develop between Gottfried and me. But half the time nothing blue showed, even though most of the things I'd stuffed into the machine were blue. Everything was really totally frustrating. Back home, I washed my sweaters in the sink. I inspected the happy young woman caressing her angora sweater on the Woolite bottle. Everybody was happy but me. To at least keep from being manipulated by commercial fantasy images of happiness, I used less Woolite than the label recommended.

Later that evening I sank into a deep depression. Aside from the fact that I had clean underwear, clean towels, and clean sweaters again, and that the coffee spills were gone from my desk, everything was still the same. All this effort just to maintain the status quo made me feel totally desolate. Struggling all your life just to spin around and around in the same place, having to defend what you've achieved anew every day—and no matter how hard you worked, all earthly things remained transitory. . . . The lace insert in my favorite panties was frayed, the elastic on two other pairs was shot. Somehow my neon-blue sweater had gotten baggy. . . . How do you change your life?

On Friday I didn't go to the women's seminar because I really had to tidy up my apartment. Tidying is good if you need time to think. I kept wondering whether Birgit had answered the ad. Maybe true romance still existed somewhere.

Toward evening I tried to call her. I wanted to know if she at least had any hope of changing her life. But her phone was busy all evening.

Saturday afternoon at two-thirty, when I was in the middle of cleaning the kitchen, Birgit called me.

"Why were you on the phone all day yesterday? Did you answer the ad?" was the first thing I asked.

"Well . . ."

"Yes or no?"

"Well, yes."

"And?"

"Well, we're going to meet this evening. He's coming over here."

"What! Tell me!"

"I thought it over a long time—actually I didn't want to do it, but since you and Juliet were so gung ho, I did write to that Knight of the Blue Blossom of Romanticism. His name's Rudi."

"That's the ad you answered?"

"Yes, and day before yesterday he got my picture and called me immediately. I must say, he has a very nice voice. And he also asked me straight out what my sign was. He's a Taurus. And I'm a Pisces. . . . I once had a boss who was a Taurus, too, and I got along very well with him."

"So he's coming to your place?"

"Yes. A bar would be too impersonal, or meeting on the street—no. I have no idea what I should wear. Should I wear a party dress? Juliet said I shouldn't get myself all dolled up. One of the girls I work with said I should appear very casual, in leisurewear, but my sister says I should have on something very sensible, with someone coming to my place who I don't know at all. Well, if Juliet didn't live in the building, I'd be kind of scared. But she said she'd be home all evening, and if he tried to kill me she'd come up and save me. We wondered whether I should tell the man my friend lives right downstairs and can hear everything that goes on in my apartment. What do you think I should wear?"

"Wear what you were wearing in the picture, so he'll recognize you."

"You think so? I don't know. . . ."

"How many people have you told that you answered the ad?"

Well, she had to find out how to act in such a situation, Birgit explained. I was surprised that she was telling the world about it after she'd resisted the whole thing so strenuously at first. I wouldn't talk about something like that till I was sure I liked the man. But Birgit didn't seem to be worried about that kind of disappointment. Or was any old man fine with her? So long as it was a man?

Birgit didn't have any more time to talk; she had to wash her hair, fix a bite to eat, and call her sister again and ask what she should wear, but she promised to let me know right away tomorrow how it had gone. I wished her luck.

I was all excited myself. What kind of man would he be, a Knight of the Blue Blossom of Romanticism? I'd never have picked that ad. Well, to each her own.

That evening I bought the weekend edition of the paper with the most personals. What was the first thing I saw? The ad I'd answered, this time printed correctly under the heading "Acquaintanceships, female." I'd gotten over my mistake and could already smile at it. My kindred soul—a woman. Actually that made sense.

Under "Acquaintanceships, male" I discovered another ad that had also been there four weeks ago and had appealed to Birgit, the one headed, "Don't claim you're sincere, just be it." I wondered why he'd run the ad again. Hadn't he found the right woman? Hadn't anyone responded? I wouldn't have replied to this ad either, I thought. But all the others were just as much out of the question. The guys in the personals couldn't compete with Albert, even: they were all midlife crisis types who wanted a woman to fuck and parade around in return for a full-time position as a cleaning lady. Not one of them could hold a candle to Gottfried. And Gottfried was free again. I felt sort of guilty because I'd been unfaithful to him. On the other hand, in my thoughts I'd been absolutely faithful.

Birgit didn't call Sunday morning. I didn't dare call her; I could imagine she hadn't gotten to bed too early, and besides, it was pretty obvious that I wasn't exactly at the top of her list of confidantes and consultants—otherwise she wouldn't have waited till I called to inform me of her rendezvous, which everyone else knew about already. Oh, well, we hadn't known each other that long anyway. But at noon I did call her after all. The phone was busy. At three it was still busy. I didn't feel like waiting any longer, so I decided to take a Sunday walk and go by Birgit's and Juliet's building. After all, on Sunday afternoon it's perfectly appropriate to drop in on friends.

I rang Birgit's bell, and she immediately buzzed me in. I rang Juliet's bell too, but she wasn't there. No wonder: she was upstairs with Birgit.

"Oh, it's you," Birgit said. She didn't seem particularly glad to see me, but Juliet said with a delighted smile, "Aha, the second romantic damsel enters the chamber."

"How was it?" I asked Birgit hopefully.

On her scrubbable coffee table stood a red rose, and under the vase was a coaster.

"Did he bring that?"

"Yes," Birgit said.

"Well, what else?" I could hardly wait, but Birgit went into the kitchen to get me a cup of coffee. While she was gone, Juliet whispered, "A major fiasco with the Taurus yesterday."

"Yes?"

"We have to rebuild Birgit's morale, watch what you say." So when Birgit came back I didn't say anything. So Birgit realized immediately that Juliet had warned me. "Juliet already told you everything," she said to me as she sat down.

"Juliet didn't tell me a thing," I said firmly, so as not to create the impression we'd been talking about her behind her back. Besides, I *didn't* know what had happened. "What did you end up wearing?" I asked.

"Oh, just a simple party suit that you can also wear as a lounging suit."

I was crushed. What kind of garment was that? I'd never owned anything remotely like it. Presumably it was one of those little boutique-y nothings that had made me wonder for years what you wore them for. I couldn't begin to picture a simple party suit that you could also wear as a lounging suit, and I looked around the room as if it might be lying somewhere, but of course Birgit's place was in perfect order. So I asked her what the suit was made of, and what color it was.

"Black georgette, and the lapels are beige satin, and there are beige satin stripes down the pantlegs. It looks darling," Birgit said, and smiled, remembering her combined party/lounging suit.

Her smile confirmed my guess that this suit must be an extremely elegant little nothing. Black georgette and beige satin. Olala! She must have looked like a Barbie doll in her Barbie doll bungalow.

"And what did the two of you do?"

Juliet sighed.

But Birgit told me very willingly what had happened. The two of them had watched TV and had something to drink. He hadn't been bad-looking: slim, blond, with a walrus mustache. Birgit hadn't asked his occupation. Table tennis and skiing were his hobbies. "He got many replies, but my photo struck him as special," Birgit said, smiling at the memory of her photo.

"And then?"

"Well, then I showed him the pictures of the birth of my sister's Benjamin."

I swallowed. That was absolutely the last thing I would do on a first date. I looked at Juliet. But Juliet was staring at the TV. It was a kiddie program, and the sound was turned off. They were showing a cartoon in which a bee was flirting with a hat covered with flowers.

"And then?" I asked.

"Well, then he got in the mood, and we went to my bed-room."

"What? You went to bed with him?" I think I almost shouted. I couldn't picture it. Birgit! Our perfect, well-behaved little Birgit did something like that! I think my mouth dropped open out of sheer astonishment. Birgit going to bed with a man on the first date! She looked at me reproachfully. I pulled myself together and snapped my mouth shut.

"You're acting as though I were still a virgin," Birgit said, dampened the tip of a finger with her tongue, picked up a cake crumb from the rug, then dropped the crumb in the spotless ashtray. "He said we had to find out first whether we were on the same wavelength emotionally, and that he found it much more romantic to come together at once, and it's true, too, that when you're meant for each other you know it right away and don't have to wait. And so there's nothing wrong with it."

I looked at Juliet, but Juliet wasn't saying anything, just star-ing unmoved at the soundless TV: another kiddie film, one that demonstrated how chewing gum was made.

"Nothing happened anyway," Birgit said.

"Are you on the pill?"

"Yes," Birgit said, "but that's not what I mean."

"Well, what?"

"It didn't work. He was impotent. Then he put on his clothes again and left. He said there was no point to it, I wasn't his type. We just weren't meant for each other." Birgit sighed. "But he wanted to keep my picture."

Without meaning to, I shook my head. Birgit was a puzzle to me. She wasn't even angry about this knight, who obviously had only wanted to fuck her. And she even let him keep her picture! He'd obviously go showing it around! "I wasn't his type," she said!

"Was he your type?" I asked.

"I don't know, maybe so, but I don't know him."

"How do you know you weren't his type?"

"He said so. He said I was too passive and not his type."

The kiddie program was over. Juliet energetically switched off the TV, and then said to Birgit, "There's no point in taking all the blame yourself." I thought so, too. "You have to try again right away, for the sake of your self-esteem," Juliet said.

Birgit said she had to work through her feelings first. I could understand that.

But Juliet said you didn't have to wallow in every feeling, certainly not in unnecessary frustration. Birgit should just forget the whole thing. "You can't change your feelings without changing external circumstances," Juliet said. "It can't be done—it's always forced."

"He wasn't the lid to your pot, only a pot holder," I said, to cheer Birgit up. But only Juliet giggled.

"The other ad, the one that appealed to you so much, was in the paper again yesterday"—it had just occurred to me. "The one with that super-honest man! I told you at the time you should write to him!"

Again Birgit's mind seemed to have gone blank.

"You know what?" Juliet said. "I'm going to run down and get the paper."

"I'm never answering an ad again," Birgit said.

"Look, anyone can make a mistake," I said to Birgit, and I said it convincingly, because I knew what I was talking about.

Juliet was back in a flash, had already found the ad, and said, "Now you just copy the same letter you wrote to that pot holder, put your wonderful picture with it, and we'll see what happens." I had to admire Juliet—it was all so easy for her. She really was completely unromantic. Maybe that was because of her marriage experience.

Birgit was still resisting, but not very strenuously. She seemed glad that Juliet was making decisions for her. But she didn't remember what she'd written. Juliet said three sentences and a phone number would be plenty; her picture would bowl anyone over.

"You needn't write any more than that, since you don't know what kind of a guy he is," I said, again speaking from experience.

"But if anything goes wrong, it's your fault," Birgit told Juliet.

"I can think of worse things," Juliet said.

Even aside from the fact that I was really anxious to see how Birgit's second attempt would work out, I found myself thinking about her a lot in the next few days. Somehow I felt a little sorry for her. She was nice, but so naive. What made her tick? She was so different from me. Even when my place had just been tidied up, it looked messy compared to Birgit's. But my place didn't have that kitschy plushy look of hers. In the living room she had little watercolors on the walls with almond-eyed girls—I hadn't noticed them on my first visit. Ghastly. And in the hall she had a porcelain plate with Charles and Di on it. I wouldn't hang something like that anywhere but the bathroom—there it would be funny.

Women like Birgit . . . where do they come from, what do they do until they go into a marriage with a self-designated Knight of the Blue Blossom of Romanticism . . . and go under in marriage? Birgit's sex life was a puzzle to me: she didn't have any, did she? Nevertheless she'd survived this one-night flop pretty much unscathed. She just wasn't his type, and she accepted that. Maybe she wasn't nearly such a goody two-shoes as I thought. Why was she on the pill? Was she permanently protected, just in case? I was on the pill, too, but I'd had an ongoing relationship until just a little while ago, and besides, I'd turned my back on bourgeois morality. But Juliet had certainly hopped into bed with Gottfried right away. Well, well. Were all women alike after all?

Juliet—she hadn't said a word about Gottfried. She actually

seemed to have written him off completely. But what was she up to now? Life was certainly easiest for her. She had absolutely no hope of romance. Maybe she'd never really loved anyone. One who's never loved has never lived, I thought spontaneously. But one who's loved doesn't have anything but frustration, either, my memories told me. Then I thought: One less experience is one less wound. But without experience there's also no salvation. I didn't know what these thoughts meant; I was sure they came from my subconscious and were profound and true.

For the entire next week I was so bored, and somehow felt so depressed, that I even called Sieglinde. Maybe she was suffering from boredom, too, because she was delighted to hear from me. "It's so nice of you to call," she exclaimed. "You absolutely must come over! Can you come tomorrow at three for coffee? That would be lovely."

I didn't have the nerve to ask if coffee also meant pastry. Just in case, I ate two waffle creams before I left the house.

They greeted me effusively. What gave? Maybe Wolf-Dietrich had bought a bigger car or Sieglinde's boss had acquired a bigger apartment building. Or had Wolf-Dietrich finally bought Sieglinde the jacket made out of little mink paws that he'd promised her for Christmas last year and the year before? Or had her boss's antiques dealer, with whom Sieglinde was also, she liked to stress, "friends," stumbled across another peasant cupboard rotting away in a chicken coop and practically given it away to his dear friends for a few lousy thousand? Sieglinde and Wolf-Dietrich looked at me expectantly. They wanted me to ask. Sieglinde was smiling oh-so-naturally. Wolf-Dietrich was smiling oh-so-modestly. I let them twist in the wind.

"Have you seen the new Nastassja Kinski film?" Sieglinde asked.

"No."

"Fantastic. Very sensitively directed."

Wolf-Dietrich grinned. "Yeah, what a hot little number."

"How's our friend the doctor?" Sieglinde asked next.

"Haven't the faintest," I said, "and I couldn't care less."

Sieglinde was still smiling that natural smile.

"Did you ever wash those Laura Ashley satin sheets in the machine?" I asked.

"No, can't be done," Wolf-Dietrich said. "They're much too delicate."

"You mean you send them out?"

"No," Sieglinde said, "we just wash them by hand."

"It's not really much work," Wolf-Dietrich said.

"We just wash them in the bathtub in warm water," Sieglinde said. " 'Course, then we have to scrub the bathtub like crazy because the fabric still bleeds."

"What?" Wolf-Dietrich shouted. "The color runs?"

"But that'll stop eventually. We've only washed them once."

Then Wolf-Dietrich talked about his career. And Sieglinde showed off her new Teflon-coated iron.

Sieglinde looked at Wolf-Dietrich. "May I tell her?" she asked.

"What?" Wolf-Dietrich grumbled.

Sieglinde beamed at Wolf-Dietrich, then beamed at me. "By the way, we're getting married."

"What month are you in?"

"That's what my mother said, too," Sieglinde said, slightly miffed.

"Sieglinde's not pregnant," Wolf-Dietrich said firmly.

"So, why didn't you tell me right away that you're getting married?"

"Wolf-Dietrich thinks it's not that important," Sieglinde said.

"It isn't," Wolf-Dietrich said.

"And what are you going to wear?" I asked Sieglinde.

"Wolf-Dietrich's having a lightweight suit made," Sieglinde said, "pale gray, an English fabric with a subtle pattern, but actually no pattern, more like a texture. My boss has a suit like that. . . ."

"Are you at least getting married in white?"

"Out of the question," Wolf-Dietrich said. "What would the old girl do with some white rag? Wear it later in the lab?"

"Well, I'd get married in white," I said. "If you're going to do it, might as well do it up right. And the bridesmaids all in pink, and all the guests, too, and the men with pink ties, and everywhere pink flowers, pink balloons, and a huge pink and white wedding cake. . . ." I could see the whole scene before me. "I could film the whole thing; I could work your wedding into my film."

But the bridal pair weren't interested in my ideas about a proper wedding.

"So why are you getting married, anyway?" I asked.

"Well, this year I made too much money, and Sieglinde doesn't earn that much, so we're getting married to take advantage of the tax deduction. And next year, when I take over Meyer-Foggenhausen's clientele, it'll really pay off—a few thousand more per year. After taxes! If not more! Of course, we're going to maintain separate property." Wolf-Dietrich went on to explain that he was having a lawyer he knew work out the prenuptial agreement, which the lawyer was of course doing for free.

"Oh, I see. You just want to save on taxes," I said.

"It's not only a question of the income tax," Wolf-Dietrich said, "there are a number of completely different considerations involved. My father wants to convey his house to me now, because I convinced him it made sense in terms of inheritance tax and so on, and if I'm married, there's a nice little loophole I can make use of."

"Well, I'm marrying for love," Sieglinde said, putting away the Teflon iron. "And the fact that Wolf-Dietrich has so much money and will soon be a homeowner doesn't make a bit of difference to me. And imagine, his mother is giving me this huge gold bracelet! Thirty-four grams of gold!" Sieglinde laughed loudly.

"Thirty-nine grams of gold," Wolf-Dietrich corrected her.

"And when *is* this happy event?"

"We're not sure yet ourselves, because Wolf-Dietrich's father is on vacation, and my mother broke her foot, and my brother's girlfriend is having a baby. And the Sennebergs, who are supposed to be best man and matron of honor, can't do it before the first of September, because school's out till then, and my boss can only come on a Wednesday afternoon or during lunch break. But Wolf-Dietrich's father can't come till the beginning of October, because he wants to stay on Majorca with his girlfriend till then. And he wants to give Wolf-Dietrich twenty-five hundred marks for the wedding, but of course only if we invite him, and his girlfriend, too."

"My father's an asshole," Wolf-Dietrich said.

"Of course we can't invite Wolf-Dietrich's father's girlfriend and Wolf-Dietrich's mother. But fortunately Wolf-Dietrich's mother isn't like that. She'll give me the bracelet even if we don't invite her to the wedding. But ultimately everything depends on when my mother's cast comes off. Because my parents want to hold a reception after the ceremony, and my mother'll make the canapés, and they'll serve champagne. My father has good connections; he can get the champagne cheaper, right, Wolf-Dietrich? But of course my mother can't make the canapés with a cast on."

"I see," I said. "So tell me, when is the happy event taking place?"

"The reception will only be for the immediate family," Sieglinde said. "And of course my boss is invited."

"I see," I said. "So you're not going to throw a party?"

"No," Wolf-Dietrich said. "And we're not going on a honeymoon either—it's not worth it. Besides, we have to save up."

"I see," I said. My stomach growled loudly. But there wasn't any pastry in sight. They'd probably hidden it in the refrigerator.

"Can you imagine how stressed out I am? I have to get all our papers together," Sieglinde said, putting on an air of despair. "I've just found out I have to apply specially to hyphenate my name."

"You're going to use a hyphenated name?"

"Of course. It sounds fantastic, doesn't it: Lamar-Schadler! Nowadays, when people don't take the distinction between 'Frau' and 'Fräulein' so seriously, you have to have a hyphenated name so people will know you're really married."

I said good-bye soon after that, because there was no coffee left. "Adieu, Frau Lamar-Schadler," I said to Sieglinde.

"And when are you getting married?" She beamed at me with her mouth closed. She looked like one of those little hamster banks that real banks give you when you open an account.

"You'll have to wait a long time for that," I said. Out of politeness I asked, "And what do you want in the way of a wedding present?"

"Oooh," Sieglinde said, and made a gesture as if to say it didn't matter that much.

I thought: I'm going to give them a receipt for a donation to the fund for unwed mothers! Wolf-Dietrich can deduct it from the income tax.

 How predictable that Sieglinde and Wolf-Dietrich would get married. Actually, people like that are born married. But the gall of Sieglinde, to say she was marrying for love when she was doing it for money. As for Wolf-Dietrich, that went without saying.

I had to tell Juliet right away. Of course, she also guessed immediately that Sieglinde was pregnant. But then she said only, "These things do happen; I wasn't pregnant either when I got married" and "Sometimes people just get married."

I thought Juliet could at least have said how bourgeois the two of them were, how fixated on money. And how this marriage wouldn't last. But she didn't say anything else about Sieglinde and Wolf-Dietrich, just told me that Birgit had mailed the letter to the sincere man on Sunday, but hadn't heard anything yet. And otherwise nothing much was happening.

Then I called Albert. It'd been three weeks since I'd heard from him, since that time he'd started a fight over his dumb coffee filter. I'd made up my mind not to be the one to call him first, but I had to tell him this news. After all, the four of us had been couples together. Even though it was Sunday evening, Albert was home, glued to the TV as usual; in the background I could hear the roar of some sports broadcast. He seemed perfectly happy to hear my voice: "To what do I owe the pleasure?"

"I was over at Wolf-Dietrich and Sieglinde's, and just imagine—"

"He called me."

"You already know? Since when?"

"Since last week."

That was typical. They *would* inform the doctor of their impending nuptials first! "Why didn't you tell me? After all, we both know them. I called you right away. . . ."

"It's not all *that* exciting," Albert said.

"Oh," I said. Albert didn't find it that exciting! I was simply amazed at how calmly everyone I knew was suddenly accepting bourgeois marriage. Maybe they all had a fetish.

"It'll pass," Albert said.

"So you don't think it'll last, either? How much time do you give them?"

"Three days."

"Why three days?"

"That's how long it always lasts."

I asked Albert what made him say that. Three days—he had to be joking!

"In three days at the outside all the crabs'll be gone."

"Crabs? What crabs? You're talking about crabs?" I yelled. "Oh, have mercy!"

"Calm down," Albert said. "I explained to Sieglinde too that they'll be gone in three days."

I still didn't get it. Finally Albert filled me in. Wolf-Dietrich had called Albert because he'd gotten crabs. And Albert had explained to Sieglinde, at Wolf-Dietrich's express command, that you could pick up crabs anywhere—in a public rest room, for instance—and that crabs weren't an STD. This calmed Sieglinde down. She didn't have crabs, only Wolf-Dietrich.

"And that they're getting married? You knew that?"

"Who's getting married?"

"Sieglinde and Wolf-Dietrich!"

"What! They're getting married! That can't be true. I'm going to die laughing," Albert said, and died laughing.

When I told Albert that Sieglinde wasn't even pregnant,

Albert laughed so hard he got the hiccups. "Of course she's not pregnant." He giggled. "She doesn't even have crabs." He giggled hysterically.

"What's so funny about her not having crabs?"

"Because they're not even married yet and already they're not sleeping together."

"Did he tell you that?"

"No, but he said he had an incredible number of crabs and was absolutely covered with them. You know, he's so hairy."

"Did he cheat on her? Where did he pick up crabs? What do they look like? Do they itch? Yuck!"

"No," Albert said. "I just told you, you can pick up crabs anywhere, it's not an STD." Then he described how you could hardly see them, they looked like freckles and hid in the pubic hair and body hair, but not on the head—those were a different kind—and actually crabs hardly itched, so you might not even notice you had them. "They also don't hop around on your body like fleas," Albert said, "they stay pretty much in one place, because they bite into the skin. Check and see whether you have any. There's an epidemic of them right now."

I shuddered. I unzipped my jeans right then and there and checked my pubic hair. Thank God there was nothing at all like freckles to be seen. Albert explained I also had to look for nits, the crabs' eggs, and those were just tiny dots, as if a hair was knotted. I looked again more closely, but fortunately couldn't find any hairs with knots. Just in case, I asked, "And what do you do if you have them?"

"Drugstores all carry a foolproof gel; you smear it on and the crabs all die immediately. But you have to rub it in for three days, because the gel doesn't bother the nits a bit, but after three days at most the last eggs hatch and are killed instantly. That's why you have to use the stuff for three days. That's it." Albert spoke very matter-of-factly, every inch the doctor. "It's not all that exciting," he said, and then he laughed again. "But it's hilarious that Sieglinde doesn't have them."

"Why?"

"Well, crabs don't breed all that fast. So if Wolf-Dietrich's completely covered with them, he's had them quite a while. If he'd sought any, um, physical contact, let's say, with his partner since catching crabs—well, in that case you do find a crab scrambling from one person's pubic hair to someone else's now and then. But if he absolutely avoids any physical contact, and if Sieglinde keeps the household's toilet and so on clinically clean, she won't catch them. Now do you get it?"

Now I got it! Very revealing. "And Sieglinde says she's marrying for love," I said.

"Love has many faces," Albert said.

Over the phone I could hear his doorbell. "What's that?" I asked.

"I think someone's at the door," he said. "I have to hang up now. Bye, it was nice talking with you again. Take care. Talk to you again soon maybe."

"Take care," I said. "Bye."

I'd have liked to talk with him a while longer, and I'd especially have liked to know who was coming to see him on a Sunday evening. Did he have a woman now who came to him instead of driving him out of the apartment? Maybe she even cooked for him, watched the sports roundup with him? Had he found his idyll now? TV, fucking, and finances—he'd never had any other interests. Too little for me. Still, it had been nice to talk with him.

52 On Wednesday I got up very early; I still had to wash my hair, pluck my eyebrows, paint my toenails, and of course also prepare mentally for my date with Gottfried. If things didn't work out again today, that was that, I'd sworn it to myself days ago. But yesterday I'd run into him in the hall on the fifth floor, and he had asked if I wanted to go to the movies with him after the seminar. He wanted to see a political film about Greenland; naturally I had a burning interest in the film. And after the movie, he'd said, we'd go somewhere else, of course. The stars were more favorable than ever before: although I didn't believe in horoscopes, I'd bought the *Evening Post* at the Kaput that night and checked the horoscope for today. I'm a Scorpio. The horoscope said: "A great surprise awaits you. Problems that caused you deep concern will be solved to your complete satisfaction." That was unambiguous.

Even before I made coffee, I washed my hair. I didn't want to blow-dry it but instead put it up in rollers and let it dry, then blow it smooth; I'd read that you have to stretch your hair while it's drying to get that wonderful shine models have in magazines. My hairdresser had confirmed this info.

When I went to the mirror to comb out my hair, I almost died: my face was studded with little red dots. I closed my eyes. When I opened them again, nothing had changed. My face was covered with pimples. From my forehead to my chin. I took my magnifying mirror and hurried into my study, where the light was better. Still, my face was absolutely covered with enormous pimples. I was paralyzed.

The pimples weren't squeezable. They had deep roots but they stuck up a ways. If you pressed them or squeezed them, nothing happened, except they turned dark red instead of light red. I'd never seen anything like it. But I still had hope. Maybe makeup would cover them? No such luck. After I'd dabbed every single one with cover stick, my face looked like a cover stick–colored volcanic landscape. Ghastly. I called Albert. He was already at the hospital. The nurse on duty said he didn't have time now. I told her he should call me immediately, it was terribly urgent. She heard the desperation in my voice and promised to tell the doctor right away. Half an hour later Albert called. "What's wrong?"

I was almost crying as I explained. He said red pimples on the face could be anything or nothing.

"It's certainly not nothing," I wailed. "What is it? You're the doctor!"

Albert guessed it might be measles. But I'd had those when I was a kid, I was sure of that, because I'd been the only one in my class to get them during Easter vacation, of all times. Albert asked if I had a fever. I did feel hot, but was it agitation or fever? I should take my temperature and call him back. I told him I couldn't take my temperature because he'd taken the thermometer when he moved out. He said I should run to the nearest drugstore and buy one. I'd need a thermometer anyway. Then I should call back.

Oh, what should I do? My hair had almost dried in the July heat, but in the excitement I hadn't combed it out. I looked gruesome: my face covered with pimples, my hair shaggy. To even comb out my hair I'd have to wet it again and rub in another batch of conditioner. When I looked at my face in the mirror, I felt sick. I tied a scarf over my damp hair, put on a pair of huge sunglasses, and ran as quick as I could to the pharmacy. Fortunately I didn't bump into anyone I knew.

I took my temperature in three different places, but it was normal. I called Albert again. In the meantime the pimples had multiplied. Albert thought I should go to the dermatologist around the corner from me. "But hurry," he said. "They're all closed on Wednesday afternoons."

Albert had been right: I found the door shut tight. This doctor had office hours only in the mornings, from eight to ten, and only on Monday, Tuesday, and Thursday. I rang anyway—I was an emergency, after all. No one opened.

I called Albert again. He said he couldn't tell anything without seeing these "furuncles." He'd be getting off work at five. At five! That was when my seminar began. But I had no choice. I told Albert I'd come to his place, so as not to lose any time.

By three the pimples had gotten even worse. Maybe it was because I'd squeezed them a bit. It was hopeless, anyway. I had to call Gottfried and tell him I couldn't come because I was sick.

He was so polite, he didn't even ask what was wrong. "Oh, that's too bad," he said. "So I have to go to that movie by myself—today's the only day it's showing." Then he kindly wished me a speedy recovery and said, "I hope we'll see each other again by next Wednesday at the latest."

Yes, I hoped so, too. And how I hoped it! How painful it was to see myself powerless in the grip of a grisly fate. Probably Gottfried had also suffered a great deal in his life. Without a doubt. Truly, nothing was handed to one. One was constantly compelled to fight for one's happiness, day in, day out.

At a quarter to five I was at Albert's, and fortunately he was already home.

"Oh dear, oh dear, you look awful," he said. "You poor thing, that's terrible!" I didn't answer; his pity just made me more aware of how awful it all was. "Maybe you're just entering puberty?" Albert said. I told him I couldn't take stupid jokes. So he said seriously, "It's probably some kind of allergic reaction."

"To what?"

"Strawberries, perfume, cauliflower, sperm, cat hair, dust, wine, cosmetics, milk, heat, cheese cubes . . . or it's psychosomatic."

"Stop!" I said. "You haven't got a clue."

"No, I haven't got a clue." Then he said the smart thing would be to go to the dermatologist first thing in the morning.

"And what should I do until then?"

"Wait and see."

I told him I couldn't wait that long, something had to be done right away. He dug around in his first-aid kit and finally showed me a tube of reddish-brown salve. He said he didn't know if it would help, but it was fairly certain it wouldn't do any harm—unless I was allergic to iodine. Why should I be allergic to iodine? I wanted to put the stuff on immediately, but Albert said, "Don't use it till you get home; you still have to drive, and with this salve on you'll look like an Indian with pimples, you poor thing." Since he wasn't sure the salve would help anyway, I gave it back and said he should give me something else, something colorless—that was all I needed, to look like a pimply Indian! While he dug around, I checked out the bathroom: no lipstick, no makeup, nothing on the bathtub ledge that suggested a woman. But on the bottom shelf of the medicine cabinet I discovered a jar of moisturizer.

"What do you need moisturizer for?"

Albert took the jar out of my hand. "Because when you're past thirty your skin begins to dry out," he said. "As you may know, I'm turning thirty next month. High time to take preventive measures."

"That's ridiculous," I said.

Albert said if I didn't believe him I could read the label myself. In other situations I always believed everything I read, he said. Of course I didn't believe a word; it was obvious his natural woman had left her natural moisturizer in his bathroom.

"And where's your silver glitter?" I asked.

"Don't get worked up. Stress is bad for the complexion," Albert said.

To calm me down, he offered me a glass of clear schnapps, and then I drove home. The way I looked, I'd even been embarrassed to have Albert see me.

On Thursday I was the first patient at the dermatologist's on the corner. I was already sitting in the waiting room by a quarter past seven. I'd hardly slept; again and again I'd reached for my hand mirror and counted the pimples. There were more and more of them, and now they were on my neck, too. By eight the waiting room was jammed, but the doctor didn't get there till a quarter to nine. He was somewhat older, ditto his office decor, and even the waiting-room magazines had been around the block a few times. Even though I'd gotten there first, three people who'd come later got in ahead of me—private patients, obviously. But since the private patients were clearly sicker than the other people in the waiting room, I didn't mind them getting preferential treatment. At nine-thirty my turn finally came.

"What's the problem?" the doctor asked.

"That's what I wanted to ask you."

"It looks relatively unspecific," he said. "I've never seen anything like it."

I was startled. Even though I usually take pride in being an unusual woman, in this case I would have honestly preferred to have something completely run-of-the-mill. But though the doctor said he'd never seen anything like my pimples, he didn't give them a closer inspection, just said he'd prescribe antibiotics, and then we could see what happened. I asked how long it would take for the pimples to disappear. He said he couldn't say. Then he asked what insurance I had. I told him I was on the student health plan. He said that was too bad, he could undertake a very promising course of treatment, but unfortunately it wasn't covered. Tears came to my eyes. "If you only knew what's at stake."

"Now don't let it get you down, Fräulein," he said kindly. "We can undertake this treatment for you, too, so long as you pay for it yourself."

"Thank you," I said, happy to be offered new hope.

He said he'd start with twenty injections of a new medication that had already achieved remarkable results with nonspecific symptoms. He now looked at my pimples a little more closely and said, "In your case there probably won't even be any scars when the inflammation has been eliminated by the treatment."

I tried to smile bravely, and asked what this was going to cost. He'd charge fifty marks an injection, he said. I calculated: twenty shots at fifty marks a pop made a thousand marks. All sorts of thoughts went through my mind at once. Would my mother lend me the money? I could work again during vacation and pay her back. I asked the doctor when I would have to come up with the money.

He said that for therapeutic and accounting reasons I had to pay before the treatment began, and he thought he could say that after ten shots I'd already see a marked improvement. Then he explained that I'd get an injection every day, because since I was paying for my own treatment I'd enjoy private patient status, and he had office hours for private patients on Wednesdays and Fridays as well. And I wouldn't have to wait; the receptionist could give me the injections. And the sooner we began the treatment, the better the healing would be. "And we'd don't want to leave any scars," he said at the end of this speech. No, anything but that!

I couldn't wait till after six to ask my mother about the money, and in this situation the few extra marks it would cost to call at the daytime rate didn't really matter. But my mother wasn't home. So I tried my aunt's, but no one answered there either.

So I had Albert paged at the hospital and told him what the dermatologist had said. Why hadn't I asked what kind of injections he wanted to give me? I couldn't let him give me just any old injections for a thousand marks! Was I nuts? I should go to the dermatology clinic at the university hospital. Then he said he'd try to find a colleague with some expertise, and he'd call me back.

Which he didn't do till evening. Then he said his colleague also advised me to go to the university clinic before I got into pricey private treatment. I didn't know what to do. It was certainly better to get a second opinion. But I couldn't go to the university clinic till Tuesday. On the other hand, the dermatologist on the corner might be one of those hyenas who lurk in their stinky little caves waiting for innocent victims. A thousand marks—that was serious money. On the other hand, by Tuesday it might be too late. I couldn't make up my mind. Finally I decided not to call my mother about the money yet—she would just get upset and then give me a lecture about smoking.

At least the pimples didn't get any worse on Friday and Saturday—or were they just getting sneakier? Going deeper under the skin, so as to leave even deeper scars later on? I stood in front of the mirror for hours and observed their development. They still weren't squeezable. But I could clearly feel the bumps under the skin. I called up Juliet and Birgit.

Both of them said they'd had pimples before. Neither of them wanted to, or could, feel for me in what I was going through. Juliet recommended a dermatologist who'd cured bad acne in a colleague of hers, and Birgit thought I should use exclusively natural cosmetics. I almost said I'd come by to prove to them that my pimples were worse than any pimples they'd ever seen. But the way I looked, I was ashamed to show my face. I didn't tell Juliet that this illness had screwed up my date with Gottfried. She didn't ask about him, and I didn't want to talk to her about him—she'd just have laughed at me. Instead I had to hear how she was looking forward to summer vacation, that a week from Friday she was going to go see her father and her stepmother, and then probably go to Italy.

Then we talked about how the summer always helps clear up skin conditions. Maybe the sun would heal me. Oh, summer vacation! The semester break came at the beginning of August. I hadn't even thought about what to do. Last year I'd gone to Brittany with Albert—at the time we hadn't really begun to fight yet. I didn't like to think about it. Until then I'd repressed any thoughts of summer vacation because I had no one I wanted to travel with, and traveling alone isn't any fun. But now everything was different. Being sick this way, I might just as well forget it. With these pimples, would I even be able to find a summer job to pay for the treatment? People went pale when they saw me. Juliet asked whether we could maybe see each other next week, but in the same breath she said she hardly had time, she still had so many things to take care of before she went away. And I said I didn't know how my illness would develop, and with the pimples I couldn't possibly go anywhere. At least she gave me a sympathetic "Get well soon," and promised to send me a postcard.

That evening Birgit called. I'd just been trying to cover my diseased face with powder, so as to be able to stand looking at myself in the mirror, but it was hopeless. Birgit was all excited: "The man from the ad called."

I forgot my pimples.

He'd said he was happy to have gotten her reply, and he absolutely wanted to meet her, except that this week and next he was totally tied up with business, unfortunately at night, too, but the week after that he absolutely wanted to meet her, and she should please be patient with him, please, he said. Juliet had said she should be very careful, and if Juliet was already gone when the rendezvous took place, she should on no account meet this man in her apartment, and certainly not in his, but rather in a bar or some other public place.

The problem was, Birgit said, that week after next she didn't have any time, because she had to go visit on her cousin Marion's birthday—that had only occurred to her afterward, and she didn't know what to do. She'd forgotten to ask the man for his number. Juliet had also said that was stupid of her, because now she had to wait around till he called back.

"Just look up the number in the phone book, call him, and tell him you don't have time week after next, it's as simple as that," I said; Birgit's jabbering was getting to be too much for me, and besides I'd remembered my pimples.

Birgit explained she couldn't call the man—his name was Karl-Heinz Müller, Karl-Heinz with a hyphen, and there were three columns of Karl-Heinz Müllers in the phone book: she couldn't call every single one. And Juliet had said that with a name like that you had to be very careful—it could be a phony! "Juliet thought at first it might be her old friend Karl-Heinz who'd put the ad in—his last name's Müller, too, but it couldn't be him, he's forty-one, and the ad said 'early thirties.' Besides, the ad said the man played golf, and Juliet said her Karl-Heinz doesn't play golf."

"First Juliet tells you to write, and then she tries to scare you," I said. I thought Juliet's warnings about men were superfluous.

"Yes, and besides, she said I should respond to another ad right away, just in case! But I won't do that!" Birgit said with determination. "If it doesn't work out with this man, I'm never answering an ad again."

Well, that didn't sound right to me, so I told Birgit she shouldn't pin all her hopes on this one guy, because there were always plenty of spares around.

"All I can do is wait," Birgit said.

"What does he do, that he has so little time? He might even be married."

Of course Birgit hadn't asked what he did, but she was convinced he wasn't married. "No, he can't be," she said, "the ad was so sincere." Then she went on and on about what she should wear for the date. I didn't feel like listening to all that, and my pimples were starting to itch furiously again. So I told Birgit that what she wore depended on the weather, and she just had to wait and see. Birgit recommended that I put camomile compresses on my face—camomile was natural, it worked on all kinds of inflammations. I should dip a towel in hot water, then dribble camomile drops on it, put the wet towel over my face, and put a dry towel over that to keep in the heat. I happened to have camomile drops on hand. I made compresses till I'd almost suffocated. Then I fell asleep.

When I looked in the mirror on Sunday morning, I couldn't believe my eyes. All the pimples were gone. Gone. Overnight! Okay, I looked troubled and tired, but I was pimple-free. Even in the magnifying mirror there wasn't a single one to be seen.

I called up Albert and reported that the danger was past. I asked him whether it had been the camomile; he didn't know, but he was glad. Grateful for his advice and happy that I'd saved a thousand marks, I invited him to lunch at the Bistro, but he said he had to be at the hospital in the afternoon, and he already had a commitment for the evening. I was so happy that it didn't even bother me. Birgit said camomile always helped, and Juliet had gone for a walk with a male friend, but she'd give her the message that I was cured. And she was thinking that she might possibly wear her beige cotton dress with the white batiste collar for the meeting with Herr Müller.

I also called up my mother to inform her of the danger her only child had been in, but of course she said that it all came of smoking. And when was I coming to see them? And my father

was working at the allotment garden and had to get his trees
sprayed, and I had vacation soon and should come and help
install the new fence; my father's slipped disk had been acting
up so much lately. I said I had to work during vacation, and I
was upset that not even my own mother thought my mysterious
and dangerous illness worthy of a longer discussion. But that's
how it always is: when you've survived a crisis, nobody wants to
hear about it.

During the three days leading up to Gottfried's seminar, I
took it real easy, to make sure my skin didn't break out again.
I was in luck. On Wednesday morning I called up Gottfried at
home, said I was well again, and asked whether our meeting that
evening was still on. "But of course," he said.

The weather was spectacularly beautiful, and I was, too. I'd
been through a bad time and was enjoying my renewed sense of
life very consciously. I took the subway to the seminar, so as not
to be burdened with my car.

Gottfried had already thought about where we could go: we
drove in his Mercedes to a wonderful café with a garden. I'd
never been there before. He was endlessly charming. We ate
sautéed liver with fried potatoes and drank red wine. It didn't
get dark till almost nine, and then the garden was lit up with
millions of tiny red, yellow, and blue lights.

"Isn't it unrealistic," Gottfried said, "that only kitschy things
are truly romantic?"

Yes, it was unrealistic.

"Would you like to come to my place for coffee? I live right
near here—only two hundred yards away."

"I'd like that." I was only two hundred yards from my goal.

53 Gottfried's apartment was fantastic. So many books! And political posters and lithographs by famous artists everywhere. Even a litho by Picasso, signed and numbered! And all of them, even the political posters, were framed in polished aluminum with nonreflecting glass. It was more than an apartment—it was a nonbourgeois ambience.

Gottfried went to his designer stereo and asked what I wanted to hear: "Joan Baez or Bach?" I let him decide. He asked if I liked jazz. He had something really hot, Mozart's *Magic Flute* in an interpretation by Louis Armstrong, with Mahalia Jackson as the Queen of the Night; the recording was a parody of bourgeois cultural philistinism. Unfortunately he couldn't find the album and put on Bob Dylan instead.

He got out two glasses and opened a bottle of red wine. We sat down on his sofa—natural wood with natural-colored linen cushions. Gottfried picked up the journal of film criticism lying on the natural wood coffee table and showed me an article of his that had appeared in it. The journal was two years old and pretty dog-eared, but the theses he'd put forward then were becoming more relevant by the day, he explained, and in this article he'd argued that confronting the needs of the masses didn't result in conformity to the masses but, on the contrary, was the prerequisite for establishing a distinction between oneself and the underprivileged. Only as an elite could intellectuals fulfill their proper function of transcending mass taste. And only if a critical, nonbourgeois film theory and the corresponding practice succeeded in transcending mass taste could they withstand attacks on true culture by upwardly mobile cultural philistines. "We intellectuals can no longer ignore the working class's mute appeal that we declare ourselves the representatives of their interests and accept that role," Gottfried pointed out.

I was filled with admiration. How intellectual he was! "Exactly," I said. "The people are dumb; they need someone to tell them what's right for them, they want a führer figure. . . ."

"I wouldn't express it that drastically," Gottfried said, "but it's not permissible to close one's eyes to this problem any longer."

I pointed to a particularly interesting passage in Gottfried's essay, about "communication transfer," how culture could be conveyed to the underprivileged masses by way of a critical nonbourgeois theory and practice of film, and asked Gottfried to explain to me more precisely his notion of "enhancement of the transparency of antagonistic cultural sensibility," but he smiled and said, "Let's forget these societal problems of ours for a while." He looked right into my eyes and said, "Constance. What a pretty name. How did your parents get the idea of naming you Constance?"

I took a deep breath. Gottfried Schachtschnabel was not to know how superficial my mother was. "My father worshiped Mozart," I breathed.

"Mozart?"

"Constanze, that was the name of Mozart's wife," I breathed. Gottfried nodded understanding. "How lovely."

"Um," was all I said. Well done. Gottfried was impressed.

"If you'd been a boy, your father would have called you Amadeus," he said.

Gottfried didn't know my father! Amadeus—right! Maybe Wolfgang. My father didn't give a hoot about Mozart. But Gottfried didn't need to know that. Let him take me for an intellectual equal. Therefore I just said, with great restraint, "Um."

Gottfried leaned back on the sofa, took my hand, and said, "What lovely fingernails you have."

My heart was in my throat, my head began to spin. I had to go to the bathroom and redo my lipstick. When I got back, Gottfried had turned out the ceiling light and lit a candle. Aha.

We'd been sitting close together on the sofa, but it wouldn't have been proper to sit down in the middle again, especially since Gottfried had edged a bit back toward his side, so I edged a bit back toward my side. Now the space between us was free. Across this distance I gave Gottfried a hundred-watt smile.

"I don't know if I should say this . . ." Gottfried said awkwardly.

"Yes?" I said, breathing in.

"It irritates me when you smile at me that way."

"Why?" I smiled, breathing in.

"You've got lipstick on your teeth," he said.

Shit! I wanted to crawl under the flokati rug. I wiped off my teeth. Even in the dark a blind man could have seen me blush. "Come on, it's not that bad," Gottfried said, gently laying his hand on my shoulder. "Basically I think it's very appropriate when women make themselves beautiful for men."

He was so understanding. The candle flickered. Gottfried moved closer to me. Would he kiss me first? Should I kiss him? That wasn't the question. Between us there were no tactics, no calculations. The phone rang.

Gottfried jumped. "I'm not answering it, not now," he said.

I wasn't really irritated that someone was calling him at twelve-thirty at night—you called unconventional people at unconventional times—but phones were ringing everywhere, not just next to the sofa, but also in the next room, where his bed was and the TV, and also in the back room, where he had his desk and bookshelves.

"Extra plugs," Gottfried said. "Very handy." He reached for my hand and put it to his lips. The phones rang. He put his hand on my left knee and slid his index finger from my knee to the middle of my thigh. I wasn't wearing stockings or a slip. The phones rang. I ran my hand through his hair. The phones rang.

"So . . . " Gottfried said, fiddling with one of my blouse buttons.

"Yes," I whispered.

"So, are you on the pill?"

I blushed again. "Of course."

The phones had stopped ringing. Gottfried went to the stereo, switched it off. "So, isn't it a little uncomfortable here?" he said, without turning around.

Somehow he'd taken me by the hand, and then somehow we were on his bed, in the dark. The phone next to the bed rang twice, then stopped, but before the echo of the other two phones had died away, it rang again.

"Hi, I have company," Gottfried said very curtly into the receiver. I must say I couldn't suppress a smile of triumph. I sat up a little in the Conran's bedding and stole a look at him from the side. It was so dark I could see only his silhouette. Suddenly his head sank to his chest.

"Oh, my God," he groaned.

Oh, my God, was he having a heart attack?

"How long have you known?" Gottfried groaned. "Oh, my God. Of course. Right away."

He put down the receiver and turned on the light. I was amazed: he looked a lot older suddenly.

"My wife is pregnant," he said.

I bit my lip. "So what do we do now?"

"We have to talk about what we do now. I'm going over there right away." He jumped up and pulled on his tennis shoes. I did the same, without saying anything.

We sped off toward Kreuzberg. At each light Gottfried groaned softly.

"Are you the father?" I asked cautiously.

"Are you crazy? Whatever gave you that idea?" he exclaimed in horror. "My wife and I've had a partnerlike relationship without possessive claims on one another for ages! Inge's with this guy from the Building Department. She just told me he said he wouldn't get a divorce just because she's pregnant, and besides, he couldn't afford to be saddled with a child! Can you imagine?" Gottfried shook his head bitterly. "This man earns three times what I do—net."

I nodded understandingly. Gottfried said with a deep sigh, "Maybe I'll adopt it." After some thought he added, "Though I'd wait till Inge redefined her relationship to me."

"Yes," I said understandingly, and wondered what he meant by that.

Gottfried remained silent till we got to the next light, then he said, "Actually, I always thought I'd like to have a child—it doesn't have to be my own; if I brought it up, it could amount to something. It's our environment that makes us what we are." This made him smile, but then he groaned again. "When I think of the difficulties of adopting a child! Gruesome. It must be gruesome, all the questions you have to subject yourself to. This whole bureaucratic adoption crap is so inhumane!"

Oh, how glad I was that I could comfort Gottfried at least on this point. "You don't have to adopt it," I said, and looked at him encouragingly. "You're married—you're automatically the father."

"But I'm not the father, don't you get that?" Gottfried said irritably.

"Doesn't matter; you're still the father in the eyes of the law." I told Gottfried I was absolutely sure of that, because recently a quite pregnant woman in our women's seminar had explained it to us in detail. "The law proceeds on the assumption that a child born during a marriage is legitimate, I'm absolutely certain."

"Oh, God!" Gottfried exclaimed. "I'm going to get a divorce! I'm not going to let some guy from the Building Department lay his egg in my nest! He's building himself a bungalow, and I'm paying for his pleasure! But he can count me out!"

"But if you get divorced, it's still your legitimate child. When a child is born up to three hundred and two days after a divorce, the law still automatically regards the ex-husband as the father."

"Why's that?"

"The bourgeois legal system assumes that a child conceived during a marriage has the husband as its father." I remembered it all so accurately because at first I hadn't grasped why the constitution stipulated 302 days, but that's the longest possible time a child takes to be born. "Even if you beget the child two hours before the divorce and it's born ten months after the divorce, you're still the father—provided the woman doesn't remarry in the meantime. Then the next husband's the father."

"But he's married himself! He sleeps around with my wife even though he's married! That irresponsible pig!" Gottfried snarled through clenched teeth.

"You can deny paternity. Even if the real father has the same blood type as you, after two years they can tell that you aren't the father. And then you can get the guy to pay back all the support payments you've made. Provided your wife admits that he could be the father."

Gottfried was zipping along at a hundred miles an hour, holding his hand over his eyes and groaning, "Oh, my God! Oh, my God!" Then he groaned, "Just imagine what people would say if I denied paternity! My esteemed colleagues would have a field day. And I don't have tenure. Oh God." He was a mess. I begged him not to drive so fast, or at least to take his hand away from his eyes. "And I have to go on paying for that asshole!" He groaned again. "How I hate these bourgeois constraints." And I knew he wasn't just saying that. Even before I'd shut the door of his Mercedes properly, he was racing off to his pregnant wife.

54

It was two in the morning when I got home, and I bet Gottfried got to bed much, much later—the poor man, what he had to go through! So I waited till late afternoon before calling him. "I'm completely done in," he said. "Inge's boyfriend doesn't want the child. She was hoping so much he'd get a divorce, but yesterday he told her no, just as cold as can be. Inge's at the end of her rope. How can he leave her dangling at a time like this? He said if Inge had the child he'd never see her again, because if his wife found out about it, she'd sue for a divorce and he'd be ruined. That was the worst blow for Inge. Of course she assumed all along that Mr. Building Department had arranged for separation of property with his wife, but he hasn't—which means he'd have to sell everything to pay off his wife. There's nothing to be done: Inge has to have an abortion." Then he said pleadingly, "Please, Constance, don't tell anyone; you know what would happen if my colleagues heard about it." He fell silent, exhausted.

"Abortion," I said, and that was all—I didn't have to assure him I wouldn't tell a soul; Gottfried could count on me.

"We're going to Holland. Inge has the address of a clinic there where they do natural abortions, and the partner's allowed to be there. See, an abortion's an incredibly important shared experience."

"You're going along? But you're not the father!"

"No one's supposed to know it's his, and if people assume the fetus is mine and I let my wife go for an abortion by herself, how am I going to look?" Then Gottfried calmed down some. "But we're not going till next Thursday; there wasn't a double room available at the clinic till then. See, they only do it on an inpatient basis, and the partner spends the night in the same room as the embryo mother and makes sure that everything takes a completely natural course." Gottfried sighed, but it was a sigh of relief that in the foreseeable future all this would be over. "I'll see you before we go," he said then.

"Where?" I asked.

"In class, on Wednesday," Gottfried said.

"Oh, yes, of course," I said, and didn't dare to ask what he had planned for the weekend.

I would have loved to tell Juliet all about it, but if Gottfried didn't want anyone to know that his wife was pregnant by another man, Juliet certainly shouldn't. That would be a breach of trust on my part. . . . I wondered how I could get the information across to her in the abstract—as something that had happened to friends of mine—but if she talked about it in purely theoretical terms, Juliet would be certain to say that if a wife was having a child by another woman's husband, and had an abortion because the other woman's husband wanted to keep it a secret from his wife, and the wife who was having the child by the other woman's husband went for the abortion with her own husband because the other woman's husband didn't have time, then in that case the husband's lover—which meant me—shouldn't get her hopes up. I wondered whether Juliet could use Gottfried's behavior as proof of her assertion that the stability of the institution of marriage was the basis of happiness. After much thought, I came to the conclusion that it was impossible to discuss the problem in an appropriate fashion with someone who wasn't involved. You really had to know the special circumstances to understand that basically Inge was to blame for everything. If she hadn't gotten pregnant, Gottfried wouldn't have all this aggravation.

Nevertheless I called Juliet Sunday afternoon. Maybe I could bring the conversation around to my problems. Subtly, of course.

"Oh, Goddess," Juliet exclaimed when she heard my voice, "you wouldn't believe what stupid games life plays. Last night Birgit met that super-sincere man who put in that super-sincere ad, and who did it turn out to be? Karl-Heinz Müller!"

"Your Karl-Heinz Müller?"

"My Karl-Heinz Müller! At least now I know how he gets to meet all those women."

"That old pig puts personals in the paper!" I yelled. "And he calls himself sincere!"

"Misogynists are always fixated on women. He just defines his hatred as honesty," Juliet said.

It pissed me off that Juliet was defending her Karl-Heinz again, but I just asked whether Birgit had hopped into bed with Karl-Heinz, too, the first evening.

"No."

"Well what, then?"

"I wasn't there. All I know is what Birgit told me. . . . She'd arranged to meet him at the Bistro, and she said she was terribly startled when she realized that the man at the table in the back on the left—that was the meeting place they'd arranged—was the Karl-Heinz she'd seen twice at my place. But then she was actually happy that it was this Karl-Heinz, because she knew him already and thought he was nice. But it was sneaky of him—of course he'd realized right away that she was my friend; he could tell by the address. He wanted to surprise her, he claimed."

"And then?"

"Birgit said he just criticized her nonstop." Juliet sighed. "Karl-Heinz is getting worse and worse. I've known him for ages, but the time has come when I'm going to have to tell him he's getting on my nerves. It's always hard when you've known a person a long time and then have to recognize that you have nothing left in common but your memories."

I was secretly glad that Juliet had realized that her Karl-Heinz was a stinking old chauvinist. But I merely asked, "And what else did Birgit say?"

"Well, she'd never respond to an ad again, is what she said. And I must admit I've come around to thinking that it's pointless in her case: she'll throw herself at anyone who comes along, just so she can get married. It's probably better for her to wait till someday a man comes along who's dazzled by her blond hair, and in return she'll love him forever, and he'll love her as long as he's dazzled by her blond hair. He'll turn up in no time, wait and see."

I was secretly amazed at how often this psychologist changed her mind, but again I didn't say so. "What else did Birgit say?"

"Ask her yourself when she gets back. She's at her sister's, giving her the blow-by-blow. I'm sure she'll be glad to give you one, too. I'm sure I'll get an earful before I leave on Friday."

Ah, yes, Juliet was leaving, I'd almost forgotten. "When are you leaving?" I asked.

"Well, on Friday I'm going to see my father and his wifette, and I'll have to listen to her whining about him grumbling, and him grumbling about her whining, and if I survive that, I may go to Italy for a good rest."

"Alone?"

"I don't know yet whether the Italy part will work out. But if it does, I'll certainly send you a postcard, like I promised."

"Oh, good," I said, because I loved to get postcards. A postcard meant someone was thinking of me, that I was loved and respected. For that reason I loved and respected postcards—although of course it was bourgeois to write postcards. On the other hand, you had to write postcards, because people only sent you postcards if you sent them postcards, so I always sent postcards to everyone who sent me one, and I always wrote that I thought sending postcards was dumb. Also, I only bought kitschy cards.

Juliet instructed me again to look out for Birgit. I felt somewhat flattered that she considered me more reliable than Birgit. But mainly I found Juliet pretty old-maidish with her constant instructions and preaching. I wondered whether she'd behaved that way toward Gottfried. I felt so sorry for the poor man.

I wished Juliet a nice vacation, and after I hung up I was glad I'd controlled myself and not brought up the subject of Gottfried in any way, shape, or form. When you're talking to a psychologist, you have to guard against subconscious revelations, so it was better not to talk about certain subjects at all.

So as not to be thinking about Gottfried constantly, I decided on Monday afternoon I would go visit Birgit in her municipal library. Since she hadn't called me, I simply went to see her—I must admit I was curious to hear what had happened with Karl-Heinz. Amazing, the experiences you can have when you respond to a personal, I kept thinking. And the fact that the dreamboats in the ads were actually Karl-Heinz Müller made me think—though I'm not sure what.

Since Birgit knew I was interested in books, I hoped she wouldn't guess I was as nosy as I actually was. I asked one of the librarians at the circulation desk where I could find her.

"Fräulein Döpp is downstairs in the children's section," the librarian whispered.

Birgit was sitting at a desk making little checks in a magazine with all the TV listings. "Oh, hi," she whispered to me.

"You had your meeting with Karl-Heinz! How was it?" I exclaimed.

"Shhhh, not so loud!" Birgit whispered.

I looked around. "There's nobody here."

"Still," Birgit whispered, "you're not supposed to talk loud here; the international library regulations apply to municipal libraries as well."

"I see," I whispered. "So tell me, how was it?"

"I'm sure Juliet already told you everything," Birgit whispered.

"She didn't tell me a thing, just that it was her Karl-Heinz Müller. Wild!" I whispered, so softly that actually only the movement of my lips could be heard. "But remember how Juliet said it couldn't possibly be her Karl-Heinz, because he's much older than it said in the ad."

"He told me that was a typo—instead of 'early forties' they'd printed 'early thirties' by mistake—but since he didn't look any older than the early thirties it didn't bother him," Birgit whispered.

"A typo? Oh, definitely. What else did he say?" I whispered.

"That I didn't look as good as in my picture. And that at my age I must be worried about becoming a spinster and that it was high time I found the right man."

"That's what he said?" I hissed. "He's a fine one to talk!"

"He said he was absolutely honest, and beige didn't suit me, and my hair would look better if I wore it longer. And he asked if I wanted to wither up as a librarian—books weren't good company for a woman, and he'd never marry one of those intellectualized women because they were no good in a marriage, but I told him I wasn't a librarian but a library employee—"

"Did he at least pick up the tab?" I asked. I was thinking of how the last time I'd seen him with Juliet he'd acted as though he was buying me a drink, but then he'd only paid for his own.

"No, when we were leaving and had to pay, he asked me whether I was liberated, and I said I wasn't liberated, and he said a little liberation wouldn't hurt. And then he said he thought it was undignified when women sold themselves. So I paid for both of us. He also mentioned how expensive the ad had been."

"And what else did he say?"

"Oh, he said he doesn't play golf. He drives a VW Golf."

"*What?*"

"Hush! He said it wasn't clear to him how anyone with a brain could interpret it any differently, but you and Juliet thought he played golf, too, right?"

"Of course! No one with a brain writes 'golf' in an ad and means a car!"

"But maybe they do, you see it quite often in ads," Birgit said, making an effort to see reason in the way men behaved.

"And what else did Mr. Wonderful say?"

"He said he often puts ads in the paper, and that hordes of the most fantastic women run after him, and he didn't need to be in any hurry to choose."

"But the ad said he wasn't interested in adventures," I said.

"He said he didn't want a woman who was involved with a lot of men—he values exclusivity. If he ever did marry, he'd only consider a virgin."

"He's lost his marbles!" I exclaimed indignantly.

"Hush!" Birgit hissed. "He interrogated me about my earlier boyfriends. It was like taking my high school finals. Then he said it was obvious that I'd had a hard time and had been frustrated with men. And then he said waiting wasn't doing anything for my looks—"

"Why didn't he tell you he was Juliet's friend the first time he called?"

"He said Juliet was at the age where she might misinterpret things, and he didn't want Juliet to know he put ads in the paper. He said he wanted to surprise her if possible."

"What did he mean, 'if possible'?"

"I didn't get a chance to ask. And I was so embarrassed

because the whole time he had his hand under my skirt, and the waitress kept looking at me funny." Birgit looked around to see whether anyone could hear our whispering. "Then he said he'd take me home—Juliet was away, after all. I told him Juliet wasn't leaving till Friday and that she'd certainly be delighted if the two of us popped in on her. At first he was taken aback and said he'd thought Juliet was leaving last Friday. Then he asked whether Juliet played mommy to me, and whether I absolutely had to report in, and of course I said I didn't have to . . ."

"And then?"

"Then he drove me home, and on the way I asked him whether he wanted children like I do, and I said I'd like to have children as soon as possible, and I told him about my sister's darling baby."

"And what did he say?"

"He said he didn't want to have children that soon, and he was tired and would rather go straight home."

"Did you make another date?"

"He said he had a lot to do in the next few weeks and if possible he'd call me again."

" 'If possible'? What's that supposed to mean?"

"How should I know!" Birgit hissed. "Anyway, there's nothing I can do but wait. Juliet said so herself yesterday."

"We'll go out together and pick up men," I whispered encouragingly.

"Absolutely not!" she exclaimed.

"Shhh," I hissed.

"Fräulein Döpp, we've been looking for you." A librarian suddenly materialized beside us. "Here, you have to look at this, now," she whispered, handing Birgit an open magazine. And suddenly there was another librarian, who asked Birgit agitatedly, "What do you think of that?" It was a photo essay on Princess Diana's last state visit. The topic under discussion was the princess's wardrobe, displayed on six double pages with the heading OUR READERS CHOOSE DIANA'S LOVELIEST OUTFIT. Because her colleagues were standing to Birgit's right and left, I could only see the pictures upside down. All of them were jabbering in whispers. The one who'd come first didn't think much of all those bows on the clothes—who was supposed to iron them? The other also found the simpler outfits more elegant, but thought that with her figure Diana could wear anything. Both of them were of the opinion that Diana looked under quite a bit of stress. Birgit said with the eye of an expert, "As a blonde, beige isn't very becoming to her."

No one was paying any attention to me, so I decided to exit. Birgit just said bye. I heard her explaining that Di would look better with longer hair.

I went up to the next floor, to the grown-up section. I'd planned to check out a book anyway, something stimulating for my screenplay—I was definitely going to work on it intensively during my summer vacation. There was a whole section of critical women's literature. I leafed through a few of the books—all first-person narratives by women who'd left their husbands and started a new life, instructions on how a woman could liberate herself. That didn't interest me—I'd been liberated like that for a long time, and after much pain and suffering I'd left my man; what I was interested in was how, as a liberated woman, you could put up with men. High up in the corner of a shelf I found an older book: *The School of Charm.* The photo on the title page fascinated me: it showed a woman with a radiant smile and an arched back falling backwards, intending somehow to drop into the coat that a man was holding for her. I looked at the photo for a long time and came to the conclusion that I wouldn't have the basic confidence to let myself fall backwards into uncertainty, supported only by the belief that somewhere a man would catch me with my coat. If that was charm, it was too risky for

me to be charming. I put the book back. Then it occurred to me
that I didn't have a card for this library, and I guessed that the
international library regulations would require a driver's license
and God knows what other I.D. before they let you borrow a
book; besides, I suddenly remembered that I still had some books
at home that I hadn't read yet. So I decided to go back downstairs to the children's section to chat with Birgit a bit more, but
Birgit and her colleagues had disappeared without a trace. I went
home and thought about her.

All the students were already there when Gottfried got to the
seminar half an hour late on Wednesday. We'd just decided to
leave. Gottfried apologized; he'd had his car in the shop; he was
setting out for Holland early next morning—he cleared his
throat—for a cinematographers' conference. It was a very work-
intensive conference, lasting until the beginning of August, so
next week the seminar would be canceled, and then it would be
summer vacation already, so we wouldn't see each other till next
semester.

"What a shame," I said involuntarily, but softly, and looked
at Gottfried in disappointment. He smiled happily.

Again I waited for him under the plane tree.

"How are you?" he asked happily.

"How about you?" I answered, and tried to smile likewise.
"Are you really going to a cinematographers' conference? I
thought . . ."

"You mustn't breathe a word of this, Constance. Of course
I'm going to the conference. We're going to combine the two
things. After all, I couldn't tell the department I was canceling
class because of . . . you know. Besides, it's very fortunate I'm
going to this conference. Of course it's being held in some
backwater where absolutely nothing else happens, but if I go the
department will pay my fare to Holland, plus expenses. And

afterwards we're going to Spain—Inge wants to take a vacation seminar on alternative forms of creativity. We'll be making pots, not out of potter's clay but out of mud that you don't have to fire but simply let dry in the sun, which is much more natural. Altogether mud is a much more natural material than clay."

"You're going on vacation with your wife?"

"We had incredibly long discussions about the impact it would have on our relationship if Inge and I went somewhere together, but then we simply said we wanted to experience it completely spontaneously."

I didn't say anything. I just gave Gottfried a hurt look. He must have noticed it, because he said, "You can't take such a narrow view; a person certainly has the right to go on vacation with his wife now and then."

"And when are you getting back?"

"I don't know—it all depends on what develops. Inge doesn't know either how long she wants to stay. I hope it all works out." Then he looked at me encouragingly and said, "Constance, I'll send you a postcard."

I waved to him as he drove away from the lot.

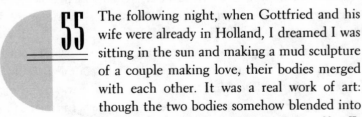

The following night, when Gottfried and his wife were already in Holland, I dreamed I was sitting in the sun and making a mud sculpture of a couple making love, their bodies merged with each other. It was a real work of art: though the two bodies somehow blended into each other, somehow they seemed free and somehow self-sufficient. I dreamed that I was just signing my work, scratching my name into the mud with a stick, when a woman grabbed my arm, tore my sculpture out of my hand, threw it on the ground, and stomped on it. Her naked foot landed right in the middle of it, separating my couple; where the breasts of the female figure had been was a hole made by the stomper's big toe. It looked as if the woman's heart had been stomped out of her body.

As suddenly as she'd come, the woman disappeared. I hadn't been able to see her face, but I knew who she was: Gottfried's wife! Bathed in sweat, I woke up. Oh, how profoundly symbolic!

I lay awake for a long time and thought. Strange, so many things had happened, and yet nothing had changed. It was already four and a half months since Albert had moved out, yet my hope that my life would take on new meaning hadn't been fulfilled. At least not yet.

What should I do till then? Read a good book? Another semester had passed and I wasn't really sure I'd learned anything. True, I'd collected experiences—but so what? It seemed pointless to wait for better times if you didn't know what you expected better times to bring. What my life lacked was an event of lasting significance. My life might just dribble away like the sand in an egg timer. A back and forth of insignificant nothings, and in the end everything was just like it was before. No, I wanted to think great thoughts, do great deeds, experience great things. Most people had the life goal of earning money. But when they finally had money, they didn't know what they wanted it for. They spent all their time worrying that they might lose it. Taking an around-the-world trip or building a house were recognized goals in life, but these goals also just came down to money. Making a film was actually my goal, but was that a goal for a lifetime? If so, it would have to be an extraordinary film—money again. And besides: one film wasn't enough for a lifetime. And if the first film flopped, would there be a chance to make a second? And if the second one wasn't a success either, that would be it. But even if the first film was a success, you'd have to worry that the second would be a failure. . . . Was the meaning of life simply that you knew what you had to worry about?

The best thing would be an event that changed everything from the ground up. Instantaneously. I thought about what that might be—an accident with lasting consequences, I thought spontaneously, that would change everything. Then your new goal in life would be to transcend the consequences, or if they couldn't be transcended, at least you'd know for sure from that point on that life didn't have any meaning. But an accident wouldn't be something you'd want to aim for. If I got married or had a child, that would be an event of lasting value, that would give my life new meaning—sure, but what kind of meaning? Was there nothing left for me besides resignation or waiting eternally for the revolution that would overthrow bourgeois property relations? Or was there something else worth waiting for?

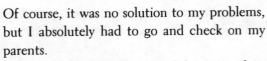

56 Of course, it was no solution to my problems, but I absolutely had to go and check on my parents.

Aside from the necessity of doing my duty as a daughter, it was a good time to get away.

On Monday and Tuesday I still had classes, but after that nothing else was going on—Gottfried had already left. The streets were practically empty—everyone was away on vacation. True, Albert was still around; I'd talked to him on the phone the day before yesterday, but we hadn't had anything to say to each other, had just exchanged notes on international cultural life. Apparently his needs were still being met by that Anna.

I arrived at my parents' on Wednesday evening. To annoy my father, I was wearing my pop T-shirt, the one where a woman was saying, "Men are all egotists," and another woman was saying, "Oh, Sister, they'll never learn from us women." Of course, my father thought my T-shirt was impossible.

He immediately launched into his favorite lecture; he obviously couldn't picture me as having any future but one of dependence on someone of his sex. I told him if that was his only worry I could always walk the streets. "But not in that T-shirt, child," my mother said. "You won't get very far with men in that."

What should I do? There was no point in trying to explain to my parents the role of woman in today's society. To make family life tolerable, I sewed myself a skirt on my mother's machine. I'd found the material in her linen closet, black with white polka dots, nothing special, but nice. My mother thought there was enough material for a dress, but that was too complicated for me, and besides, no one was wearing dresses anymore. But because my mother kept moaning about the wasted material, I went ahead and made myself a top with spaghetti straps to match the skirt. It had no darts, so it was easy to sew, and it looked cool. There was still a yard and a half of material left, and my mother the skinflint thought I could easily make a pretty blouse out of it, if I cared to go to the trouble. But no one was wearing pretty blouses anymore, and I told my mother if she cared to go to the trouble she could easily make a new cover for her umbrella with it. That finally shut her up, and she put the remnant away.

Then I dyed the sheets I'd brought home for my mother to wash. I'd been wanting to do it for a long time, but it's not allowed at Laundromats, because allegedly they have to clean out the machines afterward. I dyed two comforter covers and two pillows pink, then two sets of sheets fire engine red and two purple. Actually, I wanted to dye all the bedclothes in my trousseau, which my mother was hoarding for the great day, but my mother wouldn't hand them over. She said I wouldn't get them till I got married, and it was disgusting to dye bedclothes in the washing machine. The gaskets were totally discolored now, and who would ever get them clean?

My father got all worked up over the red sheets—what did I need those for? He was really like all men of his age: nothing but sex on his mind! But I didn't argue back, because we'd have had a blowup again.

Otherwise absolutely nothing was going on. One night I wanted to go to this club, the only one in L——, but when I saw the schoolkids hanging around outside the place, that was enough for me, and I went crawling back to the old folks, who were sitting glued to the TV. What would I have had in common with those wannabe Axl Roses and Madonnas? They had nothing on their minds but their acne, their math homework, and their motorcycles. Kid stuff.

Shopping was also impossible in that dump of a town—nothing met my standards. The only thing I bought was a really cheap silk remnant, turquoise-blue. Since I was in the swing of it, I made myself another skirt and another top with spaghetti straps. My father thought it was "very ladylike," and my mother said if I hadn't been too lazy to put in a zipper I could have made the top snugger, and it would have shown off my pretty figure to better advantage. I said if I started working the streets in the near future, I could always make it snugger, but for now I'd prefer to spend my time getting a tan, because with spaghetti straps you needed a tan, otherwise you could forget it.

After twelve days at my parents' I couldn't take it anymore. I'd helped my father put up his philistine garden-colony fence, my mother had sewed all the missing buttons onto my comforter covers, my Aunt Katharina had given me two more of her grandmother's old coffee cups, and my father had actually forked over some money. That would do for now.

Sunday morning I set out; I couldn't have stood another whole weekend in my father's garden colony. Besides, I'd told my mother that Friday was Albert's thirtieth birthday (which was true), that Albert had invited me over (which wasn't true, but it was quite possible he would), and that for Friday I had to bake a cake for Albert (which was a complete lie, but the kind that mothers like to hear). My mother gave me a jar of homemade jam for him. I'd thought a lot about a birthday present for Albert; I'd thought a lot about whether he even deserved one, and I'd decided to buy him that book on constructive ways to make your quarrels work for you. That was the right thing for him, with his total emotional block.

On the way home I gave intensive thought to the meaning this kind of family life had. My mother always said "my husband," and my father said "my wife," and I was "our child." Was it a question of possessing someone? I wasn't sure. The meaning of their lives seemed to consist in their belonging to someone, simply so they could hand over the responsibility for themselves to someone else.

As soon as I was back, I called Albert. He said he wouldn't be there for his birthday—he had to go to his parents' because his mother was ill again. Since Albert had become a doctor, his mother loved being ill. He was planning to set out very early on Thursday. But tomorrow he'd have time.

He invited me to a semi-snazzy restaurant that had just opened in his neighborhood. I'd wrapped the book on making your quarrels work for you in white glossy paper with a black ribbon around it—incredibly stylish and totally original! Along with it I gave him red roses. I was going to buy white ones, because that was more appropriate for our relationship, but then I figured Anna would be irate if she saw another woman had bought her Albert red roses. Haha. But I'd only bought ten. Thirty, for a thirtieth birthday, would have cost too much. Besides, we were just good friends now, and ten red roses would be plenty to ruin Albert's birthday for that Anna.

I got there a little late. At the last minute I'd taken off the turquoise silk top and skirt and decided to wear the black-and-white polka-dot ensemble—because it matched the wrapping paper better. Me in black and white, the book in black and white, my bright red lipstick matching the red roses, and then my gold stilettos—I looked like an ad for lipstick.

"Olala," Albert said in delight when he spotted me.

The red roses made him very happy. My mother's raspberry jam almost made him happier than the book. He asked what it was supposed to mean, especially the dedication I'd written inside: "That you may yet learn a little something in life is the wish of your old love, Constance." Since I myself hadn't really read the book and had bought it more for its subject matter, I said he'd understand when he read it, and that it was an important first step. Then we changed the subject.

He asked what plans I had for vacation. I said I didn't know yet and that I had to work on my screenplay. Albert said he was taking his vacation soon and maybe during it he'd finish his dissertation. Then I told him how my parents were and he told me how his parents were.

"How's your Anna?"

"Haven't the faintest; we're not seeing each other that much at the moment."

"Why not?"

"Dunno."

Aha, I thought. I didn't ask anything more about her. I could picture it: he'd had enough of her. Her time was up.

Then that special boredom set in that always sets in when each person would rather talk about something else but doesn't dare to. I couldn't tell Albert anything about my still-unfulfilled hopes for Gottfried Schachtschnabel. Albert's life didn't seem worth discussing, either. So for three hours we yakked about nothing. Awkward. We gave each other little pecks good-bye. I even said he should say hi to his parents for me, though I couldn't stand them. He sent greetings to my parents and special thanks to my mother for the jam. It had been a nice evening. We'd talked so harmoniously. Or noncommittally, you might say.

 I was dragging myself through the August heat to lay in a supply of canned goods when I ran into Sieglinde. She was coming home from her dentist's office, and said how lucky I was—she wished she had as much time as I did, and she was under terrible stress from the wedding preparations. Only yesterday she'd gone to the bank with Wolf-Dietrich to open a joint account, and she'd already had to sign her name "Lamar-Schadler." What a feeling! I suggested we go somewhere for ice cream. Sieglinde didn't want ice cream—she had to lose ten pounds before the wedding. So she just ordered an espresso, pulled a kitschy silver pillbox out of her bag, and put two little tablets of sweetener into her no-cal coffee.

The wedding date was definite: September 18. Still no mention of a party for their friends! Sieglinde only talked about the reception for family members and dignitaries. And she'd found a very elegant Jill Sanders suit, but Wolf-Dietrich thought it was too expensive, but maybe he would let her get it after all because the suit would be appropriate for all sorts of other occasions. Finally she inquired about me, and asked what I had planned for the summer. I shrugged suggestively.

"Albert's left on his trip already," Sieglinde said.

"He's back already—he was just at his parents' over the weekend."

"No, he's away on a trip."

"What do you mean, on a trip?" I asked, forgetting myself, and Sieglinde immediately realized her advantage. She put her hand on my arm and asked, with profound pity in her eyes, "So you don't know, you poor thing?"

At first I couldn't think what to say. Then I said, "I didn't realize you knew Albert was away."

No dice. Sieglinde knew I hadn't known; she smiled kindly. "He went with Anna. Anna wants to discover Austria."

That was too much. "You know Anna? Where from?"

"She was at our place just a little while ago," Sieglinde said, as if it were the most natural thing in the world that my ex-man should come to dinner at her house with some dietetic sour pickle.

"Has she had you over already?"

"Not exactly, but Anna copied down my recipe for grilled tartare à l'américain."

"You mean hamburger," I said slowly and scornfully, to put Sieglinde in her place.

"Albert loved it!" Sieglinde wouldn't yield an inch. I could have guessed that Sieglinde's and Wolf-Dietrich's friendship with an M.D. would survive my separation from him. Especially when his new woman also shared in the aura of this prestigious profession. Me she didn't invite over anymore. I wouldn't resurface till I had a new man to show off, and then my readmission to the lofty Lamar-Schadler circle would still depend on whether said new man had enough status. That was all perfectly clear; Sieglinde couldn't fool me.

Sieglinde was smiling smugly, like an anaconda with a litter of piglets in its gut. I stared at her, wondering what natural enemies she might have. A vulture? Nope, too weak to drag

Snake-Meat Sieglinde through the air and then smash her against a cliff. An elephant? No, an elephant would have to have terrific aim to crush her head on the first kick, before she could dig her fangs in. Would an alligator be a match for an anaconda? Iffy. But a poisonous spider! Probably there were small insects that could bring down these gigantic beasts. Crabs, for example. The thought that even the power of the Lamar-Schadler anaconda had its limits was immensely comforting.

"I was over at Albert's last week," I said, and lied: "He wanted to spend his birthday with me."

Sieglinde seemed to believe me. So I said, to make it sound like I knew everybody's secrets, "Albert had a big blowup with that Anna, and I'd be very much surprised if he was going on vacation with her."

"I'm positive they left the day before yesterday. In fact, I arranged for my boss to give Anna a special appointment on Tuesday morning. She needed a filling done on 1-4; otherwise she has excellent teeth." Sieglinde looked at me triumphantly and added, "Short-term differences of opinion occur in the best of relationships." Then she wanted to pay and leave.

It took me a few seconds to get over how well that Anna had wormed her way into my circle of acquaintances. But by the time the waiter came with our checks, I'd gotten a grip on myself. While he was standing right next to us, I put my hand on Sieglinde's arm and asked very loudly, "So how are your crabs?"

Sieglinde went red as a beet and mumbled, "I've never had crabs in my life."

"You poor thing, I know your Wolf-Dietrich didn't give you his crabs," I said even louder, and smiled like the Mona Lisa.

Pow! pow! Bang! bang! A tooth for a tooth. I hadn't done badly. But Sieglinde, the future tax consultant's wife, had won. Shit.

58 He'd been too chicken to tell me he was going away with that Anna.

Something had to be done. I called Gottfried Schachtschnabel in the middle of the night—as I'd feared, he wasn't back yet; he must still be off somewhere with his wife. At least Gottfried had been honest with me. But he hadn't kept his promise to send me a postcard yet. Every day I hoped, and every day I was disappointed; my fear grew that the Spanish sun, the Spanish wine, and the shared work with mud would solidify the marriage of Gottfried and Inge Schachtschnabel.

Something had to be done, immediately. "Love can be created"—that was what Juliet preached, right? My victim was a certain Joseph. His friends called him Joschi. True, he wasn't my type—too tall, too blond, too athletic, too young (only twenty-three)—and he was an electrician. "Technical employee of an international news organization" was what he was allowed to call himself, Joseph said, laughing. He wasn't my type, but he was nice; he treated women as equals. I'd seen him often at the Kaput. We'd said "Hi-how-are-you" a few times, and sat in nearby seats overhearing each others' conversations without consciously listening in, so I'd known him for a while, subconsciously, more or less. I also knew that blond Dagmar was always hovering around him, had been for quite a while; she adored him and blushed every time he came near her, but she didn't stand a chance with him. Life plays rough. He preferred women like me, and he was grateful when I responded to his advances.

Joschi's role was to be there while I waited for better times.

I had a guilty conscience because he loved me and I didn't love him. He was four years younger, so he automatically turned me into an older woman. "Whatever do you see in that old bag?" his pal Didi whispered to him one evening, meaning for me to hear. So what? Joseph's friends weren't my problem. My problem was my friends. Sieglinde was guaranteed to ask me what I saw in an electrician—as if I hadn't already asked myself.

But we didn't need to have any friends in common—we were an emergency alliance. I needed a regular lover as an alibi, so as to be able to remain liberated; after all, every schoolchild learns nowadays that all liberated women are frustrated. Why Joschi needed me, I didn't know. Maybe I was just his type. Our relationship worked only on the sexual level—if you accepted that, you didn't have to feel like a sex object. I was provided for, but ready to move on at a moment's notice.

This wasn't the first time I'd had a relationship like this. After Roland—the love of my youth, who lasted three years, till he got drafted, then went away to college, and the spatial separation brought emotional alienation—until I met Albert, I'd spent a year without a steady relationship. But in those days I was twenty-two, as old as Joschi was now, and the world was newer and variety was still the spice of life. Nowadays variety was a provisional solution.

In the first weeks of our liaison we met every day, sometimes at the Kaput, sometimes elsewhere. He often picked up the tab; he was generous with his money. We drank a lot and never quarreled—what would we have quarreled about? At night we went to his place or mine. He was really nice in bed. Sex: yes, even with a certain bashfulness, to distinguish the relationship from a one-night-stand; but loving kisses: no.

It was all uncomplicated when we were together, except that Joseph bored me, not a lot, but then more and more. And I was plagued by the fear that I might call him Albert by mistake. I didn't want to hurt him. And I wouldn't enjoy making comparisons with Albert, either, because Joschi just didn't measure up. But one day it slipped out: "You know, Alb—" I said to Joschi, and stopped in alarm, but he'd caught it, stared meaningfully into the distance, and didn't ask what I'd meant to say. It was embarrassing. There was no elegant way of bridging from Albert to something else. "You know, Alb . . . ania is politically an unknown quantity," I could have said, but that only occurred to me much later.

It was already the end of August when the promised card from Juliet arrived. It had a picture of two sheep kissing. I wondered what that was supposed to mean. Also I noticed that the card came from Ireland. Juliet wrote:

> Dear Constance,
> I hope things are going as well for you as for me. I'll be back next week and will call you immediately. I have a huge surprise for you!
> Keep well till then.
> Lots of love from Juliet.

I called Birgit. She'd gotten a card with Princess Di and the Queen Mother, also from Ireland, and with the same text. The huge surprise could hardly have anything to do with Gottfried Schachtschnabel, which was my first thought. But for sure some man was involved. Birgit also swore that Juliet had said she was maybe going to *Italy*. Well, I could wait till Juliet got back for the formal revelation of the secret. I figured that when she was home visiting her father she'd met someone who was going to Ireland and had invited her to come along. An old school friend, an old love from her youth, perhaps even her ex? Such spontaneous acts really only worked with men left over from earlier in your life. You couldn't fool me.

The next day a card arrived from Albert. From Austria. So Sieglinde had been right! This card showed a cow, so animal postcards seemed to be in. If I took a trip, I'd send him a card with a dachshund on it. Albert wrote:

> Dear Constance!!!
> This cow says Moo just for you!!!!!!
> It's very nice here. One hikes a lot and marvels at the Austrians. The weather is as dry as the wine. The book on constructive quarrels is also along and provides much occasion for laughter.
> Fondest greetings from Albert.

In each corner of the card he had written "MOO! MOO! MOO!"

That coward: "One hikes." Who was "one"? Anna, that nonperson? That cow. That evening I drank so much red wine I felt totally in love with Joseph.

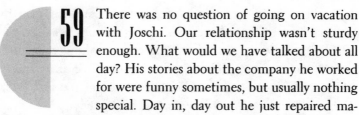

There was no question of going on vacation with Joschi. Our relationship wasn't sturdy enough. What would we have talked about all day? His stories about the company he worked for were funny sometimes, but usually nothing special. Day in, day out he just repaired machines; the only interesting thing about his job was his coworkers, who were a real pain; they'd drop a screwdriver into a machine on purpose, to make him work overtime, because as a salaried employee he didn't get paid extra.

My problem was how to spend the rest of the summer in some

meaningful way. I called up Jürgen to see if they needed any competition surveillance done. Jürgen said he hadn't the faintest idea, his own vacation started on Monday, but I should just drop by the agency and ask. He asked how I was doing, and I asked how he was doing, and since we were both fine, there wasn't much to say. So on Monday I dropped by the agency. I'd scrubbed my nails and washed my hair, and was hoping they'd ask me to stay then and there.

The personnel director remembered me perfectly. Yes, yes, I'd been a diligent worker. He didn't know if there was any competition surveillance to be done, but he'd go and ask right away. I had to wait three quarters of an hour in his office till he got back, with a distinct smell of alcohol on his breath. Yes, they might have something for me. But it was a fairly complicated assignment, so the creative director would come up and explain it to me personally.

A creative director! I got all excited. Not one but two men appeared, neither one much older than me. The creative director was called Herr Nickel. He was wearing a Lacoste polo shirt, Levi's, Adidas, a watch that you could see was a status symbol; he smoked Marlboros, and though his mustache wasn't brand-name, it looked as though it must have a Bureau of Standards number. Except for his hair color, the second man looked exactly the same, but he had on a watch that you could tell wasn't a status symbol. So the second one was clearly an underling, and the personnel director didn't call him by name, either.

Herr Nickel, the creative director, looked at me and said, "Good." Then he flopped down in one of the superchic leather chairs, gazed up at the ceiling, and said, "We need to marshal evidence in response to the charge that advertising is degrading to women." He looked at me and continued, "Recently there's been an organized campaign to discredit us. A study by some so-called women's research center has just appeared, and they assert that most advertising discriminates against women. They claim more than two-thirds of all the women in ads are portrayed in degrading poses or in sexist getups! Absolutely ridiculous, but if this keeps up it'll have a creativity-negative impact on our creativity. We have to come up with some proof!"

"Proof is what we have to come up with," said the personnel director, "to show that these accusations are complete fabrications."

"May I repeat my previous suggestion," the other man said, "that we examine a representative cross section of existing advertising so we have concrete numbers to prove that any so-called sexist advertising is merely a matter of an occasional slipup."

"Good," said Herr Nickel, the creative director.

"In accordance with my previous suggestion," No. 2 said, "we'll organize the advertising material from certain selected magazines according to the most commonly occurring female types: housewives, women in motherly roles, and women as so-called sex objects."

"Good," the creative director said. Then he said to the personnel director, "Does any other female type occur to you?"

The personnel director thought, but no other type occurred to him. Then he looked at me, so I said, "Working women."

"Good," said Herr Nickel, "let's establish another category: women as equal partners in the workplace."

"You have to organize the ads according to these types," No. 2 told me.

"But first you have to organize them according to product, because we always organize things according to product first," the personnel director said to No. 2.

"Of course," No. 2 said to the personnel director.

The creative director said to me, "Organize the ads according to product first."

"Of course," I said.

"And which advertising vehicles do you suggest?" No. 2 asked the personnel director.

He rubbed his chin, whereupon the creative director also felt called upon to check the quality of his shave. On the basis of a previous suggestion by No. 2, the gentlemen decided for the time being to analyze all the advertisements that had appeared during the previous year in various advertising vehicles. Advertising-vehicle-wise, they settled on a women's magazine that targeted "your typical lower-class woman" and a women's magazine for "your typical average woman" and a women's magazine for "your woman with upscale aspirations"—which meant, the personnel director explained to me, "your women who not only look at fashion pictures but occasionally even read a nice little article." The gentleman laughed heartily, but I didn't.

Besides, No. 2 remarked, it might be useful to include a family magazine, because of the many products advertised, and in addition a television magazine and perhaps a mass-audience magazine or two.

"Good," said the creative director. "Any other suggestions?"

"For the sake of objectivity we could also include *Der Spiegel*, so we'd have something typically male in the sample," No. 2 suggested.

I also made a suggestion: "For the sake of objectivity, maybe a girlie magazine too?"

The creative director shook his head. "We don't have any in the advertising-vehicle archive; that kind of thing disappears around here as soon as it comes in."

The gentlemen found that terribly amusing. They agreed that everything was clear now. I asked if I should cut out and paste the ads. No. 2 shook his head. For reasons of efficiency that wasn't necessary. I should just photocopy all the ads and on the back of each copy put an abbreviation for the title of the magazine and the issue number. Had I grasped that? And I could think up the title abbreviations myself.

"Good," said the creative director.

"This is a completely different project from competition surveillance," the personnel director said, shaking his index finger at me. The creative director's watch gave several sharp beeps. I looked at my watch; it was exactly twelve. "Time for lunch," the creative director said. No. 2 left with him.

The hardest part came when I was left alone with the personnel director. Because I was hoping that this new, entirely different project would bring in a lot of money, I asked what I'd be getting. Oh, ten marks an hour.

"That can't be right," I said. "I was making twelve in April."

"That can't be right," the personnel director said, astonished. "Competition surveillance is typical women's work, and we have very precise salary guidelines for temps." What could he do? he asked me. His hands were tied.

I asked in return whether he didn't have some unisex job for me. There was no such thing, he said; what was I thinking of? I said I had work experience. He said in this area it wasn't a question of experience but of speed. And I had to take into account the fact that this study wasn't being financed by someone who'd commissioned it, but was an image campaign for the German advertising industry, and the agency wouldn't get any money for it but on the contrary was paying me out of its own pocket, so as to finally have hard evidence. Finally he said he could give me fifty pfennigs more per hour, but that was the absolute maximum. He acted as if he was going to have to come up with those fifty pfennigs himself. That took the cake.

But I had no choice. I wouldn't have earned more anywhere else, and the job itself wasn't bad. Since I was getting less money, I promised myself to do less work. Honest. Besides, this study offered more interesting reading than those dumb insect journals.

But first I had to drag the magazines down from the attic to the so-called library. The secretary thought while I was at it I might as well take the old magazines from the library up to the attic. She went to the personnel director, and he backed her. What a job! My white jeans got grubby. I should have demanded a bonus for doing scutwork.

Not till Tuesday afternoon could I start on the actual project. But I still didn't get to sit down and read magazines; I spent ages at the copier, and then I really had problems organizing the stuff. On Friday afternoon No. 2 came over to the copier and asked how "our" women's research project was coming along. I showed him my organizational plan, with the ads divided by product and then subdivided by female types, fine-tuning the collection, so to speak. I showed him how many different products I'd found just for the letter *C:* Coffee, Camomile Extract, Cheese, Chips, Cat Food, Chewing Gum, Clothing, Clorox, Cooking Pots, Condensed Milk, Cosmetics, Chiropractors, Cancer Prevention, Credit, Cruises, Cookstoves, Commemorative Plates, Counseling Services.

I had lots of ads for cosmetics, but only one each for Camomile Extract, Commemorative Plates, and Condensed Milk.

No. 2 said, "This is idiotic."

I was thunderstruck. He'd said I should organize the ads by product. No. 2 told me to wait, and went off to get No. 1. Silently they looked over my heap of photocopied ads, from "Adding Machine" to "Zipper."

"That's much too complicated," No. 2 said.

The creative director didn't say anything.

"We need larger, universal categories, otherwise we'll never get done!" said No. 2.

The creative director glanced at his watch.

"She could put all comestibles and luxury items in one grouping," No. 2 said over my head to No. 1.

"Good," the creative director said to No. 2. To me he said, "Put everything edible together, and add all the beverages to that, and include all kinds of alcohol, and cigarettes, too. Have you got that?"

"Yes."

"And cars and spark plugs and motorcycles—all those go under 'Transportation,' " No. 2 explained.

"Good," said Herr Nickel. Then he asked me, "Do you know what investment instruments are?"

Before I could say no, No. 2 began to explain what investment instruments were: "That means expensive purchases that last a long time, such as homes, major electric appliances, money investments of all kinds, cars, real jewelry, machines, and the like."

"Shouldn't cars go under 'Transportation'?" I asked.

"Cars go under 'Transportation,' " the creative director said. "And cosmetics are also a separate category."

"Good," said No. 2.

The creative director's watch beeped. "Time for afternoon tea," he said. "Any other questions?"

"Where does Clorox go?"

Both of them thought about it. "Housewives' supplies," the creative director said.

No. 2 said, "You have to find organizing concepts. Try to think abstractly! If you're stumped, ask me."

"You can ask him any time," the creative director said, pointing to No. 2. Then they bustled off.

I spent the rest of the day switching the categories. I put the naked woman in the home sauna under investment instruments, the naked woman with the eternal diamond likewise; I created a category called "Medicine and Health," under which I arranged all the naked women advertising contraceptives, and the woman with nothing on but a corn pad. I could already tell that when I did the fine-tuning by female types, everything would come under sexist advertising.

Up to now I'd never given much thought to sexist advertising.

True, I'd seen millions of partly, half-, and entirely naked women in ads, but that kind of advertising didn't have any effect on me. So it didn't bother me. But there had to be a reason why advertising was so sexist—probably it had to do with sinister subliminal manipulation of lower-class women and lower-class men. Probably that was how the working class was manipulated into throwing its hard-earned money out the window for corn pads! But I'd work my tail off to unmask the practices of the ruling class! Yes, I would. Gottfried would be proud of me!

On Saturday afternoon Juliet called to say she was back. She'd gotten back yesterday, and she laughed when I asked why she'd been in Ireland instead of Italy, and what her big surprise was, and she said with a giggle that I could come over right away if I had time and felt in the mood. Since I didn't know how long I'd be at her place, I called up Joschi and told him I didn't have time to see him in the evening.

An hour later I was at Juliet's. Sitting on Juliet's sofa was a man, about thirty, medium height, medium weight, with smooth, pale blond hair. He was wearing gray checked trousers and a blue-and-white striped shirt that didn't go with the trousers.

"Hi, Constance, happy to meet you," he said, and even stood up to shake my hand. "I'm Jürgen Stöcklein."

Juliet looked at me expectantly, as if she assumed I'd break out in wild cheers or fall over dead from sheer surprise. But he was a man like any other.

"My new companion in this stage of life," Juliet said with possessive pride.

"Aha, you two were in Ireland together?"

"Right."

This Jürgen poured coffee for me, playing househusband, while Juliet adoringly eyeballed his technique. I asked how it had been in Ireland. Oh, fantastic. So many sheep. And everything so green. And the people just darling.

"How long have the two of you known each other?"

A great deal of giggling. "Since June twenty-ninth," Juliet said.

"Actually we've only known each other intimately since July fifth," Jürgen said.

I wasn't so interested in knowing the exact date, I thought, and looked down at the floor—I was certainly no prude, but there were more interesting topics in the world.

"I mean, we first met on July fifth," Jürgen said.

"Where did you meet?"

"I'm Box AZ 8314," Jürgen explained. Juliet giggled. "We sought and found each other by way of a personal."

"You answered a personal? Why didn't you tell me? When was this?"

"When we were talking Birgit into trying it again, I thought I should try it myself. Of course I wouldn't have answered just any ad, only yours." Juliet giggled at Jürgen.

"And what did he say in his ad?"

"Just a sec, let me fetch the document from my reliquary," Juliet said. She went into her bedroom and came back with a tiny newspaper clipping.

"Careful," she said, "this is a valuable memento."

I read: "Sociologist, 31, 5'8", with many interests (travel, culture), seeks not an unusual but a nice and understanding partner for a common future. Box AZ 8314."

I was fairly disappointed. "That's all?"

"You can't get any more successful than that!" Jürgen said.

"Now listen here," Juliet said, "it *is* unusual for a man to seek a nice and understanding partner instead of the usual super-dream-woman. And since Jürgen chose not to stipulate a maximum age, I wrote to him, even though I could almost be his mother." Much giggling. "See, I'm five months older than he is!"

I took a closer look at this Jürgen. He looked perfectly normal; nothing about him suggested he would put personals in the paper. "Why do you advertise?" I asked him straight out.

"I found my job through an ad, and my car, and my apartment . . . besides, I'm always putting in ads."

I guess I must have looked appalled. "Jürgen puts in help-wanteds," Juliet explained. "He's a personnel director."

"I thought: If you can seek and find something as important as your employment by advertising, why not your life's companion?" he added.

"We make a perfect team," Juliet said. "He tests adults, and I test schoolchildren."

"And Juliet's responsible for identifying the defects in the human psyche, and I'm responsible for identifying normal behavior."

"Jürgen says," Juliet exclaimed, "that my goal is understanding the problems of the behaviorally disturbed, while his goal is to define problems with the help of other normal human beings. That's what Jürgen said!"

The billing and cooing was getting on my nerves. "You'd known each other such a short time, and yet you decided to take a vacation together," I said, changing the subject.

"Childish folly," Juliet said.

"I followed Juliet, tore her away from her family, and dragged her off to Ireland."

"But you'd planned to go to Italy."

"I wanted to go to Italy, but Jürgen wanted to go to Scandinavia. So we agreed on a country in between the two. And when we got there, Jürgen admitted to me hadn't wanted to go to Scandinavia at all, but in fact to Ireland! He only said Scandinavia so the compromise would result in what he wanted anyway. Isn't that true, honey pie!" Juliet pulled her Jürgen's hair.

"Next time I'll have to come up with another scheme," he said.

"I've been warned," she said, and giggled again.

Oh, this mush-talk! We had another shot of Irish whiskey in

honor of the happy couple. I learned that when they had their
first "exploratory conversation," as Jürgen called it, they hadn't
much liked each other. "The first thing she asked me was
whether I was divorced already," Jürgen said.

"No, he wasn't divorced yet, he said. It took him a while to
admit he'd never been married! And he said he didn't want a
newly divorced woman, because the only thing women like that
did was mope over their former husbands. But then we worked
it out somehow."

I could see that. They were in love! They were the center of
the universe! It was more than I could take. I said good-bye.

I was glad I hadn't brought Joschi along. He would certainly
have been overwhelmed with respect for Juliet and this Jürgen.
"I didn't even go to an academic high school; how am I supposed
to talk to these intellectual types?" he'd said one time when I
told him about Gottfried Schachtschnabel. True, there was a
great gulf.

I called Joschi when I got home and told him I did have time
after all. As always, he was glad to put himself at my disposal.
Joschi didn't see anything special in the story of Juliet and
Jürgen. He had no sense of drama.

Every magazine is about half advertising. Whenever I'd copied all the ads in four issues—that came to four or five hundred
copies each time—I could sit down for a while and write title
abbreviations and issue numbers on the back. That was the only
part of the job where I could let my mind dwell on other things.
Mainly I wondered why other people—like Juliet, for example—
were always so lucky, while others—like me, for example—never
got their turn. Even Sieglinde would be reaching the pinnacle
of all her wishing and hoping next week. And Gottfried still
hadn't written.

But the alienated work of copying and sorting—alienated

work is when you have to do something you don't feel like doing, Gottfried once said—hardly gave me time to think. After I'd tossed out my dividers with all the different product types and arranged everything as desired in seven rough categories, I observed that simplifying made everything more complicated. The more ads I copied, the less I could tell them apart. What was the difference, say, between the blonde smiling at a tub of margarine and the one smiling at a man with snazzy shaving lotion and the one smiling because thanks to a computer she didn't have to work anymore? Once, after I'd put an ad in the cosmetics pile several times, I realized it was an ad for motor oil; I had to be more careful. To see what product was being advertised, I had to read the whole ad. Then I had to look through the corresponding category to see whether I'd already assigned a place to this product, and if I had, put the new ad there. After three days I realized that sorting was a lot easier if I went back to arranging the ads alphabetically according to product. But I didn't put in the dividers with the product types this time, in case they came to check up on me again.

Thursday I found a card from Albert in the mailbox. The card was from Vienna, and it had a photo of a Wiener schnitzel on it. Along with the schnitzel were French fries, and next to the plate a bottle of Coke. Tasteful. Albert wrote:

Dear Constance,
    The Austrian cultural heritage sends greetings, as do I.
                                            Eternally your
                                            Albert
    P.S. I'm having Sachertorte any second.

Oh, please. He was still trying to make it sound like he was alone. How stupid did he think I was? The whole next day, while I stood by the copier, I was wondering whether I shouldn't put a personal in the paper. But not as brief as Jürgen's, no way. If I did it, it had to be a really special ad, because I wanted to find a really special man. Even though it was ages till I could knock off for the day, by evening I still hadn't the slightest idea what to say in my ad.

To at least nudge my fate along, I went into a really elegant, really expensive lingerie boutique and bought myself a really elegant, really expensive silk slip. Much too expensive for my circumstances, but then, what was I working for? The slip was midnight blue, trimmed in ivory lace. It looked great under my dark blue blouse; when I left the top three buttons undone, you could see the lovely lace insert. Joschi also thought the lower part was fantastic.

On Saturday another postcard came from Albert. It had a drawing of a turtle, with huge tears dripping from its eyes, and above the turtle was a bubble with the words, "Sob! What can I do to get rid of my smooth, clear complexion? All the turtles but me have warts and pimples! Sob! Sob!"

Albert wrote:

> Dearest Constance,
> Of course I thought of you when I saw this card. I hope you're still cured.
> All the best! See you soon!! A little kiss in memory of old times!!!
> Your Albert

I was touched. It was nice of Albert to hope I was completely cured. Thank God the pimples hadn't popped up again. "A little kiss in memory of old times"—did he still love me? Or was he so in love with that Anna that he felt like hugging the whole world, with me just one among millions? That was more likely. "Let's not fool ourselves," I sighed, with my characteristic self-critical attitude.

"Everyone's happy but me," a voice whispered to me. Who was that? It was Envy.

That afternoon I quarreled with Joseph over something trivial. It got on my nerves the way he was always so accommodating. His behavior was almost obsequious. When I told him I didn't feel like going out with him that night because I wanted peace and quiet, he accepted his fate like a good boy and just asked when he should call me again. I said I'd call him. My wish was his command. How boring. So he'd go out with his buddies, he said, maybe bowling or just to the bar. "Have fun with your knuckleheads," was all I said. I couldn't stand his childish buddies, nor they me. All weekend I lay in bed feeling irritated: at Joschi—no fair, because basically he couldn't help it that he was nice but boring; at Albert—that cowardly tightwad; at Gottfried Schachtschnabel—who still hadn't written. But first and foremost I was irritated at the social circumstances my father's ideology had imposed on me: I was earning money, but except for that my life was meaningless.

In the third week I finally got everything copied and could begin fine-tuning the collection. No. 2 came and, "in order to prevent any misunderstandings," as he emphasized, dictated to me the female types I had to use for my main categories:

1. Housewives
2. Women in the Role of Mother
3. Woman as Equal Partner in the Workplace
4. Women as So-called Sex Objects

If I felt unsure which category something belonged to, I should keep such "ambiguous advertisements," as No. 2 said, separate under "Other Female Types."

As per instructions I began with "Housewives," hunting through the entire heap of "Housewives' Supplies" ads in search of housewives. What a surprise: I didn't find a single one. Household cleansers flitted through living rooms, swirled over kitchen floors, or whisked over windowpanes, but they did all that without a housewife's help. In fact, the ads said, they "worked like magic." If anybody cleaned, it was a tub-scrubbing elf or a detergent knight, a toilet giant or a toilet gnome. Or maybe a dishwasher general. These cleaning monsters, the captions said, would relieve the housewife of all her work. Obviously housewives were superfluous, so naturally they didn't appear in the ads. I looked for people working in the world of ads, but I found men, men, only men. The someone cooking was a man; the someone hanging wallpaper was a man; the someone jetting from meeting to meeting, mowing the grass, tending the kids, and picking fruit was a man. The rest of the work was taken over by the pressure cooker . . . like magic. How very busy men were around the house! And in those exceptional cases when they weren't doing everything themselves, they were explaining to the "lovely ladies and dear housewives" how to iron or polish silver.

It struck me as odd. I didn't know what to do. I went to the personnel director and said I was having problems with the housewives. He summoned the creative director by phone. But only No. 2 showed up and informed me that the creative director had delegated him to deal with this. The personnel director said, "Good."

No. 2 accompanied me to my work space. He leafed through the heap of "Housewives' Supplies"—which amounted to five thousand copies by now—and finally found one female detergent monster. He waved the copy under my nose and exclaimed, "Here, you see, she's here, the typical housewife!"

I told him I'd planned to put this ad in the category of "Woman as Equal Partner in the Workplace," since the woman in the ad was presumably a laundry detergent consultant. She couldn't be a housewife—no woman had run around in a getup like this, with a lace cap and a long ruffled apron, since the nineteenth century. And who ever wore spike heels in the kitchen?

No. 2 gave me a withering look and said, "You haven't the faintest notion of what makes for effective advertising. This isn't a working woman! This is a self-portrait of the German housewife! That's perfectly obvious!"

I didn't admit to having known that. I just said that except for this one there were no pictures of housewives. No. 2 leafed through the rest of the pile, then he said that this arrangement according to product categories was idiotic. I should have been arranging the ads according to female types from the beginning. I told him I'd been following his orders. He said he wanted to make it perfectly clear that this simply wouldn't work. And I should wait until he got back.

It was two hours, no less, before he came back with his creative director. I hadn't dared to leave, and was starving. The creative director looked through "Investment Instruments" and "Cosmetics" and said it didn't make sense to organize the ads according to product, and from now on I should organize them strictly according to female types. Then the two of them vanished. I took a deep breath and went out to get something to eat.

When I got back, No. 2 was already standing around in the library. They had decided, he told me, to introduce a further category: I should separate out all the ads in which only the product was portrayed, or no people were portrayed—this was the new category: "Product-Oriented or Informative Advertising."

So I sorted out all the ads without people. The pile of "Housewives' Supplies" dissolved, because there were no housewives in it; the products did the cleaning all by themselves. Oh well.

That evening Joschi told me that most of his work time was spent undoing things his boss had instructed him to do.

When I combed through the pile of "Investment Vehicles"

for housewives, I found a savings bank ad: in the background a home, with a man out front in the garden checking on the rose bushes, and a woman in a lawn chair watching him intently. I classified the woman as a housewife, because this idyll reminded me of my parents—although my father would no doubt fly into a rage if my mother lay around in a lawn chair while he fussed self-importantly with his roses. Otherwise I didn't find any housewifelike people of the feminine gender in this pile. I observed a moment of silence for Sieglinde Lamar-Schadler, who from today on would be married for an indefinite period of time. I wondered whether Wolf-Dietrich had let her buy that expensive suit. And how Sieglinde would look as a housewife.

After housewives I looked for "Woman as Equal Partner in the Workplace." I found only two: a well-known fashion designer who claimed she washed her face with a soap costing only 98 pfennigs, and a well-known racing driver who reported that her life had undergone a decisive change now that she could rely during those "critical days" on her superabsorbent tampon.

All the other women in the ads had as little interest in work as the housewives did. You could tell just by looking at their clothes. The simplest outfits would have been just fine at a garden party for the queen. The only time the ladies weren't wearing their jewels was when they were splashing around in their marble bathtubs. It occurred to me that my tub could use a good scrubbing one of these days.

The women who turned up in the "Transportation" category weren't quite that elegant, but then they weren't productive either. Some of them gazed adoringly at the man in the driver's seat, presumably because he had passed his driving test. Or, if a woman was alone in a car ad, she wasn't at the wheel, heavens no, she was prancing around on the hood. I certainly didn't know any women who would dent their cars on purpose or scratch the paint with their high heels. All these women from the "Transportation" category had to be assigned to "Other Female Types." I tried to think whether I knew a single man who wouldn't bring vandalism charges against a woman he caught trampling his car. No. Deep down in my heart I sensed that even Gottfried Schachtschnabel wouldn't remain emotionally neutral at the sight of a scratch in the blue paint of his Mercedes.

I went on to the next female type, "Women in the Role of Mother." It came as no surprise by now that I hardly found any mothers. Well, actually I *was* surprised, but that was how it was. In the ads you either found kids on their own—they were taken care of by the self-activating products—or the fathers were on duty again. Obviously, the women didn't have time to take care of their children; they were busy lying on the beach or in the bathtub, fooling around in bars or boutiques—if they didn't happen to be demolishing cars. Or they were adoring men and doing things with the adorees that didn't even hint at a marriage-like relationship. When a man gives a woman a great big hug because she makes such marvelous coffee, it's obvious that he's just spent the night with her for the first time. No man praises a woman twice for the same coffee.

By Friday, I had large piles of "Other Female Types," but only a handful of mothers. It wasn't my fault.

It was lucky I went straight home from the agency . . . Gottfried had written! Oh, it was a postcard of Picasso's *Guernica.* Of course I knew that this particular painting wasn't just by a famous artist but also occupied a particular political position in the history of art. Gottfried had filled the entire card with his wonderful tiny handwriting. He wrote:

Hi, Constance,
    Happy to fulfill my promise, I herewith send you greet-
ings from the land of Goya, Don Quixote, and, last but not
least, Picasso. Our fascination with the local art and culi-

naria reached a high point in the Prado, to which Picasso's grandiose indictment of the civil war has finally been returned from its exile in an American museum. My own return may be expected shortly.

All the best,

Gottfried Schachtschnabel

I soaked up his words like a sponge. Permeated by noble values, he had formulated a postcard—for me. The only thing I didn't like was the impersonal "Hi." He could certainly have written "Dear." On the other hand, that was how he was, so delightfully restrained. I did a quick calculation. The semester was starting in three weeks, so it was high time he came back.

Sighing to myself, I spent the weekend with Joschi. He was pitifully noncompetitive. I let him spend the night with me anyway. On Sunday morning, when Joschi was still lying in my bed, Albert called. He'd been back for a week already and had tried to reach me several times. I went into the other room to talk to him, but Joschi's presence made me uncomfortable. Actually, I wanted Albert to explain what he was thinking of, going away with that Anna without telling me a thing. Letting me run straight into Sieglinde's dagger! Hadn't I told him often enough that we'd separated harmoniously? But because Joschi was in the other room and the walls of my apartment were thin, I just exclaimed in a delighted voice, "Ah, so you're back!" and "How nice of you to call right away!" and "Thanks so much for all the postcards!" and "Yes, we absolutely must get together!" I laughed loudly and often into the phone. Albert was happy that I was so happy, and we arranged to meet that very evening. I told Joschi to go out with his buddies.

Albert and I had arranged to meet in a place where neither of us had ever been. My idea—it's always better to meet on neutral ground when you don't know what you're going to say to each other. "Terra incognita is the place where hope meets forgetfulness," a cowboy once said in a Western, the rest of which I've forgotten. Or had it been an article on psychology? Whatever.

Even though it didn't mean anything anymore, I wore my turquoise silk top and the matching skirt just for Albert's benefit. He appreciated ladylike elegance, like my father.

Albert was waiting outside for me, looking startling, as if he was in the middle of a midlife crisis. He'd grown muttonchops. He was wearing dark blue pants and black shoes. Had he gone color-blind? We greeted each other cordially, at the same time trying to avoid any crude familiarity.

Austria was lovely. But expensive. Vienna was very beautiful, but the Viennese were all weird birds. Albert's car had broken down on the road one night, fortunately nothing very serious. Once a huge spider "had been seen" in a hotel room. "There'd" been a lot of lazing around. Albert had put on six pounds, but had already taken off one.

"So what did you fight with Anna about?" I asked. Sneaky, as I could be when I wanted to.

Albert promptly fell into my trap. "Anna's pretty tight with money."

I almost cracked my sides laughing.

"I knew that would amuse you," Albert said. "She keeps track of every pfennig, and I mean every one, and that really got on my nerves. She would only pay for ten percent of the repairs on the car; she said the new starter would last me a long time, not just for the trip."

I was definitely going to crack my sides laughing.

"But other than that we got along well," Albert said. The defiance in his voice was unmistakable. "Because she works at the hospital we have lots in common and plenty to talk about."

"I see," I said. Then somehow we got around to Joschi, who was very generous. (We didn't get around to the fact that he was an electrician.) Later, when I asked Albert what his Anna had given him for his birthday, he just waved off the question.

"Everyone has defects," he said.

"Certainly," I said generously.

We parted without having quarreled. Albert paid for my drinks. "This is on me," he said, and he did it so naturally that I wondered whether it was a self-imposed penance for his earlier stinginess. Or was it revenge on Anna? Ah yes, the games life played. A stingy man ended up with a stingy woman. Birds of a feather flock together, haha. Served him right. I almost felt a little sorry for him. Had he really believed he would find unclouded happiness elsewhere?

Spurred by malicious satisfaction, I started picking out "Women as Sex Objects" the next morning. I decided to include not only the completely naked ones in the sexist ad category, but also the many ads in which several women at a time were gazing adoringly at a man, as if he had just invented instant coffee. Then there was this ad in which some smart alec was explaining to a woman the difference between a tube of shoe cream and a tube of sunscreen; that was sexist, too. And all the blondes shaking out canary food or squeezing a bottle of fabric softener or working the hair spray: they all deserved to be declared mentally incompetent. But they couldn't help it—I was sure these ads had all been dreamed up by men. I could only shake my head: how dumb did a man have to be to think women were that stupid?

On Tuesday, while I was wondering whether to put a disco bunny dancing on a washing machine in the "Women as Sex Object" pile or the "Other Female Types" pile, No. 2 appeared and asked how the work was coming along. I told him it was coming along nicely. When would I be finished, he wanted to know. This study had to be done by the end of the month, so if necessary I should be prepared to stay late. I asked whether they paid overtime, and he said that wasn't his department.

No. 2 looked at the many piles of "Other Female Types" and

asked what that was supposed to mean. I reported to him that there were very few mothers in the ads. He said that couldn't be true; I just hadn't worked carefully. That really pissed me off! I showed him the big pile of fathers I'd collected and the divider I'd made with "Fathers in the Role of Mother." No matter whether it was for health insurance, vitamin tablets, or oatmeal, the fathers were always the ones taking care of the children. He looked through the ads and seemed reassured that I hadn't done a sloppy job. Then he asked, "Don't you as a woman find it gratifying that advertising now places so much more value on the role of mother?"

I didn't even answer that, but said I'd only found three working women in the entire batch.

"You're not going to make me believe that!" he exclaimed.

I went to the "Women as So-called Sex Objects" pile and dug out the naked blonde at the computer and the brunette at the conference table. The brunette had on nothing but her bra. She was surrounded by men in custom-made suits. I asked him whether he would really consider these working women.

"The way you're doing this makes no sense!" No. 2 exclaimed. Then he said I shouldn't do any more till he came back.

"Fine." I went to the ladies' room, combed my hair, cleaned my fingernails, and applied some more mascara. When I got back, No. 2 and the creative director were waiting impatiently in the library.

"Oh, there you are!" No. 2 exclaimed.

Shit. The one time you left your post, they came and checked up on you. The creative director had taken an ad from the "Other Female Types" pile that showed two women sunning themselves. It was an ad for frozen potato puffs, and the text under the picture read, "A delicious meal, a breeze to prepare." The creative director said, "Those chicks are two cute secretaries on vacation; you can certainly put them with the working women." Then he wanted to know why I hadn't put the women who danced on car hoods with the working women. I asked what sort of work these women did. He couldn't say exactly, but they were so young that you couldn't assume they were housewives and mothers, and if there was no man in an ad, it was clear the women had to support themselves.

"So these are working women," No. 2 concluded. "I would suggest," he added, "that we put any women under thirty who are shown without a man in the 'Working Women' category."

"That's the logical solution," the creative director declared.

"I can't imagine what sort of occupation this woman would have," I said, and pointed to a woman paddling around in a boat on a moonlit lake. She was dressed in a lace evening gown.

"She's a model," the creative director said slyly, and No. 2 burst out laughing. "Obviously a working woman," he said.

"I thought this was supposed to be a scientific study," I said boldly, totally unconvinced.

The creative director stared at me in astonishment, furrowed his brow, and then rubbed his chin. No. 2 looked at me very suspiciously. I gave them a charming smile.

"All right, let's do it this way, then," the creative director said. "We'll expand the category!" He smiled at me. "From now on the category is called 'Woman as Equal Partner in the Workplace and' "—he paused significantly—" 'at Leisure'! Now it fits! What do you say to that?"

No. 2 was overwhelmed: " 'Woman as Equal Partner in the Workplace and at Leisure'—that's the solution! That'll give us fantastic findings!" He was obviously chagrined that this hadn't occured to him.

I was also overwhelmed. "You might just as well claim that all women shown inside a house are housewives!" I exclaimed indignantly.

"Well, what do you know," the creative director said, "you

have creative potential. That's exactly how you should organize the material." He smiled at me, and No. 2 smiled along with him. "The women inside a house are housewives, and those who are outside are equal partners in the workplace and at leisure."

"Happy hunting!" the two of them wished me as they left. Then I was alone with my conscience. I'd been the one who gave them the cue! That night I could hardly sleep; I kept wondering whether I'd become an accomplice in the degradation of my own sex. What would Gottfried Schachtschnabel say? Oh, woe!

But I had no choice. Rebelling inwardly, I spent the next two days reorganizing everything according to the gentlemen's wishes. I had to drastically reduce the pile of "Women as So-called Sex Objects," but there were still lots of ads in which women appeared naked or partially naked without the domestic setting or leisure-time props that would have pushed them into the categories of "Housewives" or "Woman as Equal Partner in the Workplace and at Leisure."

Then I went to the personnel director to tell him to report to the gentlemen that I was finished with the reorganizing.

No. 2 came, accompanied by the creative director. The only thing they were interested in was the pile with sexist advertising. Why had I put the woman wearing nothing but a pair of almost invisible pantyhose in with the sexist advertising? That was product demonstration! And the naked woman kneeling and painting her toenails, that was also product demonstration. And product demonstration was neutral portrayal of the product. And a naked person wasn't ipso facto indecent.

"Can't you picture yourself naked with a man?" the creative director asked, checking me out from my ankles to my waist.

Rage welled up in me. I wouldn't let myself be accused of being a prude! I looked scornfully at them and said that it hadn't occurred to me before now that men were so dumb that they would go out of their minds over a naked woman in a magazine. I knew no such men. A man who was turned on by that sort of thing must have something seriously wrong with him, I added sarcastically, gazing with interest at the creative director's beer belly. So haha.

The gentlemen stared back in consternation. This advertising was directed at women—you could tell just from the products. "Of course there are some women who compulsively try to repress their femininity," No. 2 said, "but our task as creators of advertising is to target the average woman."

I couldn't think of any retort to that.

"All right, start over," the creative director said to me, as if he were talking to a small child, "and this time please assign the women to the proper categories."

When they were gone and the door was shut, I stuck out my tongue at them. Completely disgusted, I did it all again, their way. This job was getting on my nerves. I wanted to get it over with as soon as possible. The swarms of bugs had been more satisfying.

The next morning I summoned the gentlemen to the library. I still had about five hundred ads in the "Women as So-called Sex Objects" pile. The creative director casually divided these ads among the "Product-Oriented or Informative Advertising" and "Woman as Equal Partner in the Workplace and at Leisure" piles. He left only one ad, which had appeared in four women's magazines altogether; it was an ad for flashlights and showed a naked woman, photographed in profile, who was holding a flashlight at penis level. "The ass on that dame is a provocation," the creative director said, and put the four copies back into the former pile of sexist ads. All the others had been redistributed. That was about enough for me.

"And how about this one?" I asked, and took the last ad he'd placed on the "Product-Oriented or Informative Advertising" heap. There was a woman in it who was naked, as far as one could see. She was drinking champagne with a man.

"Clearly a product demonstration," No. 2 said. "It's an ad for champagne, and the gal's drinking champagne."

I wasn't going to let him off that easy. "But the man's drinking champagne, too. He's demonstrating the product, too, but he's not naked!"

"Good point," the creative director said, and put the ad back. "After all, we want to be objective," he said with a smile. Then he sighed, stuck his hands in his pockets, and said, "Now comes the scientific part of the study. . . . Now the ads have to be counted, so we can determine the percentage of each female type."

"Count the whole mess!" I exclaimed. I'd earned enough money to take care of my needs, and my guilty conscience about participating in discrimination against women was still torment-ing me. I was thinking maybe I should quit then and there.

"Of course," the creative director said. "This has to be a statistically accurate study. You musn't make any mistakes in your count! The numbers will be presented to the women's organizations. You know how finicky they are."

"And you also have to count the ones that have no women in them. Don't forget!" No. 2 admonished me.

"What, those, too?" the creative director asked in astonish-ment. "But we're talking about images of women."

No. 2 whispered to the creative director, but I could hear what he was saying: "The more ads we have, the smaller the quantity of sexist advertising . . . expressed in percentages . . . you get the point?"

"Aha," the creative director said, "right!" Then he said to me, "You have to count all the ads, including those without any women in them!"

No. 2 smiled smugly.

Nice trick! No matter. I was glad to see the back of them. I counted and counted. I stacked the copies in batches of fifty at right angles to each other. I counted till eleven o'clock at night, because I wanted to get through, and because the personnel director had promised me overtime. The dumb copies stuck to my fingers. On Friday I continued counting, starting at nine. Two hours later I was finally done. I'd counted the last big category—and I could hardly believe the results: I'd found only three working women myself, but now there were 13,419 Equal Partners in the Workplace and at Leisure! No wonder No. 2 had crowed that the results of the study would be fabulous. . . . I was furious! Then filled with despair. What should I do?

I swore I'd never again buy any products with sexist advertising. From now on I'd scrutinize those ads, which up to now I'd skimmed past without a moment's thought, and I'd take careful note of the products I wouldn't buy. Yes, indeed. Somewhat calmer, I made a list of the results of the count:

Product-Oriented or Informative Advertising	5,826 ads
Housewives	6,827 ads
Men in the Role of Women	2,453 ads
Women in the Role of Mother	82 ads
Woman as Equal Partner in the Workplace and at Leisure	13,419 ads
Women as So-called Sex Objects	7 ads

In case I'd miscalculated, I checked the final tally four times, and then I was sure: all together it came to 28,614 ads. Ugh!

I dragged myself to the personnel director and gave him the list.

"Did you really make an accurate count?" he asked, and looked at me sharply.

"Yes," I said in a firm voice, although I wasn't absolutely positive that none of the copies had stuck to each other.

"Hm," the personnel director said. "Twenty-eight thousand six hundred fourteen—that's an impressive number. That's quite something. And among all of them, only seven ads that show women as so-called sex objects: that'll make a very good impression."

I didn't answer. I was beat. I wanted to go home, my job was done. I went to the secretary and made sure she recorded my overtime on my time sheet. Then she went to the personnel director and had the sheet signed. Finally she came back, saying the boss was in a great mood and I'd be getting 75 pfennigs extra per hour for the overtime. I was wondering whether I should say good-bye to the personnel director when suddenly a wild shout echoed through the whole floor: "Champagne for everybody!"

It was the personnel director. He burst out of his office with the creative director and No. 2. No. 2 shouted, "Look at these figures! Only point zero two four five percent of the ads have sexist tendencies!"

"Do you realize what that means?" the personnel director said.

"Not even three hundredths of one percent of all advertising is sexist!" No. 2 chortled.

"The libbers are making all this fuss over three hundredths of a percent! Unbelievable, their pitiful grip on reality!" the creative director exclaimed, and burst into wild laughter.

"Not even three hundredths of a percent!" No. 2 shouted.

A young woman came out into the hall, saw the laughing throng, and said, "Champagne? Did I hear someone say champagne?"

"We've just proven that there's no such thing as sexist advertising! It's statistically accurate! Only point zero two four five percent!"

"You don't say!" the woman screeched, and she, too, began to laugh hysterically. "So what are we going to do with the Women's Research Center's study that says more than two-thirds of all advertising is degrading to women?"

"You can toss that study in the trash! Not even exact figures!"
No. 2 exclaimed. "It's exactly point zero two four five percent!
Over two-thirds, ha! Who knows what sort of categories those
dames cooked up!"

"We have another splendid result to announce," the creative
director yelled. "Forty-six point eighty-nine percent of all the
women in the ads are portrayed as equal partners in the workplace and at leisure!"

"Man, that's fantastic!" screeched the woman. She hopped
up and down.

The creative director's watch beeped. "Where's our champagne?" he shouted.

The woman was still hopping up and down and shouting,
"Man, am I glad there's champagne, and no sexist advertising!"

I stole a look at the woman. How could she be taken in by
these men? Or was she a lush, ready to sell her soul for a glass
of champagne?

"Will you have a glass with us?" the creative director asked
me, gazing appreciatively at my legs.

No, I wouldn't have a glass with them. I just wanted my
money. I wasn't going to drink champagne with my enemies;
they weren't going to humiliate me any more. I dragged myself
home and fell into bed.

That evening when I met Joschi at the Kaput, I was completely done in. It had turned cold so suddenly, and I didn't
know whether it was the change in weather or my nerves that
made me feel so awful. I got drunk and Joschi comforted me.
Oh, how nice he was. He calculated that my brave intervention
had raised the percentage of sexist advertising from .014 percent
to .0245 percent. True, but what good did that do? Not until
he calculated that I'd raised the original percentage by 57 percent could I laugh again. He was right: that was something I
could be proud of.

60

Gottfried Schachtschnabel was back!

61

The blouse I was wearing when I received Gottfried Schachtschnabel in my apartment just barely veiled my midnight-blue silk slip.

How he smiled at me with his Lenin beard! Like a happy baby seal. How charming he'd been yesterday when he called me! He'd enthused over the Picasso-esque power of the Spanish landscape—what a wonderful backdrop for any film! He'd told me that at the crafts camp he'd tried at first to reproduce the feel of Picasso's *Guernica* in a mud sculpture, but then he'd learned to give in to the primal material and to shape mud the way mud would shape itself, and then he'd made wonderfully beautiful containers, which he was going to put out on his balcony next year and fill with plants. And the business with his wife had gone off without a hitch. He asked how my screenplay was coming along. I told him what I'd been up to in the last few weeks, and that I hadn't had any inspiration—just as I hadn't had him. But I didn't tell him that, I just thought it.

He'd suggested coming by to see me and had said perfectly frankly that first he had to run by his wife's to drop something off, but then . . . he could be at my place before eight. Since his call I'd cleaned the apartment; I'd almost washed the windows, but fortunately it occurred to me just in time that that would seem petty-bourgeois.

Gottfried immediately felt at home in my place. We sat in the kitchen, because that's the coziest room; I'd made a point of bringing my cassette recorder into the kitchen and had picked out my favorite cassettes. After two glasses of wine it was as if he had never been away.

"Did you redefine your relationship with your wife?" I asked cautiously.

"How do you mean?" he asked.

"I mean," I said with some embarrassment, because I didn't know how to express it to him, "I was wondering whether new structures have been introduced into your relationship?"

"Yes," he said, "of course. Everything was incredibly open at the camp. Inge fell hopelessly in love with a handsome Spaniard on the very first day. He made the most fantastic sculptures of all of us. Inge has totally unspoiled artistic taste. For Inge art is a purely sensuous experience."

"And you?"

Gottfried laughed. "You can't spend your whole life kneading mud."

"Did you and your wife . . .?"

"Inge! No way! Inge's very faithful. Oh, sometimes a little vacation flirtation. But certainly not with me; her guy from the Building Department's insanely jealous. He's not even supposed to know I was along in Spain."

Aha, so they hadn't slept with each other. Very good.

It happened the way it was supposed to happen. I know it's kitschy, but in my memories such moments are always associated with music. As we walked together from the kitchen to my bed, the tape of one of my all-time favorites, "Then He Kissed Me," was playing.

And that's how it was, too. I wasn't wearing anything but my midnight-blue silk slip. We were lying on my red-dyed sheets. Gottfried had on black briefs. Olala! He slipped them off and I did likewise. Gottfried was resting his entire weight on my right hipbone. Ouch!

"I love you," he panted.

Does he really mean me? I thought for a brief moment. Or did he mean this "I love you" only in a generic, literary sense? Or was it really true, at last? I was ecstatic. So ecstatic that when the phone rang I only recognized it as the phone ringing on the third ring. Then I was sure it must be Albert—it couldn't be Joschi because I'd sent him to the disco with his buddies, so he was busy. I, who'd been alone for so long—or rather, not alone, but without my true love—I was enjoying the moment of perfect transformation; I, who was finally lying in the arms of my proper lover, was still being besieged by my former lover, who'd come to the painful realization of what he was losing. It was vanity that seduced me into picking up the receiver, I know. But I needed the satisfaction; I'd suffered too long. Even though I really didn't want to answer, I couldn't resist. My night of revenge had come. I kissed my Gottfried lovingly, whispered, "So sorry, love," and flitted to the phone.

"This is Inge Schachtschnabel," a sweet voice said. "Could I speak to my husband for a moment?"

"Why are you calling here?" I exclaimed, completely incredulous.

"Just for a moment, it's terribly urgent."

The receiver slid out of my hand. "Your wife," I said with my last strength.

"Yes," Gottfried said, "just a moment," and pulled on his underwear under the blanket. "Yes, you're right," he said into the phone, "my geraniums . . . yes . . . better safe than sorry . . . yes, the boxes are too heavy . . . yes . . . be right over."

By the time he'd hung up, I had my midnight-blue silk slip on again.

"Inge's right," he said, and looked out the window. "We could have frost tonight. My geraniums are out on her balcony, and they have to be taken in."

"Where did she get my number?"

"From the phone book, I assume," Gottfried said, pulling on his clothes. "I probably mentioned your name to Inge one time."

Mentioned! He'd mentioned my name! "Oh," was all I said.

"Hey, listen, Constance," he said, "I'll just run over to Inge's and help her get the geraniums into the cellar, and then I'll be back."

"Oh, no need," I said, very cool.

"But you do understand I have to help Inge in this situation? She's in the middle of a very difficult identity crisis." He looked at me. "And she's right, there *will* be a frost tonight. There are four boxes of geraniums, and they don't come cheap." He laid his hand tenderly on my shoulder. "I know you understand. It's only ten-thirty. I'll be back in half an hour."

"Really, there's no need," I said, very very cool.

When I closed the door behind him, I closed it on a chapter of my life.

62

Geraniums! Jeez! The scales fell from my eyes. It was crystal-clear what kind of schmuck this Schachtschnabel was: his potted plants meant more to him than my antibourgeois sensibility. Geraniums! How petty-bourgeois could you get? He should stick to kneading mud, that cottage gardener with haha revolutionary aspirations, moaning

"I love you" so he wouldn't go to hell for having sex. I bet he picked that up in catechism class. Why not say, "Dear Lord, bless this which we are about to receive"? Good grief, how tasteless could you get? A Christian sheep in revolutionary clothing! Geraniums! Jesus Christ! What was that on his postcard? "Our fascination with the local art and culinaria." I dug out my dictionary: no *culinaria*. Mr. Intellectual Schachtschnabel didn't even know his own language. Ha! I tore the stupid postcard to bits. Picasso's *Guernica* in mud! Why not go straight for Dürer's *Praying Hands*? And then making flowerpots! For geraniums, no doubt! That would be just like him. Haha. Mr. Antimarriage Slogans! Mr. Devoted Lackey of the Institutionalization of Private Emotions, more likely. Mr. Married Gardener! Boy, had he pulled the wool over my eyes. As an unmarried woman I was merely a marginal social group for Mr. Conformist Career-Hawk. He was just exploiting my societal powerlessness. Right! I'd had it! And it was crystal-clear that Schachtschnabel was a lousy lover, too. Joschi would never throw all his weight on my poor hipbone, or get into bed with me without brushing his teeth! Jeez! Jeez! And who knows how many days he'd been wearing those hot black briefs? I called Juliet and told her every detail. She laughed herself sick. She'd suspected the whole time that Schachtschnabel would go after me again after she'd dumped him. Okay, so Juliet made it sound as though I went around picking up her discarded humps, but she laughed even harder when I told her that the bozo had gone to his wedded wife's abortion just so his colleagues would think he'd done the deed. And Juliet said he'd never get divorced unless he got another woman pregnant, because then he could remarry right away. Schachtschnabel needed the institutionalization of private emotions to disguise his inability to commit himself. He was so vain that all he needed was himself. Everyone else was just window dressing. And Juliet said she'd only put up with Gottfried Schachtschnabel's inability to make a commitment because at the time she hadn't gotten over her divorce yet. And then she guessed that I'd also been fixated on this sort of alienating relationship because I hadn't gotten over my separation from Albert yet. I didn't really buy that, but Juliet was right, Schachtschnabel would never get divorced. He lived for his vanity and his geraniums. Haha! And why should he mind his wife's using him as a stopgap? This way he could pretend he was irreplaceable. What was he thinking of? Any woman with half a brain would dump him the second she realized what kind of guy he was! Did he think he could put one over on me? That old chauvinist had another think coming. And Juliet said that when they were still together, he'd say "I've got company," every time his wife called up. He didn't even have the guts to say it was a woman, let alone mention Juliet's name—we wouldn't want Inge to feel undermined in her role! "Well, well," Juliet said, "I'm glad you got your wish, because otherwise you'd still be dreaming about Prince Gottfried Schachtcharming." Maybe she was right; after all, she'd fallen for this married nothing too. The man had no future, just a past. "A perfect example of living a lie," Juliet said. Schachtschnabel acted like a revolutionary, but actually he just wanted to wait for better times without making any sacrifices; he wanted to laze around in comfort till a miracle happened. He wanted to be a revolutionary with a nice pension. Types like that often turn into the worst reactionaries later on. And he'd just forgotten to tell Juliet he was married! Just forgotten! And to top it off he'd let me think that being married made no difference! Being married! He had some screws loose. Gottfried Schachtschnabel, that great critic of bourgeois marriage, that lapdog, bringing his mistress her slippers and taking in the geraniums. Oh, yes, excuse me, except that he wanted us unmarried women to take over the "marital obligations" so he could tell himself nothing was missing from his marriage! That was it, what he wanted was an alibi for his marriage. That exploiter! And catch that Mercedes! His entire revolutionary praxis consisted of sitting down with his wife to piece together denim seat covers for his capitalist gas-guzzler! Haha! Put him in a shooting gallery for the Movement. No more Schachtschnabel seminars for me, that I could guarantee. Juliet agreed. Good thing I hadn't done more on my film. What a waste that would've been. A film based on the Schachtschnabel philosophy would have been about as good as the Schachtschnabel life. You couldn't impose Schachtschnabel on an audience! He'd rather have a large-screen TV than a divorce! I thought: Let me give you a tip, Herr Schachtschnabel: Start saving for the family plot right now. Oh, and plant the damn thing with geraniums!

63 Three days after I'd closed the books on Schachtschnabel once and for all, Joschi arrived three-quarters of an hour late at the Kaput and said, "It's all over between us."

I immediately accepted his resignation.

It was okay. He could keep my bath bubbles, which were still in his bathroom. Joschi was tipsy, and his pal Didi waited bashfully in the door till we'd terminated our relationship in a spirit of mutual agreement.

It had been intended as an interlude. And it had become an interlude. My expectations had been fulfilled. Anyone who expected anything more would have been wallowing in illusions. This was a separation without a loser or a winner. Probably Joschi had come to recognize that a shared bed isn't enough of a basis. Or had he given in to his friends, who'd been against our relationship from the start because they were afraid of losing their bowling partner? No matter. No hard feelings against Joschi. I'd known from the beginning that it couldn't last. Why should it have lasted?

A harmonious separation is so easy when the other person doesn't mean anything to you, I thought. And something else made me think, too: I'd waited so long for something to finally happen, but now, when events were coming hot on each other's heels, it didn't really make any difference.

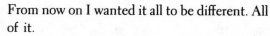

From now on I wanted it all to be different. All of it.

After long struggles our academy had finally gotten authorization for a teaching position in "Structural Criticism of Aesthetic Reception."

"Structural Criticism of Aesthetic Reception" took place on Thursdays, so I decided to shift my free day this semester to Wednesday. A person has to stay flexible.

The new instructor was called Wolfgang Klein, and he was the sort of teacher who's on a first-name basis with everyone from the start. Wolfgang brought his son along to the seminar. Daniel was eighteen months old, and Wolfgang explained that the child's mother—which meant his girlfriend—was a student and right now she needed time entirely without disruptions for writing her dissertation, and it was no problem at all for him to bring Daniel to the academy because Daniel was a child you could take anywhere, Daniel could handle anything. Daniel really did sleep peacefully in his portable bassinet for the first half hour of the seminar, and when he began to whimper Wolfgang took him in his arms. And Daniel immediately quieted down. A woman sitting diagonally across from me flicked a tear from her eye with her knitting needle. Wolfgang explained that his approach was to demonstrate that the private was the political. And we were supposed to discover together what the innate structures of our psychological fantasies were. And he didn't want to ram anything down our throats; everything was to come from us. I breathed a sigh of relief. Thank God! At least with Wolfgang I could be sure of not being ideologically manipulated.

"So, how do you folks want to proceed?" Wolfgang asked, rocking Daniel.

One of the women said she had a great idea. It would be great if kids made a film for grown-ups; up to now it had always been the other way around. We could learn from the spontaneous, unfalsified imagination of children what spontaneous, unfalsified imagination is. And Katrin, that was her daughter, was also a child who could be taken anywhere, and she could play a role in the film, provided, of course, she felt like it. But Katrin's mother was relatively sure Katrin would agree to it.

It turned out that several others in the class had children who could also be taken anywhere, and they also promised to ask their children if they'd be interested in making a film for us grownups.

"What about those of us who don't have any children?" asked a woman sitting in the front row. She seemed rather grouchy.

"They can go take a different seminar," Katrin's mother said. The woman in the first row got indignant: that was a subtle form of discrimination, she said to Katrin's mother; did she want to create a two-class society, with mothers against women? Identifying biological fate with societal fate—that was something she thought we'd left behind long ago.

Katrin's mother looked to Wolfgang for support. Wolfgang rocked Daniel. "Well, what do you folks want to do?" Wolfgang asked.

Another woman said she wanted to say quite spontaneously

that she thought it was an incredibly fantastic idea that children should make a film for grown-ups. And she was a mother, too.

Wolfgang's baby laughed, and Wolfgang said, "Daniel likes that. Daniel has an incredibly keen sense of what he likes. He's totally autonomous." Then he affirmed that there would have to be a great deal of discussion about the film, and he found the idea fantastic, too. The question was, would they get the necessary funding? And what else might we want to do besides?

"We could do a theoretical workup of the structural criticism of aesthetic reception." Chlodwig Schnell came up with this. What was he doing here? Could it be he'd turned traitor to Gottfried Schachtschnabel? Or was he trying to smuggle in some of Schachtschnabel's extra theories? I murmured approvingly when a woman asked what good a theoretical workup would do.

Wolfgang said theory was all very well and good, but it had to be relevant to us. What he wanted was a theory of personal involvement. "Millions are dying of famine in Africa—that's bad, but Africa is too far away to touch many people personally. We must ask ourselves how many people are dying here every day of broken hearts. What do we want to do about that? About the emotional suffering in our midst?"

This affected me as nothing ever had before.

Then Wolfgang asked whether one of the women would care to sign up for an oral report. Should I? Immerse myself in the new world of ideas that was opening up before me? I boldly raised my hand. Wolfgang made a note of my name: "Constance Wechselburger," he said, and added, "Great, Connie, and what do you want to do your report on?"

Well, that I didn't know. I'd thought he was going to give me a topic. So we postponed the question of the content of possible reports until a later point in time when we'd see more clearly what the structural criticism of aesthetic reception actually entailed. We weren't in any hurry; the semester had just begun.

The class broke up early because Daniel began to cry and wouldn't calm down.

65 I called Sieglinde shortly after the wedding and let her account of it wash over me. She announced that she'd invite me over when the pictures were ready. Of course that had been about two weeks ago, but I still didn't have a wedding present. Tomorrow was Saturday, so I'd have to get out early and buy something before the stores closed. What do you give a married woman? A good book, as usual? Do married women even read books? When a husband is constantly stomping around, can you still find enough peace and quiet to read a book? A cookbook—now that was an idea. After all, Sieglinde loved to cook, and you can always use a cookbook when you're married. I went to the bookstore by City Hall and told the clerk I wanted a cookbook.

"What sort of cookbook?" she asked.

I didn't know that either. My eye fell on a shelf with women's literature, so I said, "A woman's cookbook."

No such thing as a cookbook specially for women, the clerk said. "Have a look," she said.

I had a look. Either the cookbooks were too expensive or they didn't have any pictures. I couldn't make up my mind. I watched a man with a kid in a Snugli standing by books on natural foods and healthy lifestyles. The kid grabbed *Cigarette-Free in Thirty Days* and hurled it to the floor. The clerk came running over and said to the father, "Please keep an eye on what your child's doing."

The father said, "I think you'll have to take it up with Juliet herself."

The clerk picked up the book.

"Juliet doesn't see anything wrong with what she did," the father said proudly. "Smoking stinks."

I decided not to buy Sieglinde a book after all, so I left. The last thing I heard was the father saying to the clerk, "Say, you really overreacted there." The clerk didn't say anything. And then he asked her, "Do you smoke, by any chance?"

Finally I bought Sieglinde two kitchen towels; that's the kind of thing you can always use when you're married. The towels were plain white; only the hanging loop was colorful, because the designer's name was on it, and there was a large, colorful ticket attached to the towels that said that this design had been selected by *Vogue.*

Sieglinde was very pleased with the towels once she'd noticed that *Vogue* was too. Then she got out the pictures. She'd filled two of her shit-brown plastic albums, and between the pictures she'd mounted the labels from the wines served at the reception.

Sieglinde had persuaded Wolf-Dietrich to let her get the expensive Jill Sanders suit; it didn't really look very good on her, but even in the pictures you could tell it was expensive. Sieglinde in the wood-paneled room at the registry office—revolting, that wood paneling . . . Sieglinde with her bridal bouquet—salmon-pink roses and mimosa, not what I would have chosen . . . Sieglinde with Wolf-Dietrich, also not what I would have chosen. In none of the pictures was the bridegroom smiling. The mother of the bride was beaming in every picture, showing every last molar. The father of the bridegroom was plainly smashed. Sieglinde's boss ditto. As Sieglinde explained the relationships and the financial status of the wedding guests, she constantly twisted her wedding ring. Wolf-Dietrich, who was sitting there during the presentation of the pictures as though they had nothing to do with him, said the wedding ring was the best gold, not 14-karat or 18-karat but 24-karat gold. But it still looked cheap.

And only Sieglinde had one; Wolf-Dietrich had spared himself the expense.

Finally she produced something to eat. The phone in the back room rang just as Sieglinde was putting broccoli au gratin on my plate. Her husband went to the phone. I was in favor of starting without him, but Sieglinde said she'd wait till her husband came back. Well, she had nobody but herself to blame when her broccoli got cold. I ate slower than usual, but even so my plate was soon empty, and Wolf-Dietrich was still on the phone.

"Hurry, the food's getting cold!" Sieglinde called across the hall. "Shut up!" Wolf-Dietrich shouted, slamming the door. Sieglinde began to eat, too. We'd both been finished for ages when Wolf-Dietrich came back. "Guess who that was? Albert!" he shouted triumphantly.

"Albert? Why didn't you put me on?" I was peeved.

"Guess what he wanted!"

"Your broccoli's gotten all cold, and the delicious sauce—"

"Albert's getting married!"

"What?"

"Anna's pregnant by Albert!"

"What?"

 I skipped dessert—it was only fruit and cheese cubes anyway—and went home immediately; I told Wolf-Dietrich and Sieglinde I had to call Albert right away—it just couldn't be true. And Wolf-Dietrich had shouted after me that I should tell Albert that he'd send him the model prenuptial agreement first thing tomorrow, and then Albert should come to see Wolf-Dietrich for a consulta-

tion. And Sieglinde had said three times, "Ah, I'm so happy for Anna."

Albert sounded chastened. Yes, it was true, Anna was in her first month. Then he asked me, "What do you think of that?"

"You're letting yourself be blackmailed into marriage!"

"I don't even know if we're getting married. Wolf-Dietrich said I'd save a bundle on taxes because Anna doesn't earn that much, and if I have to pay child support it comes to the same thing. . . ."

"You're only getting married because of money, and your stingy Anna, too!"

"No, Anna would be willing to raise the child by herself, but if I'd have to pay child support in any case . . ."

"Then it's cheaper to save on your taxes and get a cleaning lady to boot!"

"That's not how it is. It's also a question of responsibility, my responsibility for the child. I'm its father! But I'm still not sure we're getting married. . . ."

I banged down the receiver. He didn't call back to calm me.

Unbelievable, simply unbelievable how fiendishly clever that Anna was. She just went and got pregnant. And it worked! She had no compunctions! "Responsibility for the child"! Albert, of all people! He couldn't even take responsibility for himself. Indecisive as he was, he was a plaything in the hands of events set in motion by others.

To comfort myself, I put on my all-time favorite cassette. The last cut was "Only the Lonely." I felt positively sick with loneliness. Only the lonely knew what it meant to be alone. Albert would marry Anna, just because Anna was pregnant. If I hadn't taken the pill, I would have been pregnant too, long ago, married, out of the soup. . . . All my problems in life would be solved now. . . . I'd have a profession, the most beautiful profession in the world: mother! Then no one would dare to ask me what I planned to do later with my education . . . and later I could do whatever I liked, when my child was past the worst stage—I'd wait for later, like every other woman. I could make a film about the life of my child, beginning with its birth . . . and no one would ask why and whether there was any point to making such a film. When you had a child you knew you had a future. Because the child had one, you did too. It was that easy. Albert and I—when had we slept with each other last? In April. I could be in my sixth month now. I stuck a pillow under my sweater to see how I'd look pregnant. Absolutely convincing, absolutely natural.

"We have to be very brave now," I said to my unborn sofa pillow. "Your father's left us."

The wedding was in May.

Albert wore a black suit, nipped in at the waist, with only two buttons. The material didn't have a pattern, but the weave shimmered elegantly when the light was reflected or absorbed by it; you couldn't exactly say where the shimmer came from. The shoulders were lightly padded, which made Albert seem more powerful without looking massive. The pearl-white shirt with its delicate tucks and its transparent sheen signaled to those of discriminating taste that it was the finest cotton batiste blend, at least 30 percent silk. Perfectly matched with the shirt: a narrow aquamarine bow tie with a classic hand-knotted bow. Unlike most men, Albert didn't wear those vulgar pumps but, much more elegant because much more suitable, shoes with double laces. Not patent-leather shoes, of course—Albert's shoes had a silky matte finish. Also the shoes didn't have dyed soles like cheap shoes; on his shoes you could see the natural light-colored leather between the heel and the sole. And he'd even removed the price tag that's always stuck on between heel and sole! I knew his socks were pure silk, and the buttons of his shirt were hand-polished mother-of-pearl. His hair seemed no different than usual, but I noticed that his temples had turned gray—he'd never had gray hair before. Albert's watch was also new: the case was dark oxidized chrome, and the band was of the same material, with a clasp of 14-karat gold.

The bride wore a white rag.

Before the church an incredulous crowd had gathered, mostly women, asking themselves how such a woman could have hooked such a man. Anna was smiling the smile of those who love seeing their enemies dead; she looked like Salomé demanding the head of John the Baptist. Albert followed her, walking one pace behind. He looked like a prisoner of himself.

"There goes your father," I said to my unborn child as Albert passed without noticing me—us. "Just look how happy he is."

Only invited guests were allowed to attend the nuptial ceremony. I, who bore the bridegroom's firstborn in my womb, was not invited. The lackey at the church portal turned me away. So I threw myself down to pray on the church steps, on the cold granite, for the happiness of my former lover. For him I had bought a bunch of forget-me-nots. The flowers in my hands were wilting as flowers had never wilted before. Petal after petal the flowers were closing, fading. I don't know how long I lay there, lost in prayer.

When the church doors opened again, the last notes of a chorale cut through the air: "Mecum omnes plangite!" I didn't know what it meant, but sensed that it had a terrible significance. The colorful light from the church windows that now streamed out through the open doors blinded me like the strobe lights in the old disco on Carl Orff Square.

Anna was smiling like Salomé after receiving the head of John the Baptist. Suddenly, at this moment, it began to snow, although it hadn't snowed in May since time immemorial.

"A bad omen," an old beggar woman next to me whispered, and crossed herself.

"When the heart of the bride is made of ice, it can snow at any time of year," said an old man. I couldn't make out his face; he was wearing a black cloak that covered him completely, hanging far down over his eyes. He held a scythe. Was he a peasant relative of Anna's? Not fine enough in her eyes to attend her wedding?

The newly wedded pair descended the many steps.

"Long live love!" cried a few people hired as a claque—among them I recognized Sieglinde and Wolf-Dietrich, but they seemed not to know me. The working class stood in silence.

A storm cloud tugged at Anna's veil; like a wild animal the veil billowed out, got caught in the decorative sprays of evergreens placed in buckets along the sides of the church steps. Anna tugged at her veil. The veil ripped with a groaning sound that froze the hearts of all present. The sky darkened.

"This shitty veil!" Anna said.

The crowd before the church muttered.

"When the heart of the bride is made of ice, love freezes over," the man with the scythe said softly. His voice was strangely hollow.

When I stepped in front of the wedded couple in my simple yet tasteful linen dress, everything went dim before my eyes. The sky had become a dirty yellow. Albert looked at me; in his gaze was all the disappointed love in the world. It was the gaze of a man who had sold out his love for the seeming security of capitalism. It was the look of a traitor. A traitor to eternal love. I could not tolerate this look. I lowered my eyes to stare at the forget-me-nots in my hands. The last blue flowers were closing. A starry firmament was going dark.

Without anyone being able to explain later where it had come from, an old song suddenly rang out. I, too, knew the song from my youth. Were the snowflakes singing it?

> *Only the lonely . . .*
> *dum, dum, dum, dum dee doo ah . . .*
> *only the lonely . . .*
> *oh yeah, oh yeah dee doo ah.*
> *Only the lonely . . .*
> *. . . the only lonely . . .*
> *. . . the lonely only . . .*

The sky turned sulfur yellow. Only a single ray of sun had the power to break through the toxic clouds. It fell on my hair, which gleamed as beautifully as the hair of all pregnant women gleams, fell on my flawless complexion, which glowed immaculately as the complexions of all pregnant women glow. In spite of my fierce morning sickness I smiled, raising my slim hands to offer Albert my little nosegay of forget-me-nots.

"Quiet! What's all the commotion!" Anna screeched.

"It is the song of a lonely heart, beneath which another lonely heart is beating," I said softly but bravely.

The old ladies 'round about picked up the song—where had it come from?—"Dum, dum, dum, dum dee doo ah . . . oh yeah, oh yeah, dee doo ah," their voices exhorted.

The forget-me-nots slipped from my hands, fell to the ground. Albert, as if in a trance, stooped to rescue them, but Anna lifted her foot in its cheap patent-leather shoe—although it was new, it already looked old-ladyish and down-at-heel—and brought it down on the innocent flowers, crushing them to a blue-green pulp. Only one stalk remained unharmed, and I picked it up, pressing it to my belly, as if to protect my unborn child against the coldness of this woman.

"In renunciation resides true love," said the peasant with the black cloak and the scythe.

"Who is this chick?" screeched Anna. "Is she an unwed mother?" Then she quickly whispered to Albert, "Give her five marks and the address of Planned Parenthood." Albert did not react. "Get this chick out of my sight!" Anna screeched. "I'm a married woman!" Albert still did not react.

"Have mercy, gracious lady!" cried the beggar woman.

"When the heart of the bride is made of ice, the bridegroom freezes up," said the man with the scythe; his face was as white as Albert's.

Anna pushed me away. The hard edge of her wedding ring struck my unborn child. I fell down the steps like the baby carriage in *Battleship Potemkin.*

"Only the lonely," sang the snowflakes.

And the old women looked at Anna and sang so softly that it almost sounded like humming: "Oh yeah, oh yeah, dee doo ah . . ."

Anna's glance cut through my soul like a scalpel through a butterfly's wing. Her face was of concrete; only a pimple on her nose glowed. The last flower of the last stalk of forget-me-nots closed forever. I felt my senses dimming. Only the unborn life under my simple yet tasteful linen dress still stirred. "Mama! Mama!" my little baby cried. "Don't give up; I'll be everything to you!" cried the new life within me.

"I know, darling, we'll stay together, my darling," I breathed.

My eyes blinded with tears, I did not see Albert bending over me, but I recognized him when I felt him raise my head from the granite steps and press my face to the delicate tucks of his shirt. "Constance, you're pregnant? You?" Albert whispered in my ear. "Why didn't you tell me? Why, oh why, Constance?"

"We'll make our way in the world all by ourselves. . . . I will find strength in myself for both of us. . . . I shall raise your child to be happy," I whispered. "And if it's a boy, he will be called Daniel." My voice failed me.

Albert looked at me, and in his eyes awoke a distant tenderness.

"Go with her, find happiness with her," was all I managed to breathe. Again I heard, as if from a great distance, the sounds:

> *Only the lonely . . .*
> *can feel the way I feel. . . .*
> *only the lonely . . .*
> *. . . the only lonely . . .*
> *. . . the lonely only . . .*

The song gave me the strength to speak once more: "Go, but promise me one thing, Albert . . . Whatever may come to pass, never lose faith in a harmonious separation."

Then I fell into a deep faint.

 When I came to, dawn was breaking. I turned off the tape player. I felt bereft as never before. Albert's fate had caught up with him. He was living for his money, and he would have to die for it. Die slowly and painfully in a marriage with that Anna. And later on Anna's child would fritter away Albert's estate. But it would serve him right.

To annoy him I called him constantly during the next few weeks to ask whether Anna had set a date. He claimed there was no talk of marriage; Anna had said she'd raise the child alone if it came to that, and he didn't know either whether it made sense to get married. Sense! That's not the way a happy person thinks. Yes, his stinginess had betrayed him, had sold him out. It was fitting that he should be unhappy.

But somehow I felt sorry for him, in spite of everything. First of all, Anna had tricked him, and besides, he couldn't help being so cheap. All doctors are cheap. When is a doctor a good doctor? When he's rich. The more he earns, the better a doctor he is. Albert said himself that the respect doctors enjoyed was just respect for their wealth. He said he didn't exist as a person for people. I was the only woman who was interested in him as a person—Albert had said so himself. Right.

Anna was just exploiting him as a father for her child. She'd only known Albert a few weeks! How could she do this to him? Albert said she said if he couldn't develop a bond with the child she wouldn't force him. Albert said he was happy that Anna understood his situation. Was he blind? How could he defend her when she was ready to ruin him?

"He'll get over it," Juliet said, when I told her how Albert was suffering. "Fathers aren't born, they're made." Once the baby came, Albert would get enthusiastic about it, she said. I shouldn't feel sorry for him; he'd be happy later on. Especially if he was as emotionally inhibited as I'd always claimed, he'd succumb to the charm of a baby.

"The charm of a baby?" I asked, nonplussed.

"Helplessness—that's the charm of a baby." Juliet claimed a baby communicated a sense of a person's own significance. No one with a heart, and especially no one who was emotionally unsure of himself, could hold out against it. But mainly, if Albert and Anna had a baby, that would give them a serious reason for staying together. Juliet always said that being in love wasn't a lasting basis. If I listened to nothing but my feelings, I'd spend my whole life going from man to man.

I was so depressed, Juliet's preaching didn't even piss me off. She was right: Anna would force Albert to marry her. And what was I to do?

Birgit said my horoscope wasn't favorable at the moment for major changes. Scorpios should sit tight. Even though sitting tight was the very thing Scorpios found difficult. Did I know my ascendants? No.

Once when I called to ask Albert about the wedding date again, a woman answered. Anna, for sure. I hung up. She would become a mother, and I was powerless against her. She had the tax bureau, the Church, and Albert's parents behind her. Albert's parents would take a former dietitian's assistant over a future filmmaker as the mother of their grandchild. Philistines.

Life no longer gave me any pleasure. Nothing was fun anymore. Wolfgang Klein's seminar didn't provide me with new focus. New women kept joining and almost all of them had kids. Wolfgang said we should adapt our feelings to the feelings of our children. We had to learn to learn from our children. I felt superfluous. I was envious. Envious of the mothers, mothers like Anna. Wolfgang Klein didn't seem to be interested in my report anymore, and of course he didn't take attendance; anyone who wanted credit for the course just got it. So why even go?

I sat around at the Kaput. Joschi didn't come there anymore; he'd changed his haunts. I shot the breeze with this person or that. Meaningless. Bar chat had never bothered me before, but now . . . In three weeks I'd be turning twenty-eight. What future did a woman have at twenty-eight? Any future at all? Or should I just go out and reserve a place at a nice nursing home?

I began to isolate myself from the world. I spent the whole weekend ironing; I even ironed my panties. Life had nothing more to offer me. When I found myself wondering whether I should iron the hems of my bath towels the way my aunt Katharina did, I revolted against my fate. No, I wouldn't let it get to that point. I would answer a personal ad instead.

The autumn wind blew in my face as I fought my way to the newsstand. Juliet had found happiness through an ad. Birgit hadn't, of course, but still; objectively speaking, to judge by my own circle, the chances were fifty-fifty. I bought the paper with the most ads.

What I found was the same-o same-o. The men hadn't changed in the last six months. There was no point to writing to one of these youthful dirty old men. It would be better to put in an ad myself. But what should I say? Was I an attractive girl-woman? Or a girllike intellectual? Should I say I couldn't cook? And didn't like sports? No, then I'd look bad in comparison with the other women offering themselves. I mulled over my positive characteristics for ages, but couldn't make up my mind.

What had that woman said, the one whose ad I'd answered way back when? I'd cut the ad out, and I hadn't thrown it away. So it had to be around somewhere. It was. I found it in the back of the kitchen cabinet, in my terra-cotta baking dish, which I never used. The ad forms and the price list were there, too. All very organized. I wasn't as sloppy as Albert always said.

I was fascinated all over again by the ad:

> Your fine qualities cannot be formulated in the language of advertising. . . . You have found your own path, beyond the tranquillity of stasis. . . . You feel much that others repress. . . . You seek to take up arms against philistinism per se. . . . For you, being is more important than having. Your free spirit despises norms and is open to the deeper meaning of existence. You like politics. . . . Tolerance and aesthetics are as vitally important to you as to me: you are intellectual to the depths of your soul. The laws of eroticism are terra cognita. . . .
>
> I, 32 5'6" 143 lbs., capable of enthusiasm and self-motivation, flexible and disciplined, but completely undogmatic and nevertheless reliable, have learned to orient myself in absolutely unstructured space, to discern organizing principles. I like clear language and clear people; unorthodox as I am, I prefer to view things other than stereotypes. We are seeking each other, so that all this may be self-evident. Box 48763 UZ.

I wondered whether this woman would mind if I borrowed her words for my ad? She was a kindred soul, and if I were her I wouldn't mind. Of course, I had to change the external details. I was twenty-seven—though not for long, so it was high time—and five-two and 116 pounds. Everything else fit me perfectly, and characterized perfectly the man I was looking for: a free intellectual spirit, aesthetically tolerant. So as not to miss my chance to find a man who not only thought the same as I did but also did what I did, I added two words at the end: "Hobby: movies." Terrific.

I counted the lines and checked the price list. It would be expensive. Could I afford it? Should I shorten the ad? Cut a sentence? But which one? How could I sacrifice a single word? Each one was important, full of significance, relevant. All right, the ad would cost me, but I'd just gotten my November money from my father, and for my birthday I'd get some extra from my mother and my aunt.

This time I'd ask for a new man for my birthday. My mother wanted me to buy an electric mixer—okay, it was practical, but so was a new man.

When I'd copied the ad—I had to use two forms, because it was so long—my hands were shaking, and an hour after I'd thrown the envelope in the mailbox my heart was still pounding like crazy. It was Tuesday evening; I wondered whether my ad would get into the Saturday edition. How many replies would I get? Should I meet everyone who wrote? Maybe I should just pick a few to meet. Maybe I should wait and see. When would the answers arrive? Maybe as early as Monday? No. But if a man wrote on Saturday, the letter would reach the paper by Monday; if the paper sent it right on, I'd have it on Tuesday. Or not until Wednesday. Better wait and see.

69

Box 23841 BP, that was me. My ad made it into the Saturday paper. I was so frantic I could hardly read my own text. You couldn't miss the ad. Would Albert see it? Or Juliet? Or Birgit? Or that Karl-Heinz? Would they notice it was me? Maybe I shouldn't have added "Hobby: movies"—that pointed too clearly to me. But what was done was done. Again I stayed home all weekend. I was afraid the guys at the Kaput would identify me as the enthusiastic, undogmatic, flexible intellectual (27/5′2″/116) and make dumb remarks. I didn't feel like subjecting myself to that.

Then an inconspicuous largish brown envelope appeared in my mailbox, but not until Wednesday. I recognized the newspaper's logo. Inside the envelope was another—the nicest stationery—addressed to the newspaper, and under the address was "Ref. Box 23841 BP, Nov. 9." I lit a cigarette before I opened it. Here is what I read:

Dear Seeking,

I was amazed at your personal. The same one appeared months ago in this newspaper. I wrote it myself, at the time seeking a new beginning after a failed marriage. I am writing to you because my wish has been fulfilled—a fulfillment that has brought about a complete transformation in my life. I owe my happiness to a man at the newspaper who made a mistake, so that my ad appeared in the wrong column . . . it appeared like a foreign body, among men seeking partners. . . . I received seventeen replies from women, each of whom thought my ad was a man's.

At the time I found the courage . . . after long hesitation
. . . to reply to a woman whose words moved me deeply. . . . I cannot analyze the totality of our feelings. . . .
Today we are more than a couple—we have merged into
one.

You who are still seeking, take this thought with you on
your journey:

BID MEN FAREWELL!

Two happy women
P.S. After the error, the paper printed my ad again, in the
right column. Not a single man replied. I could not even
feel sad about that. . . . On the contrary, I gained the
certainty that this part of my existence that I'd consciously
given up had merely been a constraint. Together we freed
ourselves from the bondage of convention.

What was that supposed to mean? No man had replied to this
woman? But sixteen women besides me! Why? What was the
difference between men and women? And now this woman was
with another woman . . . had become a lesbian . . . that couldn't
be true! Or could it?

The woman turned out to be right; no men wrote to me
either.

Why not become a lesbian? I asked myself. But I had no idea
how you became a lesbian. Or was it only my bourgeois upbringing? No, I wasn't a philistine. Hadn't the thought already
crossed my mind, when I found out I'd answered a woman's ad,
that I was a lesbian? Yes. Would that solve my problems? No.
I didn't know any woman I could be a lesbian with.

The next day I got another letter from the newspaper. It
contained the bill. Including value-added tax, the whole thing
came to 256 marks and 48 pfennigs. Down the drain.

70 On Saturday I ran into Sieglinde in the supermarket.

"I'm in such a rush! My husband's away, so I finally have a chance to do a good cleaning!" she announced.

"Where's he gone?"

"My husband's gone to Paris."

"What, by himself? Has he left you?"

"My husband is in Paris on business. With his colleagues, and they didn't take their wives either. In the evening the men like to go out to drink, and we wives would just be in the way."

"Well, if he says so himself, it must be true."

Sieglinde looked me over from bust to hem and asked, "And how's Albert's Anna? I'm so happy for the two of them. My husband said—"

"Why don't you ask her yourself how she is? You know each other so well."

"Why are you so hostile?" Sieglinde asked in great surprise. Then she asked gently, "Would you like to come over? We haven't seen each other in so long. You haven't even seen my new living-room rug."

"All right," I said graciously. "I can come along for a cup of coffee, Frau Lamar–Schadler."

It was ice-cold in the Lamar-Schadler apartment. So they were saving on heat, too. The new rug was supposed to have an antique look, with musty colors. It smelled musty, anyway. There were brochures lying around everywhere: "Enhance your life with good lighting," "Enhance your comfort with genuine wool carpeting," "Live better with genuine wood furniture," "Elegant kitchens," and so on.

"You see," Sieglinde said, "my husband and I are considering purchasing a condominium. My husband just has to check first on how to work it so we get the best break on our taxes."

"My stomach and I could certainly do with a cup of coffee in this cold," I said. I hadn't come along for the latest tax tips. I shivered demonstratively and gave Sieglinde a penetrating look.

"I've discovered Irish coffee," she said. "Have you ever had that?"

"No."

"It's very tasty. I got the recipe from my boss's wife, and it's already been a big hit with my guests."

I shivered demonstratively again and gave Sieglinde another penetrating look.

"Should I make an Irish coffee for us?" she finally asked.

"Good idea!"

Sieglinde sprinkled an extra spoonful of confectioners' sugar on her whipped cream. Then she came back to the subject of the condo. "My husband insists on having wall-to-wall carpeting in the new place, everywhere. I like wooden floors; you can use area rugs with them. It looks more elegant. But my husband thinks we can't afford that yet. What do you think?"

Apparently she wasn't really interested in hearing my opinion, because she got up, went back to the kitchen, and came out with a box of pralines. There were only four left. "Help yourself," Sieglinde said, gesturing generously.

I took one with hazelnuts.

When I put my hand back in the box, it was empty. No fair. There should have been two for each. "Am I wrong, or have you gained weight?" I asked slyly.

"I've hardly gained anything since my wedding . . . only as much as I'd lost beforehand. All that dieting—you wouldn't believe what it did to my nerves." Sieglinde sighed involuntarily as she thought of the period of self-denial before her marriage.

"Would you like another Irish coffee?" she asked.

"Oh, sure."

The coffee and the alcohol had warmed me up and improved my mood. I asked Sieglinde what her divine spouse was giving her for Christmas.

"Well, I saw this fox jacket at Couture Furs, magnificent workmanship! Actually, my husband wanted to buy it for me, but since we'll probably have big outlays soon for the condo, my husband says a fur jacket is out of the question. Maybe next summer—on sale, you know." Sieglinde smiled.

"You know, I'd rather get a fur jacket in the winter," I said mercilessly.

"You have to understand, it's just not possible. We have to save in any case, because my husband needs a bigger car. If we move to a better part of town, my husband has to have a fancier car." Suddenly Sieglinde sat up very straight, pulled a footstool over to her chair, modestly placed her feet on it, and said, "My husband doesn't like me to cross my legs!" She beamed.

I didn't have much to say to that.

By the time I'd finished my second Irish coffee, I couldn't stand Sieglinde's fussing anymore. Besides, it occurred to me that I'd meant to clean my kitchen. I told her I had to go now because I had work to do. She said she had to get on with the cleaning.

"What are you two doing for Christmas?" I asked at the door.

"My boss and his wife are going skiing in Saint-Moritz."

"I see. And there was something else I wanted to ask you."

"Yes?"

"What's your husband's first name?"

"Wolf-Dietrich! You mean you've forgotten?"

"I thought you had." I beat it out of there as fast as I could.

I thought and thought about why Sieglinde kept harping on

what her dear husband wanted, what her dear husband disapproved of. He didn't give a damn what she did or didn't do—the main thing for him was that he was saving on taxes. Why the big act?

Sieglinde had gotten married in order to achieve the status of a married woman; well, she'd gotten the status, but that was all. Basically she was a very undemanding little lady. Sieglinde had voluntarily gone into slavery. Now she existed only through her husband.

Nevertheless I couldn't really be mad at her. Women like her proved that it was still worthwhile for a woman to have her own identity. Compared to her, I was infinitely better off; an uncertain future is better than no future at all.

71 My birthday was going to fall on the Sunday commemorating the dead. That was all I needed this particular year. Even so, I decided on Wednesday morning, which was Penitents' Day and had weather to match, to celebrate my birthday on Sunday no matter what. Not a big party, just a kaffeeklatch. I called Juliet first. I hadn't seen her in ages—she was in love and had dropped out of my life. Typical! Juliet said she and Jürgen were terribly busy looking for an apartment.

"What? You're planning to move in together?"

"Jürgen and I don't see any problem with that."

"Nothing you do surprises me anymore!" Then I told her about my not-quite-party.

Juliet said she'd very much like to come, and her Jürgen was free, too, and could he come?

Of course. Sunday at two. Settled.

I also invited Birgit. I asked whether she wanted to bring a man along, but of course she didn't. Then I wondered whether I should invite that Bernhard for Birgit, the one I sometimes talked to in the cafeteria; he was nice, though not my type . . . or whether I should invite anyone else from school—Beate, or Klaus, or maybe Rosemarie from the Kaput? But if you invited people who only knew the hostess, you had to watch them all the time to make sure they weren't getting bored. And anyway it was better not to invite anyone from school, because what if Juliet mentioned Gottfried Schachtschnabel?

I didn't feel like inviting Sieglinde and her husband, what's-his-name. But on the spur of the moment I called up Albert.

Yes, of course he knew that my birthday was November second. And he'd be happy to come on Sunday at two.

"Don't you have to ask your Anna for permission first?"

No, he could make up his own mind. And he'd appreciate it if I didn't go on and on about Anna on Sunday when the others were there.

"All right," I said.

That same evening Juliet called and said whatever I did I shouldn't bake a cake. She'd be bringing a surprise. She couldn't say what it was, because then it wouldn't be a surprise, but I absolutely shouldn't bake or buy a cake. And how old was I going to be?

"Twenty-eight."

"Fine," Juliet said.

"Fine," said I.

A day before my birthday Juliet called up again and said she was terribly sorry, but tomorrow she and Jürgen would have to leave around five, because they'd just called up about an apartment, and they could look at it tomorrow at six. There was nothing to be done; I'd already bought stuff for supper, but fortunately nothing that would spoil quickly. So we said good-bye, but not until after Juliet had told me in detail how hard it was to find a nice apartment.

My parents called on Sunday at the crack of dawn to shower me with congratulations and advice for leading a healthy life. And Aunt Katharina spent half an hour reporting on the latest developments in her life. The phone kept ringing all morning. Ilona Reuter hadn't forgotten my birthday either, and various ancient acquaintances called to wish me happy birthday. My old roommate Christiane even called from France; she wasn't with the French teacher anymore, and in three months she would come to see me and tell me the whole story.

On the stroke of two Juliet arrived with a huge egg-liqueur cake, with Jürgen and Birgit in tow. Terrific! The chocolate lettering on the cake said "For Constance on Her Twenty-eighth." Absolutely terrific. That was really incredibly nice of her.

Typical Birgit—she gave me a book: *The Scorpio Woman and Her Men*. Terrific. She'd already glanced through it, to make sure, and it was very, very informative. Terrific. And Juliet's Jürgen gave me a white amaryllis in a nice flowerpot. I liked amaryllis, not only because they were so pretty, but also because they grew so fast; you could practically see them grow. Absolutely terrific.

At a quarter past two Albert still hadn't shown. "I bet Anna isn't going to let him come," I prophesied.

I opened a bottle of champagne my parents had sent me and toasted my twenty-eighth.

"We wish you everything you wish yourself," Jürgen said.

"What do you wish yourself?" Birgit asked.

I felt silly. "I don't really have any specific wishes."

"A new old man, perhaps?" Juliet said playfully.

"But please, not just any old man!" I said.

"Of course not just any old man! The man with whom it'll all be different."

"You have to read the book I gave you; that'll help," Birgit said.

At two-thirty Albert still hadn't shown. The coffee was ready, though, and because I'd astutely guessed that Juliet's surprise would be a cake, I had a quart of whipped cream in the refrigerator. So we started on the cake, even though it looked much too beautiful to cut.

At three Albert arrived.

He was pretty embarrassed, especially when he said hello to Juliet. Birgit immediately fell to worshiping him. He gave me a really pretty bouquet, all pink: rose-pink roses, rose-pink baby's breath, little carnations, and those round, plump flowers I can never remember the name of. And with it a huge picture book, Hollywood stars of the fifties! Wow, such an expensive book! He certainly hadn't spared any expense. I kissed him, but only on the cheek.

He got even more embarrassed and said, "I'm really sorry, but I can't stay. Anna's not feeling well at all."

"What's wrong?" someone asked.

"She has stomach cramps."

"Do you think your child's being born? On my birthday, of all days!"

"Don't start! She really isn't feeling well. I was already over there, that's why I got here late."

"But at least you can stay for a piece of cake," Jürgen said, and added proudly, "Juliet made it herself."

Well, that much time Albert could spare.

"Have you figured out when you have to get married?" I asked him.

He looked plaintively at Juliet, Birgit, and Jürgen. "She's constantly asking me that. I don't know. It's not all that easy."

"I believe you," Juliet said.

"My sister gave birth at Holy Spirit Hospital, and she says she'd do it again anytime," Birgit said.

"It hasn't reached that point yet," Albert said.

"What month is she?" Birgit asked.

"Her sixth *week.*"

"Well, you have time for another piece of cake," I said.

"No, I have to go. I promised."

He had a glass of champagne with us, at least.

"Too bad we didn't meet sooner. I wish you could've stayed," Juliet said as Albert said good-bye. Birgit was also very sad to see the handsome doctor go so soon. Albert wished Juliet and Jürgen lots of luck finding an apartment, and he said to me that maybe we could have a longer talk soon. Then he rushed off.

Everybody had to admit it: Albert didn't seem too happy. Juliet and Jürgen also didn't think it was too cool of this Anna to have his kid when she'd known him only a few months. But Birgit had to bring up the example of her sister again, who'd become pregnant and happy on seven months' acquaintance. And she added, "You two are moving in together, and you've only known each other three months."

"Moving into an apartment together seems less problematical to me than having a child together," Jürgen replied somewhat sharply.

"You can give up a shared apartment if you break up," I explained to Birgit. She looked at Jürgen in shock and incomprehension.

"This time I'm not getting married for the sake of an apartment," Juliet said. "No one can say I repeat my mistakes." She laughed.

"This time you're getting married because of me," Jürgen said.

"But I thought you were never going to marry again!" I said. "Do you . . . Are you two getting married?"

"Not right away, so relax. But now that I don't have any illusions about marriage anymore, I'd do fine," Juliet said.

"I still have illusions," Jürgen said.

"What kind of illusions?" I asked.

"When I'm married, I'll have someone I can use as an alibi. When all the guys at work want to talk shop till midnight, I can say I have to go home, because my wife is waiting for me and she'll throw fits." He grinned happily. "Besides, I need a woman to take my car to the garage. I always have to pretend I know something about cars, when it's all I can do to tell a moped from a Mercedes. A woman doesn't have to pretend to be an expert. If a mechanic wants to put something over on me, he'll do it anyway. But then he has to make fun of me, too."

"Well, you'll have to buy the meat if we're having a roast. I'm always afraid they're going to foist the worst piece off on me. I don't dare admit I don't know a thing about meat."

"Buying meat is my specialty; I've never gotten a bad cut," Jürgen said casually. "When a man goes to buy meat, they automatically assume he's a gourmet cook."

"And when we're married, you'll have to listen to my father's stories about what goes on at the plant."

"And in return you'll have to talk to my mother about astrology."

Juliet laughed again.

"But that doesn't mean you have to get married!" I exclaimed. "You can talk to Jürgen's mother and take his car to the garage just as well if you're not married. If you break up, it's much easier when you're not married."

"You know what I think?" Juliet said. "I think it's better if you can rely on the fact that you belong together, instead of having to reinvent your togetherness every day. People who say right off the bat that they don't want to take any risks because the relationship is going to dissolve anyway—well, you might just as well split up right away. Why wait?"

Why was Juliet so enthusiastic? Was it the enthusiasm of the converted? "What do you two really have in common?" I asked, kind of annoyed.

"We don't have anything in common!" Jürgen laughed loudly. "We just complement each other!"

"You don't have to do everything together; you need some distance between you. But there's no ideal distance. And there are only two possibilities: either you reduce the distance or you enlarge it. And because we want to reduce the distance, we're going to get married. Some time or other," Juliet said.

"Soon," said Jürgen.

Some people make it so easy for themselves! I sighed. To change the subject, I asked, "Do you think Albert will be happy with Anna?"

Juliet wasn't as optimistic as she had been recently. Nor was Jürgen. Nor was Birgit.

"Albert seemed pretty helpless to me; he should wait and see how things develop," Jürgen said.

Juliet gave me a serious look. I knew what she was thinking: she was thinking I wouldn't have any influence over this development. "How's your film coming?" she asked out of the blue.

My film. Ah yes. "It's stagnating." I had to admit it. "I thought," I said without thinking, "that I should solve my personal problems first. That would be better, wouldn't it?"

"You want to wait with your film project till you have a new man? First, you won't be in the mood, and second, you shouldn't place so much value on a man!" Juliet exclaimed.

"You're theorizing again," Jürgen said to her.

Juliet was firm. "I think you should concentrate on your film, not on men. Men come of their own accord. Especially when you're not thinking about them."

"You're just theorizing," I said, in solidarity with Jürgen. "Actually, I wanted to make a film about separating from Albert, but now I'm not so sure it's a good topic."

"You have to make a film about a woman who finds the love of her life!" Birgit exclaimed, beaming expectantly.

"Like Anna, maybe? No way."

"We have to go now; we're looking for the landlord of our life."

As always when Jürgen made a joke, Juliet laughed heartily. Then Birgit and I were alone. As we chatted about this and that, I was thinking about Juliet. First she got divorced and said she never wanted to marry again. Then she got involved with a man who likewise never wanted to marry again—because he was already married. Then she left this man, precisely because he was married. Then she answered a personal, and now she wanted to get married again! Was that logical? And her a psychologist!

Sure, Jürgen was very nice. But was he really the man of her dreams, or was she just taking him because she was too lazy to go on looking? He wasn't my type, this Jürgen. There was something so settled about him; he must be authoritarian. And all that billing and cooing with Juliet. And how loud his laugh was. And anyway I didn't like men with straight blond hair.

Birgit leafed through the book she'd given me.

"What does it predict for my future?"

"It doesn't have any predictions, it just says what kind of man is best for you."

"Since I haven't even *met* the man who's best for me, that would be a prediction."

Birgit disagreed. Maybe it would turn out that Albert was the man who was best for me, she said.

I could tell her she was on the wrong track, and besides, I didn't believe in horoscopes, certainly not when I didn't like what they said.

The book said my ideal partner was a Scorpio or a Cancer, or an Aquarius. In any case, someone from the water.

"There you have it: Albert's a Leo. That's probably why he's so humorless."

Birgit read other significant passages out loud: "The ideal

partner of the Scorpio woman is a man who does not impede her drive, but knows how to support it unobtrusively."

"Whether that fits Albert or not depends on how you care to see it; he neither impedes me nor supports me."

"The ideal partner of the Scorpio woman is generous." Birgit paused.

Haha. Well, I had to admit Albert's birthday gift had been generous. Especially when you considered that by now our relationship was friendly at most.

"Some people can only give when you don't expect anything of them," she said.

How very Birgit-esque this humble wisdom was. "Go on reading," I said.

It would also be ideal if my partner were down-to-earth, to balance the passionate temperament of the Scorpio woman. Well, that was certainly one respect in which Albert would be a good complement to me. He handled his feelings the way he handled his money. He was as down-to-earth as a twenty-mark bill.

Birgit didn't reply to this. She read on: "The Scorpio woman is a sophisticated lover . . . when she wants to enchant a man, she likes to wear blue. The Scorpio woman knows instinctively that this appeals to men's nature without denying her own. . . ."

"Blue—why blue?"

"It says so right here," Birgit explained.

Oh, of course. Then I thought of my blue silk slip. But no, it hadn't brought me luck. "Go on."

"The Scorpio woman would never violate the trust that is placed in her!" And suddenly Birgit became confiding. She put the book aside. She absolutely had to tell me that every Wednesday for the last few weeks such a sweet man had been coming to the library, always at two-thirty in the afternoon. I simply couldn't imagine how he looked at her, every time, so sweetly!

And he only ever checked out two books. "I'm sure he reads every book he borrows," Birgit said approvingly. "And you know what he is?"

"What is he?"

"He's a Scorpio, just like you!"

"You've gotten to know him?"

"Of course not. His birthdate is on his library card. It's next Thursday."

"What kind of books does he take out?"

"He always borrows a detective story and a science fiction novel. But recently he took out a book about aquariums. So my guess is, he has an aquarium."

"Haven't you ever spoken with him?"

"He always brings his books back on time. If he doesn't have to pay a fine, what can I say to him?"

"Just talk to him!"

"I can't do that!"

"So wish him a happy birthday next week. I guarantee you that'll make him happy."

"But then he'll think I'm throwing myself at him."

Oh, God. Birgit was hopeless. I gave her a little more wine.

"I guess I'm just the passive type," she moaned. "Last week I took a big personality test in a magazine, and it turned out I'm the passive type."

"Didn't you know that before?" I was laughing so hard I spilled my wine. Never mind, I had enough in the refrigerator.

"That's just how I am, you can't change your nature," Birgit said plaintively, but actually she seemed perfectly contented.

I looked at Birgit. Everything was spinning in a strange way. I'd meant to say something, but I couldn't think what it was. Think, Constance. I thought. It occurred to me that I had tons of cheese, ham, salami, and pickles in the fridge. And a can of sardines.

We ate tons of cheese, ham, salami, and pickles, and then we opened the sardines. Now I remembered what it was I'd wanted to say. "Listen," I said, freshly fortified. "Sometimes I get the feeling a woman can't really be happy till she's divorced. It's like this: everyone who's alone is unhappy. Everyone who has a steady relationship is unhappy. The only happy ones are the divorced—I hear it all the time. So I've come to the conclusion that I have to get married, and then I'll get divorced, and then I'll be happy. Here's to my divorce!"

"So who do you want to get divorced from?" Birgit asked slowly.

Hm, now there was a problem. I became engrossed in thought again. "I'll just find myself some rich guy; they're easier to marry—because of taxes they're all wild to get married. It's also more practical to get divorced from a rich guy."

"But it isn't good for the children when you get divorced."

"I don't want children, I want to be happy!" I was furious with Birgit, because she reminded me of Anna. "You want to wait for the father of your children, I know. And he'll be the right one for you! The person who wants you, as simple as that! It doesn't have to be the one you want!"

"I don't understand you," Birgit said slowly.

"You've got to start thinking about what you want. All you think of is what men want!"

"But—"

Now I was really picking up steam, and I knew the objections Birgit would raise, so I broke in: "You know what I read once? A woman who tries to be a good wife according to men's standards is like a Jew trying to be a good Jew according to the Nazis' standards! Tasteless, I know, but true!"

Compared to Birgit, I was a radical feminist. A nice feeling! "As long as societal conditions don't change, men won't change either," I said, wagging my index finger at her. "So you have two choices: either you stay away from men till you know what you're up against, or you go through everything I've been through so you absolutely know what you're up against." I lowered my index finger and raised my glass instead.

The look in Birgit's eyes told me she didn't have a clear picture at all. "But my yearly horoscope said a new man would enter my life," she murmured slowly.

"Maybe he's already left it."

Birgit looked unhappily at her glass: "I have to go use the potty."

I poured more wine. Birgit must have thought of her sister in the bathroom because the first thing she said when she got back was, "My sister wants to have another child as soon as possible. If Benjamin grows up an only child, that won't be good for him."

"It never bothered me to be an only child," I said, and finished up the smoked ham.

Then the phone rang. It was Juliet.

"We got the apartment!"

"Fantastic!" I yelled back.

"Get this, the landlady asked where I worked, and when I said I was at the Lessing School, that clinched it, because her grandkid goes there!"

I yelled to Birgit, "They got the apartment!"

"Fantastic," Birgit said slowly.

"You've got to come back and celebrate with us!"

"We can't possibly; we had to try the landlady's home brew. Then we had to try it some more. That did us in. But she's very nice."

"We're perfectly sober," I giggled.

But Juliet and Jürgen didn't want to come back. I said "Bye" a few more times, and "Congratulations!" and "Hic"—suddenly I had the hiccups.

So Birgit and I drank to Juliet and Jürgen's apartment by ourselves. Birgit was deeply moved that they owed their lease to the landlady's grandchild. "I want a child, too," she said mournfully. Then she sank into self-pity because in the future she'd be living all alone, and now, in the more immediate future, she had to go home alone.

Birgit moaned and groaned a bit more. Yes, it's tough being a woman in this society, especially when you're a Pisces. It was already eleven when I called a taxi for her. When I locked the outside door behind her, I had trouble finding the keyhole.

Because my hiccups wouldn't stop, I tried to distract myself by cleaning up a little. Albert's flowers already looked pretty limp. He could at least have called me again. Anna wasn't the only one feeling awful. I was sick as a dog.

72

The next morning I still felt so lousy I couldn't sit up. There was no point in getting up. My head was buzzing. When the phone rang, I just crawled under the covers. I couldn't talk, not to anyone. It was almost afternoon when I dragged myself to the refrigerator. There was a whole bowl of whipped cream left. Just the sight of it made me sick all over again.

Now I was twenty-eight. I went back to bed and waited for last-minute panic to strike. Many women who haven't gotten their lives straightened out by twenty-eight get last-minute panic—so I'd read. But I just felt sick.

I didn't feel completely normal until Wednesday. I had to make up my mind to work on my screenplay. Not only was I twenty-eight now, but if I wanted to make a film of my own I had to have my screenplay to submit to the funding commission soon.

Of course I was still unsure whether my separation from Albert was the best possible subject, but I couldn't think of anything better, and besides, personal things like that always interest people. "The personal is political," Wolfgang Klein had said—to that extent I didn't have to lower my sights. I was glad to have liberated myself from Schachtschnabel's abstract theories.

Back when I'd planned to make the film with Schachtschnabel, I hadn't known how to begin; it still wasn't clear to me, but now what was really unclear to me was how to end the story. Of course, it didn't solve all your problems when you found the love of your life. But not to have found the love of your life didn't make you especially happy either.

And writing a screenplay is like making a proclamation. I didn't have any message to proclaim. I was an abandoned woman with vague hopes of social rehabilitation. True, I'd be able to show that even as a single woman I deserved respect. I'd be able to show what profound complications I'd been caught up in. But how could I show that everything was better now?

Should I simply leave the ending open? Or fill it with symbols that would speak for themselves? Maybe an animated film . . . with me as a caterpillar, first vegetating on a wilted leaf, then spinning a cocoon, then breaking out of the cocoon and flying into the world, a brilliant butterfly? Or was that too kitschy? Plus, the butterfly symbol was good, but me as a caterpillar—that didn't fit my situation, really. Maybe a mummy that metamorphosed into a butterfly? That would be a beautiful symbol. . . . We women love symbols . . . they're so deep, so meaningful. . . .

Still, a movie was supposed to uncover the secret of life—or reveal the truth ruthlessly, one of the two, that was the least that was expected. I wanted to do both. But would the medium of film be adequate to present my relationship to the problems of our times in all its complexity? I shuddered at the thought of ending up a victim of the banality of everyday life.

If I showed love in my film, it would have to be a love that wasn't everyday . . . it would have to have the word *obsession* in the title.

I wanted my film to turn out the way my life would. But what would the right happy ending be? Maybe it was only in novels that two halves merged into a whole. In reality this merging business was more like getting stuck to each other. . . . Maybe reality really is that realistic? Were the misfortunes of my life mistakes? Maybe I shouldn't have let Albert go? Shouldn't have let him hurl himself into unhappiness? True, Albert wasn't the love I'd dreamed of, but maybe my dreams had only been theories.

A film about lost love. Lost love, that sounds like a lost house key—could you find it again?

Or was lost love more like that Czech dish called lost eggs? An intention that becomes a permanent condition?

What should I do? Now? Later? For this year I'd reached my goal. I'd planned to separate from Albert, and it had happened. But now it was almost next year. The years you start out by resolving to help old ladies cross the street are the happiest years of your life—I'd read that somewhere, and now I realized it was true.

I could drink myself to death, like my dear departed Aunt Frida. I could drink up the dowry I'd inherited from her. My parents couldn't stop me. It would be entirely in the spirit of the deceased. She always did exactly what she felt like doing. Frau Frida Küntzle—she always used the title "Frau" so no one would think she was an old maid. And she really wasn't; she'd survived—and inherited from—a fiancé and two husbands! And no children. A real role model. And I didn't even have a live husband, never mind surviving one.

I looked out the window, into the distance, and saw myself sitting in my study. On the wall hung a clock, and the clock had stopped. I sat there and looked at a calendar hanging next to the clock. The pages dropped from the calendar, like leaves off autumn trees. I looked out the window, into the distance, and I saw myself looking out the window. Outside the seasons passed: sun, snow, spring green, October storms . . . was this a vision of my future? When would the shining hero come, to set the clock of my life in motion again? Would he come some morning, or in the night? In April or December? This year? Next year? Or only in the hour of my death? I shuddered. No, I wouldn't just sit and wait. I wanted to go out. I wanted to go to the Kaput.

Maybe there were new men there, better men, men who'd just been waiting for me. Somewhere someone is always waiting for someone. I didn't remember who said that—was it Nietzsche? Socrates? Ingrid Bergman in *Casablanca*?

 There wasn't a soul in the Kaput. Only Niyazi, the proprietor.

"What's wrong?" I asked.

"Nothing," he said, in his taciturn Bavarian way.

"Where is everybody?"

"Are you interested in soccer?"

"No."

"That's what I thought."

"Why? Is there soccer on TV today?"

"What's it look like?"

I stayed anyway. Every game ends eventually. People would turn up. I sat down in the corner with a glass of wine, studying the handwritten sign on the wall: CHRISTMAS AND NEW YEAR'S FOR FOLKS WITH NOWHERE TO GO. Underneath it said that the Kaput was open on all holidays, and anyone who didn't want to return to the bosom of his family was most welcome. At Christmas Wolfgang would even play the piano and Peter the guitar, and on New Year's the Kreuzberg Kitsch Konservatory would perform. New Year's would be fun. For Christmas I had to go home to my parents'. My father was convinced that this time— since there was no male competition—I'd even stay for New Year's. But that much family life was too much for me.

"When's the game over?" I asked when I went to get my second glass of wine at the bar.

"It's going to take a while, I'm telling you. It isn't just a game."

"No?"

"Today they're showing highlights from the whole season. Every ball into the wrong goal, every brawl. It'll take a while, I'm telling you. Fucking soccer!" Niyazi was so bitter he was actually talking. "If something like this comes up again, I'm not even going to bother opening."

A car stopped in front of the Kaput.

"See, someone's coming now," I said encouragingly to Niyazi. We looked expectantly toward the door.

In came Albert.

"What are you doing here?" Niyazi and I exclaimed.

"Why aren't you watching soccer?" Niyazi exclaimed.

"Why aren't you with your wife and fetus?" I exclaimed.

But Albert said to Niyazi, "Give me a beer."

And to me he said, "I thought you'd be here, even though it's Soccer Night. I called you, and when you weren't home, I drove right over."

"Very smart. And what are you doing here on Soccer Night?"

"I want to tell you something."

We withdrew into the corner. "Well, what's up?"

"What I wanted to tell you"—Albert paused, lit a cigarette, and looked at me significantly—"Anna isn't pregnant anymore."

"What! What?"

"Don't yell!" Albert yelled. "Or rather, Anna wasn't pregnant at all. As it turned out yesterday. Remember she had stomach cramps? They weren't getting any better, so I took her to the hospital yesterday morning. They checked her out and she wasn't even pregnant. Then they sent us home . . . it wasn't our hospital . . . I didn't want any talk . . . we went to an emergency room. Anyway, last night she started to bleed. It wasn't a miscarriage; I took her to the hospital again . . . it was just a period. Late."

"What? How can that be? You're a doctor, why didn't you realize what was going on?"

"How was I supposed to realize? Anna bought a test, and it came out positive. Maybe she did something wrong, or the test had something wrong with it, or whatever. . . . My colleague in gynecology said there were probably psychic reasons why her period was so late. In any case, she doesn't have anything . . . I mean, she's perfectly healthy. It was only a passing irregularity, the colleague assured me. His supervisor said the same thing. In any case . . ." Albert put out his cigarette and didn't finish the sentence.

"You've got to buy a round to celebrate! You'll never get away this cheap again, with only three people here!"

"This is no reason for drinks. That's not proper."

What a serious old tightwad. "And now what are you going to do?"

"I don't know. Anna's pretty depressed. She cried all night. She was looking forward to the child so much. Now she wants to get pregnant again right away. Or rather, finally get pregnant." Albert didn't look at me while he was talking about Anna. "But I'm not going along. I want to marry first and then become a father." He had to look under the table to say that.

"Of course. You're so conservative."

"Don't start that again."

"So now you're going to marry Anna, and then you'll make a new embryo."

"No, I'm not going to marry Anna." Albert spoke with a decisiveness I hadn't seen in him before.

"Why not?"

"We're not compatible. I don't want to get married just to sire someone's child. Besides, Anna's too clinging for me. I'd rather marry you." Albert looked under the table again, and stared with interest at the soles of his shoes. "Why don't you marry me?" he asked.

I checked out the soles of my shoes, too. "Why should I marry you?"

"Why not?"

"Because you—" I interrupted myself, thought about what I should say first. "You're too stingy"? Maybe he'd improved a bit . . . the birthday present, for example. . . . But he was also stingy in his feelings, I knew that for a fact. And this eternal indecisiveness!

"Was that supposed to be a proposal?" I finally asked.

"I don't know."

"Jeez! That's not how you propose marriage!"

"Well, how?"

"Not in a bar, for starters. You have no class! And in any case you have to give the girl red roses!"

"How many?"

I thought carefully. "At least a hundred marks' worth," I said decisively—it did seem like a lot to me, but I wanted to give Albert a jolt.

"That's too much!" he exclaimed in horror.

"Fifty roses is the absolute minimum, and that could come to a hundred marks." I added graciously, "Maybe you can find fifty for less than that. With a quantity discount."

"Fifteen are plenty."

"You must be crazy!"

"You come on so progressive, but you're pretty darn bourgeois in your expectations, let me tell you! Why does it have to be roses, anyway?"

"Why don't you go ahead and marry Anna! You don't need to buy her roses! She'll just get what she likes and pass the bills on to you."

"Fifteen roses, tops!"

"Thirty roses is the absolute minimum for a marriage proposal! I can't come down any further!"

"All right," Albert said, "I'm going now." He got up. In silence I watched him pay for his beer at the bar. How I'd have loved to throw a couple of ashtrays at him. But Niyazi wouldn't have stood for it.

74

I went home and waited till three in the morning for Albert to call. He had to be feeling remorse. But he didn't call. Nor did he call the next day.

The damned sit in hell and wait for mail—I'd read that somewhere, and it's true, too. But much worse than waiting for mail is waiting for a call. The mail comes once a day, but the telephone . . . I was chained to the house.

On Friday morning I had to go out, to my documentary course. It didn't interest me in the slightest, but I had to go because I'd already missed two classes and otherwise I wouldn't get credit. When I got back, I could hear the phone ringing through the door. By the time I got the door open, the ringing had stopped.

Had that been Albert? Had he finally realized that he would have to invest something if he wanted me?

If I called him back now, he would think I was ready to negotiate a compromise; that was how he'd always exploited me. No!

It wasn't the roses; it was a matter of principle. My mother claimed that people who say it's not the money, just the principle of the thing, always care about the money. She was certainly right as far as Albert went, but for me it really wasn't the money. If Albert wasn't going to be the lover of my dreams, at least he could act like it from time to time. That wasn't asking too much. But he wouldn't give in. Well, all right then. Let him go to hell. Or to Anna.

On the other hand, he'd said he'd rather marry me. Over Anna! I'd done battle with a would-be pregnant woman—Laocoön's battle with the serpent was nothing compared to this— and I'd won. I hadn't even had to get pregnant first. Ha! What would my friends and acquaintances say if I married Albert? I thought of everybody I knew. Only one person would advise me against it: Gottfried Schachtschnabel. And what was his advice worth?

True, Albert wasn't the love of my life, but at least he might become it. We'd known each other almost four years now. . . . We'd been separated for almost a year. . . . If we got married after such a long separation, who knows? Maybe we could even dispense with the divorce. And besides, a wedding with the bride not pregnant . . . that would be incredibly original!

Suddenly I had my brainstorm. It was 4:45 in the afternoon. I went out and overdrew my savings. If Albert wasn't prepared to fulfill my dreams, I'd fulfill them myself. After all, I was self-sufficient. Okay. I drove to one of the best flower shops in the city. I picked thirty red roses, the most expensive kind. To be delivered to Albert Auerbach. Okay.

The woman in the flower shop said the roses couldn't be sent till tomorrow, Saturday. Better yet. He'd be sure to be at home. What time, more or less, would they be delivered? By ten in the morning, at the latest. Splendid. Did I want to fill out a card? the woman asked. Not necessary. Or was it? What if he thought the roses came from Anna? That was all I needed. I thought only a moment, then wrote:

For your marriage proposal.

Haha!

75 By 10:00 at the latest he'd get the roses.

From 10:05 on I looked out the kitchen window every minute or so—it was the only window in my apartment that had a view of the street. Every time a car drove by I looked out. It was snowing and ice-cold.

After I'd waited for four hours I went to bed, a total wreck. I'd made up my mind. . . . Had Albert gotten cold feet? Did he want revenge?

I turned on the radio and got back in bed. Christmas was coming in three days, so sang an ecstatic children's choir. A total lie—it was twenty-four days to Christmas. Then came "O Tannenbaum, O Tannenbaum," and then the children's voices twittered, "Ring, little bells ring, ring-a-ling-a-ling." Nerve-racking. But I was too limp to get up and turn it off. "Ring-a-ling-a-ling, dong dong, little bells ring, ring-a-ling-a-ling, dong dong dong, ring little bell ring." I pulled myself together and turned off the radio.

Dong, dong, dong—it was my door! It was Albert!

I opened the door and almost fainted. There was the most enormous bouquet of roses I'd ever seen. There were thirty roses . . . thirty-two roses . . . thirty-seven roses . . . forty-one roses . . . forty-five roses . . .

"Exactly fifty," Albert said.

"But I only sent you thirty!"

"Well, I bought twenty more."

Five more roses than he was willing to invest originally! If that wasn't success! It was pure insanity!

"And here, I have something else for you." He gave me a little white package that smelled of coffee. I unwrapped it. It was coffee. A pound of coffee!

"A pound of coffee?"

"Yes. And I bought something along with it."

"A special offer?"

"A one-time special offer." From his coat pocket he pulled a little blue box with a silver border. In the box was pale blue cotton . . . and a ring.

A ring just like the ring Prince Charles gave Lady Di for their engagement!

"Real silver with a synthetic sapphire, but I've forgotten what the diamonds are. It was only 89.95. A good buy, huh?"

I put the ring on my finger..

"But it looks so real," I said.

About the Author

Eva Heller is a satirical cartoonist with several published collections. She lives in Frankfurt, Germany, and is at work on her next book.